"Look around, Gabrielle." His lips dragged over hers as he spoke, making her dizzy with want. "It is only you and me."

"A girlfriend," she blurted out between kisses. It was probably a little late to be asking, but she had to know, even if she wasn't at all sure how she would deal with an answer she didn't want to hear. "Do you have a girlfriend? Are you married? Please don't tell me you're married. . . ."

"There is no one else."

Only you.

She was pretty sure he hadn't said those last couple of words, but Gabrielle heard them echo in her mind, warm and provocative, stripping her of any resistance.

Oh, he was good. Or maybe she was just that desperate for him, because that spare, unadorned pledge was all he gave her—that and the dizzying combination of his tender hands and hot, hungry mouth—and yet she believed him without a shred of doubt. She felt as if his every sense were trained on her alone. As if there were only her, only him, and this burning thing that existed between them. Had existed, from the moment he first showed up on her doorstep.

"Ohh," she gasped as the breath left her lungs in a slow sigh. She sagged against him, reveling in the feel of his hands on her skin, caressing her throat, her shoulder, the arch of her spine. "What are we doing here, Lucan?"

His low growl of humor hummed beside her ear, deep as night.

"I think you know."

"I don't know anything, not when you're doing that. Oh . . . God . . ."

"This is why I came here tonight." Lucan's voice rumbled beside her ear. "Do you understand, Gabrielle? I want you."

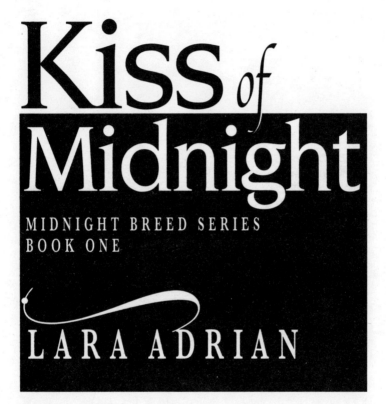

Kiss *of* Midnight

MIDNIGHT BREED SERIES
BOOK ONE

LARA ADRIAN

A DELL BOOK

KISS OF MIDNIGHT
A Dell Book

Published by Bantam Dell
A Division of Random House, Inc.
New York, New York

Dell is a registered trademark of Random House, Inc., and the colophon is a
trademark of Random House, Inc.

ISBN-13: 978-0-7394-8102-8

Printed in the U.S.A.

For John,

whose faith in me has never faltered,

and whose love, I hope, will never fade.

With much gratitude to my agent, Karen Solem, for helping chart the course, and for brilliant navigation under all manner of conditions.

My wonderful editor, Shauna Summers, rightly deserves her own page of acknowledgments for all of her support and encouragement, not to mention the superb editorial vision that always finds the heart of every story and helps bring it into focus.

Thanks also to Debbie Graves for enthusiastic critiques, and to Jessica Bird, whose talent is surpassed only by her amazing generosity of spirit.

Lastly, a special nod of appreciation to my audial muses during much of the creation of this book: Lacuna Coil, Evanescence, and Collide, whose stirring lyrics and amazing music never failed to inspire.

Kiss *of* Midnight

Prologue

Her baby wouldn't stop crying. She'd started fussing at the last station, when the Greyhound bus out of Bangor stopped in Portland to pick up more passengers. Now, at a little after 1 A.M., they were almost to the Boston terminal, and the two-plus hours of trying to soothe her infant daughter were, as her friends back in school would say, getting on her last nerve.

The man beside her in the next seat probably wasn't thrilled, either.

"I'm real sorry about this," she said, turning to speak to him for the first time since he'd gotten on. "She's usually not this cranky. It's our first trip together. I guess she's just ready to get where we're going."

The man blinked at her slowly, smiled without showing his teeth. "Where you headed?"

"New York City."

"Ah. The Big Apple," he murmured. His voice was dry, airless. "You got family there or something?"

She shook her head. The only family she had was in a backwoods town near Rangeley, and they'd made it clear that she was on her own now. "I'm going there for a job. I mean, I hope to find a job. I want to be a dancer. On Broadway maybe, or one of them Rockettes."

"Well, you sure are pretty enough." The man was staring at her now. It was dark in the bus, but she thought there was something kind of weird about his eyes. Again the tight smile. "With a body like yours, you ought to be a big star."

Blushing, she glanced down at her complaining baby. Her boyfriend back in Maine used to say stuff like that, too. He used to say a lot of things to get her into the backseat of his car. And he wasn't her boyfriend anymore, either. Not since her junior year of high school when she started swelling up with his kid.

If she hadn't quit to have the baby, she would have graduated this summer.

"Have you had anything to eat yet today?" the man asked, as the bus slowed down and turned into the Boston station.

"Not really." She gently bounced her baby girl in her arms, for all the good it did. She was red in the face, her tiny fists pumping, still crying like there was no tomorrow.

"What a coincidence," the stranger said. "I haven't eaten, either. I could do with a bite, if you're game to join me?"

"Nah. I'm okay. I've got some saltines in my bag. And anyway, I think this is the last bus to New York tonight, so I won't have time to do much more than change the baby and get right back on. Thanks, though."

He didn't say anything else, just watched her gather her few things once the bus was parked in its bay, then moved out of his seat to let her pass on her way to the station's facilities.

When she came out of the restroom, the man was waiting for her.

A niggle of unease shot through her to see him standing there. He hadn't seemed so big when he was sitting next to her. And now that she was looking at him again, she could see that there was definitely something freaky about his eyes. Was he some kind of stoner?

"What's going on?"

He chuckled under his breath. "I told you. I need to feed."

That was an odd way of putting it.

She couldn't help noticing that there were only a few other people around in the station at this late hour. A light rain had begun, wetting the pavement, sending stragglers in for cover. Her bus was idling in its bay, already reloading. But in order to get to it, she first had to get past him.

She shrugged, too tired and anxious to deal with this crap. "So, if you're hungry, go tell it to McDonald's. I'm late for my bus—"

"Listen, bitch—" He moved so fast, she didn't know what hit her. One second he was standing three feet away from her, the next he had his hand around her throat, cutting off her air. He pushed her back into the shadows near the terminal building. Back where nobody was going to notice if she got mugged. Or worse. His mouth was so close to her face, she could smell his foul breath. She saw his sharp teeth as he curled his lips back and hissed a terrible threat. "Say another word, move another muscle, and you'll be watching me eat your brat's juicy little heart."

Her baby was wailing in her arms now, but she didn't say a word.

She didn't so much as think about moving.

All that mattered was her baby. Keeping her safe. And so she didn't dare do a thing, not even when those sharp teeth lunged toward her and bit down hard into her neck.

She stood utterly frozen with terror, clutching her baby close while her attacker drew hard at the bleeding gash he'd made in her throat. His fingers elongated where he gripped her head and shoulder, the tips cutting into her like a demon's claws. He grunted and pulled deeper at her with his mouth and sharp teeth. Although her eyes were wide open in horror, her vision was going dark, her thoughts beginning to tumble, splintering into pieces. Everything around her was growing murky.

He was killing her. The monster was killing her. And then he would kill her baby, too.

"No." She gulped in air, but tasted only blood. "Goddamn you—No!"

With a desperate burst of will, she snapped her head into his, cracking the side of her skull into her attacker's face. When he snarled and reared back in surprise, she tore out of his grasp. She stumbled, nearly falling to her knees before she righted herself. One arm wrapped around her howling child, the other coming up to feel the slick, burning wound at her neck, she edged backward, away from the creature that lifted his head and sneered at her with glowing yellow eyes and bloodstained lips.

"Oh, God," she moaned, sick at the sight.

She took another step back. Pivoted, prepared to bolt, even if it was pointless.

And that's when she saw the other one.

Fierce amber eyes looked right through her, but the hiss that sounded from between his huge, gleaming fangs promised death. She thought he would lace into her and finish what the first one had started, but he didn't. Guttural words were spat between the two of them, then the new-comer strode past her, a long silver blade in his hand.

Take the child, and go.

The command seemed to come out of nowhere, cutting through the fog of her mind. It came again, sharper now, spurring her into action. She ran.

Blind with panic, her mind numb with fear and confusion, she ran away from the terminal and down a nearby street. Deeper and deeper, she fled into the unfamiliar city, into the night. Hysteria clawed at her, making every noise—even the sound of her own running feet—seem monstrous and deadly.

And her baby wouldn't stop crying.

They were going to be found out if she didn't get the baby to quiet down. She had to put her to bed, nice and warm in her crib. Then her little girl would be happy. Then she'd be safe. Yes, that's what she had to do. Put the baby to bed, where the monsters couldn't find her.

She was tired herself, but she couldn't rest. Too dangerous. She had to get home before her mom realized she had missed curfew again. She was numb, disoriented, but she had to run. And so she did. She ran until she dropped, exhausted and unable to take another step.

When she woke sometime later, it was to feel her mind coming unhinged, cracking apart like an eggshell. Sanity was peeling away from her, reality warping into something black and slippery, something that was dancing farther and farther out of her reach.

She heard muffled crying somewhere in the distance. Such a tiny sound. She put her hands up to cover her ears, but she could still hear that helpless little mewl.

"Hush," she murmured to no one in particular, rocking back and forth. "Be quiet now, the baby's sleeping. Be quiet be quiet be quiet...."

But the crying kept on. It didn't stop, and didn't stop. It tore at her heart as she sat in the filthy street and stared, unseeing, into the coming dawn.

CHAPTER
One

Remarkable. Just look at the use of light and shadow...."

"You see how this image hints at the sorrow of the place, yet manages to convey a promise of hope?"

"...one of the youngest photographers to be included in the museum's new modern art collection."

Gabrielle Maxwell stood back from the group of exhibit attendees, nursing a flute of warm champagne as yet another crowd of faceless, nameless, Very Important People enthused over the two dozen black-and-white photographs displayed on the gallery walls. She glanced at the images from across the room, somewhat bemused. They were good photographs—a bit edgy, their subject matter being abandoned mills and desolate dockyards outside Boston—but she didn't quite get what everyone else was seeing in them.

Then again, she never did. Gabrielle merely took the photographs; she left their interpretation, and ultimately, their appreciation, up to others. An introvert by nature, it made her uncomfortable to be on the receiving end of this much praise and attention... but it did pay the bills. Quite nicely, at that. Tonight, it was also paying the bills for her friend Jamie, the owner of the funky little art gallery on Newbury Street, which, at ten minutes to closing, was still packed with prospective buyers.

Numb with the whole process of meeting and greeting, of smiling politely as everyone from moneyed Back Bay wives to multipierced, tattooed Goths tried to impress one another—and her—with analyses of her work, Gabrielle couldn't wait for the exhibit to end. She had been hiding in the shadows for the past hour, contemplating a stealth escape to the comfort of a warm shower and a soft pillow, both waiting at her apartment on the city's east side.

But she had promised a few of her friends—Jamie, Kendra, and Megan—that she would join them for dinner and drinks after the showing. As the last couple of stragglers made their purchases and left, Gabrielle found herself gathered up and swept into a cab before she had a chance to so much as think of begging off.

"What an awesome night!" Jamie's androgynous blond hair swung around his face as he leaned across the other two women to clutch Gabrielle's hand. "I've never had so much weekend traffic in the gallery—and tonight's sales receipts were amazing! Thank you so much for letting me host you."

Gabrielle smiled at her friend's excitement. "Of course. No need to thank me."

"You weren't too miserable, were you?"

"How could she be, with half of Boston falling at her

feet?" gushed Kendra, before Gabrielle could answer for herself. "Was that the governor I saw you talking with over the canapés?"

Gabrielle nodded. "He's offered to commission some original works for his cottage on the Vineyard."

"Sweet!"

"Yeah," Gabrielle replied without much enthusiasm. She had a stack of business cards in her pocketbook—at least a year of steady work, if she wanted it—so why was she tempted to open the taxi window and scatter them all to the wind?

She let her gaze drift to the night outside the car, watching in queer detachment as lights and lives flickered past. The streets teemed with people: couples strolling hand in hand, groups of friends laughing and talking, all of them having a great time. They dined at café tables outside trendy bistros and paused to browse store window displays. Everywhere she looked, the city pulsed with color and life. Gabrielle absorbed it all with her artist's eye and, yet, felt nothing. This bustle of life—her life as well—seemed to be speeding by without her. More and more lately, she felt as if she were caught on a wheel that wouldn't stop spinning her around, trapping her in an endless cycle of passing time and little purpose.

"Is anything wrong, Gab?" Megan asked from beside her on the taxi's bench seat. "You seem quiet."

Gabrielle shrugged. "I'm sorry. I'm just...I don't know. Tired, I guess."

"Somebody get this woman a drink—stat!" Kendra, the dark-haired nurse, joked.

"Nah," Jamie countered, sly and catlike. "What our Gab really needs is a man. You're too serious, sweetie. It's not healthy to let your work consume you like you do.

Have some fun! When's the last time you got laid, any-way?"

Too long ago but Gabrielle wasn't really keeping track. She'd never suffered from a shortage of dates when she wanted them, and sex—on those rare occasions she had it—wasn't something she obsessed over like some of her friends. As out of practice as she was right now in that de-partment, she didn't think an orgasm was going to cure whatever was causing her current state of restlessness.

"Jamie is right, you know," Kendra was saying. "You need to loosen up, get a little wild."

"No time like the present," Jamie added.

"Oh, I don't think so," Gabrielle said, shaking her head. "I'm really not up for a late night, you guys. Gallery showings always take a lot out of me and I—"

"Driver?" Ignoring her, Jamie slid to the edge of the seat and rapped on the Plexiglas that separated the cabbie from his passengers. "Change of plans. We decided we're in the mood for celebrating, so ixnay on the restaurant. We wanna go where all the hot people are."

"If you like dance clubs, there's a new one just opened in the north end," the cabbie said, his spearmint chewing gum cracking as he spoke. "I been takin' fares over there all week. Fact, took two already tonight—fancy after-hours place called La Notte."

"Ooh, La No-tay," Jamie purred, tossing a playful look over his shoulder and arching an elegant brow. "Sounds perfectly wicked to me, girls. Let's go!"

The club, La Notte, was housed in a High Victorian Gothic building that had long been known as St. John's Trinity Parish church, until recent Archdiocese of Boston payouts on priest sex scandals forced the closings of dozens of such places around the city. Now, as Gabrielle and her friends made their way inside the crowded club, synthesized trance and techno music rang in the rafters, blasting out of enormous speakers that framed the DJ pit in the balcony above the altar. Strobe lights flashed against a trio of arched stained-glass windows. The pulsing beams cut through the thin cloud of smoke that hung in the air, pounding to the frenetic beat of a seemingly endless song. On the dance floor—and in nearly every square foot of La Notte's main floor and the gallery above—people moved against one another in writhing, mindless sensuality.

"Holy shit," Kendra shouted over the music, raising her arms and dancing her way through the thick crowd. "What a place, huh? This is crazy!"

They hadn't even cleared the first knot of clubbers before a tall, lean guy swooped in on the spunky brunette and bent to say something in her ear. Kendra gave a throaty laugh and nodded enthusiastically at him.

"Boy wants to dance," she giggled, passing her handbag to Gabrielle. "Who am I to refuse!"

"This way," Jamie said, pointing to a small, empty table near the bar as their friend trotted off with her partner.

The three of them got seated and Jamie ordered a round of drinks. Gabrielle scanned the dance floor for Kendra, but she'd been devoured in the midst of the crowded space. Despite the crush of people all around, Gabrielle could not dismiss the sudden sensation that she and her friends were sitting in a spotlight. Like they were somehow under scrutiny simply for being in the club. It was nuts to think it. Maybe she had been working too much, spending too much time alone at home, if being out in public could make her feel so self-conscious. So paranoid.

"Here's to Gab!" Jamie exclaimed over the roar of the music, raising his martini glass in salute.

Megan lifted hers, too, and clinked it against Gabrielle's. "Congratulations on a great exhibit tonight!"

"Thanks, you guys."

As she sipped the neon yellow concoction, Gabrielle's feeling of being observed returned. Or rather, increased. She felt a stare reach out to her from across the darkened distance. Over the rim of her martini glass, she glanced up and caught the glint of a strobe light nicking off a pair of dark sunglasses.

Sunglasses hiding a gaze that was unmistakably fixed on her through the crowd.

The quick flashes from the strobes cast his stark features in hard shadow, but Gabrielle's eyes took him in at once. Spiky black hair falling loosely around a broad, intelligent brow and lean, angular cheeks. A strong, stern jaw. And his mouth...his mouth was generous and sensual, even when quirked in that cynical, almost cruel line.

Gabrielle looked away, unnerved, a rush of warmth skittering along her limbs. His face lingered in her head, burned there in an instant, like an image set to film. She put down her drink and braved another quick glance to where he stood. But he was gone.

A loud crash sounded at the other end of the bar, jerking Gabrielle's attention over her shoulder. At one of the crowded tables, liquor seeped onto the floor, spilled from several broken glasses that littered the black-lacquered surface. Five guys in dark leather and shades were having words with another guy wearing a Dead Kennedys wifebeater tank and torn, faded blue jeans. One of the thugs in

leather had his arm slung around a drunk-looking plat-
inum blond, who seemed to know the punker. Boyfriend,
apparently. He made a grab for the girl's arm, but she
slapped him away and bent her head to let one of the
thugs put his mouth on her neck. She stared defiantly at
her furious boyfriend, all the while playing with the long
brown hair of the guy fastened to her throat.

"That's messed up," Megan said, turning back around
as the situation escalated.

"Sure is," Jamie added as he finished off his martini
and flagged a server to bring another round. "Evidently
that chick's mama forgot to tell her it's bad news not to
leave with the guy who brought you."

Gabrielle watched for another moment, long enough
to see a second biker move in on the girl and descend on
her slackened mouth. She accepted both of them together,
her hands coming up to caress the dark head at her neck
and the pale one that was sucking her face like he meant to
eat her alive. The punker boyfriend shouted a string of ob-
scenities at the girl, then turned around and shoved his
way into the spectating crowd.

"This place is creeping me out," Gabrielle confided,
just now noticing some clubbers openly doing lines of co-
caine off the far end of the long marble bar.

Her friends didn't seem to hear her over the driving
pound of the music. They also didn't seem to share
Gabrielle's unease. Something wasn't quite right here and
Gabrielle could not shake the feeling that eventually the
night was going to get ugly. Jamie and Megan began talking between themselves about local bands, leaving
Gabrielle to sip what was left of her martini and wait on
the other side of the small table for an opportunity to
break in and make her excuses to leave.

Essentially alone at the moment, her gaze drifted over the sea of bobbing heads and swaying bodies, as she surreptitiously searched for the sunglass-shaded eyes that had been watching her before. Was he with the other thugs—one of that gang of bikers still stirring up trouble? He was dressed like them, certainly carried the same dark air of danger about him.

Whoever he was, Gabrielle saw no trace of him now.

She leaned back in her chair, then nearly jumped out of her skin when a pair of hands came to rest on her shoulders from behind.

"Here you are! I've been looking all over for you guys!" Kendra said, sounding breathless and animated at the same time, as she leaned over the table. "Come on. I've got a table for us on the other side of the club. Brent and some of his friends want to party with us!"

"Cool!"

Jamie was already on his feet, ready to go. Megan took her fresh martini in one hand, Kendra's and her pocketbooks in the other. When Gabrielle didn't rush to join them, Megan paused.

"You coming?"

"No." Gabrielle stood up and looped the strap of her handbag over her shoulder. "You go on, have fun. I'm beat. I think I'm just going to catch a cab and head back home."

Kendra gave her a little-girl pout. "Gab, you can't go!"

"You want some company for the ride home?" Megan offered, even though Gabrielle could tell she wanted to stay with the others.

"I'll be fine. Enjoy yourselves, but be careful, right?"

"You're sure you won't stay? Just one more drink?"

"Nah. I really need to take off and get some air."

"Suit yourself, then," Kendra chided with mock venom. She stepped in and planted a quick peck on Gabrielle's cheek. As she withdrew, Gabrielle caught a whiff of vodka, and, beneath that, something less obvious. Something musky, queerly metallic. "You're a buzzkill, Gab, but I still love you."

With a wink, Kendra looped her arms with Jamie's and Megan's, then playfully tugged them toward the churning mass of people.

"Call me tomorrow," Jamie mouthed over his shoulder as the trio were slowly engulfed by the crowd.

Gabrielle immediately started her trek for the door, anxious to be out of the club. The longer she had stayed, the louder the music seemed to get, drumming in her head, making it hard to think. Hard to focus on her surroundings. People pushed at her from all sides as she tried to pass through them, squeezing her into the press of dancing, flailing, gyrating bodies. She was jostled and nudged, pawed at and groped by unseen hands in the dark, until, finally, she stumbled into the vestibule near the club's entrance, then out the heavy double doors.

The night was cool and dark. She drew in a deep breath, clearing her head of the noise and smoke and the unsettling atmosphere of La Notte. The music still throbbed out here, the strobe lights still flashed like small explosions behind the tall stained-glass windows above, but Gabrielle relaxed a bit now that she was free.

No one paid her any mind as she hurried down to the curb and waited to hail a ride home. Only a few people were outside, some passing by on the sidewalk below, others filing up the concrete steps and into the club. She spotted a yellow cab coming her way, and thrust out her hand to call it over.

"Taxi!"

As the empty cab navigated across the lanes of night-time traffic and roared up beside her, the doors of the nightclub burst open with the force of a hurricane.

"Hey, man! What the fuck!" Behind Gabrielle on the steps, a male voice rose to an octave just north of fear. "Touch me again, and I'll fuckin'—"

"You'll fuckin' what?" taunted another voice, this one low and deadly, and flanked by several others that were chuckling in amusement.

"Yeah, tell us, you little asswipe punker piece of shit. What're ya gonna do?"

Her fingers gripping the door handle of the cab, Gabrielle swiveled her head, half in alarm, half in knowing dread of what she would see. It was the gang from the bar, the bikers or whatever they were, in black leather and shades. The six of them circled the punker boyfriend like a pack of wolves, taking turns jabbing at him, toying with him like prey.

The kid threw a swing at one of them—missed—and the situation went from bad to worse in the blink of an eye.

All at once, the scuffle came crashing toward Gabrielle. The gang of thugs threw the punker up against the hood of the cab, slamming their fists into the kid's face. Blood splattered like raindrops from his nose and mouth, some of it hitting Gabrielle. She took a step back, stunned and horrified. The kid scrabbled to get away but his attackers stayed on him, beating him with a fury Gabrielle could hardly fathom.

"Get off my goddamn car!" the cabbie shouted out his open window. "Jesus Christ! Take it somewhere else, you hear me!"

One of the assailants turned his head toward the cabbie, smiled a terrible smile, then brought his large fist down on the windshield, shattering the glass into a spiderweb of cracks. Gabrielle saw the cabbie cross himself, his mouth working soundlessly within the car. There was a grinding of gears, then a piercing screech of tires as the taxi jerked into reverse, dislodging the burden from its hood.

"Wait!" Gabrielle screamed, too late.

Her ride home—her escape from this brutal scene— was gone. With a cold lump of fear lodged in her throat, she watched the cab speed off, careering into the street and its taillights disappearing into the dark.

And on the curb, the six bikers were showing their victim no mercy, too preoccupied with beating the punker senseless to give Gabrielle more than a passing thought.

She turned and bolted up the steps to La Notte's entrance, all the while fishing in her pocketbook for her cell phone. She found the slim device, flipped it open. Punched in 911 as she threw open the doors of the club and skidded into the vestibule, panic rising in her breast. Above the din of music and voices, and the thundering pulse of her own heart, Gabrielle heard only static on the other end of her cell. She pulled the phone away from her ear—

Signal faded.

"Shit!"

She tried 911 again. No luck.

Gabrielle ran for the main area of the club, shouting into the noise in desperation.

"Someone, please help! I need help!"

No one seemed to hear her. She tapped people's shoulders, tugged on sleeves, practically shook the arm of a tattooed military-looking guy, but no one paid any attention. They didn't even look at her, merely continued dancing and talking as if she wasn't even there.

Was this a dream? Some twisted nightmare where only she was aware of the violence taking place outside?

Gabrielle gave up on strangers and decided to search out her friends. As she wended through the dark club, she kept hitting *Redial*, praying for a decent signal. She couldn't get one, and she soon realized she would never find Jamie and the others in the thick crowd.

Frustrated and confused, she ran back to the club's exit. Maybe she could flag down a motorist, find a cop, anything!

Frigid night air hit her face as she pushed open the heavy doors and stepped outside. She dashed down the first set of concrete steps, panting now, uncertain what she was walking into, a woman alone against six, probably drugged-out gang members. But she didn't see them.

They were gone.

A group of young clubbers came strolling up the steps, one of them playing air guitar while his friends talked about hitting a rave later that night.

"Hey," Gabrielle said, half expecting them to walk right past her. They paused, smiling at her, even though at twenty-eight she was likely a decade older than any of them.

The one in the lead nodded his head at her. " 'Sup?"

"Did any of you—" She hesitated, not certain she should be relieved that this was not, evidently, a dream after all. "Did you happen to see the fight that was going on out here a few minutes ago?"

"There was a fight? Awesome!" said the headbanger of the group.

"Nah, man," answered another. "We just got here. We ain't seen nothin'."

They passed by, climbing the rest of the steps while

Gabrielle could only watch, wondering if she was losing her mind. She walked down to the curb. There was blood on the pavement, but the punker and his attackers had vanished.

Gabrielle stood under a streetlamp and rubbed a chill from her arms. She pivoted to look down both sides of the street, searching for any sign of the violence she had witnessed a few minutes before.

Nothing.

But then ... she heard it.

The sound drifted from a narrow alley to her right. Flanked by a concrete shoulder-high wall that acted as an acoustic aid, the almost lightless walkway betrayed its occupants whose faint animal-like grunts carried out to the street. Gabrielle could not place the sick, wet sounds that froze her blood in her veins and tripped off instinctual alarms in every nerve in her body.

Her feet were moving. Not away from the source of those disturbing sounds, but toward it. Her cell phone was like a brick in her hand. She was holding her breath. She didn't realize she wasn't breathing until she had walked a couple of paces into the alleyway and her gaze had settled on a group of figures up ahead.

The thugs in leather and sunglasses.

They were crouched down on their hands and knees, pawing at something, tearing at it. In the scant light from the street, Gabrielle glimpsed a tattered scrap of fabric lying near the carnage. It was the punker's tank top, shredded and stained.

Gabrielle's finger, poised over the *Redial* button of her cell phone, came down silently onto the tiny key. There was a quiet trill on the other end, then the police dispatcher's voice shattered the night like cannon fire.

"911. What is your emergency?"

One of the bikers swung his head around at the sudden disturbance. Feral, hate-filled eyes pinned Gabrielle like daggers where she stood. His face was bloody, slick with gore. And his teeth! They were sharp like an animal's—not teeth at all, but fangs that he bared to her as he opened his mouth and hissed a terrible-sounding foreign word.

"911," said the dispatcher once again. "Please state your emergency."

Gabrielle couldn't speak. She was so shaken, she could hardly breathe. She brought the cell phone up to her mouth, but could not make her throat form words.

Her call for help was wasted.

Knowing this with a certain, bone-deep dread, Gabrielle did the only logical thing that came to her. With trembling fingers, she turned the device toward the gang of sadistic bikers and clicked the image-capture button. A small flash lit up the alley.

They all turned toward her now, raising their hands to shield their sunglass-shaded eyes.

Oh, God. Maybe she still had a chance of escaping this hellish night. Gabrielle clicked the picture button again and again and again, all the while making her retreat back up the alley to the street. She heard murmured voices, snarled curses, the movement of feet on pavement, but she didn't dare look back. Not even when a sharp hiss of steel rang out behind her, followed by unearthly shrieks of agony and rage.

Gabrielle raced into the night on adrenaline and fear, not stopping until she reached a standing taxi on Commercial Street. She jumped in and slammed the door. She was panting, out of her mind with fear.

"Take me to the nearest police station!"

The cabbie slung his arm over the back of the seat and turned around to stare at her, frowning. "You okay, lady?"

"Yeah," she replied automatically. Then, "No. I need to report a—"

Jesus. What *did* she intend to report? A cannibalistic feeding frenzy by a pack of rabid bikers? Or the only other possible explanation, which wasn't any more believable?

Gabrielle met the cabbie's anxious eyes. "Please hurry. I just witnessed a murder."

CHAPTER
Two

Vampires.

The night was thick with them. He had counted more than a dozen in the dance club, most of them trolling the half-dressed, undulating crowds, selecting—and seducing—the women who would Host their thirst that night. It was a symbiotic arrangement that had served the Breed well for more than two millennia, a peaceful cohabitation that depended on the vampires' ability to scrub the memories of the humans on whom they fed. Before the sun came up, a good deal of blood would be spilled but in the morning, the Breed would be returned to their Darkhavens in and around the city, and the humans they had enjoyed tonight would be none the wiser.

But that was not the case in the alley outside the night-club.

For the six blood-gorged predators there, their un-sanctioned kill would be their last. They were careless in their hunger; they hadn't detected that they were being watched. Not when he was observing them in the club, nor when he had trailed them outside, surveilling them from the ledge of a second-story window of the converted church.

They were lost to the high of Bloodlust, the disease of addiction that had once been epidemic among the Breed, causing so many of their kind to turn Rogue. Like these, who fed openly and indiscriminately from the humans who lived among them.

Lucan Thorne had no particular affinity for hu-mankind, but what he felt for the Rogue vampires before him was even less. To see one or two feral vampires in a single night's patrol of a city the size of Boston was not un-common. To find several working in tandem, feeding in the open as these did, was more than a little troubling. The Rogues were growing in numbers again, becoming more bold.

Something had to be done.

For Lucan and several others of the Breed, every night was a hunting expedition aimed at routing out the diseased few who would jeopardize all that the vampire race had worked so hard to achieve. Tonight, Lucan tracked his prey alone, not caring that he was outnumbered. He had waited until the opportunity to strike was prime: once the Rogues had greedily fed the addiction that ruled their minds.

Drunk on more blood than they could safely consume, they had continued to savage and fight over the body of the young man from the club, snarling and snapping like a pack of wild dogs. Lucan had been poised to dispatch quick justice—and would have, if it hadn't been for the sudden appearance of a ginger-haired female in the darkened corridor. In an instant, she had thrown the entire night off course: following the Rogues to the alley, then unwittingly drawing their attention away from their kill.

As the light from her cell phone's flash exploded in the dark, Lucan descended from the shadowed ledge of the window and landed on the pavement without a sound. Like the Rogues, Lucan's sensitive eyes were partially blinded from that sudden spark of light amid the dark. The woman fired a series of piercing flashes as she fled the carnage, those few panicked clicks likely all that spared her from the wrath of his savage kin.

But where the other vampires' senses were clouded and sluggish with Bloodlust, Lucan's were ruthlessly clear. From beneath his dark trenchcoat, he drew his weapons—twin blades wrought of titanium-edged steel—and swung to claim the head of the nearest Rogue.

Two more followed, the bodies of the dead thrashing as they began their swift cellular decomposition from oozing acidic pulp to incinerated ash. Animal shrieks filled the alleyway as Lucan severed the head of one more, then swung around to impale another Rogue through the torso. The Rogue hissed through bared, bloody teeth, its fangs dripping gore. Pale-gold eyes held Lucan in contempt, the huge irises swelled in hunger, swallowing up pupils that were narrowed to thin vertical slits. The creature spasmed, long arms reaching for him, its mouth stretched into a hideous, alien sneer as the specially forged steel poisoned its Rogue blood and reduced the vampire to smoldering stain on the street.

Only one remained. Lucan whirled to meet the large male, both blades raised to strike.

But the vampire was gone—fled into the night before he could slay it.

Damn.

He'd never let one of the bastards escape his justice before this. He shouldn't now. He considered chasing the Rogue down, but it would mean leaving the scene of the attack unsecured. That was the greater risk here, letting the humans know the full measure of the danger that lived among them. Because of the savagery of the Rogues, Lucan's kind had been persecuted and hunted by humans throughout the Old Times; the race might not survive a new age of retribution, now that man had technology on his side.

Until the Rogues were suppressed—better yet, eliminated entirely—humankind could know nothing of the existence of the vampires living all around them.

As he set about cleaning the area of all traces of the killing, Lucan's thoughts kept returning to the woman with the sunlit hair and sweet, alabaster beauty.

How was it she had been able to find the Rogues in the alley?

Although it was widely held among human folklore that vampires could disappear at will, the truth was only slightly less remarkable. Gifted with great agility and speed, they could simply move faster than human eyes could register, an ability that was augmented by the vampires' advanced hypnotic power over the minds of lesser beings. Oddly, this woman seemed immune to both.

Lucan had seen her in the club, he realized now. His gaze had been drawn away from his quarry by a pair of soulful eyes and a spirit that seemed nearly as lost as his own. She had noticed him, too, staring at him from where she sat with her friends. Even through the crowd and the stale odor of the club, Lucan had scented the trace notes of perfume on her skin—something exotic, rare.

He smelled it now as well, a delicate note that clung to the night, teasing his senses and calling to something primitive within him. His gums ached with the sudden stretching of his fangs, a physical reaction to need— carnal, or otherwise—that he was powerless to curb. He scented her, and he hungered, little better than his Rogue brethren.

Lucan tipped his head back and dragged the essence of the woman deeper into his lungs, tracking her across the city with his keen sense of smell. The sole witness to the Rogues' attack, it was more than unwise to let her keep the memory of what she had seen. Lucan would find the female and take whatever measures were necessary to ensure the protection of the Breed.

And in the back of his mind, an ancient conscience whispered that whoever she was, she already belonged to him.

"I'm telling you, I saw the whole thing. There were six of them, and they were tearing at the guy with their hands and teeth—like animals. They killed him!"

"Miss Maxwell, we've been over this numerous times already tonight. Now, we're all tired and the night is only getting longer."

Gabrielle had been at the police station for more than three hours, trying to give her account of the horror she witnessed outside La Notte. The two officers she spoke with had been skeptical at first, but now they were getting impatient, almost adversarial. Soon after she had arrived, the cops had sent a squad car around to the club to check out the situation and recover the body Gabrielle had reported seeing. The call had come up empty. No reports of a gang altercation and no evidence whatsoever of anyone having met with foul play. It was as if the entire incident had never happened—or had been miraculously swept clean.

"If you would just listen to me . . . if you would just look at the pictures I took—"

"We've seen them, Miss Maxwell. Several times already. Frankly, nothing you've said tonight checks out—not your statement, and not these grainy, unreadable images from your cell phone."

"I'm sorry if the quality is lacking," Gabrielle replied, acidly. "The next time I'm witnessing a bloody slaughter by a gang of psychos, I'll have to remember to bring my Leica and a few extra lenses."

"Maybe you want to rethink your statement," suggested the elder of the two officers, his Boston accent tinged with the Irish brogue of a youth spent in Southie. He stroked a chubby hand over his thinning brow, then slid her cell phone back across the desk. "You should be aware that filing a false police report is a crime, Miss Maxwell."

"This is not a false report," she insisted, frustrated and not a little angry that she was being treated like the criminal here. "I stand by everything I've said tonight. Why would I make this up?"

"That's something only you can answer, Miss Maxwell."

"This is unbelievable. You have my 911 call."

"Yes," agreed the officer. "You did, indeed, make a call to emergency dispatch. Unfortunately, all we have is static on the recording. You didn't say anything, and you didn't respond to the dispatcher's requests for information."

"Yeah, well, it's hard to find the words to describe seeing someone get their throat ripped out."

He gave her another dubious look. "This club—La Notte? It's a wild place, I hear. Popular with the goths, the ravers..."

"Your point being?"

The cop shrugged. "Lotta kids get into some weird shit these days. Maybe all you saw was a little fun getting out of hand."

Gabrielle exhaled a curse and reached for her cell phone. "Does this look like fun getting out of hand to you?"

She clicked the picture recall button and looked again at the images she had captured. Although the snapshots were blurry, diffused by the flash, she could still plainly see a group of men surrounding another on the ground. She clicked forward to another image and saw the reflective glow of several eyes staring back at the lens, the vague outlines of facial features peeled back in animal fury.

Why didn't the officers see what she did?

"Miss Maxwell," interjected the younger police officer. He strolled around to the other side of the desk and sat on the edge before her. He had been the quieter of the two men, the one listening in careful consideration where his partner spewed nothing but doubt and suspicion. "It's obvious that you believe you saw something terrible at the club tonight. Officer Carrigan and I want to help you, but in order for us to do that, we have to be sure we're all on the same page."

She nodded. "Okay."

"Now, we have your statement, and we've seen your pictures. You strike me as a reasonable person. Before we can go any further here, I need to ask if you would be willing to submit to a drug test."

"A drug test." Gabrielle shot out of her chair. She was beyond pissed off now. "This is ridiculous. I am not some tripped out crackhead, and I resent being treated like one. I'm trying to report a murder!"

"Gab? Gabby!"

From somewhere behind her in the station, Gabrielle heard Jamie's voice. She had called her friend soon after she arrived, needing the comfort of familiar faces after the horror she had witnessed.

"Gabrielle!" Jamie dashed up to her and surrounded her in a warm hug. "I'm sorry I couldn't get here sooner, but I was already home when I got your message on my cell. Jesus, sweetie! Are you all right?"

Gabrielle nodded. "I think so. Thanks for coming."

"Miss Maxwell, why don't you let your friend here take you home," said the younger officer. "We can continue this at another time. Maybe you'll be able to think more clearly after you get some sleep."

The two policemen rose, and gestured for Gabrielle to do the same. She didn't argue. She was tired, bone weary, and she didn't think even if she stayed at the station all night she'd be able to convince the cops of what she witnessed outside La Notte. Numbly, Gabrielle let Jamie and the two officers escort her out of the station. She was halfway down the steps to the parking lot when the younger of the men called her name.

"Miss Maxwell?"

She paused, looking back over her shoulder to where the officer stood beneath the floodlight of the station.

"If it will make you rest any easier, we'll send someone around to check in on you at your home, and maybe talk to you a bit more, once you've had some time to think about your report."

She didn't appreciate his coddling tone, but neither could she find the anger to refuse his offer. After what she had seen tonight, Gabrielle would gladly take the security of a police visit, even a patronizing one. She nodded, then followed Jamie out to his waiting car.

From a quiet corner desk in the precinct house, a file clerk hit the print key on his computer. A laser printer whirred into action behind him, spitting out a single page report. The clerk drained the last swallow of cold coffee from his chipped Red Sox mug, rose from his rickety, putty-colored chair, and casually retrieved the document from the printer.

The station was quiet, emptied out for the midnight shift break. But even if it had been hopping with activity, no one would have paid any attention to the reserved, awkward intern who kept very much to himself.

That was the beauty of his role.

It was why he'd been chosen.

He wasn't the only member of the force to be recruited. He knew there were others, though their identities were kept secret. It was safer that way, cleaner. For his part, he couldn't recall how long it had been since he first met his Master. He knew only that he now lived to serve.

With the report clutched in his hand, the clerk shuffled down the hallway in search of privacy. The break room, which was never empty no matter the time of day, was currently occupied by a couple of secretaries and Carrigan, a fat, loud-mouthed cop who was retiring at the end of the week. He was bragging about the primo deal he had gotten on some backwater Florida condo while the women basically ignored him, the two females lunching on day-old, frosted yellow party cake and washing it all down with Diet Coke chasers.

The clerk ran his fingers through his pale brown hair and walked past the open doorway, toward the restrooms at the end of the corridor. He paused outside the men's room, his hand on the battered metal handle, as he casually glanced behind him. With no one there to see him, he moved to the next door down, the station's janitorial supply closet. It was supposed to be kept locked, but seldom was. Nothing much worth stealing in there anyway, unless you had a thing for industrial-grade toilet paper, ammonia cleanser, and brown paper towels.

He twisted the knob and pushed the old steel panel inward. Once inside the dark closet, he clicked the push-button lock from within and retrieved his cell phone from the front pocket of his khakis. He pressed speed dial, calling the sole number that was stored in the untraceable, disposable device. The call rang twice, then fell into an ominous silence as his Master's unmistakable presence loomed on the other end of the line.

"Sire," the clerk breathed, his voice a reverent whisper. "I have information for you."

He spoke quickly and quietly, divulging all of the details of the Maxwell woman's visit to the station, including the specifics of her statement about a gang killing downtown. The clerk heard a growl and the soft hiss of breath skating across the cell phone's receiver as his Master absorbed the news in silence. He sensed fury in that slow, wordless exhalation, and it chilled him.

"I ran her personal data for you, Sire—all of it," he offered; then using the dim glow of the cell's display, he recited Gabrielle's address, unlisted phone number, and more, the servile Minion so very eager to please his dreaded and powerful Master.

CHAPTER
Three

Two full days passed.

Gabrielle tried to put the horror of what she had witnessed in La Notte's alleyway out of her mind. What did it matter, anyway? No one had believed her. Not the police, who had yet to send anyone to see her as they had promised, and not even her friends.

Jamie and Megan, who had seen the thugs in leather harassing the punker inside the club, said the group left without incident sometime during the course of the night. Kendra had been too involved with Brent—the guy she picked up on the dance floor—to notice any trouble elsewhere in the club. According to the cops at the station Saturday night, the story had been the same from everyone their dispatched patrol had questioned at La Notte. A brief scuffle at the bar, but no reports of violence in or outside of the club.

•No one had seen the attack she reported. There had been no hospital or morgue admissions. Not even a damage report filed by the cabbie at the curb.

Nothing.

How could that be? Was she seriously delusional?

It was as if Gabrielle's eyes were the only ones truly open that night. Either she alone had witnessed something unexplainable, or she was losing her mind.

Maybe some of both.

She couldn't deal with all the implications in that idea, so she sought solace in the one thing that gave her any joy. Behind the sealed door of her custom-built darkroom in the basement of the townhouse, Gabrielle submerged a sheet of photo paper in the tray of developing solution. From pale nothingness, the image began to take shape beneath the surface of the liquid. She watched it come to life—the ironic beauty of strong ivy tentacles spreading over the decayed brick and mortar of an old Gothic-style asylum she had recently discovered outside the city. It came out better than she had hoped, teasing her artist's fancy with the potential of an entire series centered on the haunting, desolate place. She set it aside and developed another photo, this one a closeup of a pine sapling sprouting from between a crack in the crumpled pavement of a long-abandoned lumberyard.

The images made her smile as she lifted them out of the solution and clipped them to the drying line. She had nearly a dozen more like these upstairs on her worktable, wry testaments to the stubbornness of nature and the foolishness of man's greed and arrogance.

Gabrielle had always felt something of an outsider, a

silent observer, from the time she was a kid. She chalked it up to the fact that she had no parents—no family at all, except the couple who had adopted her when she was a troubled twelve-year-old, bounced from one foster home to another. The Maxwells, an upper-middle-class couple with no children of their own, had kindly taken pity on her, but even their acceptance had been at arm's length. Gabrielle was promptly sent to boarding schools, summer camps, and, finally, an out-of-state university. Her parents, such as they were, had died together in a car accident while she was away at college.

Gabrielle didn't attend the funeral, but the first serious photograph she took was of two maple-shaded gravestones in the city's Mount Auburn Cemetery. She'd been taking pictures ever since.

Never one to mourn the past, Gabrielle turned off the darkroom light and headed back upstairs to think about supper. She wasn't in the kitchen two minutes before her doorbell rang.

Jamie had generously stayed over the past two nights, just to make sure Gabrielle was all right. He was worried about her, as protective as a big brother she never had. When he left that morning, he had offered to come by again, but Gabrielle had insisted she would be fine by herself. She was actually in need of some solitude, and as the doorbell sounded again, she felt a niggle of mild annoyance that she might not have any alone time tonight, either.

"Be right there," she called from inside the apartment's foyer.

Habit made her check the peephole, but instead of seeing Jamie's blond sweep of hair, Gabrielle found the dark head and striking features of an unfamiliar man waiting on her stoop. A reproduction gaslight stood on the sidewalk just off her front steps. The soft yellow glow wrapped itself around the man like a golden cloak draped over night itself. There was something ominous, yet compelling, about his pale gray eyes, which were staring straight into the narrow cylinder of glass as if he could see her on the other side, too.

She opened the door, but thought it best not to remove the chain lock. The man stepped in front of the wedge of open space and glanced at the tight chain length that stretched taut between them. When his eyes met Gabrielle's again, he gave her a vague smile, as if he thought it amusing she would expect to bar him so easily if he truly wanted in.

"Miss Maxwell?" His voice stroked her senses like rich, dark velvet.

"Yes?"

"My name is Lucan Thorne." The words rolled past his lips in a smooth, measured timbre that eased some of her anxiety at once. When she didn't say anything, he went on. "I understand you had some difficulty a couple of nights ago at the police station. I wanted to come by and make sure you were all right."

She nodded.

Evidently the police hadn't completely blown her off after all. Since it had been a couple of days with no word from them, Gabrielle had not expected to see anyone from the department, despite the promise to send a patrol out to look in on her. Not that she could be certain this guy, with his sleekly styled black hair and chiseled features, was a cop.

He looked grim enough, she supposed, and apart from his dark, dangerous good looks, he didn't seem intent on causing her any harm. Still, after what she'd been through, Gabrielle thought it wise to err on the side of caution.

"Have you got ID?"

"Of course."

With deliberate, almost sensual movements, he opened a thin leather billfold and held it up to the crack of space at the door. It was nearly dark outside, which was likely why it took a second for Gabrielle's eyes to focus on the shiny policeman's badge and the picture identification card next to it, bearing his name.

"Okay. Come in, Detective."

She freed the chain lock, then opened the door and let him enter, watching as his broad shoulders filled the doorway. His presence seemed to fill the entire foyer, in fact. He was a large man, tall and thickly hewn beneath the drape of his black overcoat, his dark clothes and silky jet hair absorbed the soft light of the pendant lamp overhead. He had a confident, almost regal bearing about him, his expression gravely serious, as if he would be better suited to commanding a legion of armored knights than schlepping out to Beacon Hill to handhold a hallucinatory female.

"I didn't think anyone was going to come. After the reception I got down at the station this weekend, I figured Boston's finest had written me off as a nutcase."

He didn't acknowledge or deny it, merely strode into her living room in silence and let his gaze roam freely over the place. He paused at her worktable, where the roughs of some of her latest images had been arranged. Gabrielle trailed after him across the room, casually watching for his reaction to her work. One dark brow quirked as he perused the photographs.

"Yours?" he asked, turning his pale, piercing eyes on her.

"Yes," Gabrielle replied. "They're part of a collection I'm calling *Urban Renewal.*"

"Interesting."

He looked back to the array of images and Gabrielle felt herself frown slightly at his careful, yet indifferent response. "They're just something I'm playing around with right now—nothing I'm ready to exhibit yet."

He grunted, still considering the photographs in silence.

Gabrielle moved closer, trying to get a better handle on his reaction, or lack thereof. "I do a lot of commissioned work around the city. In fact, I'll probably be taking some pictures of the governor's place on the Vineyard later this month."

Shut up, she admonished herself. *Why was she trying to impress this guy?*

Detective Thorne didn't seem overly impressed. Saying nothing, he reached out, and with fingers entirely too elegant for his profession, gently rearranged two of the images on the table. Inexplicably, Gabrielle found herself imagining those long, deft fingers touching her bare skin, splaying into her hair, cupping the back of her skull ... guiding her head back until it rested on his strong arm and his cool gray eyes drank her in.

"So," she said, snapping herself back to reality. "I'll bet you'd rather have a look at the pictures I took outside the club Saturday night."

Without waiting for him to reply, she walked to the kitchen and grabbed her cell phone off the counter. She flipped it open, brought up an image, and held the device out to Detective Thorne.

"That's the first shot I took. My hands were shaking, so it's a little blurry. And the light from the flash washed out a lot of the detail. But if you look closely, you'll see six dark shapes huddled low to the ground. That's them—the killers. Their victim is that lump they're tearing at in front of them. They were...biting him. Like animals."

Thorne's eyes held fast to the image; his expression remained grim, unchanging. Gabrielle clicked to the next photograph.

"The flash startled them. I don't know—I think it might have blinded them or something. When I clicked these next few shots, some of them stopped to look at me. I can't really make out features, but that's the face of one of them. Those weird slits of light are the reflection of his eyes." She shuddered, recalling the yellow glow of vicious, inhuman eyes. "He was looking right at me."

More silence from the detective. He took the cell phone from Gabrielle's fingers and clicked through the remaining pictures.

"What do you think?" she asked, hoping for confirmation. "You can see it, too, can't you?"

"I see...something, yes."

"Thank God. Your buddies at the precinct tried to make me think I was crazy, or that I was some drugged-out loser who didn't know what I was talking about. Not even my friends believed me when I told them what I saw that night."

"Your friends," he said with careful deliberation. "Do you mean someone other than the man you were with at the station—your lover?"

"My lover?" She laughed at that. "Jamie is not my lover."

Thorne looked up from the cell phone's image display to meet her gaze. "He spent the past two nights with you alone, here in this apartment."

How did he know that? Gabrielle felt a jolt of outrage at the prospect of being spied on by anyone, including the police, who probably would have done so more out of suspicion than as a means of protecting her. But as she stood beside Detective Lucan Thorne in her living room, some of that anger seeped out of her, replaced by a feeling of calm acceptance. Of subtle, languid cooperation. Strange, she thought, but found herself fairly unfazed by the idea.

"Jamie stayed with me for a couple of nights because he was concerned about me after what happened this weekend. He's my friend, that's all."

Good.

Thorne's mouth didn't move, but Gabrielle felt certain she had heard his reply. His unspoken voice, his pleasure at her denial of a lover, seemed to echo from somewhere deep inside of her. Wishful thinking, maybe. It had been a long time since she'd had anything close to a boyfriend, and merely being in the presence of Lucan Thorne was doing strange things to her head. Or rather, her body.

As he stared at her, Gabrielle felt a pleasant knot of warmth begin to pool in her belly. His gaze penetrated like heat itself, physical and intimate. A picture suddenly formed in her mind: she and him, naked and writhing together in the moonlit dark of her bedroom. An instant blast of heat flooded her. She could feel his hard muscles beneath her fingertips, his firm body moving over her... his thick shaft filling her, stretching her, exploding deep within her.

Oh, yes, she thought, practically squirming where she stood. *Jamie was right. She really had been celibate for too long.*

Thorne blinked slowly, his thick black lashes shuttering stormy silver eyes. Like a cool breeze skating over flushed bare skin, Gabrielle felt some of the tightness in her limbs dissipate. Her heart was still pounding; the room still seemed oddly warm.

He turned his head away from her, and her eyes were drawn to the base of his scalp, where his hair met the collar of his tailored shirt. He had a tattoo on his neck—at least, she thought it was a tattoo. Intricate swirls and geometric-looking symbols rendered in ink just a few shades darker than his skin came up the back of his neck and around the side, disappearing beneath the thick growth of his dark hair. She wondered what the rest of it looked like, and if there was some special meaning to the beautiful pattern.

She had an almost irrepressible urge to trace the interesting markings with her fingertip. Maybe her tongue.

"Tell me what you told your friends about the attack you witnessed at the club."

She swallowed on a dry throat, shaking her head to bring herself back to the conversation. "Yes. Right."

God, what was wrong with her? Gabrielle dismissed the peculiar race of her pulse and focused on the events of the other night. She recounted the story for the detective, as she had for the other officers, and, later, her friends. She told him every horrific detail, and he listened carefully, letting her relay it all uninterrupted. Under the cool acceptance of his gaze, Gabrielle's memory of the slaying seemed more precise now, as if the lens of her recollection had been sharpened, the details magnified.

When she finished, she found Thorne clicking through the pictures on her cell phone once more. The line of his mouth had gone from grim to grave.

"What exactly do you think these images show, Miss Maxwell?"

She glanced up and met his look, those wise, piercing

eyes of his boring into her. In that instant, a word skated through Gabrielle's head—incredible, laughable, terrifyingly clear.

Vampire.

"I don't know," she said lamely, speaking over the rising whisper in her head. "I mean, I'm not sure what to think."

If the detective didn't suspect she was nuts yet, he would if she blurted out the word that was now swimming through her mind, chilling her to the bone. It was the only explanation she had for the gruesome slaying she witnessed that night.

Vampires?

Christ Jesus. She really was crazy.

"I'll need to take this device, Miss Maxwell."

"Gabrielle," she offered. Her smile felt awkward. "Do you think forensics, or whoever does that sort of thing, will be able to clean up the images?"

He gave her a slight incline of his head, not quite a nod, then pocketed her cell phone. "I will return it to you tomorrow evening. You will be home?"

"Sure." *How was it he could make a simple question sound more like an order?* "I appreciate you coming by, Detective Thorne. It's been a rough few days."

"Lucan," he said, studying her for a moment. "Call me Lucan."

Heat seemed to reach out to her from his eyes, along with a stoic understanding, as if this man had seen more horrors than she could ever comprehend. She could not name the emotion that passed through her in that moment, but it sped her pulse and made the room feel sapped of all its air. He was still looking at her, waiting, as if expecting her to comply at once with his request to speak his name.

"All right... Lucan."

"Gabrielle," he replied, and the sound of her name on his lips sent a quiver of awareness shooting through her veins.

Something on the wall behind her caught his attention. He glanced to where one of Gabrielle's most acclaimed photographs hung. His mouth pursed slightly, a sensual quirk of his lips that hinted at amusement, perhaps surprise. Gabrielle pivoted to look at the image of an inner city park that was frozen and desolate beneath a blanket of thick December snow.

"You don't like my work," she guessed.

He mildly shook his dark head. "I find it... intriguing."

She was curious now. "How so?"

"You find beauty in the most unlikely of places," he said after a long moment, his attention focused now on her. "Your pictures are full of passion...."

"But?"

To her bewilderment, he reached out, stroked a finger along the line of her jaw. "There are no people in them, Gabrielle."

"Of course there..."

She started to blurt out a denial, but before the words reached her tongue, she realized that he was right. Her gaze lit on each framed photograph she kept in her apartment, her memory touching on all the others that hung in galleries and museums and private collections around the city.

He was right. The images, no matter their subjects were all empty places, lonely places.

Not one of them contained a single face or even a shadow of human life.

"Oh, my God," she whispered, stunned at the revelation.

In just a few moments, this man had defined her work as no one ever had before. Not even she had seen the obvious truth in her art, but Lucan Thorne had inexplicably opened her eyes. It was as if he had peered into her very soul.

"I must go now," he said, already making his way to the door.

Gabrielle followed him, wishing he would stay longer. Maybe he would come back later. She nearly asked him to, but forced herself into maintaining at least a modicum of cool control. Thorne was halfway out the door when he abruptly paused on the threshold. He turned toward her, too close in the cramped space of the foyer. His large body crowded her, but Gabrielle didn't mind. She didn't so much as breathe.

"Is something wrong?"

His fine nostrils flared almost imperceptibly. "What kind of perfume are you wearing?"

The question flustered her. It was so unexpected, so personal. She felt heat rise to her cheeks, though why she should be embarrassed she had no idea. "I don't wear perfume. I can't. I'm allergic."

"Really."

His mouth curved into a harsh smile, as if his teeth had suddenly become too full for his mouth. He leaned toward her, slowly bending his head down until it was hovering at her neck. Gabrielle heard the soft rasp of his breath—felt it caress her skin in coolness then in warmth—as he drew her scent into his lungs and released it through his lips. Heat seared her throat, and she could have sworn she felt the swift pressure of his mouth brushing over her pulse, which lurched into an erratic beat as the dark head lingered so intimately close to her. She heard a low growl rumble near her ear, something very near a curse.

Thorne came away at once, and did not meet her startled gaze. He didn't offer any excuse or apology for his strange behavior, either.

"You smell like jasmine," was all he said.

And then, without looking at her, he stepped out the door and strode into the darkened street outside.

It was wrong to pursue the woman.

Lucan knew this, even as he had waited on Gabrielle Maxwell's apartment steps that evening, showing her a detective's badge and photo ID card. It wasn't his. It wasn't real, in fact, only a hypnotic manipulation that made her human mind believe he was who he had presented himself to be.

A simple trick for elders of his kind, like himself, but one he seldom stooped to use.

Yet now, here he was again, some time past midnight, stretching his slim personal code of honor even thinner as he tried the latch on her front door and found it unlocked. He knew it would be; he'd given her the suggestion while he had talked with her that evening, when he had shown her what he wanted to do with her and read the surprised, but receptive, response in her soft brown eyes.

He could have taken her then. She would have Hosted him willingly, he was certain, and knowing the intense pleasure they would have shared in the process had nearly been his undoing. But Lucan's first duty was to his Breed and the warriors who had banded together with him to combat the growing problem of the Rogues.

Bad enough that Gabrielle had witnessed the nightclub slaying and reported it to the police and her friends before her memory of the event could be erased, but she had also managed to take pictures. They were grainy, almost un-readable, but damning just the same. He needed to secure the images, before she had a chance to show them to any-one else. He'd made good on that, at least. By rights, he should be back at the tech lab with Gideon, IDing the Rogue who had escaped outside La Notte, or riding shot-gun around the city with Dante, Rio, Conlan, and the oth-ers as they hunted down more of their diseased brethren. And so he would be, once he finished this last bit of busi-ness with lovely Gabrielle Maxwell.

Lucan slipped inside the old brick building on Willow Street and closed the door behind him. Gabrielle's tanta-lizing scent filled his nostrils, leading him to her now as it had the night outside the club and at the police station downtown. He silently navigated her apartment, through the main level and up the stairs to her bedroom loft. Skylights in the vaulted ceiling summoned the moon's pale glow, which played softly over Gabrielle's graceful curves. She slept nude, as though awaiting his arrival, her long legs wrapped in twisted sheets, her hair spread out around her head on the pillow in luxurious waves of burnt gold.

Her scent enveloped him, sweet and sultry, making his teeth ache.

Jasmine, he thought, curling back his lips in a smile of wry appreciation. An exotic flower that opens its fragrant petals only under the coaxing of night.

Open for me now, Gabrielle.

But he wouldn't seduce her, he decided, not like this. He wanted only a taste tonight, just enough to satisfy his curiosity. That was all he'd permit himself. When he was through here, Gabrielle would have no memory of meeting him, nor of the horror she had witnessed in the alley a few nights ago.

His own need would have to wait.

Lucan went to her and eased his hip onto the mattress beside her. He stroked the burnished softness of her hair, brushed his fingers along the slender line of her arm.

She stirred, moaning sweetly, rousing at his light touch. "Lucan," she murmured sleepily, not quite awake, yet subconsciously aware that he had joined her in the room.

"Just a dream," he whispered, astonished to hear his name on her lips when he had used no vampire guile to place it there.

She sighed deeply, settling against him. "I knew you would come back."

"Did you?"

"Mm-hmm." It was a purr of sound in her throat, raspy and erotic. Her eyes remained closed, her mind still caught in the web of her dreams. "I wanted you to come back."

Lucan smiled at that, tracing his fingers over her placid brow. "You do not fear me, beauty?"

She gave a small shake of her head, nuzzling his palm against her cheek. Her lips were slightly parted, small white teeth gleaming in the scant light overhead. Her neck was graceful, proud, a regal column of alabaster above the fragile bones of her shoulders. How sweet she would taste, how soft against his tongue.

And her breasts...Lucan could not resist the peachy dark nipple that peeked out from under the sheet draped haphazardly across her torso. He teased the little bud between his fingers, tugging it gently and nearly growling with need as it puckered into a tight bead, hardening at his touch.

He was hardening as well. He licked his lips, growing hungry, eager to have her.

Gabrielle squirmed languidly beneath the tangled sheet. Lucan slowly drew the cotton coverlet away, baring her to him completely. She was exquisite, as he knew she would be. Petite, yet strong, her body was lithe with youth, supple and fair. Firm muscle shaped her elegant limbs; her artist's hands were slender and expressive, flexing mindlessly as Lucan trailed his fingers along her sternum and down to the concave dip of her belly. Her skin here was velvet and warm, too tempting to resist.

Lucan moved over her on the bed, and slid his palms beneath her. He lifted her to him, gently arching her up off the mattress. He kissed the sweet curve of her hip, then let his tongue play across the small valley of her navel. She gasped as he plumbed the shallow indentation, and the fragrance of her need wreathed his senses.

"Jasmine," he rasped against her heated skin, his teeth dragging lightly as his kiss ventured lower.

Her moan of pleasure as his mouth invaded her sex sent a violent jolt of lust through his veins. He was already stiff and erect; his cock throbbed beneath the constricting barrier of his clothes. She was wet and slick against his lips, her cleft a heated sheath against his questing tongue. Lucan suckled her as he would sweet nectar, until her body convulsed with the coming of her release. And still he lapped at her, bringing her to the crest of another climax, and then another.

She'd gone slack in his arms, boneless and trembling. Lucan trembled as well, his hands shaking as he carefully eased her back down onto the bed. He'd never wanted a woman so badly. He wanted something more, he realized, bemused by the impulse that he had to protect her. Gabrielle panted softly as her last climax subsided, and she curled onto her side, as innocent as a kitten.

Lucan stared down at her in silent fury, heaving with the force of his need. Dull pain tightened his mouth as his fangs stretched out from his gums. His tongue was dry. Hunger knotted in his gut. His vision sharpened as lust for blood and release slung its seductive coils around him, and his pupils elongated to catlike slivers in his pale eyes.

Take her, urged that part of him that was inhuman, unearthly.

She is yours. Take her.

Just a taste—that was what he had vowed. He would not harm her, only heighten her pleasure as he took a bit of his own. She wouldn't even remember this moment, come the dawn. As his blood Host, she would give him a sustaining sip of life, then awake later, drowsy and sated, but blissfully unaware of its cause.

It was a small mercy, he told himself, even as his body quickened with the urge to feed.

Lucan bent over Gabrielle's languid form, and tenderly swept aside the riot of ginger waves concealing her neck. His heart was hammering in his chest, urging him to slake his burning thirst. Just a taste, no more. Only pleasure. He came forward, his mouth open, his senses swamped with her intoxicating female scent. His lips pressed down against her warmth, settling over the delicate pulse that beat against his tongue. His fangs grazed the velvet softness of her throat, throbbing now, like another demanding part of his anatomy.

And in the instant before his sharp teeth penetrated her

fragile skin, his keen vision lit on a tiny birthmark just behind Gabrielle's ear.

Nearly undetectable, the diminutive mark of a teardrop
falling into the cradle of a crescent moon made Lucan rear
back in shock. The symbol, so rare among human females,
meant only one thing...

Breedmate.

He withdrew from the bed as though touched by fire,
hissing a furious curse into the dark. Hunger for Gabrielle
still pounded through him, even as he grappled with the
ramifications of what he might have done to them both.

Gabrielle Maxwell was a Breedmate, a human gifted
with unique blood and DNA properties that comple-
mented those of his kind. She and the few numbers like
her were queens among other human females. To Lucan's
kind, a race comprised solely of males, this woman was a
cherished goddess, giver of life, destined to bond in blood
and bear the seed of a new vampire generation.

And in his reckless lust to taste her, Lucan had nearly
claimed her for his own.

CHAPTER
Four

Gabrielle could count on one hand the number of erotic dreams she'd had in her life, but never had she experienced anything as hot—not to mention, *real*—as the sexfest fantasy she had enjoyed the night before, courtesy of the virtual Lucan Thorne. His breath had been the night breeze, sifting through the open window of her bedroom loft. His hair was the obsidian darkness that filled the skylights over her bed, his silver eyes the pale glow of the moon. His hands were the silken bonds of her bedsheets, twined around her splayed wrists and ankles, spreading her open beneath him, holding her fast.

His mouth had been pure heat that seared every inch of her skin, licking her like an unseen flame. *Jasmine*, he had called her in the dream, and the soft hum of the word had vibrated against her damp flesh as his warm breath stirred the flossy curls between her legs.

She had writhed and whimpered under the skill of his tongue, submitting to a torment that she hoped might have no end. But it had ended, too soon. Gabrielle had awakened in her bed, alone in the dark, gasping Lucan's name, her body wrung out and listless, aching for more.

She still ached and that bothered her even more than the fact that the mysterious Detective Thorne had stood her up.

Not that his offer to come by her place tonight was anything close to a date, but she had been looking forward to seeing him again. She was interested to know more about him since he seemed so adept at deciphering her with a single glance. Aside from getting some more answers about what she had witnessed the night outside the club, Gabrielle had been hoping for a little conversation with Lucan, maybe some wine or dinner. The fact that she shaved her legs twice and wore some sexy black lingerie beneath her long-sleeved silk blouse and dark jeans was purely incidental.

Gabrielle had waited for him until well after nine, then finally gave up on the idea and called Jamie to see if he would have dinner with her downtown.

Seated across the table from her in a windowed alcove at Ciao Bella bistro, Jamie set down his glass of pinot noir and eyed her nearly untouched *frutti de mare*. "You've been pushing that same piece of scallop around your plate for ten minutes, sweetie. Don't you like it?"

"No, it's great. The food is always amazing here."

"So, it's just the company that sucks?"

She glanced up at him and shook her head. "Not at all. You're my best friend, you know that."

"Uh-huh," he said, smiling. "But I don't compare to your wet dream."

Gabrielle's face warmed as one of the patrons at a neighboring table looked their way. "You're a shit some-times, you know that?" she whispered to Jamie. "I shouldn't have told you about it."

"Oh, honey. Don't be embarrassed. If I had a nickel for every time I woke up torqued and screaming some hot guy's name..."

"I wasn't screaming his name." No, she was gasping and moaning it, both in bed and in the shower a short while later, when she still couldn't get Lucan Thorne out of her system. "It was like he was *there*, Jamie. Right there, in my bed—so real I could touch him."

Jamie sighed. "Some girls have all the luck. Next time you see your dream lover, be a dear and send him my way when you're through."

Gabrielle smiled, knowing that her friend was hardly lacking in the romance department. For the past four years, he'd been happily monogamous with David, an an-tiques dealer, who was currently out of town on business. "You want to know the strangest thing about this, Jamie? When I got up this morning, my front door was unlocked."

"So?"

"So, you know me, I never leave it unlocked."

Jamie's tawny, manicured brows knit into a scowl. "What are you saying, you think this guy broke in while you were asleep?"

"Sounds crazy, I know. A police detective coming into my house in the middle of the night to seduce me. I must be losing my mind."

She said it casually, but this wasn't the first time she'd questioned the soundness of her own sanity. Not the first time by a long shot. She fidgeted absently with the sleeve of her blouse while Jamie observed her. He was quietly concerned now, which only increased her discomfort with the subject of her possible shaky mental stability.

"Look, hon. You've been under a lot of stress since the weekend. That can do strange things to your head. You were upset and confused. You must have forgotten to lock the door."

"And the dream?"

"Just that—a dream. Just your harried mind trying to tell you to chill out, to relax."

Gabrielle bobbed her head in an automatic nod of agreement. "Right. I'm sure that's all it is."

If only she could accept that the explanation was as reasonable as her friend made it sound. But something in the pit of her stomach rejected the idea that she might have carelessly left her door unlocked. It was something she simply would not do, no matter how stressed out or confused she was.

"Hey." Jamie reached across the table to clasp her hand. "You're going to be okay, Gab. And you know you can call me anytime, right? I'm here for you, always will be."

"Thanks."

He let her go and picked up his fork to gesture at her *frutti de mare*. "So, are you going to eat any more of that or can I scavenge it now?"

Gabrielle traded her half-eaten plate of food for his empty one. "It's all yours."

As Jamie went to work on her cold meal, Gabrielle leaned her chin on her hand and took a long sip of her wine. As she drank, her fingers moved idly over the faint marks she had found on her neck this morning after her shower. The unlocked front door wasn't exactly the strangest thing she had discovered, the twin welts below her ear took that prize, no contest.

The small nicks had not been deep enough to break her skin, but they were there. Two of them, evenly spaced, at the place where her pulse beat strongest against her fingertips. At first, she had wondered if she'd scratched herself in her sleep, maybe been swept up in the strange dream she'd had and raked her nails across her skin.

But the marks didn't look like scratches. They looked like something... else.

Like someone, or something, had nearly taken a bite out of her carotid.

Crazy.

That's what it was, and she needed to snap herself out of that kind of thinking before she did any further harm to herself. She had to get her head together and stop manufacturing paranoid fantasies about midnight visitors and horror-movie monsters that couldn't possibly exist in real life. If she wasn't careful, she might end up like her birth mother...

"Ohmigod, smack me right now because I am a complete and utter dolt," Jamie exclaimed suddenly, breaking into her thoughts. "I keep forgetting to tell you this! I got a call at the gallery yesterday about your photographs. Some bigwig downtown is interested in a private showing."

"Seriously? Who is it?"

He shrugged. "Don't know, sweetie. I didn't actually talk to the potential buyer, but based on the snooty attitude of the guy's assistant, I'd say whoever your admirer is, he—or she—is dripping with money. I've got an appointment down at one of the buildings in the Financial District tomorrow night. We're talking penthouse office, darling."

"Oh, my God," she gasped, incredulous.

"Uh-huh. *Trés* cool, girlfriend. Pretty soon you're gonna be too good for small-time art peddlers like me," he joked, grinning with shared excitement for her.

It was hard not to be intrigued, especially given everything she had been through the past few days. Gabrielle had achieved a respectable following and had won some very nice accolades for her work, but a private showing for an anonymous buyer was a first.

"Which pieces did they ask you to bring?"

Jamie lifted his wine glass and tipped it at her in mock salute. "All of it, Miss Thang. Every single piece in the collection."

From the rooftop of an old brick building in the city's busy theater district, moonlight gleamed off the lethal sneer of a black-clad vampire. Crouched in position near the ledge, the Breed warrior pivoted his dark head, then held out his hand, and gave a covert signal.

Four Rogues. One human prey. Heading straight for them.

Lucan nodded to Dante and stepped off the fifth-floor fire escape that had been his lookout perch for the past half hour. He descended to the street below in one fluid motion, landing quietly as a cat. Dual combat blades were sheathed crisscross on his back and thrust out over his shoulders like the bones of demonic wings. Lucan drew the titanium-edged weapons with barely a hiss of sound as he eased into the shadows of the narrow side street to await the evening's action.

It was just around 11 P.M., several hours past the time he should have been stopping by Gabrielle Maxwell's apartment to return her cell phone like he'd told her he would. The device was still at the tech lab with Gideon, who was processing the images and running them against the Breed's International Identification Database.

As for Lucan, he had no intention of returning the phone to Gabrielle, personally or otherwise. The images of the Rogues' attack had to stay out of human hands, and after the near fiasco he'd had in her bedroom, the farther he stayed away from the female, the better.

A goddamned Breedmate.

He should have known. Thinking back on it, there had been a few things about her that should have clued him in to the fact right away. Like her ability to see through the veil of vampire mind control permeating the dance club that night. She had seen the Rogues—Bloodlusting in the alley, and in the scrambled images of her cell phone— when other humans could not. Then, at her apartment, she had even proven resistant to Lucan's own efforts to bend her thoughts with mental suggestion, and he suspected she had succumbed more out of her own unconscious desire for the pleasure he offered than anything else.

It was no secret that human females with the genetic makeup unique to Breedmates possessed keen intelligence and flawless health. Many possessed uncanny extrasensory skills or paranormal talents that would amplify once a Breedmate was blood-bonded to a vampire male.

As for Gabrielle Maxwell, it appeared that she was gifted with a special vision that let her see what other humans could not, though just how far that vision went was anyone's guess. Lucan wanted to know. His warrior's instinct demanded he get to the bottom of it without delay.

But getting involved with the female in any form or fashion was the very last thing he needed.

So why couldn't he shake himself loose of her sweet

scent, her soft skin...her sultry sensuality? He hated that the woman had brought out such weakness in him, and his current mood was hardly improved by the fact that his body was aching with the need to feed.

The only bright spot in his night was the steady clip of Rogues' boot heels on pavement somewhere near the mouth of the side street, coming his way.

The human turning the corner a few paces ahead of them was male. Young, healthy, garbed in black-and-white houndstooth pants and a stained white tunic that reeked of a greasy restaurant kitchen and sudden, anxious perspiration. The cook checked over his shoulder where the four vampires were gaining ground. A hushed, nervous-sounding expletive hissed in the dark. The human swung his head back around and walked faster, fists clenched at his sides, his rounding eyes rooted to the lightless stretch of asphalt at his feet.

"No need to run, little man," one of the Rogues taunted, his voice scraping like gravel.

Another made a shrill, mocking squeal as he loped ahead of his three companions. "Yeah, don't run away now. It ain't like you're gonna get far."

The Rogues' laughter echoed against the buildings flanking the narrow street.

"Shit," the human whispered under his breath. He didn't turn around again, just plowed ahead at a swift clip, two seconds from breaking into a flat-out, but pointless, run.

As the frightened human neared, Lucan took a slow step out of the gloom, bracing his feet wide beneath him. Arms extended out at his sides, he blocked the street with his menacing body and twin swords. He shot a cold smile at the Rogues, his fangs stretched long in anticipation of the fight to come. "Evening, ladies."

"Oh, Jesus!" gasped the human. He made an abrupt stop, staring up into Lucan's face in horror as one of his knees buckled beneath him. "Shit!"

"Get up." Lucan gave him the briefest flick of a glance as the young man scrambled to find his feet. "Get out of here."

He scraped his two blades together before him, filling the darkened street with the harsh metallic grate of steel sliding over hard-edged, lethal steel. Behind the four Rogues, Dante leaped to the asphalt in a crouch, then drew himself up to his six-and-a-half-foot height. He had no sword, but circling his waist was a leather belt studded with a collection of deadly, hand-to-hand weaponry, including a pair of razor-sharp, curved blades that performed as hellish extensions of his dazzlingly fast hands. *Malebranche*, he called them, and evil claws they were. Dante had them poised in his grasp in an instant, one mean-ass vampire who was always ready for a round of up-close-and-personal combat.

"Oh, my God," the human cried, his voice wobbling as he took in the danger that surrounded him. Gaping up at Lucan, the man went for his wallet, hands trembling as he pulled the worn billfold out of his back pocket and tossed it to the ground. "Take it, man! You can have it. Just don't kill me, I'm begging you!"

Lucan kept his eyes trained on the four Rogues, who were checking their positions, going for their own weapons. "Get the hell out of here. Now."

"He's ours," one of the Rogues hissed. Yellow eyes fixed on Lucan in pure hatred, the pupils permanently narrowed to hungered, vertical slits. Long fangs dripped with saliva, further evidence of the vampire's advanced Bloodlust addiction.

Just like a human could fall dependent on a powerful narcotic, Bloodlust was as destructive for the Breed. The tipping point between the necessary assuaging of hunger and reckless overdose of blood was easily breached. Some vampires went willingly into that abyss, while others succumbed to the disease through inexperience or a lack of personal discipline. Gone too far, and for too long, a vampire would turn Rogue, like these feral beasts snarling before Lucan now.

Eager to smoke them, Lucan slapped his long blades together, smelling the spark of heat as one length of steel crashed against the other.

The human was still standing there, idiotic in his fear, his head swinging between the advancing Rogues and Lucan's unwavering stance. The hesitation was sure to cost the man, but Lucan shrugged off the knowledge with cold dispassion. The human wasn't his concern. Eradicating these bloodsuckers, and the rest of their diseased kind, was all that mattered.

One of the Rogues wiped a dirty hand across his slavering mouth. "Back off, asshole. Let us feed."

"Not tonight," Lucan growled, "not in my city."

"Your city?" The rest of them sniggered as the Rogue in the lead spat on the ground at Lucan's feet. "This city belongs to us. Won't be long and we're gonna own it all."

"That's right," added another of the four. "So, looks like you're the one trespassin' here."

Finally, the human had gathered his wits and started to make a break. He didn't get far. Moving with incredible speed, one of the Rogues lashed out a hand and grabbed the man by the throat. He jerked him off his feet and held him aloft, letting the human's black hightop sneakers dangle six inches off the ground. The human grunted and squirmed, struggling wildly as the Rogue squeezed harder, slowly strangling him with his bare hand. Lucan stared, unfazed, even as the vampire dropped his twitching prey and tore a hole in the man's neck with his teeth.

In his periphery, Lucan saw Dante creep up silently behind the Rogues. Fangs bared, the warrior licked his lips, eager to get busy. He wouldn't be disappointed. Lucan struck first, and then the street erupted with the clash of metal and the crush of breaking bone.

Where Dante fought like a hell-spawned demon, *malebranche* blades flashing, war cries splitting the night, Lucan maintained a cold control and deadly precision. One by one, the Rogues fell to the warriors' punishing blows. The kiss of titanium-laced steel sped through the Rogues' corrupted blood systems as poison, accelerating death and bringing on the swift stages of decomposition characteristic of the Rogues' demise.

With their enemies dispatched, their corpses reducing from flesh and bone to fine, drifting ash, Lucan and Dante surveyed the other carnage in the street.

The human was unmoving, bleeding profusely from the tattered wound in his throat.

Dante knelt beside the man, sniffing at the savaged form. "He's dead. Or will be, in another minute."

The smell of spilled blood reached Lucan's nostrils like a fist slamming into his gut. His fangs, already extended in rage, now throbbed with the urge to feed. He glared down at the dying human in disgust. Although the taking of blood was necessary to him, Lucan despised the idea of accepting Rogue leavings, in any form. He preferred to draw his sustenance from willing Hosts of his own choosing whenever he could, although those meager tastes only staved off the deeper hunger.

Sooner or later, every vampire had to kill.

Lucan didn't try to deny his nature, but on the occasions when he killed, it was by his choice, by his own rules. When he sought prey, he took primarily criminals, drug dealers, junkies, and other lowlifes. He was judicious and efficient, never slaughtering simply for the sake of it. All of the Breed adhered to a similar code of honor; it was what separated them from their lawless Rogue brethren.

His gut tightened as another whiff of blood trailed into his nose. Saliva surged into his parched mouth.

When was the last time he'd fed?

He couldn't recall. It had been a while. Several days, at least, and not enough to last him. He'd thought to curb some of his hunger—both the carnal and the systemic— with Gabrielle Maxwell last night, but that idea had taken a quick turn south. Now he was shaking with the urge to feed, and too far gone to consider anything but the necessity of his body's basic needs.

"Lucan." Dante pressed his fingers to the man's neck, feeling for a pulse. The vampire's fangs were extruded, sharp from the battle and the physiological reaction to the scent of pooling crimson life. "If we wait much longer, the blood will be dead, too."

And no use to them, for it was only fresh blood, pumping through human veins, that could quench the vampires' hunger. Dante waited, even though it was obvious he wanted nothing more than to drop his head and take his fill of the human who had been too stupid to flee when he had the chance.

But Dante would wait, even to the point of wasting prey, for it was an unwritten protocol that later generation vampires did not feed in the presence of an elder, particularly when that elder was Gen One Breed and starving.

Unlike Dante, Lucan's sire was one of the Ancients, one of eight alien warriors who came from a distant, dark planet only to crash-land thousands of years ago on unforgiving, inhospitable Earth. To survive, they had fed on the blood of humans, decimating entire populations with their hunger and savagery. In rare instances, these foreign conquerors had successfully bred with human females—the first Breedmates—who spawned a new generation of the vampire race.

Those savage, otherworldly forebears were all gone now, but their progeny lived on, in Lucan and a few scattered others. They were the closest things to royalty in vampire society—respected, and not a little feared. The vast majority of the Breed were younger, born of second, third, and some countless dozens later generations.

The hunger was strongest in Gen Ones. So was the propensity to give in to Bloodlust and turn Rogue. The Breed had learned to live with the danger. Most had learned to manage it, taking blood only when needed, and in the smallest quantities required to sustain. They had to, for once lost to Bloodlust, there was no coming back.

Lucan's slitted eyes fell to the twitching, shallowly breathing human on the pavement. The animal snarl he heard came from his own dry throat. As Lucan strode toward the scent of spilled, life-giving blood, Dante gave a slight but deferential bow of his dark head and backed off to let his elder feed.

CHAPTER
Five

He hadn't even bothered to call and leave her a message last night.

Typical.

Probably had a big date with his remote control and ESPN, or maybe after he left her place the other evening, he'd met someone else and gotten a more interesting offer than schlepping Gabrielle's cell phone back out to Beacon Hill. Hell, he might even be married, or involved with someone. Not that she'd asked, and not that asking would have guaranteed he'd have told her the truth. Lucan Thorne probably wasn't any different than any other guy.

Except he was . . . *different.*

He struck her as being very different from anyone she had ever met before. A very private man, almost secretive. Definitely dangerous. She could no more see him sitting in a recliner in front of the television than she could envision him tied down with a serious girlfriend, let alone a wife and family. Which brought her back to the idea that he must have gotten a better offer elsewhere and decided to blow her off, an idea that stung a lot more than it should have.

"Forget about him," Gabrielle scolded herself under her breath as she edged her black Cooper Mini to the side of the quiet rural road and cut the ignition. Her camera bag and gear sat beside her in the passenger seat. She gathered it up, grabbed a small flashlight from the glove compartment, pocketed her keys in her jacket, and got out of the car.

She closed the door quietly and cast a quick look around. Not a soul in sight, not surprising given that it was just nearing 6 A.M. and the building she was about to enter illegally and photograph had been shut down for about twenty years. She walked along the empty stretch of cracked pavement and cut a sharp right, heading down through a ditch then up into a pine-and-oak wooded lot that stood like a thick curtain wall around the old asylum.

Dawn was just beginning to creep over the horizon. The lighting was eerie and ethereal, a misty haze of pink and lavender shrouding the Gothic structures with an otherworldly glow. Even bathed in soft pastels, the place held an air of menace.

The contrast was what had brought her out to the location this morning. Shooting it at dusk would have been the more natural choice, capitalizing on the haunted quality of the abandoned structures. But it was the juxtaposition of warm dawn light against a cold, sinister subject that appealed to Gabrielle as she paused to retrieve her camera from the bag slung over her shoulder. She snapped off a half-dozen shots, then clapped the lens cap back on, and continued her trek toward the ghostly buildings.

A tall wire security fence loomed in front of her, barricading the property against nosy explorers like herself. But Gabrielle knew its hidden weakness. She had found it the first time she had come to the place to take exterior pictures. She hurried along the line of the fence until she reached the southwest corner, then squatted down near the ground. Here, someone had discreetly severed the links with a wire cutter, creating a breach just large enough for a curious adolescent to wriggle through—or a determined female photographer who tended to view *No Trespassing* and *Authorized Personnel Only* signs more as friendly suggestions rather than enforceable laws.

Gabrielle pushed open the flap of snipped fence, shoved her gear inside, and scrambled spiderlike on her belly through the low opening. A shiver of apprehension coursed along her limbs as she came up on the other side of the fence. She should be used to this type of covert, solitary exploration; her art often depended on her courage to seek out desolate, some might argue dangerous, places. This creepy asylum could certainly classify as the latter, she thought, her gaze drifting to graffiti spray-painted next to an exterior door that read, *BAd VIBeS.*

"You can say that again," she whispered under her breath. As she brushed the dirt and dried pine needles off her clothes, her hand drifted automatically to the front pocket of her jeans for her cell phone. It wasn't there, of course, still in the possession of Detective Thorne. Just one more reason to be pissed at him for standing her up last night.

Maybe she should cut the guy a little slack, she thought, suddenly eager to focus on something other than the ominous feeling that pressed down on her now that she was inside the asylum grounds. Maybe Thorne had been a noshow because something bad happened to him on the job.

What if he'd been injured in the line of duty and didn't come by as promised because he was incapacitated in some way? Maybe he hadn't called to apologize or to explain his absence because he physically couldn't.

Right. And maybe she had checked her brain into her panties from the second she first laid eyes on the man.

Scoffing at herself, Gabrielle picked up her things and walked toward the soaring architecture of the main building. Pale limestone climbed skyward in a steep central tower, capped by peaks and spires worthy of the finest gothic cathedral. Surrounding this was a sprawling compound of red-brick walled and tile-roofed outbuildings arranged in a batwing layout, connected by covered walkways and cloisterlike arches.

But as awe-inspiring as the structure was, there was no dismissing its air of slumbering menace, as if a thousand sins and secrets loomed behind the chipped walls and smashed mullioned-glass windows. Gabrielle strode to where the light was best and took a few pictures. There was no current point of entry here; the main door had been bolted shut and boarded up tight. If she wanted to get inside to take interior shots—and she definitely did— she had to go around to the back and try her luck with a ground-level window or basement door.

She skirted down a sloping embankment, toward the anterior of the building and found what she was looking for: wooden shutters concealed three windows that likely opened into a service area or crawl space of the structure. The shutter's rusty latches were corroded but not locked, and they broke away easily with a little encouragement from a rock Gabrielle found nearby. She pulled the wooden covering away from the window, lifted the heavy glass panel, and propped it open with the window brace.

After a perfunctory sweep of her flashlight to make sure the place was empty and not about to cave in on her head, she shimmied through the opening. As she hopped down from the window casement, the soles of her boots crunched broken glass and years of accumulated dust and debris. The foundation of gray cinderblock bricks ran about four yards in, disappearing into the gloom of the un-lit basement. Gabrielle shot the thin beam of her flashlight into the shadows at the other end of the space. She ran it back along the wall, holding the light steady when she came across a battered old service door bearing the sten-ciled words *No General Access*.

"Wanna bet?" she whispered as she approached the door and found it unlocked.

She opened it and shone some light around the other side into a long, tunnel-like corridor. Broken fluorescent light fixtures hung down from the ceiling; some of the panel coverings had fallen to the industrial-grade linoleum floor, where they lay shattered and dust-coated. Gabrielle stepped into the dark space, not certain what she was look-ing for, and a bit apprehensive of what she might find in the deserted bowels of the asylum.

She passed an open room off the corridor and her flashlight skimmed across a red vinyl dentist's chair, a little worse for wear, and poised in the center of the room as if awaiting its next patient. Gabrielle removed her camera from its case and took a couple of quick shots. She moved on, passing more examination and treatment rooms in what must have been the medical wing of the building. She found a stairwell and climbed two flights, pleased to find herself in the central tower where tall windows brought in generous amounts of soft morning light.

Through her camera lens, she looked out over wide lawns and courtyards flanked by elegant brick and limestone buildings. She snapped a few pictures of the faded glory of the place, appreciating both the architecture and the warm play of sunlight against so much ghostly shadow. It was strange looking out from the confines of a building that had once held so many disturbed souls. In the eerie silence, Gabrielle could almost hear the voices of the patients, people who had not been able to simply walk away like she could now.

People like her birth mother, a woman Gabrielle had never known beyond what she had heard as a kid through hushed conversations between social workers and the foster families who would, eventually, one by one, return her into the system like a pet that had proved more trouble than it was worth. She lost track of the number of places she'd been sent to live, but the complaints against her when she was bounced back were always the same: restless and withdrawn, secretive and untrusting, socially dysfunctional with self-destructive tendencies. She'd heard the same labels applied to her mother, along with the added distinctions of paranoid and delusional.

By the time the Maxwells came into her life, Gabrielle had spent ninety days in a group home, under the supervision of a state-appointed psychologist. She'd had zero expectations and even less hope that she might actually make another foster situation stick. Frankly, she'd been past the point of caring. But her new guardians had been patient and kind. Thinking it might help her cope with her emotional confusion, they had helped Gabrielle obtain a handful of court documents pertaining to her mother.

The young woman had been a teenage Jane Doe, presumably homeless, with no ID, and no known family or acquaintances, except for the newborn baby girl she had left, squalling and distressed, in a city garbage bin late one August night. Gabrielle's mother had been brutalized, bleeding from deep puncture wounds in her neck that had been made worse by her hysteria and panicked clawing at the injury. While she was being treated at the emergency room, she slipped into a catatonic state and never recovered.

Rather than prosecute her for the crime of abandoning her infant, the courts had deemed the woman incompetent and sent her away to a facility probably not much different from this one. Not a month into her institutionalization, she had hanged herself with a knotted bedsheet, leaving behind countless questions that would never have answers.

Gabrielle tried to shake off the weight of those old hurts but standing there, looking out the hazy glass windows, brought her past into tighter focus. She didn't want to think about her mother, or the misfortune of her birth, and the dark, lonely years that had followed. She needed to concentrate on her work. That's what always got her through, after all. It was the one constant in her life, sometimes all she truly had in this world.

And it was enough.

Most of the time, it was enough.

"Get a few shots and get the hell out of here," she scolded herself, bringing the camera up and taking a couple more photos through the subtle metalwork that was meshed between the double panes of glass in the window.

She thought about leaving the same way she had come in, but wondered if she might find another exit somewhere on the main floor of the central building. Going back down to the dark basement was not exactly appealing. She was creeping herself out with thoughts about her crazy mother, and the longer she lingered in the old asylum, the more her skin was beginning to crawl. She opened the stairwell door and felt a little better to see dim light filtering in through windows in some of the empty rooms and at the end of the adjacent hallway.

Evidently the "bad vibes" graffiti artist had made it in here, too. On each of the four walls, strange scroll-like symbols had been rendered in deep black paint. Probably gang markings, or the stylized signatures of the kids who'd been here before her. A discarded spray-paint canister lay in the corner, along with a smattering of cigarette butts, broken beer bottles, and other debris.

Gabrielle took out her camera and looked for a good angle for the shot she had in mind. The light wasn't great, but with a different lens it might prove interesting. She fished around in her bag for her lens cases, then froze when she heard a distant whirring noise coming from somewhere beneath her feet. It was faint, but it sounded impossibly like an elevator. Gabrielle stuffed her gear back into the bag, her ears tuned to the vague sounds around her, every nerve flooded with a chilling sense of foreboding.

She was not alone in here.

And now that she was thinking about it, she felt eyes on her from somewhere nearby. The prickling awareness raised the fine hairs at the back of her neck and sent a spray of goosebumps along her arms. Slowly, she pivoted her head and looked behind her. It was then that she saw it: a small closed-circuit video camera mounted in the shadowed upper corner of the corridor, monitoring the

stairwell door she had just come through a few minutes
before.

Maybe it wasn't working, just a leftover from the days
when the asylum was still in operation. It might have been
a comforting thought, except the camera looked too well-
maintained and compact to be anything less than current
issue, state-of-the-art surveillance. To test that idea,
Gabrielle took a long step toward it, placing herself almost
directly beneath the camera. Soundlessly, its base mount
tilted, angling the lens until it was staring Gabrielle in the
face.

Shit, she mouthed into that black, unblinking eye.
Busted.

From deep within the empty compound, she heard the
metal creak and crash of a heavy door. Evidently the abandoned asylum wasn't quite abandoned after all. They had
security at least, and the Boston PD could take a few
response-time lessons from these folks.

Footsteps pounded at a steady clip as whoever was on
guard started coming for her. Gabrielle turned back into
the stairwell and took off sprinting down the steps, her
gear bouncing against her hip. As she descended, light
grew scarce. She gripped the flashlight in her hand, but
hated to use it for fear of creating a beacon for security to
follow. She hit the last stair, pushed open the metal door,
and plunged into the dark of the lower-level corridor.

Back on the stairs, she heard the monitored door swing
open with a bang as her pursuer thundered down behind
her, running hard and gaining on her fast.

Finally, she reached the service door at the end of the
corridor. Throwing herself against the cold steel, she
rushed into the dank basement, and raced for the small
window that was open to the outside. A blast of fresh air

gave her strength as she slapped her hands onto the casement and hoisted herself up. She vaulted through the window and tumbled onto the pebbled earth outside.

She couldn't hear her pursuer now. Maybe she had lost him in the dark twisting hallways. God, she hoped so.

Gabrielle shot to her feet and ran for the breached corner of the perimeter fence. She found it quickly. Diving to her hands and knees, she scrambled under the snipped section of wire, heart pounding in her ears, adrenaline jetting through her veins. She was too panicked: in her haste to flee, she scraped the side of her face on a rough edge of wire. The cut burned her cheek and she felt the hot trickle of blood running near her ear. But she ignored the searing sting and the bruising crush of her camera case as she wriggled on her belly through the fence and out toward freedom.

Once clear of the fence, Gabrielle leaped up and made a mad dash across the wide, rough lawn of the outer grounds. She spared only the barest glance behind her— long enough to see that the huge security guard was still there, having exited from somewhere on the ground floor and was now bounding after her like a beast straight out of hell. Gabrielle swallowed a knot of sheer panic at the sight of him. The guy was built like a tank, easily 250 pounds and all of it muscle, capped off by a large square head, his hair buzzed military style. The big man ran up to the tall fence and stopped at last, smashing his fist against the links as Gabrielle sped into the thick cover of trees separating the property from the road.

Her car was on the side of the quiet stretch of pavement, right where she had left it. With trembling hands, Gabrielle fumbled with the locked door, petrified that G.I. Joe on steroids might catch up to her yet. Her fear seemed irrational, but that didn't stop the adrenaline from pouring through her. Dropping down into the leather seat of the Mini, Gabrielle slammed the key into the ignition and turned over the engine. Heart racing, she threw the little car into drive, stomped on the gas pedal, and ripped out onto the road, making her escape in a screech of spinning tires and burning rubber.

CHAPTER
Six

At midweek in the height of the summer tourist season, Boston's parks and avenues were clotted with humanity. Commuter trains sped people in from the suburbs, to workplaces and museums, and to the countless historic sites located around the city. Camera-toting gawkers clambered onto excursion buses and horse-drawn carriages to putter around town, while others lined up to board overpriced, overcrowded charter tours that would haul them by the hundreds out to the Cape.

Not far from the daytime bustle, secreted some three-hundred feet beneath a heavily secured mansion outside the city, Lucan Thorne leaned over a flat-panel monitor in the Breed warriors' compound and muttered a ripe curse. Vampire identification records scrolled up the screen's display with machine-gun speed as a computer program searched a massive international database for matches against the photos Gabrielle Maxwell had taken.

"Anything yet?" he asked, slanting an impatient look at Gideon, the machine's operator.

"Zip, so far. But my search is still clocking. IID's got a few million records to scan." Gideon's sharp blue eyes flashed over the rims of sleek silver shades. "I'll get a lock on your suckheads, don't worry."

"I never do," Lucan replied, and meant it. Gideon had an IQ that was off the charts, compounded by a streak of tenacity that ran a mile wide. The vampire was as much relentless bloodhound as he was flat-out genius, and Lucan was damned glad to have him on his side. "If you can't flush them out, Gideon, no one can."

Beneath his crown of cropped, spiky blond hair, the Breed's computer guru bared a cocky, confident grin. "That's why I get the big bucks."

"Yeah, something like that," Lucan said, drawing away from the screen's nonstop roll of information.

None of the Breed warriors who had signed on to protect the race from the scourge of the Rogues did so for any kind of payback. They never had, not from the first forming of their alliance in what was mankind's medieval era to now. Each warrior had his reasons for choosing this dangerous way of life, and some of them were, admittedly, more noble than others. Like Gideon, who had worked the field independently until seeking out Lucan after his twin brothers—little more than children—were killed by Rogues outside the London Darkhaven. That was three centuries ago, give or take a few decades.

Even then, Gideon's skill with a sword had been rivaled only by his rapier-sharp mind. He had slain many Rogues in his time, but much later, devotion and a private pledge to his Breedmate, Savannah, had made him give up combat in exchange for wielding the weapon of technology in service to the Breed.

Each of the six warriors who currently fought beside Lucan had their personal talents. They had their own personal demons as well, though none of them were the touchy-feely types looking to have Dr. Phil crawl up their ass with a flashlight. Some things were better left to the dark, and probably the only one of them who felt that more than Lucan himself was the Breed warrior called Dante.

Lucan acknowledged the young vampire as he strode into the tech lab from one of the compound's numerous chambers. Dante, wrapped in his standard basic black attire, was wearing biker's leathers and a fitted tank that showcased both his inked tattoos and his more elaborate Breed markings. His thick biceps were banded with intricate scrollwork, which, to human eyes would seem oddly abstract, a series of interlocking symbols and geometric designs rendered in deep henna hues. Vampire eyes would see the symbols for what they truly were: *dermaglyphs,* naturally occurring marks inherited from the Breeds' forebears, whose hairless skin had been covered in the changeable, camouflaging pigments.

Glyphs typically were a source of pride for the Breed, unique indications of lineage and social rank. Gen Ones like Lucan bore the marks in greater numbers and deeper saturation. His own *dermaglyphs* covered his torso, front and back, stretched down onto his thighs and along his upper arms, with still more running up the back of his neck and onto his scalp. Like living tattoos, the *glyphs* changed hues according to a vampire's emotional state.

Dante's were currently deep russet-bronze, indicating

satiation from a recent feeding. No doubt, once he and
Lucan had parted company after hunting Rogues the
night before, Dante had gone on to find the bed—and the
ripe, juicy vein—of a willing female Host topside.

"How goes it?" he asked, dropping into a chair and
putting one large booted foot up on the desk in front of
him. "Figured you'd have those bastards bagged and
tagged for us already, Gid."

Dante's voice held the trace accent of his eighteenth-
century Italian ancestry, but tonight the cultured tone bore
a rough edge that said the vampire was restless and itching
for action. As if to make the point, he drew one of his ever-
present signature curved blades from the sheath at his hip
and began idly toying with the polished claw of steel.

Malebranche, he called the arced blades, a reference to
demons inhabiting one of the nine levels of hell, though
sometimes Dante wryly adopted the word as a surname for
himself when he was out among humankind. That was
about all the poetry the vampire had in his soul; everything
else inside of him was unapologetic, cold, dark menace.

Lucan admired that about him, and had to admit
watching Dante in combat with those ruthless blades was a
thing of beauty, enough to put any artist to shame.

"Nice work last night," Lucan said, well aware that
praise from him was rare, even when it was deserved. "You
saved my ass out there."

He wasn't talking about the confrontation with the
Rogues, but what had happened afterward. Lucan had
gone too long without feeding, starvation being something
almost as dangerous to their kind as the addictive
overindulgence that plagued the Rogues. Dante's look said
he understood the meaning, but he let the fact slide with
his usual cool nonchalance.

"Shit," he replied, drawing the word out around a deep chuckle. "After all the times you've had my back? Forget it, man. Just returning the favor."

The lab's glass entry doors slid open with a smooth hiss as two more of Lucan's brethren strode in. They were quite a pair. Nikolai, tall and athletic, with sandy hair, strikingly angular features, and piercing ice-blue eyes a shade colder than the winter of his Siberian homeland. The youngest of the group by far, Niko had come of age during the height of the humans' so-called Cold War. A gearhead right out of the cradle, he was a high-octane thrill-seeker and the Breed's first line of defense when it came to things like guns, gadgets, and everything in between.

Conlan, by contrast, was soft-spoken and serious, a consummate tactician. He was as graceful as a big cat next to Niko's brash swagger, a wall of bulky muscle, his copper hair shorn beneath the black triangle of silk that wrapped his skull. The vampire was late generation Breed—a youth by Lucan's standards—his human mother the daughter of a Scottish chieftain. The warrior carried himself with a bearing that was nothing short of regal.

Hell, even his beloved Breedmate, Danika, affectionately referred to the highlander as *My Lord* a lot of the time, and the five-eleven female was hardly the subservient type.

"Rio's on the way," Nikolai announced, his mouth widening into a sly grin that put twin dimples in his lean cheeks. He gave Lucan a nod of his head. "Eva said to tell you we can have her man only after she's done with him."

"If there's anything left," Dante drawled, holding out his hand to greet the others with a smooth grazing of palms, then a knock of briefly connected knuckles.

Lucan met Niko and Conlan with like respect, but he

settled in with mild annoyance at Rio's delay. He didn't begrudge any vampire his chosen Breedmate, but Lucan personally saw no point in strapping himself down with the demands and responsibilities of a blood-bonded female. It was expected of the general population of the Breed to take a woman to mate and bear the next generation, but for the warrior class—those select few males who willingly shunned the sanctuary of the Darkhavens in favor of a life of combat—Lucan saw the process of blood-bonding as sentimental at best.

At its worst, it was an invitation to disaster if a warrior was tempted to put feelings for his mate above his duty to the Breed.

"Where's Tegan?" he asked, his thoughts leading naturally to the last of their number at the compound.

"Not yet returned," Conlan answered.

"Has he called in his location?"

Conlan exchanged a look with Niko, then gave a slight shake of his head. "No word."

"This is the longest he's been MIA," Dante remarked to no one in particular, running his thumb over the curved edge of his blade. "What's it been—three, four days?"

Four days, going on five.

But who the hell was counting?

Answer: they all were, but no one spoke up to voice the concern that had been running through their ranks of late. As it was, Lucan had to work hard to stifle a surge of venom that rose in him when he thought about the most reclusive member of their cadre.

Tegan had always preferred to hunt alone, but his secretive nature was beginning to wear on the others. He was a wild card, more and more lately, and Lucan, frankly, was finding it hard to trust the guy, not that mistrust was anything new when it came to Tegan. There was bad blood between the two of them, no question, but that was ancient history. It had to be. The war they had both pledged themselves to so long ago was more important than any animosity they held for each other.

Still, the vampire bore close watching. Lucan knew Tegan's weaknesses better than any of the others could; he wouldn't hesitate to make a move if the male stepped so much as a toe out of line.

The lab's doors whisked open again and in came Rio at last, tucking the loose tail of a sleek, white, designer shirt into tailored black pants. Some of the buttons were missing from the crisp silk, but Rio wore his postsex dishevelment with the same air of cool that hung over him in everything he did. Under the hank of thick dark hair that swung over his brow, the Spaniard's topaz-colored eyes danced. When he smiled, the tips of his fangs glimmered, not yet receded after the passion with his lady had drawn them out. "I hope you saved a few Rogues for me, my friends." He rubbed his hands together. "I'm feeling good, ready to party."

"Have a seat," Lucan drawled, "and try not to bleed all over Gideon's computers."

Rio's long fingers went up to the crimson rosebud mark at his throat where Eva had apparently bitten him with her blunt human teeth and sipped from his vein. Even though she was a Breedmate, she was still genetically Homo sapiens. Despite the long years that she and others like her would share through the blood-bond with a mate, none of her kind would grow fangs or take on any other traits of the vampire males. It was a widely accepted practice that a vampire would feed his mate from a self-inflicted gash on his wrist or forearm, but passions ran wild in the

ranks of the Breed warriors. And in their chosen women.
Sex and blood were a potent combination—sometimes,
too much so.

Grinning, unrepentant, Rio threw himself into a loose
sprawl in one of the swivel chairs and leaned back, prop-
ping his big bare feet on the clear Lucite console. He and
the other warriors began reviewing the previous night's
tallies, exchanging laughs as they one-upped one another
and discussed the finer techniques of their profession.

While hunting their enemies gave some of the Breed
pleasure, Lucan's own drive was based in hatred, pure and
simple. He didn't try to hide it. He despised everything
that the Rogues were and had vowed, long ago, that he
would eradicate their kind, or die trying. Some days, he
didn't really care what came first.

"Here we go," Gideon said finally, when the records
scrolling on his monitor came to a stop. "Looks like we hit
pay dirt."

"What've you got?"

Lucan and the others turned their attention to an oversized flat-screen panel above the lab's bank of micro-
processors. The faces of the four Rogues slain by Lucan
outside the nightclub came up on the display next to those
of Gabrielle's cell phone images of the same individuals.

"IID records have all of these down as missing persons.
Two from the Connecticut Darkhaven last month, another
out of Fall River, and the last one is local. They're all current generation, the youngest wasn't even thirty years old."

"Shit," Rio said, whistling low. "Stupid kids."

Lucan said nothing, felt nothing, for the loss of young
lives gone Rogue. They weren't the first, and they sure as
hell wouldn't be the last. Living in the Darkhavens could
seem pretty dull to an immature male with something to

prove. The allure of blood and conquest was deeply in-grained, even in the later generations, who were the furthest removed from their savage forebears. If a vampire went looking for trouble, particularly in a city the size of Boston, he generally found it in spades.

Gideon punched a quick series of commands on his computer keyboard, bringing up more photos from the database. "Here are the last two records. This first individual is a known Rogue, repeat offender here in Boston, although he's apparently been keeping low under the radar for more than three months. That is, he was, until Lucan smoked him in the alley over the weekend."

"And what about him?" Lucan asked, eyeing the last remaining image, that of the only Rogue who'd managed to elude him outside the club. His photo record came up in the form of a video still, presumably captured during some sort of interrogation session, based on the restraints and electrodes the vampire was wearing. "How old is this image?"

"About six months," Gideon replied, calling up the date stamp. "Came out of one of the West Coast operations."

"L.A.?"

"Seattle. But according to the file, L.A.'s got a warrant for him, too."

"Warrants," Dante scoffed. "Fucking waste of time."

Lucan had to agree. For most of the vampire nation in the United States and abroad, enforcement of the law and apprehension of individuals gone Rogue was governed by specific rules and procedures. Warrants were written, arrests were made, interrogations were conducted, and, given ample evidence and due process, convictions were handed down. It was all very civilized. And rarely effective.

While the Breed and its Darkhaven populations were

organized, motivated, and mired in layers of bureaucracy, their enemies were rash and unpredictable. And unless Lucan's gut was wrong, after centuries of anarchy and general chaos, the Rogues were gearing up to recruit.

If they weren't already months into the process.

Lucan stared at the image on screen. In the video still, the captured Rogue was strapped to an upright metal table, stripped naked, his head shaved bald to better accommodate the currents that were likely being sent into his skull during his questioning. Lucan felt no sympathy for the torture the Rogue had undergone. Interrogations of that nature were often necessary, and like a human jacked up on heroin, a vampire afflicted with Bloodlust could take ten times the pain of his Breed brethren without breaking.

This Rogue was big, with a heavy brow and thick, primitive features. He was snarling in the video frame, his long fangs gleaming, his amber eyes wild around the elliptical slashes of his fixed pupils. He was draped with wires from the top of his huge head and corded neck to his muscle-girded chest and hammerlike arms.

"Assuming ugly's not a crime, what did Seattle bust him for?"

"Let's see what we've got." Gideon spun back to his bank of computers and brought a record up on another screen. "Picked him up for trafficking—weapons, explosives, chemicals. Oh, this guy's a bloody charmer. Into some real nasty shit."

"Any idea whose arms he's been running?"

"Nothing listed here. They didn't get that far with him, evidently. The record states he broke out of containment right after these images were taken. He killed two of his guards during the escape."

And now he'd escaped again, Lucan thought grimly,

wishing to hell he had popped the SOB when he had him in his sights. He didn't tolerate failure well, least of all in himself.

Lucan glanced to Niko. "You ever run across this guy?"

"No," said the Russian, "but I'll check him out with my contacts, see what I can find."

"Get on it."

Nikolai gave a curt nod and headed out of the tech lab, already dialing someone on his cell phone.

"These are damning pictures," Conlan said, peering over Gideon's shoulder at the photos Gabrielle had taken during the slaying outside the nightclub. The warrior blew out a curse. "Bad enough humans have witnessed some of these Rogue slayings over the years, but now they're pausing to take snapshots?"

Dante put his feet down with a thump, stood up, and started pacing, as if he was growing restless with the inactivity of the meeting. "Whole world up there thinks they're friggin' paparazzi."

"The guy who took these shots must've pissed himself real good when he saw two-hundred pounds of Breed warrior gunning for him," Rio added. Grinning, he looked at Lucan. "Did you bother to scrub his memory first, or did you just take the sucker out on the spot?"

"The human who witnessed the attack that night was female." Lucan stared into the faces of his brethren, revealing none of his feelings about the news he was about to impart. "Turns out she's a Breedmate."

"Madre de Dios," Rio swore, raking his fingers through his dark hair. "Breedmate—you're sure?"

"She bears the mark. I saw it with my own eyes."

"What did you do with her? Cristo, you didn't..."

"No," Lucan replied sharply, agitated by the implication

in the Spaniard's hedging tone. "I didn't harm the woman. There is a line that even I won't cross."

He hadn't claimed Gabrielle as his own, either, although he'd come damned close to it that night in her apartment. Lucan clamped his teeth together, a wave of dark hunger hitting him when he thought about how tempting Gabrielle had looked, curled up and dreaming in her bed. How bloody sweet she had tasted against his tongue. . . .

"What will you do with her, Lucan?" This time the concern was coming from Gideon's direction. "We can't very well leave her topside for the Rogues to find her. She's certain to have gotten their attention when she snapped these pictures."

"And if the Rogues should realize she's a Breedmate . . ." Dante added, his trailing comment drawing grim nods from the other warriors.

"She'll be safest here," Gideon said, "under Breed protection. Better still, she should officially be admitted to one of the Darkhavens."

"I know the protocol," Lucan growled. He felt too much anger at the thought of Gabrielle in the hands of the Rogues, or those of another member of the Breed if he were to do the right thing and send her off to one of the nation's Darkhaven sanctuaries. Neither option seemed acceptable to him at the moment, thanks to the streak of possessiveness that was burning through his veins, unbidden and unwanted.

He delivered a cold stare to his warrior brethren. "The female is my responsibility for now. I will decide how best to proceed in this."

None of the others spoke up to contradict him, nor did he expect they would. As Gen One, he was elder; as the founder of the warrior class within the Breed, he was the most proven, by blood and by steel. His word was law, and all in the room respected that.

Dante got to his feet, flipping the *malebranche* blade between long, nimble fingers, and sheathing it in one fluid motion. "Four hours to sunset. I'm outta here." He shot an arch look over at Rio and Conlan. "Anyone game to spar before things get interesting topside?"

Both males rose eagerly to the idea, and with respectful nods in Lucan's direction the three big warriors strode out of the tech lab and into the corridor leading to the compound's weapons training area.

"You got anything more on this Rogue out of Seattle?" Lucan asked Gideon, as the glass doors slid closed and just the two of them remained in the lab.

"I'm running a cross-check of all record sources right now. Should only take a minute to come back one way or the other." The keys clacked as he typed a flurry of strokes, then, "Bingo. Got a hit from a West Coast GPS feed. Looks like intel gathered prior to our boy's arrest. Have a look."

The monitor screen filled with a series of nighttime satellite images homed in on a commercial fishing wharf off Puget Sound. The surveillance focused on a long black sedan that sat idling behind a dilapidated building at the end of the docks. Leaning into the back passenger window of the car was the Rogue who had managed to escape Lucan a few days ago. Gideon scrolled through the next few frames of feed that showed an apparently lengthy conversation between the Rogue and whoever was concealed behind the vehicle's darkened windows. As the images advanced, they showed the rear door opening from within to admit the Rogue inside.

"Hold up," Lucan said, his gaze narrowing on the hand of the hidden passenger. "Can you tighten this frame at all? Zoom in on the open car door."

"Let me try."

The image magnified incrementally, although Lucan hardly needed a better visual to confirm what he was seeing. Barely discernible, but there it was. In the slice of exposed skin between the passenger's big hand and the French cuff of his long-sleeved shirt was an impressive array of Gen One *dermaglyphs*.

Gideon saw them now, too. "I'll be damned, will you look at that," he said, staring at the monitor. "Our Seattle suckhead was keeping some interesting company."

"Maybe still is," Lucan replied.

They didn't come more badass than a Rogue with first generation vampire blood in its veins. Gen Ones fell to Bloodlust faster and harder than the later Breeds, and they made deadly vicious enemies. If one of them had designs on leading the Rogues in an uprising, it would be the start of a hellacious war. Lucan had fought that battle once before, long ago. He had no wish to do so again.

"Print everything you've got, including some zooms of those *glyphs*."

"You got it."

"Anything else you dig up on these two individuals, bring it directly to me. I'll handle it personally."

Gideon nodded, but the glance he flicked over the tops of his silver shades was hesitant. "You can't expect to take them all out single-handedly, you know."

Lucan pinned him with a dark look. "Says who?"

No doubt the vampire had a dissertation on probability and the law of averages perched at the tip of his genius tongue, but Lucan wasn't in the mood to hear it. Night was coming, and with it another chance to hunt his enemies. He needed to use the remaining hours to clear his mind, prepare his weapons, and decide where best to strike. The predator in him was pacing and hungry, but not for the battle he should be craving with the Rogues.

Instead, Lucan found his thoughts drifting to a quiet Beacon Hill apartment, back to a midnight visit that never should have happened. Like her jasmine scent, the memory of Gabrielle's soft skin and warm, willing body coiled itself around him. He tensed, his sex rousing at the very thought of her.

Damn it.

This was the reason he hadn't already brought her under Breed protection here at the compound. At a distance, she was distracting. In close quarters, she would prove a bloody disaster.

"You all right?" Gideon asked, his chair spun around, so that he faced Lucan. "That's some major fury you're wearing, buddy."

Lucan snapped out of his dark musings long enough to realize that his fangs had begun to lengthen in his mouth, his vision sharpened by the slivering of his pupils. But it wasn't rage that transformed him. It was lust, and he was going to have to slake it, sooner than later. With that thought pounding in his veins, Lucan grabbed Gabrielle's cell phone from the desktop where it lay, and stalked out of the lab.

CHAPTER
Seven

Ten more minutes to heaven," Gabrielle said, peering into her opened oven and letting the rich aroma of homemade baked manicotti waft into the kitchen of her apartment.

She closed the windowed door, reset the digital timer, then poured herself another glass of red wine and carried it with her into the living room. An old Sarah McLachlan CD was playing softly on the sound system. At a few minutes past seven in the evening, Gabrielle was finally beginning to unwind from her little morning adventure at the abandoned asylum. She had gotten a couple of decent shots that might amount to something, but best of all, she had managed to escape the scary-looking bruiser who'd apparently been running security detail for the place.

That alone was worth celebrating.

Gabrielle folded herself into the cushioned corner of her sofa, her skin warm beneath dove-gray yoga pants and a pink, long-sleeved tee-shirt. Her hair was still damp from her recent bath, loose tendrils slipping out of the careless ponytail fixed haphazardly at the nape of her neck. Freshly scrubbed and chilling out at last, she was more than glad to settle in for the night and enjoy her solitude.

So when the doorbell rang not a minute later, she cursed under her breath and considered ignoring the unwanted intrusion. It rang a second time, insistent, followed by a sharp rap delivered by a rather powerful hand that didn't sound like it was going to take no for an answer.

"Gabrielle."

She was already on her feet and cautiously walking halfway to the door when she heard a voice she recognized at once. She shouldn't know it with such certainty, but she did. Lucan Thorne's deep baritone came through the door and into her bones like a sound she'd heard a thousand times before, soothing her even as it kick-started her pulse into a sudden flutter of anticipation.

Surprised, more pleased than she wanted to admit, Gabrielle unfastened the multiple locks and opened the door to him.

"Hi."

"Hello, Gabrielle."

He greeted her with an unsettling familiarity, his eyes intense beneath the dark slashes of his brows. That piercing gaze traveled a slow, downward path, from the top of her mussed head, to the silk-screened peace sign stretched across her braless chest, to the bare toes peeking out from the flared legs of her low-slung pants.

"I wasn't expecting anyone." She said it as an excuse for her appearance, but Thorne didn't seem to mind. In fact, as his attention came back to her face, Gabrielle felt a sudden flush of heat fill her cheeks for the way he was looking at her.

Like he wanted to devour her where she stood.

"Oh, you have my cell phone," she said, blurting out the obvious when she spotted the gleam of silver metal in his big hand.

He held it out to her. "Later than intended. My apologies."

Was it her imagination, or did his fingers deliberately brush hers as she took the device from his grasp?

"Thanks for returning it," she said, still caught in the hold of his gaze. "Were you, ah...were you able to do anything with the images?"

"Yes. They were very helpful."

She exhaled a sigh, relieved to hear that the police might, at last, be on her side in this. "Do you think you'll be able to catch the guys in the photos?"

"I'm certain of it."

His tone was so dark, she didn't doubt him for a second. Actually, she was getting the feeling that Detective Thorne was a bad guy's worst nightmare.

"Well, that's great news. I've got to admit, this whole thing has been making me a little jumpy. I guess witnessing a brutal murder will do that to a person, right?"

He gave her only the barest nod of agreement. A man of few words, evidently, but then who needed conversation when you had soul-stripping eyes like his?

To her relief and annoyance, from behind her in the kitchen, the oven timer started beeping. "Shit. That's, um—that's my dinner. I'd better grab it before the smoke alarm goes off. Wait here for a sec—I mean, do you want to—?" She took a calming breath, unused to being so rattled by anyone. "Come in, please. I'll be right back."

Without hesitation, Lucan Thorne stepped inside the apartment as Gabrielle turned to set down her cell phone and liberate her manicotti from the oven.

"Am I interrupting something?"

She was surprised to hear him in the kitchen with her so quickly, as if he had been silently on her heels from the instant she invited him in. Gabrielle lifted the pan of steaming pasta out of the oven and set it down on the range top to cool. She stripped off her hot mitts and turned to give the detective a proud grin.

"I'm celebrating."

He cocked his head to regard the quiet space around them. "Alone?"

She shrugged. "Unless you want to join me."

The mild incline of his chin seemed guarded, but he removed his dark coat and draped it over the back of a counter stool. He was a peculiar, distracting presence, all the more so now that he was standing in her small kitchen—this heavily muscled stranger with the disarming gaze and slightly sinister good looks. He leaned back against the counter and watched her attend to the bubbling dish of baked pasta. "What are we celebrating, Gabrielle?"

"I sold some of my photographs today, in a private showing at a chichi corporate office downtown. My friend Jamie called about an hour ago with the news."

Thorne smiled faintly. "Congratulations."

"Thank you." She pulled an extra glass from the cupboard, then held up her opened bottle of chianti. "Would you like some?"

He shook his head slowly. "Regretfully, I cannot."

"Ah. Sorry," she said, reminding herself of his profession. "On duty, right?"

A muscle jumped in his strong jaw. "Always."

Gabrielle smiled, reaching up to hook some of her loose, curling hair behind her ear. Thorne's gaze followed the movement, and narrowed on the small scratch that marred her cheek.

"What happened to you?"

"Oh, nothing," she replied, not thinking it was a good idea to tell a cop how she spent part of the morning trespassing out at the old asylum. "Just a scrape—hazard of the job from time to time. I'm sure you know how that goes."

She laughed lightly, a bit nervously, because suddenly he was moving toward her, his expression very serious. Just a few smooth paces brought him right up in front of her. His size—his obvious strength—was overwhelming. This close, she could see the thick slabs of muscle that bunched and moved under his black shirt. The fine knit fabric clung to his shoulders, arms, and chest, as if tailored to fit him perfectly.

And he smelled amazing. She didn't detect cologne, only the trace scents of mint and leather, and something darker, like an exotic spice she could not name. Whatever it was, it drenched her senses in something elemental and primal that drew her closer to him when she probably should be backing away.

She sucked in her breath as he reached out to her, the tips of his fingers tenderly grazing her jaw. Heat spread out from that bare contact, flooding her neck as he splayed his hand along the sensitive skin below her ear and around to her nape. With his thumb, he traced the abrasion on her cheek. The scrape had stung when she cleansed it earlier in the day, but now, under his unexpectedly soft caress, she felt no discomfort. Nothing but languid warmth and a slow, swirling ache at her very core.

To her astonishment, he leaned down and dropped a kiss on her marred cheek. His lips lingered there, long enough for her to understand that this was meant as a prelude to something more. She closed her eyes, heart racing. She didn't move, hardly breathed, as she felt Lucan's mouth drift toward hers. He kissed her lips meaningfully, a faint bite of hunger cushioned within the warm press of his mouth. She opened her eyes to find him staring at her. His gaze held an animal wildness that sent a thrill of anxiousness shooting up her spine.

When she finally found her voice, it came out in a small, breathless rasp. "Should you be doing this?"

That penetrating gaze stayed rooted on her. "Oh, yes."

He bent down to her again, brushing his lips over her cheeks, her chin, her throat. She sighed, and he caught her little gasp with a searing kiss, thrusting his tongue between her parted lips. Gabrielle took him in, vaguely aware that his hand was behind her now, slipping beneath the hem of her tee-shirt. He stroked the arch of her bare back, his fingers tenderly brushing her spine. His caress traveled lazily downward, over the fabric of her pants. His strong fingers cupped the curve of her ass, squeezed her tightly. She didn't resist at all as he kissed her deeper and gradually pulled her forward, until her pelvis mashed against the hard muscle of his thigh.

What the hell was she doing? What was she thinking here?

"No," she said, her conscience struggling to surface. "No, wait. *Stop.*" God, how she hated the sound of that word when his mouth was feeling so damned good on hers. "Are you ... Lucan ... are you with someone?"

"Look around, Gabrielle." His lips dragged over hers as he spoke, making her dizzy with want. "It is only you and me."

"A girlfriend," she blurted between kisses. It was probably a little late to be asking, but she had to know, even if she wasn't at all sure how she would deal with an answer she didn't want to hear. "Do you have a girlfriend? Are you married? Please don't tell me you're married. . . ."

"There is no one else."

Only you.

She was pretty sure he hadn't said those last couple of words, but Gabrielle heard them echo in her mind, warm and provocative, stripping her of any resistance.

Oh, he was good. Or maybe she was just that desperate for him, because that spare, unadorned pledge was all he gave her—that, and the dizzying combination of his tender hands and hot, hungry mouth—and yet she believed him without a shred of doubt. She felt as if his every sense was trained on her alone. As if there was only her, only him, and this burning thing that existed between them.

Had existed, from the moment he first showed up on her doorstep.

"Ohh," she gasped as the breath left her lungs in a slow sigh. She sagged against him, reveling in the feel of his hands on her skin, caressing her throat, her shoulder, the arch of her spine. "What are we doing here, Lucan?"

His low growl of humor hummed beside her ear, deep as night. "I think you know."

"I don't know anything, not when you're doing that. Oh . . . *God.*"

He broke their kiss for an instant, looking into her eyes as he ground into her with a slow, meaningful thrust. His sex was rigid at her abdomen. She could feel the solid length of him, could feel the sheer size and strength of his shaft, even through the barrier of their clothes. A flood of moist heat surged between her legs at the thought of taking him inside of her.

"This is why I came here tonight." Lucan's voice rumbled beside her ear. "Do you understand, Gabrielle? I want you."

The feeling was more than mutual. Gabrielle moaned, her body writhing against his with a heat she had no power to control.

This wasn't happening, not really. It had to be another crazy dream, like the one she'd had after the first time she met him. She wasn't actually standing in her kitchen with Lucan Thorne, letting this man she hardly knew beyond his name seduce her. She was dreaming—had to be—and before long she was going to wake up on her sofa, alone as usual, with her glass of red wine dumped on the carpet and her dinner burning in the oven.

But not yet.

Oh, God, please . . . not yet.

Feeling him stroke her skin, burning under the skill of his tongue, was better than any dream, even the delicious one she'd had of him before, if that could be possible.

"Gabrielle," he whispered. "Tell me you want this, too."

"Yes."

She felt his hand working between them, urgent tugging, his breath hot against her neck. "Feel me, Gabrielle. Know how badly I need you."

His fingers were light on hers, guiding her to where his stiff erection protruded, freed from its confines. Gabrielle wrapped her hand around him and gave the velvety shaft a slow, admiring stroke. He was large here as everywhere, and brutally strong, yet so very smooth. The weight of his sex in her hand intoxicated her like a drug. She tightened her grasp and pulled the hard flesh, her fingertips skimming over the thick head.

As she worked her hand along his length and girth, Lucan's body jerked. She felt his hands shake a bit as he moved them from her hips to the loose ties of her pants. He yanked at the knotted cord, his hot exhalation feathering across her scalp in a foreign-sounding oath. There was a rush of cool air against her belly, then the sudden heat of Lucan's palm as he slid his hand inside her panties.

She was wet for him, out of her mind and burning with desire.

His fingers slipped easily through the narrow thatch of curls between her legs, then into her slippery cleft, teasing her with the play of his hand against her aching flesh. She cried out as hunger washed over her in a shivering wave.

"I need you, too," she confessed, her voice threadbare, raw with desire. In response, he eased one long finger inside of her, then another. Gabrielle writhed around that questing, not quite filling caress. "More," she gasped. "Lucan, please . . . I need . . . more."

A dark growl boiled out from between his lips as he leaned down and claimed her mouth in another hungry kiss. Her pants came off in a hasty tug of falling fabric. Her panties were next, thin lace snapping under the strength of Lucan's impatient hands. Gabrielle felt air hit her suddenly naked skin, but then Lucan sank down to his knees in front of her and she was on fire before she could take her next breath. He kissed her and licked her, his hands braced hard and unrelenting against her inner thighs, spreading her wider for his carnal desires. The feel of his tongue spearing her flesh, suckling her deep into his mouth, turned Gabrielle's limbs to liquid.

She came swiftly, harder than she could have imagined. Lucan held her firmly in his hands, pressing her damp core to him, giving no quarter as her body quivered and bucked, her breath falling to a strangled gasp as he stroked her toward the crest of another climax. She closed her eyes and dropped her head back on her shoulders, surrendering to him, and to the insanity of this most unexpected encounter. Gabrielle clawed at Lucan's shoulders to hold herself up while her legs went boneless beneath her.

Release bore down on her again. It seized her in a fierce grasp, spun her high into a sensual dreamland, then let her go, and she was falling, falling. . . .

No, she was being lifted she realized from within her sexual daze. Lucan's arms held her tenderly, curved beneath her back and under her knees. He was naked now, and so was she, though she couldn't recall taking off her shirt. She looped her arms around his neck as he carried her out of the kitchen and into the living room, where Sarah McLachlan's voice poured out of the speakers, singing about holding someone down and kissing their breath away.

The soft crush of chenille cushioned her as Lucan placed her down on the sofa and braced himself above her. It wasn't until that moment that she was able to see him fully, and what she saw was magnificent. Six-and-a-half feet of solid muscle and sheer masculine power caging her beneath him, his strong arms hemming her in on either side.

And as if the raw beauty of his body wasn't enough, Lucan's gorgeous skin was decorated with a jaw-dropping array of intricate tattoos. The complex design of arcing lines and interlocking patterns swirled around his pecs and ribbed abdomen, up over his broad shoulders, then down his thick biceps. Their color was elusive, variegated in shades of sea green, sienna, and wine-dark red that seemed to pulse toward richer hues the longer she stared at them.

When he tilted his head downward to lavish attention on her breasts, Gabrielle saw the tattoo that stretched up the back of his neck and into his dark hairline. She had wanted to trace the intriguing markings the first time she saw Lucan. Now, she gave in to the urge with abandon, letting her hands travel all over him, marveling at both the mysterious man and the unusual art he wore.

"Kiss me," she begged him, reaching down to clutch at his tattooed shoulders.

He started to rise up over her and Gabrielle arched into him, fevered with hunger, needing to feel him inside her. His erection was a heavy length of steely heat where it pressed between her thighs. Gabrielle slid her hands down and stroked him, lifting her hips to welcome him in.

"Take me," she whispered. "Fill me, Lucan. Now. Please."

He did not deny her.

The thick head of his sex pulsed, hard and demanding, at the entrance of her body. He was trembling, she realized dimly. His massive shoulders shook beneath her hands, as if he had been holding himself back all this time and was now about to burst. She wanted him to come apart like she had. She needed to have him inside her or she was going to die. He gave a strangled groan, his mouth at the sensitive crook of her neck.

"Yes," she urged him, shifting beneath him so that the shaft of his cock now cleaved the center of her. "Don't be gentle. I won't break."

His head reared up at last, and for an instant he stared down into her eyes. Gabrielle looked up at him from beneath heavy lids, startled by the untamed fire that met her gaze. His eyes fairly glowed, twin flames of palest silver, engulfing his pupils and boring into her with preternatural heat. The bones of his face seemed sharper, his skin stretched taut across his angular cheeks and stern jaw.

It was so peculiar, the way the dim light of the room played across his features....

That thought had hardly formed before the living room lamps blinked off as one. She might have considered it strange, but as the dark settled around them, Lucan breached her body with a deep, mind-numbing thrust. Gabrielle could not bite back her moan of pleasure as he filled her, stretched her, impaled her to her core.

"Oh, my God," she nearly sobbed, accepting every hard inch of him. "You feel so good."

He dropped his head to her shoulder and grunted as he drew back, then plunged even farther than before. Gabrielle clutched at his strong back, pulling him closer, as she lifted her hips to meet his hard thrusts. He cursed under his breath, and it was a black, feral sound. His cock leaped within her, seeming to swell even greater with each relentless flex of his hips.

"I need to fuck you, Gabrielle. I've needed to fuck you from the moment I first saw you."

The frank words—his admission that he'd wanted her as much as she had wanted him—only inflamed her more. She twined her fingers in his hair, gasping wordless, pleasured cries as his tempo increased. He thrust and withdrew, pistoning between her legs now. Gabrielle felt the rush of orgasm coiling in her belly.

"I could do this all night," he growled, his breath hot against her neck. "I don't think I can stop."

"Don't, Lucan. Oh, God...don't stop."

Gabrielle held on to him as he pumped into her. It was all she could do as a raw scream tore from her throat and she was coming and coming and coming again.

Lucan stepped off Gabrielle's front stoop and headed down her dark, quiet street on foot. He'd left her sleeping in her bedroom loft, her breathing rhythmic and sated, her delectable body spent after more than three nonstop hours of passion. He had never fucked so hard, so long, or so completely.

And still he was hungry for more.

More of her.

That he'd been able to conceal the lengthening of his fangs and the wild, desire-swamped cast of his eyes from her was a miracle.

That he hadn't given in to the relentless, pounding need to sink his sharp teeth into her sweet throat and drink to inebriation was even more astounding.

Nor did he trust himself to linger anywhere near her when every fevered cell in his body ached to do just that.

Coming to see her tonight had likely been a monstrous mistake. He had thought that sex with her would purge some of the heat she fueled in him. He'd never been more wrong. Taking Gabrielle, being inside of her, had only further exposed his weakness for her. He had wanted her with an animal need, and had pursued her like the predator he was. He wasn't sure he would have taken no for an answer. He didn't think he would have been capable of leashing his desire for her.

But she hadn't denied him.

Christ, no.

In retrospect, it would have been an act of mercy if she had. Instead, Gabrielle had accepted every measure of his sexual fury, demanding he give her nothing less.

If he turned around right now and stalked back into her apartment to wake her, he could spend another few hours between her gorgeous, welcoming thighs. That would at least satisfy part of his need. And if he could not slake the other, growing torment within him, he could wait out the sun and let the killing rays scorch him into oblivion.

If duty to the Breed didn't have such a hold on him, he might consider that option as a damned attractive possibility.

Lucan hissed a curse as he turned out of Gabrielle's neighborhood and strolled deeper into the nightscape of the city. His hands were shaking. His vision was sharp, his thoughts sliding toward feral. His body was twitchy, anxious. He snarled with frustration, knowing the signs well enough.

He needed to feed again.

It was too soon since the last time when he had taken enough blood to sustain him for a week, maybe more. That had been just a few nights ago, yet his stomach gnawed as though starving. For a long time, his cravings had been getting worse. Close to unbearable, the harder he tried to suppress them.

Denial.

That's what had gotten him through this far.

Sooner or later, he was going to reach the end of that rope. And then what?

Did he really think he was so different from his father?

His brothers hadn't been, and they'd both been older,

stronger, than him. Bloodlust had ultimately claimed them both: one took his life by his own hand when the addiction became too much; the other went deeper still, turning Rogue, and then losing his head to the killing blade of a Breed warrior.

Being born first generation had gifted Lucan with a great deal of strength and power—and instant respect that he knew he didn't deserve—but it was every bit as much a curse. He wondered how much longer he could fight the darkness of his own savage nature. Some nights, he grew goddamned tired of the fact that he had to.

Passing among the evening population on the streets, Lucan let his gaze roam. Although he was stoked for battle if he found it, he was pleased there were no Rogues in sight. Only a scattered number of late-generation vampires from the area's Darkhaven: one pack of young males mixing with a giggly group of human partygoers and surreptitiously trolling, as he was now, for viable blood Hosts.

He saw the youths nudge each other, heard them whisper the words *warrior* and *Gen One* as he moved toward them on the stretch of pavement. Their open awe and curiosity were annoying, though not unusual. Vampires born and raised in the Darkhavens rarely had the opportunity to see one of the warrior class, let alone the founder of the once-vaunted, now long-antiquated Order.

Most knew the old stories of how, several centuries past, eight of the fiercest, most lethal Breed males came together as a group to slay the last of the savage Ancients and the army of Rogues who served them. Those warriors became legendary, and in the time since, their Order had gone through many changes, increasing in numbers and locations under periods of Rogue conflict, only to trail off during the long stretches of peace between.

Now, the warrior class was comprised of a covert hand-ful of individuals around the globe, operating largely inde-pendently, and not without a little contempt from the society as a whole. In this enlightened age of fair treatment and due process within the vampire nation, warrior tactics were considered renegade, and but a shade this side of the law.

As if Lucan, or any of the warriors on the front lines with him, gave a shit about public relations.

With a snarl tossed in the direction of the gaping youths, Lucan cast out a mental invitation to the nattering human females the vampires had been chatting up on the street. Every pair of feminine eyes latched on to the raw power he was knowingly throwing off in waves. Two girls—a chesty blonde and a redhead just a degree or two lighter than Gabrielle's tresses—immediately broke away from the pack to approach him, their friends and the other males instantly forgotten.

But Lucan needed only one of them, and the choice was easy. He dismissed the blonde with shake of his head. Her companion settled under his arm, petting him as he led her off the street and into a discreet, unlit alcove of a nearby building.

He got down to business without hesitation.

Sweeping the girl's smoke-and-beer scented hair away from her neck, Lucan licked his lips, then plunged his ex-tended fangs into the flesh of her throat. She spasmed un-der his bite, her hands coming up instinctively as he pulled the first long draught from her vein. He sucked hard, no desire to draw things out. The female moaned, not in alarm or discomfort, but in the pleasure that was unique to the letting of blood under the thrall of a vampire.

Blood surged into Lucan's mouth, warm and thick.

Against his will, he flashed on a mental picture of Gabrielle in his arms, letting himself imagine for the briefest second that it was her neck he suckled now.

Her blood, coursing down the back of his throat and into his body.

God, to think what it would be like to draw from her vein as his cock pumped into her heat, spilling deep within her...

Christ.

He thrust the fantasy away with a vicious snarl.

Never gonna happen, he warned himself harshly. Reality was a bitch, and he'd better not lose sight of it.

Fact was, this wasn't Gabrielle, but an anonymous stranger, just the way he preferred it. The blood he took now wasn't the jasmine-tinged sweetness he craved, but a bitter copper tanginess, corrupted by some mild narcotic his Host had recently ingested.

He didn't care what she tasted like. All he needed was to smooth the edge off his hunger, and for that, anyone would do. He drew more from her and drank it down with haste, expedient in his feeding as was always his way.

When he finished, he smoothed his tongue over the twin punctures to seal them, then backed out of the unwanted embrace. The young woman was panting, her mouth slack, her body languid as though fresh off an orgasm.

Lucan put his palm on her forehead and let it drift down to close her dazed, heavy-lidded eyes. That touch would scrub all recollection of what just occurred between them.

"Your friends are looking for you," he told the girl when his hand came away from her face and she blinked up at him in confusion. "You should go home. The night is full of predators."

"Okay," she said, nodding agreeably.

Lucan waited in the shadows as she wobbled back around the corner of the building to find her companions. He sucked in a deep breath through teeth and fangs, every muscle in his body tense, tight, pulsing. His heart was hammering in his chest. Just thinking about what Gabrielle's blood might taste like in his mouth had given him a raging hard-on.

His physical appetite might be calmer now that he'd fed, but he was hardly content.

He still...wanted.

With a low growl, he stalked out into the street once more, surlier than ever. He set his sights on the roughest part of town, hoping he'd meet up with a Rogue or two before dawn started to rise. He suddenly needed a fight in a bad way. Needed to hurt something—even if that something ended up being himself.

Whatever it took to keep him far as hell away from Gabrielle Maxwell.

CHAPTER
Eight

At first, Gabrielle thought it had just been another erotic dream. But waking up late that next morning, naked in her bed, her body spent, parts of her aching in all the right places, she knew that Lucan Thorne had definitely been there, in the flesh. And God, what amazing flesh it had been. She'd lost track of how many times he'd made her climax. If she added up every orgasm she'd had for the past two years, it probably wouldn't even come close to what she'd experienced with him last night.

Yet she'd been wishing for just one more as she dragged her eyelids open and realized with disappointment that Lucan hadn't stayed. Her bed was empty, the apartment was quiet. He'd evidently left sometime during the night.

As exhausted as she was, Gabrielle could have slept a full day, but lunch plans with Jamie and the girls got her

out of the house and downtown about twenty minutes after noon. As she wandered into the Chinatown restaurant,
she felt heads turning in her direction: appreciative glances
from a group of advertising types over at the sushi bar, half
a dozen suited young executives watching her stroll past
them as she made her way toward her friends' booth near
the back.

She felt sexy and confident in her dark red V-neck
sweater and black skirt, and she didn't care if it was obvious to everyone in the place that she'd just had the most incredible sex of her life.

"Finally, she graces us with her presence!" Jamie exclaimed as Gabrielle reached the table and greeted her
friends with quick hugs.

Megan bussed her cheek. "You look great."

Jamie nodded. "Yeah, you do, sweetie. Love the outfit.
Is it new?" He didn't wait for an answer, just plopped back
down into the booth and wolfed down a fried dumpling in
one gulp. "I was starving, so we already ordered a few ap-
petizers. Anyway, where've you been? I was just about to
send a posse out for you."

"Sorry. I slept in a little today." She smiled and sat
down next to Jamie on the paisley vinyl bench. "Isn't
Kendra coming?"

"MIA again." Megan took a sip from her teacup, and
shrugged. "Not that it matters. She's all about her new
boyfriend lately—you know, that guy she picked up at La
Notte last weekend?"

"Brent," Gabrielle said, weathering a jolt of unease at
the mention of that terrible night.

"Yeah, him. She even managed to switch her shift from
graveyard to days at the hospital so she can spend every
night with him. Evidently, he has to travel a lot for work or

something and is generally out of touch during the day. I can't believe Kendra is letting some guy dictate her life like this. Ray and I have been dating for three months, but I still make time for my friends."

Gabrielle raised her brows. Of the four of them, Kendra was the most free-spirited, unapologetically so. She preferred to maintain a stable of ready dates and was committed to staying single at least until she turned thirty. "You think she's in love?"

"Lust, honey." Jamie pinched the last dumpling with his chopsticks. "It can make you do crazier things than love sometimes. Trust me, I've been there."

As he chewed on his appetizer, Jamie's gaze held Gabrielle's for a long moment, before it swept over her loosely tousled hair and suddenly flushing cheeks. She attempted a casual smile, but couldn't keep her secret from betraying her to him in the happy gleam of her eyes. Jamie set his chopsticks down on his plate. He cocked his head at her, his bobbed blond hair swinging around his chin.

"Oh. My. God." He grinned. "You did it."

"Did what?" A soft laugh bubbled out of her mouth.

"You *did it*. You got laid, didn't you?"

Gabrielle's laughter dissolved into a blushing, girly giggle.

"Oh, sweetie. You're wearing it well, I must say." Jamie patted her hand, laughing along with her. "Let me guess; Detective Dark-and-Sexy of the Boston PD?"

She rolled her eyes at the silly nickname, and nodded.

"When?"

"Last night. Practically all night."

Jamie's whoop of enthusiasm drew attention from some of the surrounding tables. He simmered down, but beamed at her like a proud mother hen. "He was good, huh?"

"Amazing."

"Okay, how come I don't know anything about this mystery man?" Megan interjected now. "And he's a cop? Maybe Ray knows him. I could ask—"

"No." Gabrielle shook her head. "Please don't say anything about this to anyone, you guys. It's not like I'm dating Lucan. He came over last night to return my cell phone, and things just got...well, out of control. I don't even know if I'll see him again."

She had no idea about that, actually, but God, she hoped so.

Part of her warned that what happened between them was reckless behavior, foolish thinking. It was. She couldn't really argue that. It was crazy. She had always considered herself a reasonable, careful person—the one who would caution her friends against careless impulses like the one she'd indulged in last night.

Stupid, stupid, stupid.

And not just because she'd allowed herself to get so caught up in the moment that she had forgone any kind of protection. Getting intimate with a practical stranger was seldom a good idea, but Gabrielle had the terrible feeling that it would be a very easy thing to lose her heart to a man like Lucan Thorne.

And that, she was sure, was nothing short of idiotic.

Still, sex like she'd had with him didn't happen all the time. At least, not for her. Just thinking about Lucan Thorne made her insides twist with sweet longing. If he happened to walk into the restaurant right now, she'd probably leap over the tables to jump him.

"We had an incredible night together, but right now, that's all it is. I don't want to read anything more into it."

"Uh-huh." Jamie put his elbow on the table and leaned in conspiratorially. "Then why can't you stop smiling?"

"Where the hell have you been?"

Lucan smelled Tegan before he saw the vampire round the corner of the residence corridor inside the compound. The male had been hunting recently. He still carried the metallic, sweet odor of blood on him—both the human and Rogue variety.

When he saw Lucan waiting for him outside one of the apartments, he paused, his hands fisted in the pockets of his low-slung jeans. Tegan's gray tee-shirt was shredded in places, filthy with dirt and splattered blood. His pale green eyes were hooded, ringed with dark circles. Long, unkempt tawny hair drooped into his face.

"You look like shit, Tegan."

He glanced up from under that hank of light brown hair and smirked, wiseass, as usual.

Glyphs tracked up his forearms and thick biceps. The scrolling, elegant markings were just a shade darker than his own golden skin tone, their color betraying nothing of the vampire's current mood. Lucan didn't know if it was sheer will that kept the male's attitude locked on permanent apathy, or if the darkness of his past had truly deadened all feeling in him.

God knew, he'd been through enough to break a full cadre of warriors.

But Tegan's personal demons were his own. All that mattered to Lucan was making sure the Order remained

strong and on point. There was no room for weak links in
the chain.

"You've been out of contact for five days, Tegan. I'll say
it again, where the fuck have you been?"

He scoffed. "Piss off, man. You're not my mother."

When he started to walk away, Lucan closed the space
between them with blinding speed. He seized Tegan by the
throat and shoved his back against the corridor wall to get
his attention.

Lucan's fury was ripe: in part for the general disregard
Tegan showed the others in the Order lately, but more for
the sorry lack of judgment that had made Lucan think he
could spend one night with Gabrielle Maxwell and then
put her out of his mind.

Neither blood nor the extreme violence he'd brought
down on two Rogues in the hours before dawn had been
enough to dim the lust for Gabrielle that still pounded
through him. Lucan had prowled the city like a wraith all
night and came back to the compound in a seething, black
rage.

The feeling persisted as he closed his fingers around his
brethren's throat. He needed an outlet for his aggression
and Tegan, feral-looking and secretive, was more than
prime for the role.

"I'm tired of your shit, Tegan. You need to get a grip
on yourself, or I'll do it for you." He squeezed tighter on
the vampire's larynx, but Tegan hardly flinched under the
certain pain. "Now tell me where you've been all this time,
or you and I are going to have real problems."

The two males were evenly sized, and a more than fair
match in terms of strength. Tegan could have fought back,
but he didn't. He showed no emotion whatsoever, just
stared at Lucan with steely, indifferent eyes.

He felt nothing, and even that pissed off Lucan.

With a snarl, he took his hand away from the warrior's throat, trying to clamp a lid on his rage. It wasn't like him to lash out like this. It was beneath him.

Christ.

And he was standing there telling Tegan to get a grip? Great advice. Maybe he ought to take it himself.

Tegan's flat gaze said pretty much the same thing, although the vampire wisely kept his mouth shut.

As the two uneasy allies considered each other in dark silence, behind them some distance down the hallway, a glass door slid open with a hiss. Gideon's sneakers squeaked on the polished floor as he came out of his private quarters and into the corridor.

"Hey, Tegan, great work on the recon, man. I ran some surveillance on the T after we talked last night. That hunch you had about Rogues staking out the Green Line seems like a good one."

Lucan didn't so much as blink while Tegan held his stare, scarcely acknowledging Gideon's praise. Nor did Tegan rise to defend himself against the erroneous suspicion. He just stood there for a long minute, saying nothing. Then he strode past Lucan and continued his progress down the compound's corridor.

"You'll want to check this out, Lucan," Gideon said as he headed for the lab. "Looks like something's about to go down."

CHAPTER
Nine

Holding the warm cup in both hands, Gabrielle sipped her weak oolong tea while Jamie polished off the last of her lo mein. He would wheedle her fortune cookie away from her as well—he always did—but she didn't mind. It was nice simply to be out with her friends, life getting back to some sense of normalcy after everything that had happened last weekend.

"I have something for you," Jamie said, breaking into Gabrielle's thoughts. He fished around in a cream-colored leather bag that sat between them on the bench and pulled out a white envelope. "Proceeds from the private showing."

Gabrielle tore open the seal and pulled out the gallery check. It was more than she expected. A few grand more. "Wow."

"Surprise," Jamie singsonged, grinning broadly. "I highballed the price. Figured what the hell, you know. And they pounced on it without any haggling whatsoever. Think I should have asked for more?"

"No," Gabrielle said. "No, this is, um . . . wow. Thanks."

"Nothing to it." He pointed to her fortune cookie. "You gonna eat that?"

She slid it across the table to him. "So, who's the buyer?"

"Ah, that remains a big mystery," he said, crushing the cookie inside its plastic wrapper. "They paid in cash, so obviously they were serious about the 'anonymous' part of the sale. And they sent a cab over to pick me up with the collection."

"What are you guys talking about?" Megan asked. She stared at the two of them, frowning in confusion. "I swear, I am the last to know everything."

"Our talented little artiste here has a secret admirer," Jamie supplied with ample drama. He pulled out the fortune, read it, and rolled his eyes as he discarded the slip of paper onto his empty plate. "What happened to the days when these things actually meant something? Anyway, a few nights ago, I was summoned to present Gabby's entire collection of photographs to an anonymous buyer downtown. They purchased them all—every last one."

Megan's eyes widened in Gabrielle's direction. "That's wonderful! I'm so happy for you, sweetie!"

"Whoever it was that bought them has a serious cloak-and-dagger fetish."

Gabrielle glanced at her friend as she slipped the check into her purse. "What do you mean?"

Jamie finished munching a shard of broken fortune

cookie, then brushed the crumbs off his fingers. "Well, once I arrive at the address they gave me—one of those corporate suite places, with multiple tenants—I'm met in the lobby by some kind of bodyguard. He doesn't say anything to me, just mumbles something into a wireless mouthpiece, then leads me into an elevator that takes us up to the top floor of the building."

Megan's brows rose. "The penthouse?"

"Yeah. But here's the thing. The place is empty. All the lights are on in the suite, but there are no people inside. No furniture, no equipment, nothing. Just walls of windows, looking out over the city."

"That's bizarre. Don't you think so, Gabby?"

She nodded, a creeping sense of unease spreading over her as Jamie continued.

"So, the bodyguard tells me to take the first photograph out of the portfolio and walk it over to the north bank of windows. It's dark outside, and I've got my back to him now, but he tells me that I am to hold each photo up in front of me until he instructs me to put it aside and get another."

Megan laughed. "With your back to him? Why would he want you to do that?"

"Because the buyer was watching from another location," Gabrielle answered softly. "Somewhere in view of the penthouse windows."

Jamie nodded. "Apparently so. I couldn't hear anything, but I'm sure the bodyguard—or whatever he was— was taking directions through his earpiece. To tell you the truth, I was getting a little nervous about the whole thing, but it was cool. In the end, no harm done. All they wanted were your photographs. I only made it to the fourth one before they asked me for a price on all of them. So, like I said, I pitched high and they took it."

"Weird," Megan remarked. "Hey, Gab, maybe you've caught the interest of a devastatingly handsome, but reclusive, billionaire. This time next year, we could be dancing at your lavish wedding on Mykonos."

"Ugh, please," Jamie gasped. "Mykonos is so last year. All the pretty people are in Marbella, darling."

Gabrielle shook off the odd niggle of wariness that was gnawing at her from Jamie's strange account. Like he said, no harm done, and she had a fat check in her purse besides. Maybe she would treat Lucan to dinner, since the meal she'd made in celebration last night went to waste on her kitchen counter.

Not that she could summon the slightest bit of remorse for the loss of her manicotti.

Yeah, a romantic dinner out with Lucan sounded great. Hopefully, they'd have dessert in . . . breakfast, too.

Her mood instantly lightened, Gabrielle laughed along as her friends continued trading outlandish ideas about who the mysterious collector might actually be, and what it could mean to her future and by association, theirs as well. They were still at it after the table was cleared and the bill was paid, and the three of them exited the restaurant to the sunlit street outside.

"I have to dash," Megan said, giving Gabrielle and Jamie each a quick hug. "See you guys soon?"

"Yes," the two replied in unison, waving as Megan started up the sidewalk toward the office building where she worked.

Jamie raised his hand to hail a cab. "You heading right home, Gabby?"

"No, not yet." She patted the camera case that hung

from her shoulder. "I thought I'd walk over to the Common, maybe burn a little film for a while. You?"

"David's due back from Atlanta in about an hour," he said, smiling. "I'm playing hooky for the rest of the day. Maybe tomorrow, too."

Gabrielle laughed. "Give him my best."

"I will." He leaned in and bussed her cheek. "It's good to see you smiling again. I was really worried about you after last weekend. I've never seen you so shook up. You're gonna be all right, right?"

"Yes. I'm fine, really."

"And you have Detective Dark-and-Sexy looking after you now, so that's not half bad."

"No. That's not bad at all," she admitted, warmed again just thinking about him.

Jamie embraced her in a brotherly hug. "Well, honey, if there's anything you need that he can't give you—which I highly doubt—you just give me a call, you understand? I love you, sweetie."

"Love you, too." They separated as a taxi pulled up to the curb. "Have fun with David." She lifted her hand to wave goodbye as Jamie climbed into the cab and the car eased back into the busy lunchtime traffic.

It took only a few minutes to walk the handful of blocks from Chinatown to the park at Boston Common. Strolling along the expansive grounds, Gabrielle snapped off a few photographs, then paused to observe a group of children playing blindman's bluff in a grassy picnic area. She watched the girl in the center of the game, eyes covered with a blindfold, her blond pigtails bouncing as she spun first one way, then another, her hands outstretched as she tried to tag her dodging friends.

Gabrielle lifted her camera and lined up a shot of the

darting, giggling kids. She zoomed in, following the fair-haired girl's blindfolded face with her lens, hearing the peals of laughter that fell from the children's lips and carried across the park. She didn't take any pictures, just watched the carefree play from behind her camera and tried to remember a time when she might have felt so content and secure.

God, had she ever?

One of the adults supervising the kids from nearby summoned them to lunch, breaking up their raucous game. As the children dashed over to the picnic blanket to eat, Gabrielle swung her camera's focus back across the Common. In the blur of movement through the lens, she glimpsed someone looking back at her from within the shade of a large tree.

She brought her camera away from her face and glanced to where a young man stood, partially concealed by the trunk of the old oak.

He was an unremarkable presence in the busy park, albeit a vaguely familiar one. Gabrielle noted his mop of ashy brown hair, his drab button-down shirt and standard-issue khaki pants. He was the type of person who'd blend in easily in a crowd, but she was certain she'd seen him somewhere recently.

Hadn't he been at the police station last weekend when she'd given her statement?

Whoever he was, he must have realized she'd spotted him because he pulled back suddenly and ducked around the back of the tree to begin heading out of the park toward Charles Street. He dug a cell phone out of his pants pocket, then threw a glance over his shoulder at her as he strode at a fast clip toward the street.

The back of Gabrielle's neck tingled with suspicion and a sinking feeling of alarm.

He had been watching her—but why?

What the hell was going on here? Something was definitely up, but she wasn't about to stand around and guess at it any longer.

With her eyes trained on the guy in khakis, Gabrielle started after him, stuffing her camera back into its case and shrugging the straps of the small padded backpack up onto her shoulders as she walked. The kid was ahead of her about a block by the time she cleared the park's wide lawn and stepped onto Charles.

"Hey!" she called after him, breaking into a jog.

Still on his phone, he pivoted his head to look at her. He said something urgent into the receiver, then flipped the cell closed and fisted it in his hand. Turning away from her, his quick pace became a full-on sprint.

"Stop!" Gabrielle shouted. She drew the curious attention of other people on the street, but the kid continued to ignore her. "I said stop, damn it! Who are you? Why are you spying on me?"

He tore up crowded Charles Street, vanishing into the sea of strolling pedestrians. Gabrielle followed, dodging tourists and office workers on lunch break, her eyes fixed on the bobbing bulk of the kid's backpack. He turned down one street, then another, wending deeper into the city, away from the shops and businesses on Charles and back toward the tightly clustered area of Chinatown.

She didn't know how far she'd tracked the kid, or even where exactly she'd ended up, but all of a sudden she realized she'd lost him.

She spun around near a busy corner, utterly alone, unfamiliar surroundings closing in on her. Shopkeepers stared at her from under shaded awnings and doors left open to welcome the summer air. Passersby threw her annoyed looks as she stood stockstill in the middle of the sidewalk, blocking the flow of foot traffic.

It was then she felt a menacing presence behind her on the street.

Gabrielle glanced over her shoulder and saw a black sedan with dark-tinted windows slowly moving between the other cars. It moved gracefully, deliberately, like a shark cutting through a school of minnows in search of better prey.

Was it coming toward her?

Maybe the kid who'd been spying on her was inside. Maybe his appearance, and that of this ominous-looking car, had something to do with whomever had purchased her photographs from Jamie.

Or maybe it was something worse.

Something to do with the horrific attack she had witnessed last weekend. Her report to the police. Maybe it had been a gang slaying she stumbled upon after all. Maybe those vicious creatures—she couldn't quite convince herself that they were men—had decided she was their next target.

Icy fear lanced through her as the vehicle veered into the near lane, which hugged the sidewalk where she still stood.

She started walking. Picked up her pace.

Behind her, the car's accelerator roared.

Oh, God.

It *was* coming after her!

Gabrielle didn't wait to hear the peal of rubber being laid behind her. She screamed, and took off in a blind run, her legs pumping as fast as they could.

There were too many people around. Too many obstacles in her direct path. She dodged the milling pedestrians, too rattled to offer apologies as some of them clucked their tongues and swore at her in reproach.

She didn't care, certain this was life or death.

A quick look behind her would prove to be disastrous. The car was still roaring through the traffic, hot on her heels. Gabrielle put her head down and dug in harder, praying she could make it off the street before the vehicle plowed into her.

In her haste, her ankle twisted beneath her.

She stumbled, losing balance. The ground came up and she fell hard onto the rough concrete. Her bare knees and palms broke the worst of her tumble, both getting chewed up in the process. The searing burn of torn flesh brought tears to her eyes, but she ignored it. Gabrielle surged to her feet. She was hardly up off the ground before she felt the hard clamp of a stranger's hand gripping her at the elbow.

She sucked in a sharp gasp, panic pouring through her.

"You okay, lady?" The grizzled face of a municipal worker swung into her line of vision. His wrinkled blue eyes flicked down at her abrasions. "Aw, jeez. Look at that, you're bleedin'."

"Let go of me!"

"Didn't you see those pylons right there?" He hooked his thumb over his shoulder at the orange cones she'd blown right past. "I got this section of sidewalk all torn up here."

"Please, it's okay. I'm fine."

Caught in his helpful but hindering grasp, Gabrielle looked just in time to see the dark sedan pull up to the corner where she'd been standing only a moment ago. It rocked to an abrupt halt at the curb. The driver's door opened and a broadly built, towering man stepped out.

"Oh, God. Let go!" Gabrielle yanked her arm away from the man who was trying to assist her, her gaze rooted on that monstrous black car and the danger that was crawling out of it. "You don't understand, they're after me!"

"Who is?" The muni worker's voice was incredulous. He looked to where she was gaping and let out a laugh. "You mean that guy? Lady, that's the friggin' mayor of Boston."

"Wha—"

It was true. Her eyes were wild as she watched the activity at the corner with new understanding. The black sedan wasn't after her at all. It had pulled up to the curb and the driver now waited, holding open the back door. The mayor himself came out of a restaurant, flanked by suited bodyguards. They all climbed into the backseat of the vehicle.

Gabrielle closed her eyes. Her raw palms were burning. Her knees, too. Her pulse was still pounding, but all the blood seemed to have drained from her head.

She felt like a complete fool.

"I thought . . ." she murmured as the driver closed the door, got in the front, then eased the official's car back into traffic.

The worker let go of her arm. He walked away from her, back to his sack lunch and coffee, shaking his head. "What's a matter with you? You crazy or somethin'?"

Shit.

She wasn't supposed to see him. His orders had been to observe the Maxwell woman. Note her activities. Determine her habits. Report everything back to his Master. Above all, he was to avoid detection.

The Minion spat another curse from where he was hiding, his spine flat against the inside of a nondescript door in a nondescript building, one of many such places nestled among the Chinatown markets and restaurants. Carefully, he drew open the door and peered around it to see if he could spot the woman somewhere outside.

There she was, right across the busy street from him.

And he was pleased to see that she was leaving the area. He could just make out her coppery hair as she wended through the traffic on the sidewalk, her head down, her pace agitated.

He waited there, watched her until she was well out of sight. Then he slipped back onto the street and headed in the opposite direction. He'd blown more than an hour on lunch break. He'd better get back to the police station before he was missed.

CHAPTER
Ten

Gabrielle ran another paper towel under the cold water running in her kitchen sink. Several others lay discarded in the basin already, sopping wet, stained pink with her blood and gray with grime from the sidewalk grit she'd washed out of her palms and bare knees. Standing there in her bra and panties, she squirted some liquid soap onto the wad of damp toweling, then gingerly scrubbed at the abrasions on each of her palms.

"Ow," she gasped, wincing as she ran over a sharp little stone embedded in the wound. She dug it out and tossed it into the sink with the other shards of gravel she'd recovered in her cleanup.

God, she was a mess.

Her new skirt was torn and ruined. The hem of her sweater was frayed from scraping the pavement. Her hands and knees looked like they belonged to a clumsy tomboy.

And she'd make a public, total ass of herself besides.

What the hell was wrong with her, freaking out like she had?

The mayor, for chrissake. And she had run from his car like she feared he was a . . .

A what? Some kind of monster?

Vampire.

Gabrielle's hand went still.

She heard the word in her mind, even if she refused to speak it. It was the same word that had been nipping at the edge of her consciousness since the murder she'd witnessed. A word she would not acknowledge, even alone, in the silence of her empty apartment.

Vampires were her crazy birth mother's obsession, not hers.

The teenaged Jane Doe had been deeply delusional when the police recovered her from the street all those years ago. She spoke of being pursued by demons who wanted to drink her blood—had, in fact, already tried, as was her explanation for the strange lacerations on her throat. The court documents Gabrielle had been given were peppered with wild references to bloodthirsty fiends running loose in the city.

Impossible.

That *was* crazy thinking, and Gabrielle knew it.

She was letting her imagination, and her fears that she might one day come unhinged like her mother, get the best of her. She was smarter than this. More sane, at least.

God, she had to be.

Seeing that kid from the police station today—on top of everything else she'd been through the past several days—

just set something off in her. Although, now that she was thinking about it, she couldn't even be sure the guy she saw in the park actually was the clerk she'd seen at the precinct house.

And so what if he was? Maybe he was out in the Common having lunch, enjoying the weather like she was. No crime in that. If he was staring at her, maybe he thought she looked familiar, too. Maybe he would have come over and said hi to her, if she hadn't charged after him like some paranoid psycho, accusing him of spying on her.

Oh, and wouldn't that be lovely, if he went back to the station and told them all how she'd chased him several blocks into Chinatown?

If Lucan were to hear about that, she would absolutely die of humiliation.

Gabrielle resumed cleansing her scraped palms, trying to put the whole day out of her head. Her anxiety was still at a peak, her heart still drumming hard. She dabbed at her surface wounds, watching the thin trickle of blood run down her wrist.

The sight of it soothed her in some strange way. Always had.

When she was younger, when feelings and pressures built up inside of her until there was nowhere for them to go, often all it took to ease her was a tiny cut.

The first one had been an accident. Gabrielle had been paring an apple at one of her foster homes when the knife slipped and cut into the fleshy pad at the base of her thumb. It hurt a little, but as her blood pumped out, a rivulet of glossy bright crimson, Gabrielle hadn't felt panic or fear.

She'd felt fascination.

She'd felt an incredible sort of...peace.

A few months after that surprising discovery, Gabrielle cut herself again. She did it deliberately, secretly, never with the intent to harm herself. Over time, she did it frequently, whenever she needed to feel that same profound sense of calm.

She needed it now, when she was anxious and jumpy as a cat, her ears picking up every slight noise in the apartment and outside. Her head was pounding. Her breath was shallow, coming rapidly through her teeth.

Her thoughts were careening from the flash-bright memories of the night outside the club to the creepy asylum she'd taken pictures of the other morning, to the confusing, irrational, bone-deep fear she'd experienced this afternoon.

She needed a little peace from all of it.

Even just a spare few minutes of calm.

Gabrielle's gaze slid to the wooden block of knives sitting on the counter nearby. She reached over, took one in her hand. It had been years since she'd done this. She'd worked so hard to master the strange, shameful compulsion.

Had it truly ever gone away?

Her state-appointed psychologists and social workers eventually had been convinced that it had. The Maxwells, too.

Now, Gabrielle wondered as she brought the knife over to her bare arm and felt a surge of dark anticipation wash over her. She pressed the tip of the blade into the fleshy part of her forearm, though not yet firm enough to break the skin.

This was her private demon—something she had never

openly shared with anyone, not even Jamie, her dearest friend.

No one would understand.

She hardly understood it herself.

Gabrielle tipped her head back and took a deep breath. As she brought her chin back down on the slow exhale, she caught her reflection in the window over the sink. The face staring back at her was drawn and sorrowful, the eyes haunted and weary.

"Who are you?" she whispered to that ghostly image in the glass. She had to choke back a sob. "What's wrong with you?"

Miserable with herself, she threw the knife into the sink and backed away as it clattered against the stainless basin.

The steady percussion of helicopter rotors chopped through the quiet of the night sky above the old asylum. From out of the low cloud cover, a black Colibri EC120 descended, coming to a soft touchdown on a flat expanse of rooftop.

"Cut the engine," the leader of the Rogues instructed his Minion pilot after the craft had settled on its makeshift helipad. "Wait here for me until I return."

He climbed out of the cockpit, greeted at once by his lieutenant, a rather nasty individual he'd recruited out of the West Coast.

"Everything is in order, sire." The Rogue's thick brow bunched over his feral yellow eyes. His large bald head still bore the scars from electrical burns inflicted during a bout of Breed interrogation he'd undergone about a half a year ago. However, amid the rest of his hideous features, the numerous scorch marks were merely a footnote. The

Rogue grinned, baring huge fangs. "Your gifts tonight have been very well-received, sire. Everyone eagerly awaits your arrival."

Eyes hidden behind dark sunglasses, the leader of the Rogues gave a slight nod, strolling at an easy pace as he was led into the building's top floor, then on toward an elevator that would take him into the heart of the facility. They went deep below the ground-level floor, getting off the elevator to travel a network of curving, tunneled walkways that comprised part of the general garrison of the Rogue lair.

As for the leader himself, he'd been based in private quarters elsewhere in Boston for the past month, privately reviewing operations, assessing his obstacles, and determining his strongest assets in this new territory he meant to control. This was to be his first public appearance—an event, as was fully his intention.

It wasn't often he ventured into the filth of the general population; vampires gone Rogue were a crude, indiscriminate lot, and he had come to appreciate finer things during his many years of existence. But an appearance was due, however brief. He needed to remind the beasts of whom they served, and so he had given them a taste of the spoils that would await at the end of their latest mission. Not all of them would survive, of course. Casualties tended to mount in the midst of war.

And war was what he was selling here tonight.

No more petty conflicts over turf. No more divisive infighting among the Rogues or pointless acts of individual retribution. They would unite and turn a page not yet imagined in the age-old battle that had forever split the vampire nation in two. For too long, the Breed had ruled, striking an unspoken treaty with the lesser humans while striving to eliminate their Rogue kin.

The two factions of the vampire race were not so different from each other, separated only by degrees. All that stood between a Breed vampire fulfilling his hunger for life and the Bloodlust addiction of the Rogue's unquenchable thirst for blood was a mere few ounces. The bloodlines of the race had diluted in the time since the Ancients, as new vampires grew to adulthood and paired with human Breedmates.

But no amount of human genetic corruption would completely obliterate the stronger vampire genes. Bloodlust was a specter that would haunt the Breed forever.

The way the leader of this budding war saw it, one could either fight the innate urge of his kind, or use it to one's best advantage.

He and his lieutenant guard had reached the end of the corridor now, where the pulsing drone of loud music reverberated through the walls and under their feet. Behind battered steel double doors, a party raged. In front of those doors, a Rogue vampire on watch sank down heavily on one knee as soon as his slitted pupils registered who waited before him.

"Sire." There was reverence in the gravel of his rough voice, deference in the way he did not glance up to meet the eyes shaded behind dark glasses. "My lord, you honor us."

He did, in fact. The leader gave a slight nod of acknowledgment as the watchman came to his feet. With a grimy hand, the guard pushed open the doors to permit his superior entry to the raucous assembly gathered within. The leader dismissed his companion, freeing himself to private observation of the place.

It was an orgy of blood and sex and music. Everywhere he looked, Rogue males groped and rutted and fed on a rich assortment of humans, both men and women. They knew little pain, whether or not they attended this event willingly. Most had been bitten at least once, drained enough to be riding a wave of lightheaded, sensual bliss. Some were further gone, slumped like pretty cloth dolls into the laps of wild-eyed predators who would not cease feeding until there was nothing left to devour.

But then, that was to be expected when one threw tender lambs into a pit of ravenous beasts.

As he strode into the thick of the gathering, his palms began to sweat. His cock tightened behind the carefully pressed fall of his tailored pants. His gums began to throb and ache, but he bit his tongue in an effort to keep his fangs from stretching long in hunger the way his sex had so greedily responded to the erotic barrage of sensory stimulation hitting him from all angles.

The mingled scents of sex and spilling blood called to him like a siren's song—one he knew well, though that was in his very distant past. Oh, he still enjoyed a good fuck and a juicy open vein, but those needs no longer owned him. It had been a hard road back from the place he'd once been, but in the end, he had won.

He was Master now, of himself, and, soon, much, much more.

A new war was beginning, and he was poised to deliver Armageddon itself. He was cultivating his army, perfecting his methods, aligning allies who would later be sacrificed without hesitation on the altar of his personal whim. He would wreak a bloody vengeance on the vampire nation and the human world that existed only to serve his kind.

When the great battle was over, the dust and ash finally cleared, there would be none to stand in his way.

He would be a goddamned king. As was his birthright.

"Mmm...hey, handsome...come in and play with me."

The husky invitation reached his ears over the din of noise. From out of the writhing pit of slick, naked bodies, a female hand had risen to grasp at his thigh as he walked past. He paused, glancing down at her with open impatience. There was a faded beauty under her smeared dark makeup, but her mind was utterly lost to the delirium of the orgy. Twin rivulets of blood ran down her pretty throat and over the tips of her perfect breasts. She had other open bites elsewhere as well: at her shoulder, on her belly, and on her inner thigh, just below the narrow strip of hair that shadowed her sex.

"Join us," she begged, pulling herself out of the twisting jumble of arms and legs and rutting, howling Rogue vampires. The woman was all but drained, a scant few ounces this side of dead. Her eyes were glassy, unfocused. Her movements were languid, as if her bones had turned to rubber. "I have what you want. I'll bleed for you, too. Come, taste me."

He said nothing, merely pried the pale, bloodstained fingers from the fine weave of his expensive silk pants.

He frankly wasn't in the mood.

And like any successful dealer, he never touched his own product.

With his large hand flat against her chest, he pushed the woman back into the churning fray. She squealed as one of the Rogues caught her in a rough hold, then savagely flipped her over his arm to bear her down beneath him and enter her from behind. She shrieked and moaned as he rammed into her, but choked silent an instant later, when the Bloodlusting vampire sank his huge fangs into her neck and sucked the last drop of life from her depleted body.

"Enjoy these spoils," said the one who would be king, his deep voice ringing out magnanimously over the animal roars and the skull-battering blast of the music. "Night is on the rise, and you will soon earn all of the rewards I see fit to give you."

CHAPTER
Eleven

Lucan rapped on Gabrielle's apartment door again.

Still no response.

He had been standing on her front stoop in the dark for about five minutes, waiting for her either to open the damn door and invite him in, or curse him as a bastard from behind the perceived safety of her multiple locks and tell him to get lost.

After the hard-core moves he'd put on her the night before, he wasn't sure which reaction he deserved. Probably the irate kiss-off.

He dropped his knuckles onto the door once more, hard enough that the neighbors likely heard it, but there was no movement from within Gabrielle's apartment. Only quiet. Too much stillness on the other side.

She was in there, though. He could sense her through

the layers of wood and brick that stood between them.
And he smelled blood, too—not a lot, but trace amounts
somewhere near the door.

Son of a bitch.

She was inside, and she was hurt.

"Gabrielle!"

Concern ran like acid through his arteries as he
calmed his mind enough to focus his mental powers on
the chain lock and double bolts that were set on the other
side of the door. With effort, he turned one lock, then the
other. The chain slid free of its channel, swinging loose
against the doorjamb with a metallic scrape.

Lucan threw open the door, his boots pounding over
the tiled foyer. Gabrielle's camera bag lay directly in his
path, likely fallen where she dropped it in her haste. The
jasmine-sweet scent of her blood slammed into his nostrils
just an instant before an erratic trail of small crimson
splatters caught his eye.

A bitter tang of fear laced the air of the apartment as
well. Its odor had faded, some hours old, but lingering like
fog.

He strode through the living room, about to head for
the kitchen where the blood droplets continued. As he
stalked farther inside, his gaze snagged on a stack of photos lying on the sofa table.

They were rough cuts, an odd assortment of images.
Some he recognized from Gabrielle's work-in-progress,
the one she was calling *Urban Renewal.* But there were a few
shots he hadn't seen before. Or maybe hadn't looked close
enough to notice.

He noticed them now.

Goddamn, did he ever.

An old warehouse near the wharf. An abandoned paper

mill just outside the city. Several other forbidding-looking structures that no human—let alone an unsuspecting woman like Gabrielle—ought to be getting anywhere near.

Rogue lairs.

Some of them were defunct now, forced into that status by Lucan and his warriors, but a few others were active cells. He spotted several that Gideon currently had under surveillance. Sifting through the others, he wondered how many other photos she had here of Rogue locations not yet on the Breed's radar.

"Jesus Christ," he whispered tightly, fingering through a couple more images.

She even had some exterior shots of local Darkhavens, obscure entryways and masking signage meant to conceal the vampire sanctuaries from easy detection, whether from nosy humans or the enemy Rogues.

Yet Gabrielle had found all of these places. How?

It sure as hell wasn't by chance. Her extraordinary visual sense must have led her to them. She had already proven to be all but immune to the regular tricks of vampire guile—mass hypnotic illusion, mind control…now this.

With a curse, Lucan shoved a few pictures into the pocket of his leather jacket, then tossed the rest back onto the table.

"Gabrielle?"

He moved into the kitchen, where something even more disturbing waited for him.

The scent of Gabrielle's blood grew stronger here, drawing him to the sink. He froze in front of it, something cold clamping down around his chest as he stared into the basin.

It looked like someone had tried to clean up a crime

scene, and had done a piss-poor job of it. More than a dozen waterlogged, bloodstained paper towels were clumped in the sink along with a paring knife that had been removed from the wooden block on the counter.

He picked up the sharp blade and gave it a quick inspection. It hadn't been used, but all the blood in the sink and spattered on the floor from the foyer to the kitchen belonged solely to Gabrielle.

And the torn clothing that lay in a discarded heap near his foot carried her scent, too.

God, if anyone had touched her—

If anything had happened to her . . .

"Gabrielle!"

Lucan followed his senses down to the basement level of her apartment. He didn't bother with lights; his vision was most acute in the dark. Tearing down the stairs, he called her name into the quiet.

At the back corner of the space, Gabrielle's scent grew strongest. Lucan found himself standing before another closed door, this one framed in thick weatherstripping to block out all exterior light. He tried the latch, rattling the door on its meager lock.

"Gabrielle. Can you hear me? Baby, open the door."

He didn't wait for a reply. He didn't have the patience for that, or the focus to carefully release the hook and eye closure on the other side. With a growl of fury, Lucan smashed his shoulder into the door and burst inside.

His eyes instantly found her in the lightless space. Her body was curled up on the floor of the cramped darkroom, naked except for a skimpy lace bra and bikini underwear. She jerked awake with the sudden crash of his arrival.

Her head came up fast. Her eyelids were heavy, puffed from recent crying. She'd been sobbing in here, and for some length of time by his guess. Exhaustion poured off her in waves. She looked so small, so vulnerable.

"Ah, God. Gabrielle," he whispered, dropping into a low crouch beside her. "What the hell are you doing in here? Did somebody hurt you?"

She shook her head, but didn't answer right away. With dragging hands, she pushed her hair out of her face, trying to find him in the dark. "Just... tired. I needed quiet... peace."

"So you locked yourself down here?" He blew out a sharp breath, relieved, except for the fact that her body did bear injuries that had only recently stopped bleeding. "You're sure you're all right?"

She nodded, listing toward him in the dark.

Scowling, Lucan reached for her, smoothed his palm over the top of her head. She seemed to take his touch as an invitation, crawling into his arms like a child in need of comforting and warmth. It wasn't good, how natural it felt to hold her, how strong the inclination was to reassure her that she was safe with him. That he would protect her as his own.

His own.

Impossible, he reminded himself. More than impossible; it was ludicrous.

He looked down, silently considering the soft bundle of warm, beautiful woman wrapped around him in a delicious state of near nakedness. She couldn't have any inkling of the dangerous world she was now involved in— not least of all, from the deadly vampire male who held her against him now.

He was the last one who should offer a Breedmate protection from harm. With Gabrielle, just the faintest scent of her brought his blood hunger raging into the danger zone.

He stroked her neck and shoulder, trying to ignore the steady beat of her pulse beneath his fingertips. He had to fight like hell to ignore the memory of when he'd last been with her, or how badly he needed to have her again.

"Mmm, you feel good," she murmured dazedly into his chest, her voice a sleep-heavy purr that sent a jolt of heat down his spine. "This another dream?"

Lucan groaned, incapable of answering. It wasn't a dream, and personally he didn't feel good at all. He felt every bit the ancient, haggard beast as she nestled into him even more, all tender trust and innocence.

Searching for distraction, he found one all too quickly. A glance up over their heads made every muscle in his body go rigid with a new kind of tension.

His eyes locked onto more of Gabrielle's photographs clipped to a drying line in the darkroom. Hanging among various other insignificant shots were a handful more taken of vampire locations.

For God's sake, she even had a photograph of the warriors' compound. The daylight shot had been taken from the road outside the secured estate. There was no mistaking the enormous, scrolled wrought-iron gate that blockaded the long drive, and the high-security mansion at its end, from the public at large.

Gabrielle must have been standing right outside the property to take this picture. Based on the leafy summer foliage of the surrounding trees, the image couldn't be more than a few weeks old. She'd been there, just a few hundred yards from where he lived.

He had never been one to subscribe to the notion of fate, but it seemed pretty damned clear that one way or another this female was meant to cross his path.

Oh, yeah. Cross it like a black cat.

Just his luck that after centuries of dodging cosmic bullets and messy emotional entanglements, the twisted sisters of fate and reality would decide to put him on their shit lists at the same time.

"It's all right," he told Gabrielle, even though things were quickly progressing way south of that point. "Let's get you upstairs and dressed, then we'll talk." Before the continued sight of her in those flimsy scraps of lace and satin did him in.

Lucan gathered her into his arms, then carried her out of the darkroom and up the stairs to the main floor. Holding her this close, his keen senses registered the details of the sundry wounds she bore: raw scrapes on her hands and knees, evidence of a pretty vicious fall.

She had been running away from something—or someone—in terror when she had taken a spill. Lucan's blood boiled to know who had caused this harm, but there would be time for that soon. Gabrielle's comfort and well-being was his primary concern now.

Lucan walked with her through her living room, to the steps to her bedroom loft. His intent was to help her into some clothes, but as he passed the adjoining bathroom, he mentally flipped on the water. The two of them really needed to talk, and things probably would go down a bit easier for her after she'd had a warm soak.

With Gabrielle's arms wrapped around his shoulders, Lucan carried her into the bathroom. A small nightlight gave off an ambient glow, just enough illumination for his liking. He brought his languid armload over to the tub and seated himself on the edge, balancing Gabrielle in his lap.

He unsnapped the front closure on the wispy piece of satin, baring her breasts to his suddenly fevered eyes. His hands itched to touch her, so he did, brushing his fingertips along the buoyant curves, flicking his thumb over the dusky pink of her nipples.

God help him, the soft mewl of pleasure that curled up from her throat hardened his cock to painful degrees.

He skimmed his palm down her torso, to the matching scrap of glossy fabric that covered her sex. His hands were too large, too careless with the flimsy satin, but he somehow managed to peel the panties off and slide them down Gabrielle's long legs.

Blood surged through him like molten lava at the sight of her, nude before him once more.

Maybe he should feel guilty for finding her so incredibly desirable even in her current vulnerable state, but he wasn't much better at bowing to shame than he was at playing the nurturer. And he'd already proven to himself that trying to muster any kind of control around this particular female was a battle he might never win.

Next to the tub sat a bottle of liquid bubble bath. Lucan poured a generous dollop under the stream of running water. As the lather built, he carefully eased Gabrielle down into the warm bath. She moaned with clear appreciation as she sank into the foaming water, her limbs going visibly slack, her shoulders drooping against the towel Lucan quickly supplied as a cushion to keep her back from resting against cold tile and porcelain.

The small bathroom was filled with steam and Gabrielle's own faintly jasmine scent.

"Comfortable?" he asked her, as he shrugged out of his jacket and tossed it over the pedestal sink.

"Mmm," she moaned.

He couldn't resist putting his hands on her. With a gentle caress of her shoulder, he said, "Slide farther down and wet your hair. I'll wash it for you."

She obeyed, letting him guide her head under the water, then back up, her long ginger tresses darkened to a sleek auburn. She was silent for a long moment, then she slowly lifted her eyelids, smiling at him as if she had just come back to consciousness and was surprised to find him there. "Hi."

"Hi."

"What time is it?" she asked around a stretch and a stifled yawn.

Lucan shrugged. "Around eight, I guess."

Gabrielle sank back against the tub, closing her eyes with a moan.

"Bad day?"

"Not one of my best."

"So I gathered. Your hands and knees are a little worse for wear." Lucan reached over and turned off the water. He grabbed a tube of shampoo from nearby and squeezed some into his hands. "Wanna tell me what happened?"

"I'd rather not." A crease formed between her slim brows. "I did something stupid this afternoon. You'll hear all about it soon enough, I'm sure."

"How so?" Lucan asked, working up the lather in his palms.

As he massaged the thick foam into her scalp, Gabrielle opened one eye and slid him a sideways glance. "The kid from the station didn't say anything to anyone?"

"What kid?"

"The one who clerks down at the precinct house. Tall, lanky, kind of average-looking? I don't know his name, but I'm pretty certain he was there the night I gave my statement about the murder. Today I saw him in the Common. I thought he was watching me, actually, and I..." She trailed off, shaking her head. "I ran after him like a crazy person, accusing him of spying on me."

Lucan's hands stilled in her hair, his warrior's instincts coming to full attention. "You what?"

"I know," she said, obviously misinterpreting his reaction. She dispersed a mound of bubbles with a sweep of her hand. "I told you it was stupid. Anyway, I chased the poor kid all the way into Chinatown."

Although he didn't say as much, Lucan knew that Gabrielle's initial instincts had been spot-on about the stranger watching her in the park. Since the incident had occurred in broad daylight, it couldn't have been the Rogues—a small blessing—but the humans who served them could be equally dangerous. The Rogues employed Minions in all corners of the world, humans enslaved by a draining bite of a powerful vampire that rid them of their conscience and free will, leaving only unquestioning obedience in its wake.

Lucan had no doubt whatsoever that the man who had been observing Gabrielle was doing so in service to a Rogue who commanded him.

"Did this *person* hurt you? Is that how you got those injuries?"

"No, no. That was my own doing. I got myself all freaked out over nothing. After losing track of the kid in Chinatown, I just lost it. I thought a car was coming after me, but it wasn't."

"How can you be sure?"

She gave him a sheepish look. "Because it was the mayor, Lucan. I thought his chauffeured car was coming after me and I started running. To top off a perfectly awful day, I fell flat on my face in the middle of a crowded sidewalk and then had to limp home with bloodied hands and knees."

He cursed under his breath, realizing just how close she had come to danger. For chrissake, she had actually gone after the Minion by herself. The thought chilled Lucan more than he'd like to admit.

"You need to promise me you'll be more careful," he said, knowing he was scolding but unwilling to bother with politeness when she might have gotten herself killed today. "If something like this happens again, you need to tell me right away."

"It's not going to happen again because it was my mistake. And I wasn't about to call you or anyone else at the station about this. Wouldn't they just love it if I phoned in to report that one of their file clerks was stalking me for no apparent reason?"

Shit. His lie about being a cop was tripping him up damned good now. Even worse, it might have put her in jeopardy if she'd called the station looking for "Detective Thorne" and attracted the attention of an embedded Minion instead.

"I'm going to give you my cell phone number. You can always reach me there. I want you to use it anytime, understand?"

She nodded as Lucan turned on the faucet, then ran clear water into his hands and over her silky, burnished waves.

Frustrated with himself, he grabbed a washcloth from an overhead shelf and thrust it down into the water. "Now let me see your knee."

She lifted her leg from under the flotilla of bubbles. Lucan held her foot in one palm, carefully washing the angry-looking abrasion. It was just a scrape, but it was bleeding again now that the warm water had soaked the wound. Lucan ground down hard on his jaw as the fragrant, scarlet threads wove a delicate trail down her skin and into the pristine foam of the bath.

He finished cleansing both of her injured knees, then gestured for her to let him attend her palms next. He didn't trust his voice to work when the combined one/two punch of Gabrielle's nude body and the scent of her fresh, trickling blood was slamming into his skull like a jackhammer.

With an economy of attention, he dabbed at the scrapes on her palms, painfully aware of her rich, dark gaze following his every movement, the pulse at her wrist beating quickly under the pressure of his fingertips.

She wanted him, too.

Lucan started to release her, but as her arm twisted slightly on its retreat, he spotted something troubling. His eyes lit at once on a series of faint marks that spoiled the flawless peach skin. The marks were scars, tiny slices cut into the underside of her forearms. And she had more on her thighs.

Razor cuts.

As if she'd endured repeated and hellish torture when she was little more than a girl. "Jesus Christ." He swiveled his head back to look at her, fury no doubt rampant in his expression. "Who did this to you?"

"It's not what you think."

He was fuming now, not about to let this one slide. "Tell me."

"It's nothing, really. Just forget—"

"Give me a name, goddamn it, and I swear, I will kill the son of a bitch with my bare hands—"

"I did it," she blurted out in a quiet rush of breath. "It was me. No one did this, just me."

"What?" Holding her fragile wrist in his hand, he turned her arm over once more so he could inspect the faded network of crisscrossing, purplish scars. "You did this? *Why?*"

She withdrew from his loose grasp and sank both arms under the water, as if to shield them from his further inspection.

Lucan swore low under his breath, and in a language he rarely spoke anymore. "How often, Gabrielle?"

"I don't know." She shrugged, avoiding his gaze now. "I haven't done it in a long time. I got over it."

"Is that why there's a knife lying in the sink downstairs?"

The look she gave him was pained and defensive. She didn't like him prying, no more than he would like it himself, but Lucan wanted to understand. He could hardly fathom what might drive her to dig a blade into her own flesh.

Over and over and over again.

She scowled, staring at the dissipating suds surrounding her. "Look, can we just drop the subject? I really don't want to talk about—"

"Maybe you should talk about it."

"Oh, sure." Her small laugh held an edge of irony. "Is this the part where you suggest I need to see a shrink, Detective Thorne? Maybe go someplace where I can be put in a medicated stupor and under a doctor's close watch for my own good?"

"Did that happen to you?"

"People don't understand me. They never have. I don't understand myself sometimes."

"Don't understand what? That you have a need to hurt yourself?"

"No. That's not it. That's not why I did it."

"Then why? Good God, Gabrielle, there must be upwards of a hundred scars."

"I didn't do it because I wanted pain. It wasn't painful to me." She drew in a breath and pushed it out between her lips. It took her a second to speak, and when she did, Lucan could only stare at her in stunned silence. "It was never about causing hurt, not to anyone. I wasn't burying traumatic memories or trying to escape some kind of abuse, despite the opinions of several so-called experts appointed by the state. I cut myself because . . . it soothed me. Bleeding calmed me. It didn't take much, only a small cut, never very deep. When I'd bleed, everything that was out of place and strange about me suddenly felt . . . normal."

She held his unwavering gaze with a new air of defiance, as if a gate had been opened somewhere deep inside her and a heavy burden had been freed. In some small way, Lucan realized that was just what he'd witnessed here. Except she still was missing a crucial piece of information that would make things click into place for her.

She didn't know that she was a Breedmate.

She couldn't know that one day a member of his race would take her as his eternal beloved and show her a world unlike she had ever dreamed of. Her eyes would be opened to a pleasure that only existed between blood-bonded pairs.

Lucan found himself hating that nameless male who would have the honor of loving her.

"I'm not crazy, if that's what you're thinking."

Lucan gave a slow shake of his head. "I am not thinking that at all."

"I despise pity."

"So do I," he said, detecting the warning in her words.

"You don't need pity, Gabrielle. And you don't need medicine or doctors, either."

She had been retreating into herself from the moment he had first discovered her scars, but now he felt her hesitation, her tentative trust in him slowly returning.

"You don't belong to this world," he told her, not sentiment but fact. He reached out, cupping her face in his palm. "You are far too extraordinary for the life you've been living, Gabrielle. I think you've known it all along. One day, it will all make sense to you, I promise. Then you'll understand, and you will find your true destiny. Maybe I can help you find it."

He meant to resume bathing her, but the awareness that she was watching him made his hands still. The profound warmth in her answering smile put an ache in his chest. Snared in her tender regard, he felt his throat constrict strangely.

"What is it?"

She gave a small shake of her head. "I'm surprised, that's all. I didn't expect a big tough cop like you to speak so romantically about life and destiny."

The reminder that he had, and was still, coming to her under false pretenses jolted some of his wits back into his brain. He plunged the washcloth back into the soapy water and let it float among the suds. "Maybe I'm just full of shit."

"I don't think so."

"Don't give me so much credit," he said, forcing a casualness into his tone. "You don't know me, Gabrielle. Not really."

"I'd like to know you. Really." She sat up in the water, the tepid little waves lapping around her nude body the way Lucan wanted to do with his tongue. The tops of her breasts rode just above the surface, pink nipples hard as buds, surrounded in frothy white foam. "Tell me, Lucan. Where do you belong?"

"Nowhere." The answer slipped out of his mouth in a growl, a confession closer to the truth than he cared to admit. Like her, he despised pity and was relieved that she was looking at him more in curiosity than sympathy. He ran his finger along the pert, freckle-spattered bridge of her nose. "I am the original misfit. I've never really belonged anywhere."

"That's not true."

Gabrielle's arms circled around his shoulders. Her soft brown eyes held his gaze tenderly, with the same care he'd given her as he'd brought her out of the locked darkroom and into the warm bath. She kissed him and, as her tongue swept his lips, Lucan's senses were swamped with the heady perfume of desire and sweet, feminine affection.

"You've taken such good care of me tonight. Let me take care of you now, Lucan." She kissed him again, a deep plundering with her slick little tongue that forced a groan of pure male pleasure from deep within him. When she finally broke contact, she was breathing hard, her eyes afire with carnal need. "You're wearing too many clothes. Take them off. I want you naked with me in here."

Lucan obeyed, shucking his boots, socks, pants, and shirt to the floor. He wore nothing else, standing before Gabrielle fully nude.

Fully engorged and eager for her.

He was careful to keep his eyes tilted away from hers now that his pupils had narrowed with hunger, and he was mindful of the throbbing press of his fangs, which had stretched long behind his lips. If not for the bare trace of light from the night lamp near the sink, she would have surely seen him in all his ravenous glory.

And that would be quite a buzzkill for an otherwise promising moment.

He wasn't about to take that chance.

With a sharp mental command, he shattered the small bulb behind the night light's plastic cover. Gabrielle startled at the sudden pop, but then she sighed as blissful darkness surrounded them. Her body was making lovely, slippery noises in the tub.

"Turn on another light, if you want."

"I'll find you without it," he promised, speech a tricky thing now that lust had a firm hold on him.

"Then come," bid his siren from the warm pool of her bath.

He stepped into the water, sinking down to face her in the dark. He wanted nothing more than to haul her close—drag her into the cradle of his thighs and sheath himself to the hilt in one long stroke. But he would let her set their pace for now.

Last night he had come there hungry and taking; tonight he would give.

Even if the restraint killed him.

Gabrielle glided toward him through the thinning clouds of foam. Her feet went around his hips and linked loosely over his ass. She bent forward at the waist, her fingers finding his thighs beneath the surface of the bath. She squeezed the taut muscles, kneaded them, then firmly rode their length in slow, delicious torment.

"You should know, I'm not usually like this."

His groan of interest sounded strained in his ears. "You mean, hot enough to reduce any male to cinder at your feet?"

She exhaled a soft laugh. "Is that what I do to you?"

He brought her teasing hands up to the jutting thickness of his cock. "What do you think?"

"I think you're amazing." She didn't withdraw her touch after his hands left hers. She traced his shaft and balls, then lazily brought her fingers up around the bulbous head that more than breached the surface of the bathwater. "You're not like anyone I've ever known. And what I meant was, I'm not usually so...well, aggressive. I don't date a lot."

"You don't take a lot of men to your bed?"

Even in the dark, he sensed her sudden blush. "No. It's been a very long time."

In that moment, he didn't want her to take any other male—human or vampire—into her bed.

He didn't want her fucking anyone else ever again.

And God help him, he would hunt down and disembowel the Minion bastard who might have harmed her today.

The thought hit him with a savage rush of possessiveness as her fingers squeezed his sex, wringing a drop of slick wetness from the tip. When she bent down over him and drew his cock into her mouth, suckling him deeply, he arched up as tight as a bowstring.

Forget tearing out the Minion's entrails, he would settle for nothing less than flat-out, bloody murder.

Lucan lowered his hands onto Gabrielle's shoulders as she worked him into a mindless frenzy. Her fingers, her lips, her tongue, her breath rasping against his bare abdomen as she took him deeper and deeper into her hot mouth—all of it driving him to the brink of extraordinary madness. He couldn't get enough. When she drew off of him, he swore roundly at the loss of her sweet suction.

"I need you inside me," she told him, panting.

"Yes," he snarled. "God, yes."

"But..."

Her hesitation confused him. Angered that part of him that was more savage Rogue than considerate lover.

"What's wrong?" It came out more of a demand than he meant.

"Shouldn't we...? Last night, things got out of hand before I could mention it...but shouldn't we, you know, use something this time?" Her discomfort sliced through his passion-drenched mind like a blade. He grew still, and she pulled away from him as if to get out of the tub. "I have some condoms in the other room...."

His hand clamped down around her wrist before she could move to rise.

"I can't make you pregnant." Why did that sound so harsh to him now? It was plain truth. Only bonded pairs—Breedmate women and the vampire males who exchanged blood from each other's veins—could successfully produce offspring. "As for anything else, you don't have to worry about protecting yourself. I'm healthy, and nothing we do together will hurt either one of us."

"Oh. Me, too. And I hope you don't think I'm prudish for asking—"

He drew her closer to him, silencing her awkwardness with a slow kiss. When their lips parted, he said, "I think, Gabrielle Maxwell, that you're an intelligent woman who respects her body and herself. I respect you for having the courage to be careful."

She smiled against his mouth. "I don't want to be careful when I'm near you. You make me wild. You make me want to scream."

With her hands splayed on his chest, she pushed him

down, until he was leaning against the back of the tub. Then she rose up over the heavy spear of his sex and moved her slick cleft along its length, sliding up and down, almost—but *fuck*, not quite!—sheathing him in her warmth.

"I want to make you scream," she whispered near his ear.

Lucan groaned with the pure agony of her sensual dance. He fisted his hands at his sides in the water to keep from grabbing her and impaling her on his nearly bursting erection. She kept up her wicked game, until he felt his climax knotting in his shaft. He was about to spill, and she was still teasing him mercilessly.

"Fuck," he swore through gritted teeth and fangs, tipping his head back. "For chrissake, Gabrielle, you are killing me."

"I want to hear it," she coaxed.

And then her juicy sex was inching down over the head of his cock.

Slowly.

So damned slowly.

His seed boiled up, and he shuddered as a trickle of hot liquid spurted into her body. He moaned, never so close to losing it as he was just then. And Gabrielle's tightness enveloped him further. The tiny muscles inside her clenched at him as she sank lower on his shaft.

He could hardly bear any more.

Gabrielle's scent surrounded him, wafting on the steam of the bath and mingling with the intoxicating perfume of their joined bodies. Her breasts bobbed near his mouth like fruit just ripe for his picking, but he didn't dare sample them when his control was so near to snapping. He wanted to pull her peachy mounds into his mouth, but his fangs were throbbing with the need to draw blood—a need only heightened in the midst of sexual release.

He turned his head aside and let out a howl of anguish, torn in so many tempting directions, not the least of which was the pressure to come inside Gabrielle, filling her with every drop of his passion. He shouted a curse, and then he truly was screaming, roaring a deep oath that only gained in strength as she sank down hard on his starving cock and wrung him dry, her own orgasm following quickly behind his.

Once his head stopped ringing and his legs regained strength enough to hold him, Lucan wrapped his arms around Gabrielle's back and started to rise with her, holding her in place on his already rousing erection.

"Where are we going?"

"You've had your fun. Now I'm taking you to bed."

The shrill ring of his cell phone jolted Lucan out of a heavy sleep. He was in bed with Gabrielle, both of them spent. She was curled up beside him, her naked body gloriously draped over his legs and torso.

Jesus, how long had he been out? Had to be hours, which was amazing considering his usual itchy state of insomnia.

The phone rang again and he was on his feet, heading for the bathroom, where he'd left his jacket. He dug the cell out of one of the pockets and flipped it open.

"Yeah."

"Hey." It was Gideon, and there was something odd about his voice. "Lucan, how fast can you get to the compound?"

He looked over his shoulder to the adjacent bedroom

loft. Gabrielle was sitting up now, drowsy from sleep, her bare hips wreathed in tangled sheets, her hair a wild mess around her face. He'd never seen anything so bloody tempting. Maybe it was better that he did leave soon, while he still stood a chance of getting away before the sun came up.

Wrenching his gaze away from the arousing sight of her, Lucan growled an answer into the phone. "I'm not far. What's going on?"

A lengthy silence stretched on the other end.

"Something's happened, Lucan. It's bad." More quiet, then some of Gideon's natural calm cracked. "Ah, fuck, there's no easy way to say it. We lost one tonight, Lucan. One of the warriors is dead."

CHAPTER
Twelve

The sounds of a female's mourning reached Lucan's ears as soon as he stepped out of the elevator that had delivered him to the subterranean depths of the compound. Heart-rending cries of deep anguish, the Breedmate's keening sorrow was raw, palpable, the only thing audible in the stillness of the long corridor.

It clawed at Lucan, the stunning weight of loss.

He didn't know yet which of the Breed warriors had perished that night. He wouldn't strive to guess. His footsteps were brisk, all but running toward the infirmary chambers from where Gideon had called him a few minutes ago. He rounded a bend in the corridor just in time to see Savannah leading a grief-stricken, wailing Danika from one of the rooms.

A fresh wave of shock hit him.

So, it was Conlan who was gone, then. The big Highlander with the easy laugh and deep, unfailing honor ... dead now. Soon to be dust.

Jesus, he could hardly grasp the hard truth of it.

Lucan paused, respectfully bowing his head low to the warrior's widow as she passed him. Danika was clinging hard to Savannah, the latter's strong, mocha-skinned arms seeming to be all that prevented Conlan's tall blond Breedmate from collapsing in despair.

Savannah acknowledged Lucan where her weeping charge was unable. "They're awaiting you inside," she told him gently, her deep brown eyes glistening with tears. "They will need your strength and guidance."

Lucan gave Gideon's woman a sober nod, then took the few short strides that would bring him into the infirmary.

He entered in silence, unwilling to disturb the solemnity of the fleeting time that he and his brethren would have to spend with Conlan. The warrior had sustained staggeringly severe injuries; even from across the room, Lucan could smell terrible blood loss. His nostrils filled with the foul, mingled odors of gunpowder, electrical heat, twisted metal shrapnel, and melted flesh.

There had been an explosion, with Conlan caught in the center of it.

Conlan's remains lay on a shroud-draped examination table, his body divested of clothing except for the wide strip of embroidered white silk that covered his groin. In the short while since he'd been returned to the compound, Conlan's skin had been cleaned and annointed with a fragrant oil, all in preparation for the funeral rites that would take place with the next rising of the sun, not a few hours from now.

Around the table that held the warrior, the others had gathered: Dante, rigid in his stoic observation of death; Rio, head bent down, fingers clutching a string of rosary beads as he moved his lips silently to the words of his mother's human religion; Gideon, attending cloth in hand, dabbing carefully at one of the many savage lacerations that had torn open nearly every inch of Conlan's skin; Nikolai, who had been on patrol that night with Conlan, his face paler than Lucan had ever seen it, his wintry eyes stark, his skin marred with soot and cinder and small, bleeding cuts.

Even Tegan was there, paying respects, although the vampire stood just outside the circle of the others, his eyes hooded, sullen in his solitude.

Lucan strode up to the table to take his place among his brethren. He closed his eyes and prayed over Conlan in prolonged silence. Some longtime later, Nikolai broke the quiet of the room.

"He saved my life out there tonight. We'd just smoked a couple of suckheads outside the Green Line station and were heading back when I saw this dude get on the train. I don't know what made me look at him, but he shot us this big, shit-eating grin, like he was daring us to come after him. He was packing some kind of gunpowder on him. He stank of that and some other shit I didn't have time to get a read on."

"TATP," Lucan said, scenting the acrid stuff on Niko's clothing even now.

"Turned out the bastard was carrying a belt of wired explosives on him. He jumped off the train just before we started rolling, and took off running down one of the old tracks. We chased him, Conlan cornered him. That's when we saw the bombs. They were on a sixty-second clock, and it was counting down below ten. I heard Conlan roar at me to get back, and then he launched himself at the guy."

"Christ," Dante swore, raking a hand through his black hair.

"A Minion did this?" Lucan asked, figuring it to be a safe presumption.

The Rogues had no qualms about spending human lives like dust in order to carry out their petty turf wars or to settle matters of personal retribution. For a long time, human religious fanatics weren't the only ones to employ the weak of mind as inexpensive, expendable, yet highly effective tools of terror.

But that didn't make the ugly reality of what happened to Conlan any easier to swallow.

"This wasn't a Minion," Niko replied, shaking his head. "This was a Rogue, wired up with enough TATP to take out half a city block by the look and stench of it."

Lucan wasn't the only one in the room to grind out a savage curse at that bit of troubling news.

"So, they're not content sacrificing just Minion pawns anymore?" Rio remarked. "Now the Rogues are moving bigger pieces on the board?"

"They're still pawns," Gideon said.

Lucan glanced to the quick-witted vampire and understood what he was getting at. "The pieces haven't changed. But the rules have. This is a new brand of warfare, not the minor firefighting we've been dealing with in the past. Someone within Rogue ranks is bringing a degree of order to the anarchy. We're coming under siege."

He turned his attention back to Conlan, the first casualty of what he feared was to be a new dark age. In his aged bones, he felt the violence of a long ago past rising up to repeat itself. War was brewing again, and if the Rogues were making moves to organize, to go on the offensive, then the entire vampire nation would find itself on the front lines. The humans, too.

"We can discuss this more at length, but not now. This time is Conlan's. Let us honor him."

"I've said my goodbyes," Tegan murmured. "Conlan knows I respected the hell out of him in life, as I do in death. Nothing's ever gonna change on that score."

A heavy wave of anxiety swept the room as everyone waited for Lucan to react to Tegan's abrupt departure. But Lucan wasn't about to give the vampire the satisfaction of thinking he'd pissed him off, which he had. He waited for the retreat of Tegan's boot falls to fade down the corridor, then he nodded to the others to resume the rite.

One by one, Lucan and each of the four other warriors sank down on their knee to pay further respects. They spoke a single prayer, then rose together, and began to withdraw to await the final ceremony that would put their fallen comrade to rest.

"I will be the one to carry him up," Lucan announced to the departing vampires.

He caught the exchange of looks between them, and knew what it meant. Elders of the vampire race—Gen Ones, especially—were never asked to bear the burden of the dead. That obligation fell to the later generation Breed who were further removed from the Ancients, and who, as such, could better withstand the burning rays of the rising sun for the time required to lay a vampire to proper rest.

For a Gen One like Lucan, the funeral rite would be a torturous eight minutes of exposure.

Lucan stared at the lifeless form on the table, unwilling to look away from the damage Conlan had suffered.

Damage suffered in his place, Lucan thought, sick with

the knowledge that it should have been him on patrol with Niko, not Conlan. Had he not sent the Highlander out at the last minute as his own replacement, Lucan might have been lying on that cold metal slab, his limbs and face and torso charred from hellish fire, his gut blasted open with shrapnel.

Lucan's need to see Gabrielle tonight had trumped his duty to the Breed, and now Conlan—his grieving mate, as well—had paid the ultimate price.

"I will take him topside," he repeated sternly. He slid a bleak scowl at Gideon. "Summon me when the preparations are completed."

The vampire inclined his head, granting Lucan more respect than he was due in that moment. "Of course. It won't be long."

Lucan spent the next couple of hours alone in his private quarters, kneeling in the center of the space, head dropped in prayer and somber reflection. Gideon arrived at the door, as promised, nodding to indicate that it was time to remove Conlan from the compound and surrender him to the dead.

"She's pregnant," Gideon said grimly as Lucan rose. "Danika is three months with child. Savannah just told me. Conlan had been trying to work up the courage to tell you that he was leaving the Order once the baby arrived. He and Danika were planning to withdraw to one of the Darkhavens to raise their family."

"Christ," Lucan hissed, feeling even worse for the happy future Conlan and Danika had been robbed of, and for the son who would never know the man of courage and honor who had been his father. "Everything is in prepara-tion for the ritual?"

Gideon inclined his head.

"Then let's do this."

Lucan strode forward. His feet and head were bare, as was the rest of his body beneath a long black robe. Gideon was robed as well, but wearing the formal belted tunic of the Order, as were the other vampires who awaited them in the chamber set aside for all manner of Breed ritual—from marriages and births, to funerals, like this one. The three females of the compound were present as well, Savannah and Eva in ceremonial hooded black gowns, Danika garbed in the same manner, but in deepest scarlet, to signify her sacred blood-bond with the departed.

At the front of the gathering, Conlan's body lay on an ornate altar, cocooned in a thick shroud of snowy silk wrappings.

"We begin," Gideon announced simply.

Lucan's heart was heavy as he listened to the service, to the symbolism of infinity in each of the ceremony's rites.

Eight ounces of perfumed oil to anoint the skin.

Eight layers of white silk shrouding the body of the fallen.

Eight minutes of silent, daybreak attendance by one member of the Breed, before the dead warrior would be released to the incinerating rays of the sun. Left alone, his body and soul would scatter to the four winds as ash, a part of the elements forever.

As Gideon's voice came to a slow pause, Danika stepped forward.

Turning to face the gathering, she lifted her chin and spoke in a hoarse, but proud, voice. "This male was mine, as I was his. His blood sustained me. His strength protected me. His love fulfilled me in all ways. He was my beloved, my only one, and he will be in my heart for all eternity."

"You honor him well," came the hushed, unison reply from Lucan and the others.

Danika now turned to meet Gideon, her hands extended, palms upturned. He unsheathed a slim golden dagger and placed it in her hands. Danika's hooded head dipped down in acceptance, then she turned to stand over Conlan's wrapped form. She murmured soft, private words meant only for the two of them. Her hands came up near her face, and Lucan knew that the Breedmate widow was now scoring her lower lip with the edge of the blade, drawing blood that she would then press to Conlan's mouth from over the shroud as she kissed him one final time.

Danika bent toward her lover and remained there for a long while, her body shaking with the force of her grief. She came away from him sobbing into the back of her hand, her scarlet kiss glowing fiercely on Conlan's mouth amid the field of white that covered him. Savannah and Eva brought her into a joined embrace, leading her away from the altar so that Lucan could continue with the one task that yet remained.

He approached Gideon at the fore of the assembly and pledged to see Conlan depart with all the honor that was due him, the vow spoken by all of the Breed who walked the same path that awaited Lucan now.

Gideon stepped aside to grant Lucan access to the body. Lucan took the massive warrior into his arms and turned to face the others as was required.

"You honor him well," murmured the low chorus of voices.

Lucan progressed solemnly and slowly across the ceremonial chamber to the stairwell leading up and out of the compound. Each long flight, each of the hundreds of steps he took, bearing the weight of his fallen brother, was a pain he accepted without complaint.

This was the easiest part of his task, after all.

If he were going to break, it would be in a few minutes from now, on the other side of the exterior door that loomed ahead of him just a dozen more paces.

Lucan shouldered the steel panel open and drew the crisp air into his lungs as he walked to the place where he would lay Conlan to rest. He went to his knees on a patch of crisp green grass, slowly lowering his arms to place Conlan's body down on terra firma before him. He whispered the prayers of the funeral ritual, words he'd only heard a scant few times over centuries long passed, yet called up now by rote.

As he spoke them, the sky began to glow with the coming of dawn.

He bore the light in reverent quiet, training all thought on Conlan and the honor that had marked his long life. The sun continued to stretch over the horizon, less than halfway through the ritual. Lucan dropped his head down, absorbing the pain as Conlan surely would have done for any one of the Breed who fought alongside him. Searing heat washed over Lucan as dawn rose, ever stronger.

His ears filled with the repeated words of the old prayers, and, before long, the faint hiss and crackle of his own burning flesh.

CHAPTER
Thirteen

Police and transportation officials still aren't certain what caused the apparent explosion last night. However, I spoke with a representative for the T just a few moments ago who assured me that the incident was isolated to one of the old, unused tracks, and that no injuries were reported. Stay tuned to Channel Five for more news on this breaking story as it—"

The dusty, late-model television mounted to a wall rack clicked off abruptly, cowed into silence solely by the force of the vampire's supreme irritation. Behind him, across the length of a bleak, dilapidated room that had once been the asylum's basement cafeteria, two of his Rogue lieutenants stood, fidgeting and grunting, as they awaited their next orders.

There was little patience in the pair; Rogues, by their

addictive natures had puny attention spans, having abandoned intellect to pursue the more immediate whims of
their Bloodlust. They were wanton children, little better
than hounds in need of regular whippings and spare rewards to keep them obedient. And to remind them of
whom they currently served.

"No injuries reported," sniggered one of the Rogues.

"Maybe not to the humans," added the other, "but the
Breed took a damn big hit. I hear there wasn't much left of
the dead one for the sun to claim."

More chuckling from the first idiot, followed by an ex-
pulsion of foul, blood-soured breath as he mimicked the
detonation of the explosives that had been set off in the
tunnel by the Rogue bomber assigned to the task.

"A pity the other warrior with him was left to walk
away." The Rogues fell silent as their leader turned at last
to face them. "Next time, I'll put the two of you to the task,
since you find failure so amusing."

They scowled, grunting like the beasts they were, their
slitted pupils wild within the engulfing yellow-gold sea of
their fixed irises. Their gazes turned down as he began to
stride toward them with slow, measured paces. His anger
was tempered only by the fact that the Breed had, indeed,
suffered a healthy loss.

The warrior who fell to the bomb was not the actual
target of last night's assignment; however, any dead member of the Order was good news for his cause. There
would be time to eliminate the one called Lucan. Perhaps
he might even do it himself, face-to-face, vampire to vampire, without the benefit of weapons.

Yes, he thought, there would be more than a little pleasure in taking that one down.

Call it poetic justice.

"Show me what you've brought me," he ordered the Rogues before him.

The two departed at once, pushing open a swinging door to retrieve the baggage left in the corridor outside. They returned an instant later, dragging behind them several lethargic, nearly bled-out humans. The men and women, six in all, were bound at their wrists and loosely shackled at their feet, though none appeared fit enough to even consider an attempt at escape.

Catatonic eyes stared off into nowhere, slack mouths incapable of screaming or speech drooped on their pale faces. At their throats, bite marks scored their skin where their Rogue captors had struck to subdue them.

"For you, sire. Fresh servants for the cause."

The half-dozen humans were shuffled in like cattle— for that they were, flesh and bone commodities that would be put to work, or to death, whenever he deemed it useful.

He looked over the evening's catch with little interest, idly sizing up the two men and four women by their potential for service. He felt an itchy impatience as he drew near to the lot of them, some of their bitten necks still oozing with a lazy trickle of fresh blood.

He was hungry, he decided, his assessing look lighting on a petite brunette female with a pouty mouth and ripe, full breasts straining against the dull teal green of her baglike, ill-fitting hospital garb. Her head lolled on her shoulders, too heavy to stay upright, although it was apparent that she was struggling against the torpor that had already claimed the others. Her irises were listless, rolling upward into her skull, yet she fought the pull of catatonia, blinking dazedly in an effort to remain conscious and aware.

He had to admire her pluck.

"K. Delaney, R.N.," he mused, reading from the plastic name tag that rode the plump swell of her left breast.

He took her chin between his thumb and forefinger, lifting her face up for his persual. She was pretty, young. And her freckled skin smelled sweet, succulent. His mouth watered greedily, his pupils narrowed behind the cover of his dark glasses.

"This one stays. Take the rest down to the holding cages."

At first, Lucan thought the piercing trill was just part of the agony he'd been living for the past several hours. His entire body felt scorched, flayed, and lifeless. His head had, at some point, ceased pounding and now plagued him with a prolonged bell of pain.

He was in his private quarters at the compound, in his own bed; that much he knew. He recalled dragging himself there with his last ounce of strength, after he had stayed with Conlan's body topside for the full eight minutes required of him.

He had stayed even longer than that, another searing few seconds, until the dawn's rays had ignited the fallen warrior's shroud and erupted in an awesome shower of light and flames. Only then did he move for the cover of the compound's subterranean walls.

The extra time exposed had been his personal apology to Conlan. The pain he endured now was to let him never forget what truly mattered: his duty to the Breed and to the Order of honorable males sworn likewise into that same service. There was no room for anything else.

He'd let that oath slip last night, and now one of his best warriors was gone.

Another blast of shrill ringing from somewhere in the room assailed him. Somewhere too near where he rested; the splitting grate of it jackhammered into his already caving skull.

With a hissed curse that barely made it out of his parched throat, Lucan peeled his eyes open and glared into the dark of his private bedchamber. A small light blinked from within the pocket of his leather jacket as the cell phone rang again.

Stumbling, his legs lacking their usual athletic control and coordination, he dropped out of his bed and made a graceless lunge for the offending device. It only took him three tries to finally find the small key that would silence the ringer. Furious for the taxing that the brief series of movements had on him, Lucan held the glowing display up to his swimming vision and forced himself to read the caller's number.

It was a Boston exchange . . . Gabrielle's cell phone.

Beautiful.

Just what he fucking needed.

He'd resolved on the climb with Conlan's body up those several hundred stairs to the outside that whatever he was doing with Gabrielle Maxwell had to stop. He hadn't been entirely sure what he was doing with her anyway, short of exploiting every available opportunity he could find to get her on her back beneath him.

Yeah, he'd been brilliant at that tactic.

It was the rest of his objectives he was beginning to suck at, so long as Gabrielle was in the picture.

He had it all planned out in his head, the way he was going to deal with the situation. He would have Gideon go to her apartment that night, tell her in logical, understandable terms all about the Breed and about her destiny—her true belonging—within the vampire nation. Gideon had a lot of experience dealing with females, and he was a consummate diplomat. He would be gentle, and he sure as hell had a better way with words than Lucan himself. He could make sense of it all for her, including the very real need for her to seek sanctuary—and, eventually, a suitable mate—at one of the Darkhavens.

As for Lucan, he was going to do what was required for his body to heal. A few more hours of recovery, a much-needed feeding tonight—once he was able to stand up long enough to hunt—and he would come back stronger, a better warrior.

He was going to forget he'd ever met Gabrielle Maxwell. For his own sake, if not for the Breed as a whole.

Except...

Except, he had told her just last night that she could reach him on his cell phone whenever she needed him. He had promised he would always answer her call.

And if she was trying to get a hold of him now because the Rogues or their walking-dead Minions had come sniffing around her again, he figured he damned well needed to know.

Lying in a supine sprawl on the floor, he punched the *Talk* button.

"Hello."

Jesus, he sounded like shit. Like his lungs were made of cinder and his breath was ash. He coughed and felt his head split with pain.

Silence held for a second on the other end, then Gabrielle's voice, hesitant, anxious. "Lucan? Is that you?"

"Yeah." He worked to force sound from his arid throat. "What is it? You okay?"

"Yes, I'm fine. I hope it's all right that I called. I just..."

Well, after the way you left last night, I've been a little worried. I suppose I just needed to know that nothing had happened to you."

He didn't have the energy to speak, so he lay back, closed his eyes, and merely listened to the sound of her voice. The clear, rich tones washed over him like a balm. Her concern was an elixir, something he had never tasted before—hearing that someone was worried about him. The affection was unfamiliar, warm.

It soothed him, despite his fierce need to deny it.

"Time..." he croaked, then tried again. "What time is it?"

"Not quite noon. I wanted to call you as soon as I got up this morning, but since you generally work the evening shift, I waited as long as I could. You sound tired. Did I wake you up?"

"No."

He attempted to roll onto his side, feeling stronger just for the few minutes on the phone with her. Besides, he needed to get his ass out of its sling and back onto the street, starting tonight. Conlan's murder had to be avenged, and he meant to be the one to dispense justice.

The more brutal that justice, the better.

"So," she was saying now, "everything's okay with you, then?"

"Yeah. Fine."

"Good. I'm relieved to hear that, actually." Her voice took on a lighter, teasing tone. "You ran out of my place so fast last night, I think you left skid marks on the floor."

"Something came up. I had to go."

"Hmm," she said, after he let the silence stretch out,

not volunteering to elaborate. "Top secret detective business?"

"You could say that."

He struggled to put his feet beneath him, and winced, both at the pain lancing through his body and for the truth he couldn't tell Gabrielle about what had really made him race out of her bed. The stark reality of the war that lay ahead of him and the rest of his kind would land on her plate soon enough. Tonight in fact, when Gideon paid her a visit.

"Listen, I have yoga class tonight with a friend of mine, but it lets out around nine. If you're not on duty, would you like to come over? I could cook you dinner. Think of it as a raincheck for the manicotti you missed earlier this week. Maybe we'll actually eat the food this time."

His facial muscles burned with the involuntary pull of his mouth as Gabrielle's flirty humor wrung a smile from him. The suggestion of the passion they'd shared together was wringing something else from him as well; and the flare of his arousal amid all of his other agony didn't hurt half as bad as he wished it had.

"I can't see you, Gabrielle. I have . . . things I must do."

Chief among them, getting some blood into his depleted cells, and that meant keeping her as far away from him as possible. Bad enough she tempted him with the promise of her body; in his current state, he would be a danger to any human who was fool enough to get near him.

"Don't you know what they say about all work and no play?" she asked, a world of invitation in the purr of her voice. "I'm a bit of a night owl, so if you get off work and decide you want some company—"

"I'm sorry. Maybe another time," he said, knowing full

well there would be no other time. He was standing on wobbly legs now and managing a halting, painful step toward the door. Gideon would be in the lab and that was all the way at the end of the corridor. Sheer hell to make that in his condition, but Lucan was more than willing to try. "I'm sending someone over to see you tonight. He's a...an associate of mine."

"What for?"

His breath rasped out of him in a labored wheeze, but he was walking. His hand swung out and caught the latch of the door. "Things are too dangerous topside right now," he said in a strained rush of words. "After what happened to you downtown yesterday..."

"God, can we forget that? I'm sure I was just overreacting."

"No," he said, cutting her off. "I'll feel better knowing you're not alone...having someone look in on you."

"Lucan, really. It's not necessary. I'm a big girl. I'm fine."

He ignored her protests. "His name is Gideon. You'll like him. The two of you can...talk. He will help you, Gabrielle. Better than I can."

"Help me—what do you mean? Has something happened with the case? And who is this Gideon guy? Is he a detective, too?"

"He will explain it all to you." Lucan stepped out into the corridor where dim lights illuminated polished tile floors and crisp chrome and glass fixtures. From behind the door of another private apartment, Dante's metal music thumped heavily. Trace smells of oil and recently fired weaponry filtered out from the training facility down one of many hallways that spoked off the main corridor. Lucan weaved on his feet, unsteady amid the sudden barrage of sensory stimulation. "You'll be safe, Gabrielle, I swear to you. I have to go now."

"Lucan, wait a second! Don't hang up. What is it you're not telling me?"

"You're going to be all right, I promise. Goodbye, Gabrielle."

CHAPTER
Fourteen

Gabrielle's call to Lucan, and his strange behavior on the other end of the line, had troubled her all day. It still bothered her, as she and Megan came out of yoga class that evening.

"He just sounded so weird on the phone. I can't decide if he was in extreme physical pain, or if he was trying to find a way to tell me that he didn't want to see me anymore."

Megan sighed, waving her hand in dismissal. "You're probably reading too much into it. If you really want to know, why don't you go down to the station and pop in on him?"

"I don't think so. I mean, what would I say?"

"You say, 'Hi, baby. You sounded so down this afternoon, I thought you could use a little pick-me-up, so here I am.' Maybe bring him coffee and a doughnut for good measure."

"I don't know...."

"Gabby, you've said yourself the guy has been nothing but sweet and caring when he's with you. From what you told me about your conversation with him today, he sounds very concerned about you. So much so, that he would send one of his buddies over to look in on you while he's on duty and can't be there himself."

"He did stress how dangerous it was topside—and what do you suppose *topside* means? That doesn't sound like cop talk, does it? What is it, some kind of military terminology?" She shook her head. "I don't know. There's a lot about Lucan Thorne that I just don't know."

"So ask him. Come on, Gabrielle. At least give the guy the benefit of the doubt."

Gabrielle considered her black yoga pants and zippered hoodie, then felt to see how wilted her ponytail had become during the forty-five minute session of stretches. "I should go home first, at least take a quick shower, change my clothes...."

"Wow! I mean, really, wow." Megan's eyes went wide and bright with amusement. "You're afraid to go down there, aren't you? Oh, you want to, but you probably have a million excuses ready for why you can't. Admit it, you really like this guy."

It wasn't as if she could deny it, even if her sudden smile didn't give her away. Gabrielle met her friend's knowing look and shrugged her shoulders. "Yeah, I do. I like him. A lot."

"Then what are you waiting for? The station is three blocks away, and you look gorgeous as always. Besides, it's not like he hasn't seen you a little sweaty before. He might actually prefer this look on you."

Gabrielle laughed along with Megan, but inside, her stomach was twisting. She really did want to see Lucan—didn't want to wait another minute, in fact—but what if he had been trying to let her down gently when they spoke that afternoon? How ridiculous would she look then, traipsing into the police station like she thought she was his girlfriend? She would feel like an idiot.

No more so than if she got the news secondhand from his friend Gideon, sent to see her on some pity mission.

"Okay. I'm going to do it."

"Good for you!" Megan slung the strap of her rolled yoga mat up on her shoulder, beaming. "I'm meeting Ray at my place after his shift, but call me first thing in the morning and tell me how it went, you hear me?"

"All right. Tell Ray I said hi."

As Megan dashed off to make the 9:15 train, Gabrielle headed for the police station. Along the way, she remembered Megan's advice and made a quick pit stop, picking up a sweet roll and a cup of coffee: full-strength black, since she had a hard time thinking Lucan would be the type to wuss his down with cream, sugar, or decaffeination.

With these gifts in hand as she reached the door of the precinct house, Gabrielle took a courage-building breath, then stepped over the threshold and strode casually inside.

The worst of his burns had begun to heal by nightfall. New skin grew firm and healthy beneath the feathery peels of the old as the outward damage sloughed away. His eyes, still hypersensitive to even artificial light, registered no pain in the cool darkness topside. Which was good, because he needed to be out here to quench the searing thirst of his recuperating body.

Dante stared at him as the two of them emerged from out of the compound and prepared to part company for a night of recon and hell's own retribution on the Rogues.

"You don't look so good, man. You say the word, I'm out there hunting for you, bring you back something young and strong. You sure as shit need it. And no one has to know you didn't score the sustenance on your own."

Lucan swung a grim look at the male and bared his teeth in a sneer. "Fuck you."

Dante chuckled. "Had a feeling you'd say that. You want me to ride shotgun for you, at least?"

The slow shake of his head sent a knife of pain lancing through his head. "I'm good. Be better, once I feed."

"No doubt." The vampire was silent for a long moment, just looking at him. "You know, that was pretty friggin' impressive, what you did for Conlan today. He wouldn't have seen that coming in a hundred years, but damn, I wish he knew you were the one walking those final steps with him. Way to honor him, man. Truly."

Lucan absorbed the praise without letting it warm him. He'd had his reasons for performing the funeral rite, and winning the admiration of the other warriors wasn't one of them. "Give me an hour to hunt, then contact me back here with your location so we can deal some death to our enemies tonight. In Conlan's memory."

Dante nodded, and rapped his knuckles against Lucan's fist. "You got it."

Lucan hung back as Dante retreated into the dark, his long-legged stride cocky in anticipation of the battles that awaited him on the streets. He drew his twin weapons from their sheaths and raised the curved *malebranche* blades high over his head. The gleam from those claws of polished steel and Rogue-slaying titanium sparked in the thin glow of moonlight overhead. With a low whoop of a battle cry, the vampire vanished into the shadows of the night.

Lucan followed not long after, taking a similar path into the lightless arteries of the city. His stealthy gait held less bravado than purpose, less eager arrogance than stone-cold need. His hunger was worse than it ever had been, and the roar he sent up into the canopy of stars above was filled with feral rage.

"Can you spell that last name again, please?"

"T-H-O-R-N-E," Gabrielle told the station receptionist, who had already come up empty on her first search of the directory. "Detective Lucan Thorne. I don't know what department he works in. He came to my house after I was in here reporting an attack I witnessed last weekend—a murder."

"Oh, so you want homicide, then?" The young woman's long manicured fingernails clacked over the keyboard in rapid strokes. "Hmm...nope, sorry. He's not listed in that department, either."

"That can't be right. Could you check again for me? Doesn't that system let you search on just the name?"

"It does, but I have no listing anywhere for a Detective Lucan Thorne. You sure he works out of this precinct?"

"I'm certain of it, yes. Your computer system must be out of date or—"

"Oh, hold on! There's someone who can help you out," the receptionist interjected, gesturing toward the entrance doors of the station. "Officer Carrigan! You got a second?"

Officer Carrigan, Gabrielle registered miserably. The aging cop who had given her such a hard time last weekend, all but calling her a liar and a cokehead as he refused to believe her statement about the nightclub slaying. At least now, with Lucan having processed her cell phone pictures with the police lab, she could take comfort in knowing that, regardless of this man's input, the case was moving forward in some fashion.

Gabrielle had to fight to contain her groan as she turned her head and saw the rotund officer taking his sweet time to strut over. When he saw her standing there, the expression of arrogance that seemed so natural on his fleshy face took on a decidedly contemptuous edge.

"Ah, Jay-zuss. You again? Just what I don't need, my last day on the job. I'm retiring in four more hours, darlin'. You'll have to tell it to someone else this time."

Gabrielle frowned. "Excuse me?"

"This young lady is looking for one of our detectives," said the receptionist, sharing a sympathetic look with Gabrielle at the officer's dismissive demeanor. "I can't find him in the system, but she thinks he might be one of yours. Do you know Detective Thorne?"

"Never heard of him." Officer Carrigan started to walk away.

"Lucan Thorne," Gabrielle said with force, setting Lucan's coffee and bagged danish down on the reception counter. She took an automatic step after the cop, nearly reaching for his arm when it seemed he was simply going to leave her standing there. "Detective Lucan Thorne—you must be familiar with him. You folks sent him to my apartment earlier this week to get some additional infor-

mation on my statement. He brought my cell phone photos into the lab for analysis—"

Carrigan was chuckling now, having paused to look at
her as she blurted out the details of Lucan's arrival at her
home. She didn't have the patience to deal with the officer's belligerence. Not when her nape was crawling with
the feeling that things were about to get weird.

"Are you telling me that Detective Thorne hasn't
shared any of this with you?"

"Lady. I'm telling you that I don't know what the hell
you're talking about. I've been working out of this station
for thirty-five years, and I've never heard of any Detective
Thorne, let alone sent him out to your place."

A knot began to form in her stomach, cold and tight,
but Gabrielle refused to process the dread that was taking
shape beneath her confusion. "That's not possible. He
knew about the murder I witnessed. He knew I'd been
here, at the station, filing a statement about it. I saw his ID
badge when he came to my house. I just talked to him today, he said he was working tonight. I have his cell phone
number...."

"Well, I'll tell you what. If it will get you outta my hair
any faster, let's give your Detective Thorne a call,"
Carrigan said. "That ought to clear things right up, eh?"

"Yes. I'll call him now."

Gabrielle's fingers were trembling a little as she dug her
cell phone out of her pocketbook and punched in Lucan's
number. It rang, unanswered. She tried again, waiting for
an agonizing eternity while her call rang and rang and
rang, and Officer Carrigan's expression smoothed from
dubious impatience to a tentative, sympathetic look she'd
seen on more than one social worker's face when she was
a kid.

"He's not there," she murmured as she brought the phone away from her ear. She felt awkward and confused, made all the worse for the careful expression on Carrigan's face. "I'm sure he's just tied up with something. I'll try him again in a minute."

"Ms. Maxwell, do you have anyone else we can call? Family, maybe? Someone who can help us make sense of what you might be going through?"

"I'm not going through anything."

"Seems to me like you are. I think you're confused. You know, sometimes people invent things to help them cope with other problems."

Gabrielle scoffed. "I'm not confused. Lucan Thorne is not a figment of my imagination. He's real. These things that have been happening around me are real. The murder I saw last weekend, those . . . men . . . with their bloody faces and sharp teeth, even that kid who was watching me the other day at the Common . . . he works here at the station. What did you do, send him to spy on me?"

"Okay, Ms. Maxwell. Let's see if we can work this out together." Evidently, Carrigan had finally found a scrap of diplomacy underneath the crust of his boorish nature. But there was still a big dose of condescension in the way he took her by the elbow and tried to guide her toward one of the lobby benches for a seat. "Let's just take a few deep breaths, here. We can get you some help."

She shook him off, pulling away. "You think I'm crazy. I know what I saw—all of it! I'm not making this up, and I don't need any help. I just need the truth."

"Sheryl, honey," Carrigan said to the receptionist who was staring at them with apprehension in her eyes. "You wanna give Rudy Duncan a quick call for me? Tell him I could use him down here."

"Meds?" she inquired lightly, the phone already hugged between her ear and shoulder.

"Nah," Carrigan replied, looking back to Gabrielle. "No cause for alarm just yet. Ask him to come down to the lobby, nice and easy, have a little talk with Ms. Maxwell and me."

"Forget it," Gabrielle said, rising off the bench. "I'm not staying here another second. I have to go."

"Look, whatever you're going through, there are people who can help you—"

She didn't wait for him to finish, simply gathered what was left of her dignity, then strode over to the receptionist desk to retrieve the cup and bag from the countertop, and pitched both into the trash on her way out the door.

The night air was crisp against her flushed cheeks, soothing her somewhat. But her head was still spinning. Her heart was still pounding hard with confusion and disbelief.

Had the whole world gone mad around her? What the hell was going on?

Lucan had been lying to her about being a cop, that was pretty much a no-brainer. But just how much of what he'd told her—God, how much of what they'd done together—had been part of that deception?

And why?

Gabrielle paused at the bottom of the concrete steps leading out of the precinct house and took deep lungfuls of air. She blew it out slowly, then looked down to find her cell phone still clutched in her hand.

"Shit."

She had to know.

This strange ride she was on had to stop right now.

The *Redial* button brought up Lucan's number. She

sent the call, then waited, uncertain what she was going
to say.

It rang six times.

Seven.

Eight...

CHAPTER
Fifteen

Lucan grabbed his cell phone from out of his leather jacket, a curse rolling hard off his tongue.

Gabrielle...again.

She had called him earlier as well, but he'd had to let it go unanswered. He'd been stalking a drug dealer whom he'd first spotted selling crack to a teenaged streetwalker outside a seedy tavern. Lucan had mentally steered his prey down a quiet back alley, and was just about to lunge in attack when Gabrielle's first call of the night had rung like a car alarm going off in his pocket. He had clicked the device into silent mode, berating himself for the uncustomary lack of sense that had made him carry the damned thing on his hunt in the first place.

Hunger and injury had made him careless. But the

sudden bark of noise in the darkened street had proved a benefit to him in the end.

His strength was subpar and the cagey dealer had scented danger on the wind, even though Lucan had kept to the shadows, trailing his quarry unseen. The guy had been twitchy, anxious. He'd drawn a handgun halfway down the narrow street, and while bullet wounds were seldom fatal to Lucan's kind—unless you were talking a head shot, delivered at pointblank range—he wasn't sure his compromised, recovering body would be able to absorb the impact of a further injury today.

Not to mention the fact that it just would have pissed him off, and he was already in a seriously foul mood.

So, when the ring of the cell phone sent the dealer into a startled left-right-left spin as he tried to determine the source of the noise behind him, Lucan had sprung on him. He had taken the guy down fast, sinking his fangs into the vein in the human's neck, which bulged tautly in that instant before terror forced breath enough through the man's lungs for him to scream.

Blood gushed against his tongue, nasty with the taint of drugs and disease. Lucan choked it down, swallow after swallow, clutching at his convulsing, gasping prey without mercy. He would kill this one, and he wouldn't care less. All that mattered was feeding the hunger. Assuaging the pain of his mending body.

Lucan fed quickly, drinking his fill.

More than his fill.

He nearly drained the dealer, and still he was ravenous. But it would be pushing it to feed any more than he already had tonight. Better to give this nourishment a chance to take hold before he risked getting greedy, and taking a tailspin toward Bloodlust.

Lucan stared with scorn at the phone ringing in his hand, knowing he ought to just let the damned thing go unanswered.

It kept on, insistent, and in the second before it cut off, he picked up. He said nothing at first, just listened as the soft sound of Gabrielle's exhale blew across the receiver. Her breath shook a little, but her voice was strong, despite the fact that she was obviously pretty upset.

"You've been lying to me," she said by way of greeting. "How long, Lucan? About how much? Everything?"

Lucan took in the lifeless body of his prey with contempt. He crouched low, making a quick search of the greasy lowlife. He found a rubber-banded wad of cash, which he would leave for the street vultures to fight over. The dealer's party favors—a couple grand worth of crack and heroin—would take a bath down one of the city's sewer drains.

"Where are you?" he barked into the cell phone, thinking no more of the predator he'd eliminated. "Where's Gideon?"

"Aren't you even going to try to deny it? Why would you do something like this?"

"Put him on the phone, Gabrielle."

She ignored his demand. "There's another thing I'd like to know: how did you get into my apartment last night? I had all the locks set, including the chain. What did you do, pick them somehow? Did you steal my keys when I wasn't looking and have another set made?"

"We can talk about this later, once I know you're safe at the compound."

"What compound?" Her sharp gasp of laughter took him aback. "And you can cut the benevolent protector act. I know you're not a cop. All I want is a little honesty. Is that too much to ask, Lucan? God—is that even your real name? Is anything you've told me remotely close to the truth?"

Suddenly Lucan knew that this anger, this hurt, wasn't coming at him as a result of Gabrielle getting a crash course from Gideon on the Breed or her destined role within it. A role that wasn't going to include Lucan.

No, she didn't know any of that yet. This was something else. This wasn't fear of the facts. This was a fear of the unknown.

"Where are you, Gabrielle?"

"What do you care?"

"I do . . . care," he admitted, albeit reluctantly. "Damn it, I don't have the head for this right now. Look, I know you're not at your apartment, so where are you? Gabrielle, you need to tell me where you are."

"I'm at the police station. I came down here tonight to see you, and guess what? Nobody's ever heard of you."

"Ah, Christ. You asked for me there?"

"Of course I did. How could I have known you were playing me for a fool?" Again the brittle scoff. "I even brought you coffee and a sweet roll."

"Gabrielle, I will be there in a few minutes—less than that. Do not move. Stay where you are. Stay someplace public, somewhere inside. I'm coming for you."

"Forget it. Leave me alone."

Her sharp command drew him up short on the street. Just before his boots started hitting the pavement at a determined clip.

"I'm not sticking around to wait for you, Lucan. In fact, you know what? Just stay the hell away from me."

"Too late," he drawled into the phone.

He was already rounding the last corner before he

would turn onto the street where the police station was located. He moved over the concrete and through the thin knots of milling pedestrians like a ghost. He felt the blood he'd ingested begin to merge with his cells, adhering to muscle and bone, strengthening him, until he was nothing but a cold draft on the back of the necks of those he passed.

But Gabrielle, with her Breedmate's extraordinary perception, saw him at once.

He heard the sudden intake of air skate across the receiver of her cell phone. She drew the device away from her ear as though in slow motion, disbelief widening her eyes as she stared at his swift approach.

"My God," she whispered, the sound of it reaching his ears a mere second before he was standing in front of her, reaching out to take her by the arm. "Let go of me!"

"We need to talk, Gabrielle. Not here. I'll take you someplace—"

"Like hell you will!" She wrenched herself out of his grasp and backed away from him on the sidewalk. "I'm not going anywhere with you."

"You are not safe out here anymore, Gabrielle. You've seen too much. You're a part of it now, whether or not you want to be."

"A part of what?"

"This war."

"War," she echoed, doubt lacing the word.

"That's right. It's a war. Sooner or later, you're going to have to pick a side, Gabrielle." He ground out a curse. "No. Screw that. I'm choosing a side for you right now."

"Is this some kind of joke? What are you, one of those military rejects who gets off on acting out authority fantasies? Maybe you're something worse than that."

"This is no joke. It's not a goddamned game. I have seen a lot of combat and death in my time, Gabrielle. You can't even begin to imagine all that I've seen, all that I've done. But it's nothing like the current storm that's building. And I'm not going to stand by and watch you get caught in the crossfire." He thrust out his hand. "You're coming with me. Now."

She dodged his reach. Fear and outrage clashed in her dark eyes. "Touch me again, and I swear I'll get the cops. You know, the real ones back there in the station house. They carry real badges. And real guns."

Lucan's temperature, already high, began to rise. "Do not threaten me, Gabrielle. And don't think the police can give you any kind of protection. Certainly not from the danger that's pursuing you. For all we know, half the precinct could be infested with Minions."

She shook her head, adopting a calmer stance. "Okay, this conversation is going from strange to deeply disturbing. I'm done with it, understand?" She was speaking to him slowly and quietly, as if attempting to soothe a frothing dog that was crouched before her, ready to spring in attack. "I'm going to leave now, Lucan. Please...don't follow me."

When she took the first step away from him, what little was left of Lucan's control snapped its tether. He locked his gaze down hard on hers and sent a fierce command into her mind, ordering her to cease resisting him.

Give me your hand.

Now.

For a second, her legs stopped moving. Her fingers grew a little restless at her side, then, slowly, her arm began to lift toward him.

And, suddenly, his hold on her broke.

He felt her force him out of her thoughts, disconnecting him. The power of her will was an iron gate slamming down between them, one he would have had a hard time penetrating even if he'd been in optimal condition.

"What the *hell*?" she gasped, registering the trick for what it was. "I heard you, just now, inside my head. *My God*. You've done this to me before, haven't you?"

"You're not leaving me much choice, Gabrielle."

He tried again. Felt her push against him, more desperate this time. More afraid.

The back of her hand came up against her mouth, but could not quite stifle the broken cry that leaked out of her.

She stumbled back off the curb.

Then bolted across the darkened street to escape him.

"Yo, kid. Grab the door for me, will ya?"

It took a second for the Minion to realize he was being spoken to; he'd been so distracted by the sight of the Maxwell woman on the street below the police station. Even now, as he pulled open the door to let a pizza delivery guy carrying four steaming pie boxes enter, his attention remained rooted on the woman as she stepped off the curb and ran across the street.

Like she was trying to leave someone in the dust behind her.

The Minion looked to where a huge figure in black stood, watching her flee. The male was immense—easily six-and-a-half-feet tall, shoulders beneath his dark leather jacket like they belonged on a linebacker. He radiated an air of menace that could be felt all the way from the street to where the Minion now stood, dumbstruck, still holding the station door open, even though the pizzas were currently parked at the receptionist desk inside.

Although he had never seen one of the vampire warriors his Master so openly despised, the Minion knew without a doubt that he was witnessing precisely that now.

It was an opportunity sure to win him much esteem, alerting his Master to the presence of both the woman and the vampire with whom she seemed familiar, if not a little terrified.

The Minion stepped inside the precinct house, his palms moist with anticipation of the glory that awaited him. Head down, positive in his ability to move around all but ignored, he started across the lobby at a hasty clip.

He didn't even see the pizza guy moving into his path until he had crashed into him, head-on. A cardboard box jabbed into his midsection and emitted a blast of garlic-ripe steam before tumbling to the filthy linoleum, spilling its contents around the Minion's feet.

"Aw, man! That's my next delivery you're standing on. Don't you watch where you're goin' dude?"

He didn't apologize, or even pause to kick the greasy cheese and pepperoni off his shoe. Shoving his hand into the pocket of his khakis, the Minion found his cell phone and searched for somewhere private to make his important call.

"Hold up a second, sport."

It was the aging, balding officer standing in the lobby who shouted after him now. Stuffed into his uniform for what he'd boasted was his final few hours on the job, Carrigan had been wasting time bullshitting with the lobby receptionist.

The Minion disregarded the cop's thunderous voice behind him and kept walking, dropping his chin down and

making a beeline for a stairwell door located near the public john just off the lobby.

Carrigan puffed out his chest and gaped with obvious
disbelief as his self-perceived authority was utterly ignored.

"Hey, pencil neck! I'm talking to you. I said, get back
here and help clean this mess up—and I mean now, shit-
for-brains!"

"Clean it up yourself, you arrogant slob," the Minion
muttered under his breath, then shoved open the metal
door to the stairs and began a quick jog down to a level
below.

Above him, that same door crashed open, hitting the
other side of the wall and shaking the steps like a sonic
boom. Carrigan leaned over the rail, his jowls corpulent
with rage. "What'd you just say to me? What the *fuck* did
you just call me, asshole?"

"You heard me. Now leave me alone, Carrigan. I have
better things to do."

The Minion took out his cell phone, intending to contact the only one who truly commanded him. But before
he could press the speed-dial button that would connect
him to his Master, the burly cop was launching himself
down the stairwell. A hamlike hand cuffed the side of the
Minion's head. His ears rang, vision swimming with the
impact, as the cell phone jettisoned out of his grasp and
clattered onto the floor, several steps below.

"Thanks for giving me something to smile about my
last day on the job," Carrigan taunted. He ran a fat finger
around the front of his too-tight collar, then casually
reached up to pat the sole remaining wisps of hair on his
brow back down where they'd been pasted before. "Now,
get your scrawny ass back up those stairs before I hand it to
you on a platter. Ya get me?"

There was a time, before he'd met the one he called Master, that a challenge like that—particularly from a blowhard like Carrigan—would not have gone unmet.

But the sweating, sputtering cop glaring down on him now was insignificant in light of the duties entrusted to chosen ones like himself. The Minion simply blinked a few times, then turned to retrieve his cell phone and continue with his task at hand.

He only made it down two stairs before Carrigan was on him again, heavy fingers clamping down hard on his shoulder and forcibly wheeling him around. The Minion's eyes lit on a fancy ballpoint pen stuck into the shirt pocket of Carrigan's uniform. He recognized the commemorative service emblem on the clip as he took another hard knock to the skull.

"What are you, deaf *and* dumb? Get the hell outta my sight, or I'll—"

The abrupt choke and wheeze of Carrigan's voice snapped the Minion back to his senses. He saw his own hand clutching the officer's pen as it came down for a second brutal plunge, the point of it burrowing deep into the fleshy skin of Carrigan's neck.

The Minion struck again and again with the makeshift weapon, until the cop sank down to the floor in a savaged, lifeless heap.

He loosened his fist and the pen dropped into a pool of blood on the stairs, all but forgotten in the instant it took him to dash down and grab up his cell phone once more. He meant to place his crucial call immediately, but his eyes kept drifting to this new mess he'd made, something that wasn't going to get swept away as easily as the pizza in the lobby.

This had been a mistake, and any approval won from

informing his Master of the Maxwell woman's where-
abouts could be lost once it was discovered that he'd acted
so impulsively here. Killing without sanction might negate
everything.

But perhaps there was an even more certain path into
his Master's good graces—a path that could be paved by
apprehending and delivering the woman to his Master in
person.

Yes, thought the Minion, *that was a prize bound to impress.*

Pocketing the cell phone, he turned back to extract
Carrigan's weapon from its holster. Then he stepped over
the corpse and hurried out a back entrance to the station
parking lot.

CHAPTER
Sixteen

He should let her go.

He'd screwed things up so badly, he didn't think there would be any reasoning with Gabrielle tonight. Maybe not ever.

From the opposite curb, he watched her taking long strides down the other side of the street, heading God knew where. She looked ashen and stunned, like she'd just taken a sucker punch to the chest.

Which she had, he admitted darkly.

Maybe it was for the best that he let her run off thinking he was a liar and a dangerous lunatic. The assumption was not all that far from fact, after all. But her opinion of him wasn't key here, anyway. Getting a Breedmate to safety was.

He could let her go home, give her a few days to cool

off, take some time to come to terms with his deception. Then he could send Gideon to smooth things over and bring her calmly under Breed protection where she belonged. Gabrielle could choose a new life in any one of the Darkhavens secreted around the world. She could be happy, secure, and find a mate who would be a true partner for her.

She wouldn't even have to see him again.

Yeah, he thought, that was the best course of action at this point.

But regardless, he found himself stepping off the curb and into the street after her, unable to just walk away from Gabrielle now, even if that's what she needed most.

As he crossed the lanes of light evening traffic, his attention was wrenched to the squeal of car tires up ahead of him. A late model American rust bucket tore out of a side alley near the police station and careened into the middle of the street. The accelerator roared, laying rubber as the driver stomped on the gas and aimed the nose of the rumbling beast toward his target up the road.

Gabrielle.

Son of a bitch.

Lucan vaulted into a dead run. His boots chewed up the pavement, moving with all the speed he could summon.

The car launched up onto the curb a few feet in front of Gabrielle, blocking her path. She jolted to a stop. A low command came at her from the open window of the car. She shook her head violently, then screamed, her face going stark with recognition as the vehicle door opened and a human male jumped out.

"Jesus Christ. Gabrielle!" Lucan shouted, his mind

grasping for a hold on her assailant and getting nothing but disconnect, unreachable, dead air.

Minion, he realized with contempt. Only the Rogue Master who owned this human could command his thoughts. And the mental effort Lucan had spent attempting to do so had slowed him physically. A few seconds lost, but too damned many.

Gabrielle made a fast break to her left, racing into a small playground with her pursuer right on her heels.

Lucan heard her cry out, saw the human that was chasing her suddenly throw out his hand and grab a fistful of the ponytail swinging behind her.

The bastard dragged her down to the ground. Fumbled a pistol out from the back waistband of his khakis.

Thrust the barrel of the weapon into Gabrielle's face.

"No!" Lucan roared, coming right up on them and kicking the human off of her with one fierce blow of his booted foot.

The weapon went off as the guy rolled, a wild shot firing up into the trees. But Lucan smelled blood. The metallic odor of it clung to both Gabrielle and her attacker. Not hers, he determined quickly, and with relief, as he noted the absence of Gabrielle's unique jasmine scent.

The spilled blood was fresh on the front of the Minion's shirt, and hunger flared in that deadly part of Lucan that was still starving and trying to heal. His mouth throbbed in response to the feeding impulse, but rage burned hotter at the idea of Gabrielle being harmed by this scum. His stare locked in deadly heat on the Minion, Lucan offered Gabrielle his hand to help her up from the ground.

"Did he hurt you?"

She shook her head no, but a small sound caught in her

throat, half sob, half hysterical moan. "He's the one, Lucan—the one I saw watching me in the park the other day!"

"He's a Minion," Lucan said, growling the word through gritted teeth. He didn't care who the human was. In a few minutes it would be history, anyway.

"Gabrielle, you need to get out of here, sweetheart."

"W-what? You mean leave you with him? Lucan, he has a gun."

"Go now, baby. Just run back out the way you came and get yourself home. I'll make sure you're safe there."

The Minion was doubled over on the ground, still clutching the handgun, coughing in an effort to catch the breath Lucan had kicked out of him. He spat a mouthful of blood, and Lucan's stare tightened on the crimson spray soaking into the dirt. His gums ached with the stretching of his fangs.

"Lucan—"

"Goddamn it, Gabrielle! Leave!"

The command rushed out of him in a furious snarl, but there was little he could do to contain the beast within him. He was going to kill again—his anger was so out of control, he *needed* to—and he refused to let her see it.

"Run, Gabrielle. Go now!"

She ran.

Head reeling, heart practically exploding, Gabrielle took off at Lucan's bellowed command.

But she wasn't about to go home like he said and leave him all alone. She fled the playground area, praying that the street and the station house full of armed cops, wouldn't be far. Part of her hated leaving Lucan at all, but another part of her—a part that was desperate to do what she could to help him—sent her legs flying out beneath her.

As mad as she was at his deception, as frightened as she was of everything she didn't understand about him, she needed him to be all right.

If anything were to happen to him—

The thought was cut short as a round of gunfire cracked behind her in the dark.

She froze, all the breath sucked out of her lungs.

She heard a strange, animal roar.

Another two shots rang out, rapid sequence, then...nothing.

Only a heavy, wrenching silence.

Oh, God.

"Lucan?" she screamed. Panic lodged in her throat. "Lucan!"

She was running once more, back where she'd come from. Back to where she feared her heart was going to shatter into a million pieces if Lucan wasn't standing there unharmed when she reached him.

She felt a vague sense of worry that the kid from the police precinct—*Minion, that was the odd word Lucan had called him*—might be waiting for her, or already coming after her to finish her off as well. But concern for her own personal safety was shoved aside as she neared the little corner of the moonlit playground.

She just needed to know that Lucan was okay.

Above everything else in that moment, she needed to be with him.

She saw the silhouette of a dark figure on the grassy yard—Lucan, standing with legs braced apart, arms held down at his sides in a menacing angle. He stood over his assailant who was evidently ass-planted on the ground in front of him and attempting to scrabble out of Lucan's reach.

"Thank God," Gabrielle whispered under her breath, instantly relieved.

Lucan was all right, and now the authorities could deal with the deranged psychotic who might have killed them both.

She hurried a little closer.

"Lucan," she called, but he didn't seem to hear her.

Towering over the man at his feet, he bent at the waist and reached down to grab him. Gabrielle's ears registered a queer strangling sound, and she realized with not a little shock that Lucan was holding the man by the throat.

Hauling him up off the ground with one hand.

Her steps slowed, but she couldn't halt them altogether as her mind struggled to make sense of what she was seeing.

Lucan was strong, there was no doubting that, and the kid from the police station probably weighed only about fifty pounds more than she did, but to lift him with the power of one arm alone...she could hardly imagine it.

She watched in peculiar detachment as Lucan raised his arm higher, letting the man squirm and fight the clawing grip that was slowly cutting off his air. A terrifying roar began to fill her ears, building slowly, until everything else faded away.

In the moonlight, she saw Lucan's mouth. It was open, teeth bared. His mouth, making that terrible, otherworldly noise.

"Stop," she murmured, her eyes rooted on him now, suddenly sick with dread. "Please...Lucan, stop."

And then the keening howl went silent, replaced by a

new horror as Lucan brought the spasming body down before him and calmly sank his teeth into the flesh below the man's jaw. A jet of blood spurted from the deep puncture, crimson rendered black against the darkness of night that surrounded the terrible scene. Lucan remained fixed, holding the gushing wound to his mouth.

Feeding from it.

"Oh, my God," she moaned, her hands trembling as she brought them up to hold back a scream. "No, no, no, no...Oh, Lucan...*no*."

His head came up abruptly, as if he'd heard her quiet misery. Or maybe he'd suddenly sensed her presence not a hundred yards from where he stood, savage and terrifying, looking like nothing she'd ever seen before.

Not true, her stricken mind contradicted.

She had seen this brutality once before, and if reason had forbade her from giving a name to the horror then, it rose up within her now like a cold, bleak wind.

"Vampire," she whispered, staring at Lucan's blood-stained face and feral, glowing eyes.

CHAPTER
Seventeen

The smell of blood wreathed him, pungent and metallic, his nose swamped with the sweet, coppery tanginess. Some of it was his own, he realized with a dull sense of curiosity, grunting as he looked down and noted the gunshot wound to his left shoulder.

He felt no pain, only the swelling energy that always filled him after he fed.

But he wanted more.

Needed more, came the answering cry of the beast within him.

That voice was rising. Demanding. Urging him toward the edge.

But then, hadn't he been heading there for a long time, anyway?

Lucan clamped his jaws together so hard his teeth

should have shattered. He had to get a grip, had to get the hell out of there and back to the compound, where he might be able to pull his shit together.

He had been walking the darkened streets for two hours, and still his blood was drumming hard in his temples, rage and hunger still ruling all but a sliver of his mind. He was a danger to all in this condition, but his restless body would not be still.

He stalked the city like a wraith, moving without conscious thought even though his feet—his every sense—led him on a purposeful path toward Gabrielle.

She hadn't gone home. Lucan wasn't sure where she had run, until the unseen thread that connected him to her by scent and senses brought him in front of an apartment building in the city's North End. A friend of hers, no doubt.

A light was on in an upstairs window, that bit of glass and brick was all that separated him from her.

But he wasn't going to try to see her, and not merely because of the red Mustang parked outside with the police light propped on the dash. Lucan didn't have to see his reflection in the windshield to know that his pupils were still narrow in the center of his huge irises, his fangs still protruding behind the rigid set of his mouth.

He looked every bit the monster he was.

The monster Gabrielle had seen firsthand tonight.

Lucan growled, forced to remember her horrified expression again and again since he'd slain the Minion.

He could still see her take a faltering step backward, her eyes wide with terror and revulsion. She had seen him for what he truly was—had even flung the word at him in accusation the instant before she'd fled.

He hadn't tried to stop her, not with words or by force.

All he'd known in that moment was the pure rush of fury as he drained his prey dry. Then he'd dropped the body like the rubbish it was, feeling a further surge of rage when he considered what might have happened to Gabrielle had she fallen into Rogue hands. Lucan had wanted to tear the human apart—nearly had, he acknowledged, vividly recalling the savagery he had wrought.

He, the cool one, so fierce in his control.

What a fucking joke.

His carefully held mask had been slipping from the moment he had first met Gabrielle Maxwell. She made him weak, exposed his flaws.

Made him want things he could never have.

He stared up at that second-floor window, chest heaving as he battled a fierce urge to leap up there, smash his way in, and take Gabrielle someplace where he could keep her all to himself.

Let her fear him. Let her despise him for what he was, so long as he could press her warm body down beneath him, easing his pain as only she could do.

Yes, the beast within him snarled, knowing only want and need.

Before the impulse to have her could win out, Lucan fisted his hand and brought it down hard on the hood of the off-duty police officer's car. The vehicle alarm howled, and as curtains parted in every nearby window at the disturbance, Lucan leaped off the curb and jogged into the shadows of the waning night.

"Everything's okay," Megan's boyfriend said, coming back into her apartment after he'd gone out to investigate the sudden trip of his car alarm. "Damn thing's always had a hair trigger. Sorry 'bout that. Not like we needed any added tension tonight, eh?"

"Probably just kids causing trouble," Megan added from beside Gabrielle on the sofa.

Gabrielle nodded in vague agreement at her friend's attempt to soothe her, but she didn't believe it for a second.

It was Lucan.

She had felt him outside with an inner sense she couldn't begin to describe. It wasn't fear or dread, just a marrow-deep awareness that he was close by.

That he needed her.

Wanted her.

God help her, but she had actually been hoping he'd come to the door, haul her out of there, and help her make sense of the horror she had witnessed a short while ago.

He was gone now, however. She felt his absence as strongly as she'd known he had followed her to Megan's.

"Are you warm enough, Gabby? Would you like more tea?"

"No, thanks."

Gabrielle held on to the tepid cup of chamomile with two hands, feeling a chill inside of her that no amount of blankets or hot water could chase away. Her heart was still racing, her head still reeling from confusion and stark disbelief.

Lucan had torn open that guy's throat.

With his teeth.

He'd put his mouth to the wound and drank the blood that gushed out over his face.

He was a monster, like something out of a nightmare. Like those same fiends who attacked and killed the punker outside the nightclub—something that seemed so far in her past now that she could hardly believe it happened.

But it had, just as tonight's slaying had happened, too: this time with Lucan at the center of it.

Gabrielle had gone to Megan's out of desperation, needing to be somewhere familiar, yet too afraid to go to her own apartment in case Lucan's friend might be waiting for her there. She had told Megan and her boyfriend, Ray, how she'd been accosted on the street by the psycho from the police station. She'd relayed the facts that he'd also been spying on her a few days earlier, and when he'd confronted her tonight, he did so with a gun in his hand.

She wasn't sure why she'd left Lucan entirely out of the story, crucial as his presence was. She supposed it was partly because regardless of his methods, he had killed tonight in order to protect her, and she felt a need to offer some of the same consideration to him.

Even if he was a vampire.

God, it sounded ridiculous even to think it.

"Gab, honey. You need to report what happened. The guy sounds seriously unhinged. The police need to hear about this, they need to get him off the street. Ray and I can take you. We'll go downtown and find your detective friend—"

"No." Gabrielle shook her head, setting her cold tea onto the sofa table with only the slightest quiver in her hands. "I don't want to go anywhere tonight. Please, Megan? I just need to rest for a little while. I'm so tired."

Megan took Gabrielle's hand and squeezed it gently. "Okay. I'll get you a pillow and another blanket. You don't have to go anywhere until you're ready, sweetie. I'm just so glad you're all right."

"You were fortunate to get away," Ray interjected as Megan picked up Gabrielle's cup and carried it into the kitchen before heading to a linen closet down the hall.

"Someone else might not be so lucky. Now, I'm off duty, and you're Meg's friend, so I'm not gonna force the issue, but you have a responsibility not to let this guy get away with what he did tonight."

"He's not going to hurt anyone else," Gabrielle whispered. And even though they were all talking about the man who'd pulled a gun on her, she couldn't help thinking that they could have been saying the same things about Lucan.

He couldn't remember how he'd gotten back to the compound, or even how long he'd been there. Based on the sweat he'd worked up in the weapons room of the training facility, he had to guess it to be hours.

Lucan hadn't bothered with the lights. His eyes were killing him enough in the dark, anyway. All he needed was the burn of his muscles as he forced them to work, to regain control of his body as his system slowly came down from a high that had been perilously close to Bloodlust.

Lucan reached for one of the daggers on the counter beside him, his fingers testing the razor-sharp edge as he turned back toward the alleylike corridor of the practice range. He could sense, more than see, the target at the end, and when he let the blade loose into the dark, he knew the hard thump meant a dead-center hit.

"Hell, yeah," he murmured, his voice still rough, his fangs not yet receded.

His aim had much improved. He hadn't been a hair off a killing strike in the past several tries with the blades. He wasn't about to quit until he had shaken off the last of the effects of his feeding. That could take a while yet, he thought, still feeling ill from the near overdose of blood he'd consumed.

Lucan strode down the length of the practice range to retrieve his weapon from the target. He pulled the dagger free, noting with satisfaction the deep set of the wound he would have delivered had the target been a Rogue or Minion, and not a practice dummy.

As he turned to start back for another round, there was a soft click somewhere ahead of him in the range, then searing light flooded the length and breadth of the training facility.

Lucan recoiled as his head exploded with the sudden assault. He tried to blink some of his daze away, squinting into the glare of light that bounced off the mirrored walls lining the defense and weapons training section adjacent to the practice range. It was there he saw the large form of another vampire, leaning a thick shoulder against the wall.

One of the warriors had been watching him from out of the shadows.

Tegan.

Jesus. How long had he been standing there?

"Feeling all right?" he asked, apathetic as ever in his dark tee-shirt and loose-fitting jeans. "If the light is too much for you—"

"It's fine," Lucan growled. Stars blinded him as he struggled to adjust to the harsh illumination. He lifted his head and forced himself to meet Tegan's stare across the room. "I was just about to leave, anyway."

Tegan's eyes stayed rooted on him, his gaze too knowing as he stared at Lucan. Tegan's nostrils flared infinitesimally, and the wry twist of his mouth took on an edge of surprise. "You've been hunting tonight. And you're bleeding."

"So?"

"So, it's not like you to take a hit. You're too fast for that, usually."

Lucan exhaled a curse. "You mind not sniffing around my ass right now? I'm not in the mood for company."

"No shit. Feeling a little tense, are we?" Tegan swaggered forward to peruse the weapons laid out for training. He wasn't looking at Lucan now, but he read his torment as if it were spread before him on the table along with the collection of daggers, knives, and various other blades. "Got some aggression you need to work out? Hard to concentrate with all that buzzing in your head, I'll bet. Blood gets running so fast, it's all you can hear. All you can think about is the hunger. Next thing you know, it owns you."

Lucan tested the heft of another blade in his hand, trying to appreciate the tang and balance of the handcrafted dagger. His eyes couldn't focus for longer than a second. His fingers itched to use the weapon for something more than target practice. With a snarl, he cocked his arm back and let the dagger fly down the range. It struck hard in the dummy at the other end, a direct chest shot, right through the heart.

"Get the fuck out of here, Tegan. I don't need the commentary. Or the audience."

"No, you don't like anyone watching you too closely. I'm beginning to see why."

"You don't know dick."

"No?" Tegan stared at him for a long moment, then slowly shook his head, exhaling a low curse. "Be careful, Lucan."

"Jesus Christ," he spat harshly, turning on the vampire in a black rage. "You giving me advice, T?"

"Whatever." The male lifted his shoulders in a negligent shrug. "Maybe it's a warning."

"A warning." Lucan's bark of laughter echoed into the cavernous space. "That's fucking rich. Coming from you."

"You're walking the edge, man. I can see it in your eyes." He shook his head, tawny hair falling down around his face. "The pit is a deep one, Lucan. I'd just hate to see you fall."

"Spare me the concern. You're the last person I need to hear it from."

"Yeah, you've got it all under control, right?"

"That's right."

"You keep telling yourself that, Lucan. Maybe you'll believe it. Because looking at you now, I sure as hell don't."

The accusation spiked Lucan's anger off the chart. In a blur of speed and fury, he fell on the other vampire, fangs bared in a vicious hiss. He didn't even realize he had a blade in his hand until he saw the silver edge of it pressing hard into Tegan's throat. "Get the fuck out of my face. You reading me clearly now?"

"You wanna cut me, Lucan? You need to make me bleed? Do it. Fucking do it, man. I could give a rat's ass."

Lucan threw the dagger down and roared, grabbing two fistsful of Tegan's shirt. Weapons were too easy. He needed to feel flesh and bone under his hands, feel them tearing and cracking, bowing to the beast that was so close to ruling his mind.

"Shit." Tegan started chuckling, his insolent gaze latching onto the frenzied wildness that was surely flashing in Lucan's eyes. "You've already got one foot in the hole. Don't you?"

"Fuck you," Lucan growled to the vampire who had

once, long ago, been a trusted friend. "I should kill you. I should have killed you then."

Tegan didn't so much as flinch from the threat. "You're looking for enemies, Lucan? Then take a look in the mirror. That's the one son of a bitch who's going to beat you every time."

Lucan hauled Tegan around and slammed him against the opposite wall of the training room. The mirrored glass crunched with the impact, shattering outward around Tegan's shoulders and torso like a haloing starburst.

Despite his efforts to deny the truth in what he was hearing, Lucan caught his own savage reflection, replicated a hundred times in the network of broken pieces. He saw the slivered pupils, the glowing irises—a Rogue's eyes—staring back at him. His huge fangs were stretched long in his open mouth, his face contorted into a hideous mask.

He saw everything he hated, everything he had pledged his life to destroy, just like Tegan said he would.

And now, coming through the doors behind him and into the many reflections that had so transfixed him, Lucan saw Nikolai and Dante, their expressions wary as they strode into the training facility.

"Nobody told us we're having a party," Dante drawled, even though the look he shot between the two would-be combatants was anything but casual. "What's going on? Everything cool here?"

A long, tense silence fell over the room.

Lucan released Tegan from the punishing hold, slowly drawing away from him. He lowered his eyes, a knee-jerk reaction meant to shield their wildness from the other warriors. The shame he felt was something new to him. He didn't like the bitter taste of it; he couldn't speak for the bile that rose up from within him.

Finally, Tegan broke the silence. "Yeah," he said, his stare never leaving Lucan's face. "We're cool."

Lucan whirled away from Tegan and the others, his thigh smashing into the table of weapons and sending it into a metallic shudder as he stalked toward the exit.

"Damn, he's jacked up tonight," Niko murmured. "Smells like a fresh kill, too."

As he stepped through the training facility's doors to the hall outside, Lucan heard Dante's quiet reply. "No, man. He smells like overkill."

CHAPTER
Eighteen

More," the human female moaned, draping herself over his lap and arching her neck up under his mouth. She pulled at him with greedy hands at his nape, her eyes drooping as though drugged. "Please...take more of me. I want you to take it all!"

"Perhaps," he promised idly, already growing bored with his pretty toy.

K. Delaney, R.N., had proven entertaining enough sport the first several hours he'd had her in his private quarters, but like all humans gripped by the power of a vampire's draining kiss, she had eventually stopped fighting and now craved an end to her torment. Naked, she writhed against him like a feline in heat, rubbing her bare skin across his lips, whimpering when he refused to give her his fangs.

"Please," she said again, whining now, and beginning to annoy.

He couldn't deny the pleasure he'd taken with her, both in her willing body and the delicious, deeper fulfillment as she Hosted him at her sweet, succulent throat. But he was finished with that now. Finished with her, unless he meant to sap the last of the female's humanity and make her one of his Minion servants.

Not yet. He might decide to play again.

But if he didn't remove himself from her current needy grasping, he might be tempted to drain Nurse K. Delaney past that delicate tipping point and right into death.

He dumped her off his lap without ceremony and rose to his feet.

"No," she complained, "don't go."

He was already crossing the room. The sumptuous folds of his silk robe skated around his calves as he strode out of the bedchamber and into his study across the hall. This room, his secret sanctuary, was filled with every luxury he desired: exquisite furnishings, priceless art and antiques, rugs that had been woven by Persian hands at the height of Earth's religious crusades. All mementoes of his own past, objects collected over countless ages for the pleasure they gave him, and recently brought here, to the New England base of his budding army.

There was another recent artistic acquisition, too.

This one—a series of contemporary photographs—did not please him at all. He stared at the black-and-white images of various Rogue lairs around the city and could not contain his snarl of fury.

"Hey . . . those aren't yours. . . ."

He flicked an irritated glance to where the female now sat, having crawled after him from the other room. She slumped on the palace rug behind him, her face screwed into a little-girl pout. Head lolling on her shoulders and blinking dully as if scarcely able to hold her focus, she was staring at the collection of photographs.

"Oh?" he asked, not really interested in playing games, but curious enough to know what it was about the images that had managed to sink through her muddled head. "Whom do you think they belong to?"

"My friend...they're hers."

His eyebrows rose in response to the innocent revelation. "You know this artist, do you?"

The young woman nodded sluggishly. "My friend... Gabby."

"Gabrielle Maxwell," he said, turning around, his attention distracted truly now. "Tell me about your friend. What is her interest in these places she photographs?"

He had been rolling that question over in his mind since Gabrielle had first come to his attention as an inconvenient witness to a killing carelessly perpetrated by some of his new recruits. He'd been irritated, though not alarmed, to hear about the Maxwell woman from the Minion at the police station. Seeing her inquisitive face on the asylum's closed-circuit security feed hadn't exactly pleased him, either. But it was her apparent attention to documenting vampire locations that piqued a dark sort of interest in him.

He had, until now, been occupied with other, more crucial things that required his attention. He'd been focused elsewhere, and had been satisfied with merely keeping a close eye on Gabrielle Maxwell. Perhaps her interest and activities might bear closer scrutiny. She might, in fact, warrant hard interrogation. Torture, if it pleased him.

"Let's talk about your friend."

His tiresome playmate tossed her head, then flopped back on the rug, throwing out her arms like a petulant child being denied something she wanted. "No...don't talk about her," she murmured, as her hips arched up off the floor. "Come here...kiss me first...talk about me... about us..."

He took a step toward the female, but his intentions were hardly obliging. The slivering of his pupils might have fooled her into thinking he desired her, but it was anger pulsing through his body. There was contempt in his hard grasp as he stood over her and hauled her to her feet before him.

"Yes," she sighed, nearly his to command already.

With the flat of his palm, he guided her head back onto her shoulder, baring the pale column of skin that was still scored and bleeding from his last taste of her. He lapped roughly at the wound, his fangs surging with rage.

"You'll tell me everything I want to know," he whispered, lethal in his control as he stared into her bleary gaze. "From this moment forward, you, Nurse K. Delaney, will do whatever I tell you to do."

He bared his teeth, then struck as fiercely as a viper, draining every last bit of her conscience and her feeble human soul in one savage bite.

Gabrielle made a perimeter check of her apartment, taking care that all the locks on her doors and windows were secure. She had been back home since mid-afternoon, having left Megan's place in the morning after her friend went to work. Meg had offered for her to stay as long as she wanted, but Gabrielle couldn't hide forever, and she hated the idea that she might drag her friend any deeper into a

situation that was becoming more terrifying and unexplainable by the hour.

At first, she'd avoided returning to her apartment and
had walked around the city in a paranoid haze, all but giving in to the rising hysteria. Instinct warned her to prepare
herself for a fight.

One that she knew would be coming sooner than later.

She worried that she'd find Lucan, one of his bloodsucking friends, or something even worse waiting for her
when she arrived home. But it had been broad daylight,
and she'd returned, at last, to find her apartment empty,
not a thing out of place.

Now, as darkness settled outside, her anxieties returned
tenfold.

Wrapping her arms around her cocoon of an oversized
white sweater and jeans, she walked back into the kitchen
where her answering machine was blinking with two new
messages. They were both from Megan. She'd been phon-
ing for the past hour, since her original message about the
body recovered in the playground area where Gabrielle
had been assaulted the night before.

Megan was frantic, telling Gabrielle about the police
report she'd gotten from Ray, describing how her attacker
had apparently been mauled by animals not long after
he'd tried to hurt Gabrielle. And there was more. A police
officer had been murdered in the station; it was his weapon
recovered from the savaged body found on the grounds of
the children's park.

"Gabby, please call me as soon as you get this. I know
you're scared, honey, but the police really need your statement. Ray's about to go on break from duty. He says he
can come and pick you up, if you'd feel safer—"

Gabrielle hit the erase button.

And felt the hairs at the back of her neck begin to rise. She was no longer alone in the kitchen.

Heart lurching into overdrive, she whirled around to face her intruder, not at all surprised to see that it was Lucan. He stood in the door from the living room, watching her in thoughtful silence.

Or maybe he was just sizing up his next meal.

Curiously, Gabrielle realized she wasn't so much afraid of him as she was angry. He looked so normal, even now, standing there in a dark trenchcoat, tailored black pants, and an expensive-looking shirt that was a few shades darker than the mesmerizing silver of his eyes.

There was no trace of the monster she had witnessed last night. Just a man. The dark lover she only thought she knew.

She found herself wishing that he would have shown up with fangs bared and fury sparking in his strangely transformed eyes, as the terror he'd betrayed himself to be last night. It would have been more fair than this outward semblance of normalcy that made her want to pretend everything was all right. That he was actually Detective Lucan Thorne of the Boston Police, a man pledged to protect the innocent and uphold the law.

A man she might have been able to fall in love with—perhaps already was.

But everything about him had been a lie.

"I told myself I wasn't going to come here tonight."

Gabrielle swallowed hard. "I knew you would. I know you followed me last night, after I ran from you."

Something flickered within his penetrating gaze, which held her too intensely. Too much like a caress. "I wouldn't have hurt you. I don't want to hurt you, now."

"Then leave."

He shook his head. Took a step forward. "Not until we've talked."

"You mean, not until you've made sure I won't talk," she replied, trying not to be lulled into complacency simply because he looked like the man she had trusted.

Or because her body—even her idiot heart—responded to him on sight.

"There are things you need to understand, Gabrielle."

"Oh, I do understand," she said, amazed that her voice held no tremor. Her fingers came up near her neck, feeling for the cross pendant she hadn't worn since her first communion. The delicate talisman seemed like ridiculously flimsy armor now that she was standing in front of Lucan, with nothing to separate them except a few strides of his long, muscular legs. "You don't have to explain anything to me. It's taken me a while, granted, but I think I finally understand it all."

"No. You don't." He came toward her, pausing to notice the knot of chalky white bulbs tied above his head in the door of the kitchen. "Garlic," he drawled, and exhaled an amused chuckle.

Gabrielle retreated a pace from him, her Keds squeaking on the kitchen tiles. "I told you, I was expecting you."

And she'd done a bit of other prep work before he arrived. If he looked around, he would find the same threshold decoration in every room of the apartment, including the front door. Not that he seemed to care.

Multiple locks hadn't stopped him and neither had this further attempt at a security measure. He walked under Gabrielle's homemade vampire repellant unfazed, his eyes dark and fixed on her intently.

As he stepped closer, she backed up farther into the kitchen, until the counter came up behind her. A trial-sized mouthwash bottle lay on the polished granite top. It no longer contained Scope but a little something else she had picked up on her way home that morning, when she'd stopped in at St. Mary's for a long overdue confession. Gabrielle grabbed the plastic bottle off the counter and held it close to her chest.

"Holy water?" Lucan asked, coolly meeting her gaze. "What are you going to do with that, throw it on me?"

"If I have to."

He moved so quickly, she saw only a dizzying blur in front of her as he reached out and snatched the small vial out of her grasp and emptied it into his hands. He smoothed his dripping fingers over his face and into his glossy black hair.

Nothing happened.

He tossed the useless container aside and took another step toward her.

"I'm not what you think, Gabrielle."

He sounded so reasonable, she almost believed him. "I saw what you did. You murdered a man, Lucan."

He calmly shook his head. "I killed a human who was no longer a man—hardly human at all, in fact. What had once been human in him was bled out by the vampire who made him into a Minion slave. He was as good as dead already. I merely finished the job. I regret that you had to see it, but I cannot apologize. And I won't. I would kill anyone, human or otherwise, who means to do you harm."

"Which makes you either dangerously overprotective, or just plain psychotic. To say nothing of the fact that you sliced that guy's throat open with your teeth, and drank his blood!"

She waited for another composed reply. Some other rational explanation that might make her consider that even something as unbelievable as vampirism could actually make sense—could actually exist—in the real world.

But Lucan didn't give her any such response.

"This isn't how I wanted things to go between us, Gabrielle. God knows, you deserve better." He muttered something low under his breath, in a language she could not understand. "You deserve to be brought into this gently, by a male who will say the right words, and do the right things for you. That's why I wanted to send Gideon—" He raked his fingers through his hair in a gesture of frustration. "I am no emissary for my race. I am a warrior. At times, an executioner. I deal in death, Gabrielle, and I am not accustomed to making excuses to anyone for my actions."

"I'm not asking you for excuses."

"What, then—the truth?" He gave her a wry smile. "You saw the truth last night when I killed that Minion and drained him dry. That was truth, Gabrielle. That is who I truly am."

She felt a keen sickness in her belly that he hadn't even tried to deny the horror of what he was telling her. "You're a monster, Lucan. My God, you're something out of a nightmare."

"According to human superstitions and folklore, yes. Those same stories would tell you to fight my kind with garlic or holy water—all farce, as you've just seen for yourself. In fact, our races are very closely intertwined. We are not so different from each other."

"Really?" she scoffed, hysteria clutching at her as he took a step closer, forcing her to retreat again. "Last time I checked, cannibalism wasn't high on my to-do list. Then again, neither was screwing the undead, but I seem to be doing that with a bit of regularity lately."

He exhaled a humorless laugh. "I assure you, I am not undead. I breathe, like you. I bleed, like you. I can be killed, though not easily, and I have been living for a long, long time, Gabrielle." He came toward her, closing the small distance that separated them in the kitchen. "I am every bit as alive as you are."

As if to prove it, his warm fingers closed around hers. He brought her hand up between their bodies and pressed her palm against his chest. Through the soft fabric of his shirt, his heart pounded strong and steady. She felt his breath flowing in and out as his lungs expanded and contracted, the warmth of his body seeping into her fingertips, permeating her weary senses like a soothing balm.

"No." She pulled away from him. "No, damn you! No more tricks. I saw your face last night, Lucan. I saw your fangs, your eyes! You said that was who you truly are, so what is this? Everything you present yourself to be now—everything I feel when I am near you—are they illusions?"

"I am real, as I stand here now . . . and as you saw me last night."

"Then show me. Let me see the other you again instead of this one. I want to know what I'm really dealing with, it's only fair."

He scowled as though her mistrust wounded him. "The change cannot be forced. It is a physiological one that comes on with hunger, or during times of intense emotion."

"So, how much of a head start will I have before you decide to rip open my jugular and go for broke? A couple of minutes? A few seconds?"

His eyes flashed at her provocation, but his voice remained level. "I will not hurt you, Gabrielle."

"Then why are you here? To fuck me again, before you turn me into something awful like you?"

"Jesus," he ground out harshly. "That's not how it—"

"Or are you going to make me your personal vampire slave, like that one you killed last night?"

"Gabrielle." Lucan's jaw went rigid, as if his teeth were clenched hard enough to shatter steel. "I came here to protect you, goddamn it! Because I need to know that you are safe. Maybe I'm here because I see that I've made mistakes with you, and I want to try to fix this somehow."

She stood immobile, absorbing his unexpected candor, and watching the play of emotion on his harsh features. Anger, frustration, desire, uncertainty...she read all of it in his penetrating gaze. God help her, but she felt all of that and more churning like a tempest within herself as well.

"I want you to leave, Lucan."

"No, you don't."

"I never want to see you again!" she cried, desperate for him to believe her. She raised her hand to slap him, but he caught her easily, before she could strike. "Please. Just get out of here, now!"

Ignoring her completely, Lucan took the hand that would have lashed out at him, and brought it tenderly to his mouth. His lips parted slowly as he pressed her palm into his hot, sensual kiss. She felt no bite of fangs, only the tender heat of his mouth, the moist caress of his tongue as it teased the sensitive flesh between her fingers.

Her head swam with the delicious feel of his lips on her skin.

Her legs weakened beneath her, her limbs, and her resistance, beginning a slow meltdown that started at her core.

"No," she said, hurling the word at him as she pulled her hand out of his loose grip and shoved him away from her. "No. I can't let you do this to me, not now. Everything between us has changed! It's all different now."

"The only thing different, Gabrielle, is that you see me now with your eyes open."

"Yes." She forced herself to look at him. "And I don't like what I see."

His smile held no mercy whatsoever. "You only wish you could say the same about how I make you feel."

She wasn't sure how he did it—how he could move so fast in the time it took for her to blink—but in that same instant, Lucan's breath was skating close below her ear, his deep voice rumbling along her neck as he pressed his body against hers.

It was too much to process: this terrifying new reality, the questions she didn't even know how to begin asking. And then there was the other disorientation brought on by the exquisite power of Lucan's touch, his voice, his lips softly grazing her tender skin.

"Stop it!" She tried to push him, but he was a wall of muscle and cool, dark purpose. He withstood her anger, and the futile blows she threw at his massive chest didn't seem to faze him in the least. His placid expression remained as unmoving as his body. She backed away from him in frustration, in anguish. "God, what are you trying to prove here, Lucan?"

"Only that I am not the monster you want to believe I am. Your body knows me. Your senses tell you that you are safe with me. You need only listen to them, Gabrielle. And listen to me, when I tell you that I did not come here to frighten you. I will never strike you, nor will I ever take your blood. On my honor, I will never harm you."

She let out a choked laugh, a knee-jerk reaction to the idea of a vampire possessing anything close to honor, let alone pledging it to her now. But Lucan was unwavering, solemn. Maybe she was crazy, because the longer she held his silver stare, the weaker her grasp on the doubt she wanted so desperately to cling to.

"I am not your enemy, Gabrielle. For centuries, my kind and yours have needed each other to survive."

"You feed on us," she whispered brokenly, "like parasites."

Something dark moved across his features, but he did not rise to the contempt in her accusation. "We have protected you as well. Some of my kind have even cherished yours, sharing life together as blood-bonded mates. It is the only way the vampire race continues. Without human females to bear our young, we would eventually be extinct. It is how I came to be, and how all those like me came into being as well."

"I don't understand. Why can't you...mix with women of your own kind?"

"Because there are none. Through a genetic failure, Breed offspring are solely male, from the very first of the line, down through hundreds of generations."

This last revelation, among all the other astonishing news she was hearing, gave her pause. "So, that means your mother is human?"

Lucan gave a slight nod. "She was."

"And your father? He was..."

Before she could say the word vampire, Lucan replied. "My father, and the seven other Ancient Ones like him, were not of this world. They were the first of my kind, beings from another place, very different from this planet."

It took her a second to absorb what she had heard, particularly on the heels of everything else she was coming to grips with at the moment. "What are you saying—they were aliens?"

"They were explorers. Savage, warminded conquerors, in fact, who crash-landed here a very long time ago."

Gabrielle stared at him. "Your father was not only a vampire, but an alien besides? Do you have any idea how insane that sounds?"

"It is the truth. My father's people did not call themselves vampires but, by human definition, that is what they were. Their digestive systems were too advanced for Earth's crude protein. They could not process the plants or animals as humans did, so they learned to take their nourishment from blood. They fed without restraint and wiped out entire populations in the process. You've heard of some of them, no doubt: Atlantis. The Mayan kingdom. Countless other unnamed, unrecorded civilizations that vanished seemingly overnight. Many of the mass deaths historically attributed to plagues and famine were not that at all."

Good Lord.

"Assuming you can be taken seriously about any of this, you're talking about thousands of years of carnage." A chill spread over her limbs when he said nothing to deny it. "Do they they...do you—God, I can't believe I'm having this conversation. Do vampires feed on any living thing, like each other maybe, or are we humans the main course?"

Lucan's expression was grave. "Human blood alone contains the specific combinations of nutrients we need in order to survive."

"How often?"

"We must feed every few days, a week sometimes. More

is required if we are injured and need strength to heal from wounds."

"And you . . . kill when you feed?"

"Not always, seldom, in fact. Most of the race feeds from willing human Hosts."

"People actually volunteer to let you torture them?" she asked, incredulous.

"There is no torture involved, unless we will it. When a human is relaxed, the bite of a vampire can be very plea- surable. When it's over, the Host recalls nothing because we leave no memory of ourselves behind."

"But you do kill sometimes," she said, finding it hard not to sound accusing.

"At times, it is necessary to take a life. The Breed shares an oath never to prey on the innocent or infirm."

She scoffed. "How noble of you."

"It is noble, Gabrielle. If we wanted to—if we gave ourselves over to that part of us that is still the warring con- queror of our forebears, we could enslave all of mankind. We could be kings, with every human existing only to feed and amuse us. That very idea is at the core of a long, deadly battle between my kind and our enemy brothers, the Rogues. You saw some of them yourself, that night out- side the dance club."

"You were there?"

As soon as she said it, she knew he had been. She re- called the striking face and sunglass-shaded eyes that had watched her through the crowd. She'd felt a connection to him even then, in that brief glance that had seemed to reach out to her through the smoke and darkness of the club.

"I'd been tracking that group of Rogues for about an

hour," Lucan said, "watching for the prime opportunity to move in and take them out."

"There were six of them," she remembered vividly, seeing in her mind the half-dozen terrible faces, their glowing, feral eyes and snapping fangs. "You were going to confront them by yourself?"

His shrug seemed to say that it was not unusual odds, him against many. "I had some help that night—you and your cell phone camera. The flash surprised them, gave me the chance to strike."

"You killed them?"

"All but one. I'll get him, too."

Looking at his fierce expression, Gabrielle had no doubt that he would. "The cops sent a squad car out to the club after I reported the killing. They didn't find anything. No evidence at all."

"I made sure they wouldn't."

"You made me look like a fool. The police insisted I was making all of it up."

"Better that, than tipping them off to the very real battles that have been taking place on human streets for centuries. Can you imagine the wide-scale panic if substantiated reports of vampire attacks were to start making news around the world?"

"Is that what's happening? These kinds of killings are going on all the time, everywhere?"

"More and more, lately. The Rogues are a faction of blood addicts that care only about their next fix. At least, that had been their mode until very recently. Something's going on now. They're preparing. Becoming organized. They've never been more dangerous than they are now."

"And thanks to the pictures I took outside that club, these Rogue vampires are coming after me."

"The incident you witnessed brought you to their attention, no doubt, and any human makes good sport for them. But it is the other pictures you've taken that have likely put you in the most jeopardy."

"What other pictures?"

"That one."

He indicated a framed photograph hanging on the wall of her living room. It was an exterior shot of an old warehouse in one of the sketchier parts of town.

"What made you decide to photograph that building?"

"I don't know, exactly," she said, not even sure why she had decided to frame the picture. Just looking at it now gave her a little chill down her spine. "I never would have set foot in that part of town, but I remember I'd taken a wrong turn that night and ended up lost. Something just drew my eye to the warehouse—nothing I can really explain. I was nervous as hell to be there, but I couldn't leave without taking a few shots of the place."

Lucan's voice was gravely serious. "I, along with several other Breed warriors who work with me, raided that location a month and a half ago. It was a Rogue lair, housing fifteen of our enemies."

Gabrielle gaped at him. "There are vampires living in that building?"

"Not anymore." He strode past her to the kitchen table, where a few other shots lay, including some from the abandoned asylum, taken just a couple of days ago. He picked up one of the photographs and held it out to her. "We've been surveilling this location for weeks. We have reason to believe it might be one of the largest colonies of Rogues in New England."

"Oh, my God." Gabrielle stared at the image of the asylum, a slight tremble in her fingers as she set it back down on the table. "When I took these pictures the other morning, a man found me there. He chased me off the property. You don't think he was—"

Lucan shook his head. "Minion, not a vampire, if you saw him after dawn. Sunlight is poison to us. That much of the old folklore is true. Our skin burns quickly, like yours would if you held it under a very powerful magnifying glass at the height of morning."

"Which is why I've only seen you in the evening," she murmured, thinking back on each of Lucan's visits, from that very first time when he began his deception with her. "How could I have been so blind when all the clues were right in front of me?"

"Maybe you didn't want to see them, but you knew, Gabrielle. You suspected that the slaying you witnessed was something more than what your human experiences could explain. You nearly said as much to me, the first time we met. On some level of your consciousness, you knew it was a vampire attack."

She did know, even then. But she had not suspected that Lucan was a part of it. Part of her still wanted to reject the idea.

"How can this be real?" she moaned, dropping into the nearest chair. She stared at the pictures scattered on the table in front of her, then looked back up at Lucan's grim face. Tears threatened, burning in her eyes, a knot of desperate denial forming in her throat. "This can't be real. God, please tell me that this is not really happening."

CHAPTER
Nineteen

He had laid a lot on her to deal with—not everything, but more than enough for one night.

Lucan had to give Gabrielle credit. Aside from a bit of irrationality with the garlic and holy water, she had maintained an amazingly level head through a conversation that was, no doubt, pretty hard to swallow. Vampires, ancient alien arrivals, the rising war with the Rogues, who, by the way, were gunning for her now, too.

She had taken it all in with a stalwartness that most human men would not possess.

Lucan watched her struggling to process the information as she sat at the table with her head in her hands, stray tears only just beginning to stream down her cheeks. He wished there was a way to make her path easier. There wasn't. And things were going to go from bad to worse for her, once she learned the full truth of what lay ahead of her.

For her own safety and that of the Breed, she was going to have to leave her apartment, her friends, her career. Leave behind everything that had been a part of her life so far.

And she was going to have to do it tonight.

"If you have any other photographs like these, Gabrielle, I need to see them."

She nodded, lifting her head. "I have everything on my computer," she said, pushing her hair out of her face.

"What about the ones in the darkroom?"

"They're on disk, too, along with every image I've sold through the gallery."

"Good." Her mention of art sales tripped an alarm in his memory. "When I was here a few nights ago, you mentioned having sold an entire collection to someone. Who was it?"

"I don't know. It was an anonymous purchase. The buyer arranged a private showing in a rented penthouse suite downtown. They looked at a few images, then paid cash for all of them."

He swore and Gabrielle's already stressed expression slipped toward true terror.

"Oh, my God. Are you thinking it was the Rogues who bought them?"

What Lucan was thinking was that if he were the one standing at the helm of the Rogues' current operation, he would be most interested in acquiring a weapon that could home in on his opponents' locations. To say nothing of crippling his enemies' ability to use said weapon for their own gain.

Gabrielle would be an extraordinary asset in Rogue

hands, for many reasons. And once they had her in their possession, it wouldn't take them long to discover her Breedmate mark. She would be abused like the meanest brood mare, forced to take their blood and bear their spawn until her body simply gave out and died. It could take years, decades, centuries.

"Lucan, my best friend took those photographs into the showing that night, by himself. It would have killed me if anything had happened to him. Jamie walked in there without knowing anything about the danger he was in."

"Be glad for that, because it's probably the only reason he walked out alive."

She recoiled as if he'd slapped her. "I don't want my friends getting hurt because of what's happening to me."

"You're in more danger than anyone right now. And we need to get moving. Let's download those pictures off your computer. I want to take all of them into the lab at the compound."

Gabrielle led him over to a neat corner desk in her living room. She powered up the desktop workstation and as it cycled through its startup, she pulled a couple of flash memory sticks out of their store packaging and popped one into the computer's USB drive.

"You know, they said she was crazy. They called her delusional, a paranoid schizophrenic. They locked her away for believing she had been attacked by vampires." Gabrielle laughed softly, but it was a sad, empty sound. "Maybe she wasn't crazy after all."

Behind her, Lucan moved closer. "Who would that be?"

"My birth mother." After beginning the copying procedure, Gabrielle spun around in her chair to look up at Lucan. "She was found late one night in Boston, injured, bloody, disoriented. She didn't have a wallet or purse, or any kind of ID on her, and in the brief periods when she was lucid, she couldn't tell anyone who she was so the police processed her as a Jane Doe. She was just a teenager."

"She was bleeding, you say?"

"Multiple throat lacerations—presumably self-inflicted, according to the official records. The courts deemed her incompetent to stand trial and locked her away in a mental institution once she was released from the hospital."

"Jesus."

She gave a slow shake of her head. "But what if everything she said was true? What if she wasn't crazy at all? Oh, God, Lucan...all these years, I've blamed her. I think I've hated her, even, and now I can't help but think—"

"You said the police and the courts processed her. You mean, for some kind of crime?"

The computer beeped to indicate the memory stick was full. Gabrielle turned back to continue with the next copying function, and she stayed there, giving him her back. Lucan put his hands down gently on her shoulders and brought the swivel chair back around.

"What was your mother charged with?"

For a long moment, Gabrielle didn't say anything. Lucan saw her throat working. There was a great deal of hurt in her soft brown eyes. "She was charged with abandoning her child."

"How old were you?"

She shrugged, shook her head. "Young. An infant. She stuffed me in a trash bin outside an apartment building. It was only about a block from where the police picked her up. Fortunately for me, one of the cops decided to check the surrounding area. He heard my crying, I guess, and took me out of there."

Holy Christ.

A jolt of recollection flashed hard in Lucan's mind as she spoke. He saw a dark street, wet pavement gleaming in the moonlight, a wide-eyed female standing in transfixed horror as a Rogue vampire sucked at her throat. He heard the shrill wailing of the tiny baby nestled in the young mother's arms.

"When did this happen?"

"A long time ago. Twenty-seven years ago this summer, to be exact."

To one of Lucan's age, twenty-seven years ago was a blink of time. He clearly remembered interrupting the attack at the bus station. Recalled stepping between the Rogue and its prey, sending the terrified female off with a stern mental command. She'd been bleeding profusely, some of it raining down on her baby.

After he'd killed the Rogue and cleared the scene, he had gone to look for the woman and her child. He hadn't found them. He'd often wondered what had happened to the both of them, and cursed himself for not having been able to at least remove the horrific memories of the assault from the victim's mind.

"She committed suicide in the mental facility not long afterward," Gabrielle said. "I was already a ward of the state."

He couldn't stop himself from touching her. Gently sweeping aside her long hair, he cupped the delicate line of her jaw, stroked the proud lift of her chin. Her eyes were moist, but she didn't crack. She was a tough one, all right. Tough and beautiful and so incredibly special.

In that moment, he wanted nothing more than to pull her into his arms and tell her as much.

"I'm sorry," he said, meaning it with utmost sincerity.

And regret, something he wasn't used to feeling. But, then, since he'd first laid eyes on her, Gabrielle made him feel a lot of things that were entirely new to him. "I'm sorry for both of you."

The computer beeped again.

"That's all of them," she said, reaching up as if she might stroke his hand, but couldn't quite bring herself to touch him yet.

He let her back out of his caress and felt a sharp pang of remorse for the way she silently turned away.

Shutting him out like the new stranger he was.

He watched her remove the last memory stick and place it with the other. When she began to close the application, Lucan said, "Not yet. I need you to delete the image files from the computer and from any backups you might have. The copies we take out of here have to be the only ones remaining."

"What about print copies? The ones on the table there, the ones I have downstairs in my darkroom?"

"You wrap up here. I'll get the prints."

"Okay."

She got right to work, and Lucan made a quick sweep of the rest of the apartment. He gathered all the loose snapshots and took down her framed images as well, wanting to leave nothing behind that could be of use to the Rogues. He found a large duffel bag in Gabrielle's bedroom closet and brought it downstairs to load it up.

As he finished packing and zipping the bag closed, he heard the low rumble of a muscle car coming to a stop outside the townhouse. Two doors opened, then slammed shut, followed by urgent footsteps coming toward the apartment.

"Someone's here," Gabrielle said, sending him a stark look as she shut down her computer.

Lucan's hand was already inside his trenchcoat and snaked around to the base of his spine, where a custom Beretta 9mm was tucked into the back waistband of his pants. The gun was loaded with maximum blast, Rogue-smoking, titanium rounds—one of Niko's latest innovations. If a Rogue stood outside that door, the Bloodlusting son of a bitch was about to get a belly full of hurt.

But it wasn't Rogues, he realized at once. Not even Minions, which also would have given Lucan a bit of satisfaction in blowing away.

There were humans on the front stoop. A man and a woman.

"Gabrielle?" The doorbell rang several times in rapid succession. "Hello? Gabby! Are you in there?"

"Oh, no. It's my friend Megan."

"The one you went to last night?"

"Yes. She's been calling here most of the day, leaving messages. She's worried about me."

"What did you tell her?"

"She knows about the assault in the park. I told her how I was attacked, but I didn't tell her anything about you . . . what you did."

"Why not?"

Gabrielle shrugged. "I didn't want her involved. I don't want her to be put in any danger because of me. Because of all this." She sighed, shaking her head. "Maybe I didn't want to say anything about you until I had some answers for myself."

The doorbell rang again. "Gabby, open up! Ray and I need to talk to you. We need to know that you're okay."

"Her boyfriend's a cop," Gabrielle said softly. "They want me to file a report about what happened last night."

"Is there a back way out of here?"

She nodded, then seemed to change her mind and shook her head. "The slider opens onto a shared backyard, but there's a tall fence—"

"No time," Lucan said, discarding the option. "Go to the door. Let your friends come in."

"What are you going to do?" She saw that his hand had just slipped back out of his trenchcoat, easing off the weapon concealed behind him. Panic flooded into her expression. "Do you have a gun back there? Lucan, they won't do anything to you. I'll make sure they don't say anything."

"I won't have to use the weapon on them."

"Then what will you do?" After so deliberately avoiding any physical contact with him, now she finally did touch him, her small hands clutching at his arm. "God, please tell me you won't hurt them—"

"Open the door, Gabrielle."

Her legs moved sluggishly beneath her as she approached the front door. She twisted the deadbolt and heard Megan's voice on the other side.

"She's in there, Ray. She's at the door. Gabby, open up, honey! Are you all right?"

Gabrielle slid the chain free, saying nothing. Not sure whether she should assure her friend that she was okay, or shout for Megan and Ray to get the hell out of there.

A look behind her at Lucan gave her no indication either way. His sharp features were emotionless and still. His silver eyes were rooted on the door, cool and unblinking.

His powerful hands were empty, down at his sides, but Gabrielle knew he could spring into motion with no warning at all.

If he wanted to kill her friends—even her, for that matter—it would be done before any of them knew to take the first breath.

"Let them in," he told her in a low growl.

Gabrielle slowly turned the knob.

The door was barely open a crack before Megan pushed inside, her boyfriend, still in uniform, right behind her.

"Holy shit, Gabby! Do you have any idea how worried I've been? Why haven't you returned my calls?" She pulled her into a fierce hug, then released her, only to frown at Gabrielle like a frantic mother hen. "You look tired. Have you been crying? Where have you—"

Megan broke off abruptly, her eyes, and Ray's, catching a sudden glimpse of Lucan in the middle of the living room behind Gabrielle.

"Oh...I didn't realize you had someone here...."

"Everything okay here?" Ray asked, stepping past the two women and letting his hand rest lightly on his holstered weapon.

"Fine. Everything's fine," Gabrielle quickly replied. She held her hand out toward Lucan. "This is, uh...a friend of mine."

"Going somewhere?" Megan's boyfriend strolled forward, and gestured to the stuffed duffel bag that lay on the floor beside Lucan's feet.

"Um, yeah," Gabrielle interjected, walking swiftly past Ray and putting herself between him and Lucan. "I've been a little shaken up tonight. I thought I'd go to a hotel and chill out. Lucan stopped by to give me a ride."

"Huh." Ray was trying to peer around her to where Lucan remained rudely stoic and silent. Lucan's scathing stare said he had already sized up the young cop—and dismissed him in that same instant.

"I wish you hadn't come, you guys," Gabrielle said. And that was the God's honest truth. "Really, you don't have to stay."

Megan walked over and took Gabrielle's hand protectively in hers. "Ray and I were hoping you'd consider coming with us to the police station, honey. It's important. I'm sure your friend would agree with us. You're the detective Gabby's mentioned, right? I'm Meg."

Lucan shifted a step. The small movement brought him right up in front of Megan and Ray. It was such a slight flex of muscle, so fast, time seemed to slow around him. Gabrielle saw him take those handful of impossibly quick strides, but her friends blinked and found Lucan standing in their faces, crowding them with his massive size and a menace that vibrated in the air around him.

Without any warning at all, he lifted his right hand and took Megan by the forehead.

"Lucan, no!"

Meg cried out, a half-uttered noise that died in her throat as she stared into Lucan's eyes. With viper speed, he reached out with his left hand and clamped Ray in a similar hold. The officer struggled for a mere second before his face drooped into a trancelike stupor. Lucan's strong, clutching fingers seemed to be all that was holding the pair upright.

"Lucan, please! I'm begging you!"

"Get the memory sticks and the duffel bag," he told her, his voice calm. Coldly commanding. "I have a car waiting outside. Get in, and wait for me. I'll be right out."

"I'm not going leave you here to bleed my friends dry."

"If that had been my intent, they'd already be dead on the floor."

He was right. God, but she had no doubt that this man—this dark being she had admitted into her life—was dangerous enough to do just that.

But he hadn't. And he wouldn't; she trusted that much about him.

"The pictures, Gabrielle. Now."

She jolted into action, hefting the bulky duffel bag over her shoulder and dropping the two flash drives into the front pocket of her jeans. On the way out, she paused to look at Megan's blank face. Her eyes were closed now, as were Ray's. Lucan was murmuring something to them in a voice so low she could hardly hear it.

The tone of his words didn't sound threatening, but oddly soothing, persuasive. Almost lulling.

With one last glance at the bizarre scene taking place in her living room, Gabrielle dashed out the open front door and down onto the street. A sleek sedan waited at the curb, parallel parked in front of Ray's red Mustang. It was an expensive vehicle—incredibly expensive, from the looks of it—and the only other car around.

As she approached, the front passenger door opened as if it had been willed to do so.

Willed by the sheer strength of Lucan's mind, she knew, wondering just how far his preternatural powers might reach.

She slid into the deep leather seat and closed the door. Not two seconds later, Megan and Ray appeared on her front stoop. They calmly walked down the steps and right past her on the sidewalk, eyes straight ahead of them, neither of them saying a word.

Lucan was directly behind them. He closed the apartment door and came around the car where Gabrielle waited. He climbed in, stuck a key in the ignition, and started the Maybach's engine.

"Not a good idea to leave these behind," he said, dropping her purse and camera bag into her lap.

Gabrielle stared at him across the subtly lit cockpit of the vehicle. "You did some kind of mind control on them, like you've tried to do with me before."

"I suggested to your friends that they had never been at your apartment tonight."

"You erased their memory?"

He inclined his head in a vague nod. "They won't recall anything about this evening, or your having been at Megan's apartment last night after the Minion's attack on you. Their minds are no longer burdened with any of it."

"You know, right now, that sounds pretty damn good. So, what do you say, Lucan? Will you do me next? You can start erasing right before I made the terrible decision to go to that nightclub a couple of weeks ago."

He held her gaze, but she didn't feel him so much as trying to get into her head. "You aren't like those two humans, Gabrielle. Even if I wanted to, I couldn't change any of the things that have happened to you. Your mind is stronger than most. In many ways, you are...different from most."

"Gee, I feel so lucky."

"The best place for you now is with us, where the Breed will protect you as one of our own. We have a secured compound in the city. You can stay there to start."

She frowned. "What, you're offering me the vampire equivalent of the Witness Protection Program?"

"It's a bit more than that." He turned his head, looking out through the windshield. "And it is the only way."

Lucan hit the gas and the sleek black car shot up the narrow road with a low, silky growl. Clutching the leather seat on the passenger side, Gabrielle swung her head around to watch as darkness slowly swallowed up her residential block on Willow Street.

As the distance grew wider, she saw the vague silhouettes of Megan and Ray getting into his Mustang to leave her apartment, none the wiser. Gabrielle felt a sudden jolt of panic that made her want to leap out of the car and run back to them, back to her old life.

Too late.

She knew that.

This new reality had her in a tight grasp, and she didn't think there would be any turning back, only a steady march forward. She turned away from the rear window and sank into the seat's butter-soft leather, staring straight ahead as Lucan wheeled sharply around the corner and drove her deep into the night.

CHAPTER
Twenty

She didn't know how long they'd been driving, or even in what direction. They were still in the city, that much she could tell, but the many turns and back alley routes that Lucan took had since become a jumble in Gabrielle's mind. She stared out the dark-tinted window of the sedan, vaguely aware that they were slowing down at last, approaching what appeared to be the expansive grounds of an old estate.

Lucan braked outside a tall, black-iron gate. Twin beams of red light shot down from a pair of small devices perched on both sides of the high-security perimeter fence. Gabrielle blinked away the sudden shot of light that flashed in front of her face, then watched as the heavy gate began to slide open.

"This is yours?" she asked, turning to speak to Lucan

for the first time since they'd left her apartment. "I've been here before. I took a photograph of this gate."

They rolled through, then up a long, curving, tree-lined driveway.

"The estate is part of our compound. It belongs to the Breed."

Evidently, being a vampire was quite lucrative. Even in the dark, Gabrielle could see the old-money quality of the well-tended grounds and the ornately carved limestone work on the pale façade of the mansion as they approached. Double rotundas flanked the lacquered black doors and soaring portico of the main entrance, above which rose four elegant stories.

Ambient light glowed from many of the arched windows, but Gabrielle hesitated to call the effect welcoming. The mansion loomed like a watchful sentry in the gloom of the surrounding night, stoic and forbidding, with its collection of snarling gargoyles that stared down from the roof and twin balconies overlooking the drive.

Lucan wheeled past the front entrance and around to a large hangar in the back. A gate lifted, and he rolled the purring Maybach to a stop inside, then cut the engine. A row of lights went on as the two of them climbed out of the car, the soft clicks of motion sensors illuminating a fleet of glossy, high-end machinery.

Gabrielle gaped in astonishment. Between the Maybach, which cost about as much as her modest Beacon Hill condo, and the collection of cars, SUVs, and motorcycles, she had to be looking at millions of dollars' worth of vehicles. Multimillions.

"This way," Lucan said, the duffel bag of photographs gripped in his hand as he guided her past the impressive fleet to an unmarked door near the back of the garage.

"Just how rich are you people?" she asked, trailing after him in amazement.

Lucan gestured for her to enter as the door opened then he followed her inside the elevator and pushed a button on the console. "Some members of the vampire nation have been around a very long time. We've learned a few things about managing our money wisely."

"Uh-huh," she said, feeling a little off balance as the elevator began a smooth but swift descent, down, and down, and down. "How do you keep all of this hidden from the public? What about the government and taxes? Or are you strictly a cash-and-carry operation?"

"The public can't get past our security, even if they tried. The entire perimeter of the grounds is wired. Anyone foolish enough to get close to the compound would get a fourteen-thousand-volt ass kicking and a mind scrub. We pay our taxes—through fronted corporations, of course. Our properties around the world are owned by private trusts. Everything the Breed does is legit and aboveboard."

"Legit and aboveboard. Right." She laughed, a bit nervously. "Just nevermind all the bloodsucking or the extraterrestrial lineage."

Lucan leveled a dark glance on her, but she was relieved to see the corner of his mouth lift in something that might have passed for a smile.

"I'll take the backups now," he said, his penetratingly clear gray eyes watching her as she dug the memory sticks out of her jeans pocket and placed them in his hand.

He let his fingers close around hers for a second. Gabrielle felt heat in his touch, but she didn't want to acknowledge it. She didn't want to admit what just the slightest brush of his skin made her feel, even now.

Especially now.

The elevator finally came to a stop, and the door slid open to reveal a pristine room constructed of glass walls reinforced with gleaming metal frames. The floor was white marble, inlaid with a series of geometric symbols and interlocking designs. She recognized some of the designs as similar to the ones that Lucan bore on his body—those strange, beautiful tattoos that covered his back and torso.

No, not tattoos, she realized now, but something . . . else.

Vampire markings.

On his skin, and here, in this underground bunker where he lived.

Beyond the elevator, a corridor stretched and wended along a path that must have been several hundred yards long. Lucan paused to look at Gabrielle when she hesitated to follow him.

"You're safe here," he said, and God help her, but she actually believed him.

She walked out onto the snowy marble with Lucan, holding her breath as he placed his palm against an authentication panel and the glass doors ahead of him opened. Cool air bathed Gabrielle and she could hear a muffled rumble of male voices talking somewhere down the hall. Lucan led her toward the deep rhythm of conversation, his long stride sharp and purposeful.

He paused in front of another glass door, and as Gabrielle drew next to him, she saw what appeared to be a control room of sorts. There were monitors and computers lining a long, U-shaped console, digital readers flashing some kind of coordinates from another bank of equipment, and in the center of it all, moving on his rolling chair between the many workstations like a concert maestro, was a geeky-looking young man, his cropped blond hair spiked around his head in amusing disarray. He glanced up, crisp blue eyes registering a greeting, and then mild surprise, as the door slid open and Lucan strode inside with Gabrielle beside him.

"Gideon," Lucan said, inclining his head in a nod.

So, this was the associate he had spoken of, Gabrielle thought, noting the easy smile and friendly demeanor of the other man. He got up from his chair and nodded his head at Lucan and then at Gabrielle.

Gideon was tall and lean, with boyish good looks and obvious charm. Nothing like Lucan. Nothing at all like she would imagine a vampire to be, not that she had a lot of experience in that area.

"Is he—"

"Yes," Lucan answered, before she could whisper the rest of her question. He put the duffel bag down on a table. "Gideon is of the Breed. As are the others."

It was then that Gabrielle noticed the conversation she'd heard in the room on their approach had since gone silent.

She felt more eyes on her from somewhere at her back, and as she turned to face the source of the sensation, all the breath seemed to be sucked from her lungs. Three large men occupied the space behind her: one in dark, tailored pants and a loose silk shirt, elegantly sprawled in a leather club chair; another wearing head-to-toe black leather, thick arms crossed over his chest as he leaned against the back wall; and the last, in jeans and a white tee-shirt, was hunched over a table where he'd been cleaning the disassembled parts of some complicated type of handgun.

They were all staring at her.

"Dante," Lucan said, indicating the broody one in leather, who gave her a slight nod of greeting—or maybe it was more of a male appraisal, based on the lift of his dark brows as his sly gaze returned to Lucan.

"The gearhead over there is Nikolai." At Lucan's introduction, the sandy-haired male offered Gabrielle a quick smile. He had starkly cut features, amazing cheekbones, and a strong, stubborn jaw. Even as he looked at her, his nimble fingers were working flawlessly on the weapon, as if he knew the components of the piece instinctually.

"And that's Rio," Lucan said, turning her attention to the smolderingly handsome one with the immaculate sense of style. From his casual lounge in the chair, he sent her a dazzling smile that oozed with innate sex appeal, with an unmistakable current of danger behind his topaz-colored eyes.

That threat emanated from each of them, their muscular builds and unconcealed weapons giving the distinct warning that despite their relaxed appearances here, these were men accustomed to battle. They might even thrive on it.

Lucan placed his hand on the small of Gabrielle's back, startling her with the sudden contact as he brought her closer to him before these three other males. She wasn't totally sure she trusted him yet, but as it stood, he was her sole ally in a room full of armed vampires.

"This is Gabrielle Maxwell. For the time being, she will be staying at the compound."

He left the statement hanging without further explanation, as if he dared any one of the lethal-looking men to question him. None did. Watching Lucan, a commanding force in the midst of so much dark strength and power,

Gabrielle realized that he was not merely one of these warriors.

He was their leader.

Gideon was the first to speak. He had come around from behind the computers and monitors and offered Gabrielle his hand. "Good to meet you," he said, his voice tinged with a vaguely English accent. "Fast thinking, getting those cell pictures of the attack you witnessed. They've been a big help to us."

"Um, no problem."

She briefly shook his hand, surprised to find him so personable. So normal.

But then, Lucan had seemed relatively normal to her as well, and look how that turned out. At least he hadn't been lying entirely when he told her he'd taken her cell phone into the lab for analysis. He'd only neglected to tell her it was a vampire CSI lab, and not the Boston police.

A loud beep sounded from the bank of computers nearby, spurring Gideon into a quick jog back to his monitors.

"Yes! You beautiful bucket of bolts," he shouted, dropping into a spin in his chair. "Guys, you'll want to see this. Especially you, Niko."

Lucan and the other warriors gathered around the monitor that bathed Gideon's face in a pale blue glow. Gabrielle, feeling a bit awkward standing alone in the center of the room, slowly trailed over as well.

"I just hacked into the security feeds over at the T," Gideon said. "Now, let's see if we can get some footage from the other night, maybe find out what the bastard who took out Conlan was really about."

Gabrielle watched quietly from the periphery as several computer screens filled with closed-circuit images from a handful of the city's train platforms, the feed scrolling by in fast-forward motion. Gideon rolled his chair along the line of workstations, pausing to type commands onto several of the keyboards before continuing on to the next, and then the next. Finally, his frenetic energy came to a halt.

"Okay, here we go. Green Line, coming up." He backed away from the monitor in front of him, allowing the others a clear view. "This is footage of the platform beginning three minutes before the confrontation."

Lucan and the others closed in as the feed displayed an influx of people pouring on and off the train. Peering between the massive sets of shoulders, Gabrielle caught the now familiar face of Nikolai on the monitor screen as he and his companion, a menacingly large male outfitted in dark leather, strode onto the commuter car. They had hardly gotten seated before one of the other passengers caught the attention of Nikolai's companion. The two warriors stood up, and just before the doors closed for departure, the guy they'd been watching suddenly leaped out of the car and onto the platform. Onscreen, Nikolai and the other man jumped to their feet, but Gabrielle's attention was rooted on the person they meant to follow.

"Oh, my God," she gasped. "I know that guy."

Five pairs of hard male eyes turned toward her in question.

"I mean, I don't know him personally, but I've seen him before. I know his name. It's Brent—at least, that's what he told my friend Kendra. She met him at the dance club the night I witnessed the killing. She's been seeing him every night since, pretty seriously, in fact."

"You're certain?" Lucan asked.

"Yes. That's him, I'm positive."

The warrior called Dante hissed a violent oath.

"He's a Rogue," Lucan said. "Or rather, was. A couple of nights ago, he walked onto the Green Line train wearing a belt of explosives. Niko and another of our brethren chased him down an old track. He blew himself up before they could take him out. One of our best warriors died with him."

"Oh, God. You mean that unexplained explosion I heard about on the news?" She looked at Nikolai, whose hard jaw was clamped tight. "I'm very sorry."

"If not for Conlan throwing himself on that suckhead coward, I wouldn't be standing here. That's for damn sure."

Gabrielle was truly saddened for the loss Lucan and his men had suffered, but a new dread had lodged itself in her chest when she thought of how close her friend had come to the kind of evil Brent had apparently delivered.

What if Kendra was hurt? What if he had done something to her, and she needed help?

"I have to call her." Gabrielle started digging in her purse for her cell phone. "I have to call Kendra right now and make sure she's all right."

Lucan's hand clamped down around her wrist, firmly yet beseechingly. "I'm sorry, Gabrielle. I can't let you do that."

"She's my friend, Lucan. And I'm sorry, but you can't stop me."

Gabrielle flipped open the phone, more resolved than ever to make the call. Before she could dial Kendra's number, the device flew from her fingers and appeared in Lucan's hand. He closed it, then slipped the phone into his jacket pocket.

"Gideon," he said conversationally, even while his steely gaze remained locked on Gabrielle. "Ask Savannah to come and see Gabrielle to more comfortable quarters while we finish here. Get her something to eat."

"Give it back to me," Gabrielle said, ignoring the current of surprise that ran through the other men when she challenged Lucan's attempt to control her. "I need to know that she's okay, Lucan."

He came toward her, and for a second she feared what he might do to her as he reached out to touch her face. In front of the others, he stroked her cheek tenderly, possessively. He spoke softly. "Your friend's well-being is out of your hands. If she's not yet been bled dry by this Rogue—and believe me, that's a very real possibility—then he poses no further danger to her now."

"But what if he did something to her? What if he turned her into one of those Minions?"

Lucan shook his head. "Only the most powerful of our kind can create Minions. That gutter trash who blew himself up in the tunnel was incapable. He was nothing but an expendable pawn."

Gabrielle moved out of his caress despite the comfort his touch gave her. "What if that's how he saw Kendra? What if he turned her over to someone who does have more power than him?"

Lucan's expression was grim, but unwavering. His tone was as gentle as she'd ever heard it, which only made his words harder to accept. "Then you should forget her entirely, because she is already as good as dead."

CHAPTER
Twenty-one

I hope the tea isn't too strong. If you'd like a little milk in it, I can get you some from the kitchen."

Gabrielle smiled, truly warmed by the hospitality of Gideon's mate. "The tea is perfect, thank you."

She had been surprised to learn that there were other women in the compound, and felt she'd made an instant friend in the beautiful Savannah. As soon as she'd arrived to fetch Gabrielle on Lucan's order, Savannah had gone to great lengths to ensure that Gabrielle was comfortable and relaxed.

As relaxed as she could be, at any rate, surrounded by heavily armed vampires in a maximum-security bunker housed several hundred feet below the ground.

Not that she would have guessed that, seated as she was now, across from Savannah at a long, dark cherry table in a tastefully appointed dining room, sipping an exotic, spicy tea from a delicate bone china cup while music played softly in the background.

This chamber, and the spacious residential suite adjoining it, belonged to Gideon and Savannah. From all appearances, they lived as a normal couple within the compound, in comfortable living quarters, surrounded by sumptuous furniture, countless books, and beautiful *objets d'art*. Everything was of the finest quality and all of it impeccably maintained, no different than one might expect to find in a pricey Back Bay brownstone. If not for the absence of windows, it would have been close to perfect. And even that lack was compensated for, with a breathtaking collection of paintings and photographs adorning nearly every wall.

"Aren't you hungry?"

Savannah gestured to a silver tray of pastries and cookies that lay between them on the table. Next to that was another gleaming platter of dainty finger sandwiches and aromatic sauces. Everything looked and smelled wonderful, but Gabrielle had pretty much lost her appetite the night before when she'd watched Lucan shred the Minion's throat with his teeth and then proceed to drink his blood.

"No, thank you," she said. "This is more than enough for me right now."

She was amazed she could hold down anything at all, but the tea was hot and soothing, and she welcomed its warmth both inside and out.

Savannah watched her drink in silence from across the table, her dark eyes friendly, her thin brows knit into a sympathetic furrow. She wore her tight black curls short against her shapely skull, but the effect was more sophisticated than gamine when paired with her striking features and pretty, feminine curves. She had the same open, easy demeanor as Gideon, something Gabrielle greatly appreciated, after having dealt with Lucan and his dominating ways the past few hours.

"Well, maybe you can resist temptation," Savannah said, reaching for one of the crumbly scones, "but I can't."

She spooned a dollop of thick cream onto the biscuit then broke off a piece and moaned happily as she popped the bite into her mouth. Gabrielle knew she was staring, but could hardly help it.

"You eat real food," she said, more a question than the statement it sounded like.

Nodding, Savannah dabbed the corners of her mouth with her napkin. "Yes. Of course. A girl has to eat."

"But I thought? If you and Gideon...Aren't you like him?"

Savannah frowned, shaking her head. "I'm human, same as you. Didn't Lucan explain anything to you?"

"Some." Gabrielle shrugged. "Enough to make my head spin, but I still have a lot of questions."

"Of course, you do. Everyone does, when we're first introduced to this new, other world." She reached out, gave Gabrielle's hand a gentle squeeze. "You can ask me anything. I'm one of the newer females myself."

The disclosure made Gabrielle sit up with piqued interest. "How long have you been here?"

Savannah glanced upward for a moment, as if counting time. "I left my old life in 1974. That's when I met Gideon, and fell madly in love."

"More than thirty years ago," Gabrielle wondered aloud, taking in the youthful features, radiant mocha skin, and bright young eyes of Gideon's woman. "You don't look even twenty years old to me."

Savannah's smile beamed. "I was eighteen when Gideon took me as his mate. He saved my life, actually. He took me away from a bad situation, and so long as we are bonded, I will remain as I am now. Do I really look so young to you?"

"Yes. You're beautiful."

Savannah giggled softly as she took another bite of her scone.

"How...?" Gabrielle asked, hoping it wasn't rude to press, but she was so curious and astonished that she couldn't help blurting out questions. "If you're human, and they can't turn us into...what they are...then, how can this be? How is it that you haven't aged?"

"I am a Breedmate," Savannah answered, as if that should explain it all. When Gabrielle frowned, confused, Savannah went on. "Gideon and I are bonded, mated. His blood keeps me young, but I'm still one hundred percent human. That never changes, even after we are bonded to one of them as his mate. We don't grow fangs, and we don't crave blood in the same way that they do in order to survive."

"But you gave up everything to be with him, like this?"

"What have I given up? I am spending my life with a man I completely adore, and who loves me just as much. We're both healthy, happy, surrounded by others like us, who are our family. Aside from the threat of the Rogues, we have no worries here. If I have sacrificed anything, it pales to what I have with Gideon."

"What about sunlight? Don't you miss it, living down here as you do?"

"None of us are forced to remain in the compound all

of the time. I spend a lot of time in the gardens of the estate during the day, when I want to. The grounds are very well-secured, and so is the mansion, which is huge. I must have spent three weeks exploring it when I first came here."

From the brief glimpse Gabrielle had gotten of the place, she could imagine it would take some time to get familiar with everything.

"As for going into town during the day, we do that sometimes, too—not very often, though. Anything we need can be ordered over the internet and delivered to us." She smiled, giving a little shrug of her shoulder. "Don't get me wrong, I love salon time and shopping as much as the next girl, but it's always something of a risk to venture outside the compound without the protection of our mates. And they worry when we are somewhere they cannot provide for us. I suppose females living in the Darkhaven sanctuaries have a bit more daytime freedom than those of us who are bonded to members of the warrior class. Not that you will hear any of us complaining."

"Are there more Breedmates living here?"

"There are two others, besides me. Eva is bonded to Rio. You'll like the both of them—they're the life of any party. And Danika is one of the sweetest people you will ever meet. She was Breedmate to Conlan. He was killed recently, in a confrontation with a Rogue."

Gabrielle nodded soberly. "Yes, I heard about that just before you came to bring me here. I'm sorry."

"It's different without him, quieter. I'm not sure how Danika's going to cope, to be honest with you. They were together for many, many years. Conlan was a good warrior, but an even better mate. He was also one of the oldest members in this compound."

"How old do they get?"

"Oh, I don't know. Very old, by our standards, anyway. Conlan was born to the daughter of Scottish chieftain around the time of Columbus. His father was a Breed vampire of that current generation, five-hundred years ago."

"You're saying Conlan was five-hundred years old?"

Savannah lifted a slender shoulder. "Give or take, yes. There are some much younger, like Rio and Nikolai, who were both born in the 1900s, but none of them are as long-lived as Lucan. He's first generation, born to one of the original Ancients and the first line of Breedmates to carry their alien seed to full term. From what I understand, those first Breed offspring occurred long after the Ancients arrived here, by many centuries, according to the history. The Gen Ones were conceived unpleasantly and entirely by chance, when the vampires' wholesale rapes happened to include human females whose unique blood properties and DNA were strong enough to sustain a hybrid pregnancy."

Gabrielle got an instant, sickening picture of the brutality that must have taken place at that time. "They sound like animals, the Ancients."

"They were savages. The Rogues operate in much the same way, and with the same disregard for life. If not for warriors like Lucan, Gideon, and the few others of the Order who hunt them down around the world, our lives— all of human life—would be very bleak."

"And what about Lucan?" Gabrielle asked softly. "How old does all of this make him?"

"Ah, he is a rarity, if for his lineage alone. There are few left of his generation." Savannah's expression held a trace of awe and more than a little respect. "Lucan can be no less than nine-hundred years, possibly more."

"Oh, my God." Gabrielle fell back against her chair. She laughed at the absurdity of the idea, and yet realized that it made perfect sense. "You know, the first time I saw him, I thought he looked like he should be on horseback, brandishing a sword and leading an army of knights into battle. He just has that carriage about him. Like he owns the world, and has seen so much that nothing surprises him. Now, I know why."

Savannah was looking at her sagely, her head tilted. "I think you've been something of a surprise to him."

"Me? What do you mean?"

"He brought you here, to the compound. He's never done that, not in all the time I've known him, and not before either, from what I gathered from Gideon."

"Lucan says he's brought me here for my own protection, because the Rogues are after me, now. God, I didn't want to believe him—about any of this—but it's all true, isn't it?"

Savannah's smile was warm, sympathetic. "It is."

"I saw him kill someone last night—a Minion. He did it to protect me, I know, but it was so violent. It was horrific." A shiver snaked its way up her limbs when she pictured the gruesome scene that took place in the children's park. "Lucan bit into the man's throat and fed off him like some kind of..."

"Vampire," Savannah answered softly, with neither accusation nor condemnation in her voice. "That's what they are, Gabrielle, how they were born. It's not a curse or a disease. It's just the way they live, a different kind of consumption than what we as humans have grown to accept as normal. And vampires don't always kill to feed.

In fact, that's rare, at least among the Breed's general population, including the warrior class. It's completely unheard of with blood-bonded vampires, like Gideon or Rio, since their nourishment is provided regularly by their Breedmates."

"You make it sound so normal," Gabrielle said, frowning as she ran her finger around the edge of her teacup. She knew that what Savannah was telling her had a certain logic, despite its surrealism, but accepting it was not going to be easy. "It terrifies me to think about what he really is, how he lives. I should despise him for it, Savannah."

"But you don't."

"No," she confessed quietly.

"You care for him, don't you?"

Gabrielle nodded, reluctant to speak the words.

"And you're intimately involved with him."

"Yes." Gabrielle sighed, and shook her head. "And really, how stupid is that? I don't know what it is about him that makes me want him like I do. I mean, he's lied to me and deceived me on so many levels I can't begin to count them, but even still, just thinking about him makes my knees weak. I've never known this kind of need with another man."

Savannah was smiling over the rim of her cup. "They are more than men, our warriors."

Gabrielle took a sip of her tea, thinking that it probably wasn't wise to consider Lucan as her *anything*, unless she planned to put her heart under his boot heels and watch as he ground it to dust.

"These males are passionate in all they do," Savannah added. "And there is nothing that can compare to the giving and receiving of the blood-bond, especially while making love."

Gabrielle shrugged. "Well, the sex is amazing, I won't even try to deny that. But I haven't shared any kind of a blood-bond with Lucan."

Savannah's smile faltered slightly. "He hasn't bitten you?"

"No. God, no." She shook her head, wondering if she should feel more appalled than she did. "He hasn't even tried to take my blood, as far as I know. Just tonight he swore to me that he never would."

"Oh." Savannah carefully set down her teacup.

"Why? Do you think he will?"

Gideon's mate seemed to consider that for a moment, then gave a slow shake of her head. "Lucan has never made a promise lightly, nor would he about something like this. I'm sure he means exactly what he told you."

Gabrielle nodded, relieved, yet curious why Savannah's assurance sounded almost like a condolence.

"Come," she said, rising from the table and indicating for Gabrielle to follow. "I'll show you the rest of the compound."

"Anything come back yet on those *glyphs* we spotted on our West Coast subject?" Lucan asked, tossing his leather jacket over one of the chairs next to Gideon.

It was just the two of them alone in the lab now, the other warriors having gone to chill out for a few hours before Lucan gave orders for the night's sweep of the city. He was glad for the relative privacy. His head was beginning to pound with the onslaught of another splintering headache.

"I got squat, sorry to say. Nothing came up on the criminal check, or the census search. Apparently our boy's not in the system, but that's not so unusual. The IID records are vast, but far from perfect, especially when it comes to you Gen Ones. There are only a few of you around anymore, and for various reasons, most have never volunteered to be processed or catalogued—yourself included."

"Shit," Lucan hissed, pinching the bridge of his nose but feeling no relief from the pressure building in his head.

"You feeling all right, man?"

"It's nothing." He didn't look at Gideon, but he could sense the vampire watching him with concern. "I'll get over it."

"I, ah ... I heard about what happened the other night between you and Tegan. The guys said you came back off a hunt, looking a bit ragged. Your body's still recovering from those solar burns, you know. You've got to take things easy, feed the healing—"

"I said, I'm fine," Lucan snapped, feeling his eyes flash anger, his lips curled back off his teeth in a snarl.

Between the prey he'd taken in the street and the Minion he'd drained in the park, he'd had more than enough blood to sustain him through his recovery. The fact was, despite his physical satiation, he still craved more.

He was on damned slippery ground, and he knew it.

Bloodlust was just a careless stumble away.

Keeping a lid on his weakness was getting harder all the time.

"Got a present for you," Lucan said, anxious to change the subject. He slapped the two memory sticks down on the Lucite workspace in front of Gideon. "Load them up."

"Really? A gift for me? Darling, you shouldn't have," Gideon said, back to his jovial self. He was already popping one of the portable drives into a USB port of the machine nearest to him. A folder opened onscreen, displaying a long list of file names on the monitor. Gideon turned and shot Lucan a pensive look. "These are image files. Gads, a friggin' lot of them."

Lucan gave a slight nod. He was pacing now, growing edgy and too warm in the bright lights of the room. "I need you to go through each one, compare it against every known Rogue location in the city—past, present, and suspected."

Gideon clicked open a random image and blew out a low whistle. "This is the Rogue lair we took out last month." He opened two more, tiling them on the monitor's display. "And the warehouse we've been watching for a couple of weeks...Jesus, is this other one a shot of the building that fronts the Quincy Darkhaven?"

"There's more."

"Son of a bitch. Most of these images are of vampire locations—both Rogue and Breed." Gideon scrolled through a dozen more photos. "She took all of these?"

"Yeah." Lucan paused to look at the screen. He pointed to a number of files with date stamps from the current week. "Go to this group."

Gideon brought up the photos with a series of fast clicks. "You gotta be kidding me. She's been out to the asylum, too? That place might house hundreds of suckheads."

Lucan's gut clenched at the idea, dread mixing with the acid burn already swimming in the pit of his stomach. His insides were cramping up, gnarled with the need to feed. He mentally forced the hunger down, but his hands were trembling, and a sheen of sweat was breaking out on his brow.

"A Minion found her, chased her off the property," he said, his voice rough gravel in his throat, and not just because his body was under full assault. "She was damned lucky to get away."

"I'll say. How did she find this location? How did she find any of them, for that matter?"

"She says she doesn't know why she's drawn to them. It's a unique instinct of some sort. Part of the same Breedmate ability she has that exempts her from vampire mind control, and lets her see us move where other humans don't."

"Call it what you will, skills like hers could be damned useful to us."

"Forget it. We're not going to involve Gabrielle anymore than she already is. She's not a part of this, and I won't put her in any further danger. She won't be staying here long, anyway."

"You don't think we can protect her?"

"I won't have her sitting on the front lines while there's a war brewing just outside our gates. What kind of life would that be?"

Gideon shrugged. "Seems to be working out all right for Savannah and Eva."

"Yeah, and it's been a fucking laugh riot for Danika lately, too." Lucan shook his head. "I don't want Gabrielle anywhere near this violence. She's going to go to one of the Darkhavens as soon as possible. Someplace far away, remote, where the Rogues won't ever get to her."

And where she would be safe from him, as well. Safe from the beast that was churning inside of him, even now. If Bloodlust finally claimed him—and lately, he felt it was more a question of when than if—he wanted Gabrielle as far away from the fallout as possible.

Gideon was very still as he looked at Lucan. "You care for her."

Lucan glared at him, feeling like he wanted to punch something. Destroy something. "Don't be ridiculous."

"I mean, she's beautiful, and clearly she's as courageous as she is creative, so it's not hard to see why anyone would be attracted to her. But...damn. You really care about her, don't you?" Evidently, the vampire didn't know when to give it a rest. "Never thought I'd see the day that you'd let a female get under your skin like this—"

"Do I look like I want to join the same pathetic hearts-and-flowers club that you and Rio did? Or Conlan, with his fatherless whelp on the way? Trust me, I have no interest in binding myself to this woman or any other one." He ground out a furious curse. "I'm a warrior. My first—*my only duty*—has always been to the Breed. There's never been room for anything else. As soon as I secure a place for her at one of the Darkhavens, Gabrielle Maxwell is gone. Forgotten. End of story."

Gideon was quiet for a long while, just watching him pace and fume and roar with an uncharacteristic lack of control.

Which only spiked Lucan's temper further into the red.

"You got something else to add, or can we get off this dead topic now?"

The vampire's wise blue eyes held him in a maddeningly level stare. "I'm just wondering who it is you need to convince more. Me or yourself?"

CHAPTER
Twenty-two

Gabrielle's tour of the warriors' labyrinthine compound took her past private living quarters, meeting facilities, a training room outfitted with an astounding assortment of weaponry and combat equipment, a banquet room, some sort of chapel, and countless other hidden chambers of various purposes that had since begun to blur in her mind.

She'd met Eva as well, who was everything Savannah said she'd be. Vivacious, charming, and as beautiful as a supermodel. Rio's Breedmate had insisted on hearing all about Gabrielle and her life topside. Eva was from Spain, and talked one day of returning there with Rio where the two of them might raise a family in time. It had been a pleasant introduction, interrupted only by the arrival of Rio himself. Once he showed up, Eva was lost to her mate and Savannah had steered Gabrielle on toward other parts of the compound.

It was impressive, how immense yet efficient the head-quarters were. Any notions she might have had about vampires living in cavernous, musty old crypts were blown away by the time she and Savannah had concluded their casual stroll.

These warriors and their mates were living in high-tech style, with virtually every luxury one could want, although none appealed to Gabrielle as much as the chamber where she and Savannah were now. Floor-to-ceiling bookcases lined two of the room's tall walls, the polished dark wood containing easily thousands of volumes. No doubt, most of them were rare, given the number of heavily tooled leather bindings, and the gold inlay on their spines, which gleamed in the soft light of the library chamber.

"Whoa," she gasped, walking into the center of the room and turning around to admire the staggering collection of books.

"You like it?" Savannah asked, lingering at the open door.

Gabrielle nodded, too busy taking it all in to speak. As she pivoted, her gaze landed on a lush tapestry that covered the back wall. It was a nighttime depiction of a huge knight in black and silver chain mail, seated on a dark, rearing horse. The knight's head was uncovered, leaving his long ebony hair flying in the wind, like the pennants snapping at the tip of his bloodied lance and on the parapet of the smoldering hilltop castle in the background.

The needlework was so intricate and precise, Gabrielle could make out the man's piercing, pale gray eyes and lean, angular cheekbones. There was a familiar twist to his cynical, almost contemptuous mouth.

"Oh, my God," she murmured. "Is that supposed to be—"

Savannah answered with a shrug of her shoulder and an amused little laugh. "Would you like to stay in here for a while? I need to check on Danika, but that doesn't mean you have to leave, if you'd rather—"

"Sure. Yes. I'd love to hang out in here, are you kidding? Please, take your time, and don't worry about me."

Savannah smiled. "I'll be back shortly, then we'll see about making up a guest room for you."

"Thanks," Gabrielle replied, in no rush at all to be taken out of this unexpected haven.

As the other woman stepped away, Gabrielle didn't know what to look at first: the treasure trove of literature, or the medieval work of art starring Lucan Thorne, circa what appeared to be the fourteenth century.

Both, she decided, plucking a gorgeous—and, presumably, first edition—volume of French poetry from the shelf and carrying it over to a leather reading chair arranged beneath the tapestry. She set the book down on a delicate antique table, and for a minute, all she could do was stare up at Lucan's likeness, woven so expertly in silk threads. She reached out, but didn't dare touch the museum-quality piece.

My God, she thought, awed, as the incredible reality of this strange other world sank in fully.

All this time, they had existed alongside the human world.

Incredible.

And how small her own world felt in light of this new knowledge. Everything she thought she knew about life had been eclipsed in a matter of hours by the long history of Lucan and the rest of his kind.

A sudden stirring of the air around her sent a clamor of alarm through Gabrielle's limbs. She whirled away from the tapestry, startled to find the real, flesh-and-bone Lucan standing behind her at the room's threshold, one massive shoulder leaning against the doorjamb. His hair was shorter than the knight's, his eyes perhaps a bit more haunted now, not as mercilessly eager as they had been rendered by the artist's needle.

Lucan was far more handsome in person, radiating an innate power even in stillness. Even scowling at her in broody silence, as he was now.

Gabrielle's heart accelerated with a mix of anticipation and fear as he moved away from the door frame and walked into the room. She looked at him, really looked at him, for what he was: ageless strength, wild beauty, unfathomable power.

A dark enigma, both seductive and dangerous.

"What are you doing in here?" There was a note of accusation in his tone.

"Nothing," she replied quickly. "Well, to be honest, I couldn't help admiring some of these beautiful things. Savannah's been showing me around the compound."

He grunted, his scowl still in place as he pinched the bridge of his nose.

"We had some tea together, and talked a bit," Gabrielle added. "Eva joined us, too. They're both very nice. And this place is really impressive. How long have you and the other warriors lived here?"

She could tell he had little interest in conversation, but he answered, lifting one shoulder in a casual shrug. "Gideon and I established this location in 1898 as a headquarters for hunting Rogues who had moved into the region. From there, we recruited a team of the best warriors to fight alongside us. Dante and Conlan were the first. Nikolai and Rio joined us later. And Tegan."

This last name was completely unfamiliar to Gabrielle. "Tegan?" she said. "Savannah didn't mention him. He wasn't there when you introduced me to the others, either."

"No, he wasn't."

When he didn't elaborate, curiosity got the best of her. "Is he one you've lost, like Conlan?"

"No. Not like that." Lucan's voice was clipped when he spoke of this last member of his cadre, as if the topic was a sore one that he preferred not to open.

He was still staring intently at her, still standing close enough that she could see the rise and fall of his chest as he breathed, the bands of hard muscle expanding beneath his fitted black shirt, the warmth of his body radiating toward her in waves.

Behind him on the wall, his needleworked likeness stared out from the tapestry with fervent purpose, the young knight grimly determined, sure to conquer whatever prize lay in his path. Gabrielle saw a darker shade of that determination in Lucan now, as his gaze slowly took her in from head to toe.

"This weaving is amazing."

"It's very old," he said, staring at her as he came nearer. "But I guess you know that, now."

"It's beautiful. And you look so fierce, like you were ready to take on the world."

"I was." He glanced at the wall hanging, scoffing lightly. "I had the piece made a few months after the death of my parents. That castle burning in the background belonged to my father. I razed it to ash after I took his head for killing my mother in a fit of Bloodlust."

Gabrielle gasped. She hadn't been expecting anything like that. "My God. Lucan..."

"I found her lying in a pool of gore in our great hall, her throat savaged. He didn't even try to fight me. He knew what he'd done. He'd loved her, as much as one of his kind could, but his thirst was stronger. He couldn't deny his nature." Lucan shrugged. "I did him a favor by ending his existence."

Gabrielle looked at his cool expression, feeling as stricken by what she'd just heard as she was by the blasé tone in which he relayed it. Any romantic appeal she had imagined in the tapestry just a minute ago dimmed under the weight of the tragedy it truly depicted.

"Why would you want to have a beautiful reminder of such a terrible thing?"

"Terrible?" He shook his head. "My life began that night. I never had much of a purpose until I stood up to my ankles in my family's blood and realized I had to change things—for myself, and for the rest of my race. That night, I declared war on the last remaining Ancients of my father's alien kind, and on all the members of the Breed who had served them as Rogues."

"That's a long time to be fighting."

"I should have started a lot sooner." He pierced her with a steely stare. Gave her a chilling smile. "I'll never stop. It's what I live for—dealing death."

"Someday you'll win, Lucan. Then all the violence can finally be over."

"You think so," he drawled, a trace of mockery in his tone. "And you know this to be certain, based on what? A short twenty-eight years of life?"

"I base it on hope, for one thing. On faith. I have to be-lieve that good will always come out on top. Don't you?

Isn't that why you and the others here do what you do? Because you have hope that you can make things better?"

He laughed. Actually looked straight at her, and laughed. "I kill Rogues because I enjoy it. I'm damn good at it. I won't speak for anyone else's motives."

"What's going on with you, Lucan? You seem..."— *Pissed off? Confrontational? A tad psychotic?*—"You're acting different here than you were with me before."

He pinned her with a scathing glare. "In case you hadn't noticed, sweetheart, you're in my domain now. Things *are* different here."

The callousness she was seeing in him now took her aback, but it was the rage burning in his eyes that really put her on edge. They were too bright, hard as crystals. His skin was flushed, too tight across the stark cut of his cheekbones. And now that she was looking closer, she could see a thin sheen of sweat on his brow.

Pure, white-hot anger rolled off of him in waves. Like he wanted to tear something apart with his bare hands.

And, as it happened, the only thing in his path at the moment was her.

He walked past her in silence, toward a closed door near one of the tall bookcases. It opened without him touching the latch. Inside, it was so dark, she thought it was a closet. But then he stepped into the gloom and she heard his hard footsteps falling on a stretch of hardwood as he strode down what was apparently a hidden corridor of the compound.

Gabrielle stood there, feeling like she'd just missed being trampled by a brutal storm. She released a pent-up breath. Maybe she should let him go. Count herself lucky just to be out of his way right now. He sure didn't seem to want her company, and she wasn't all that sure she wanted his when he was like this.

But something was up with him—something was seriously wrong—and she needed to know what it was.

Swallowing past her own prickling of fear, she followed after him.

"Lucan?" There was no light at all in the space beyond the door. Only blackness, and the steady clip of Lucan's boot heels. "God, it's so dark in here. Lucan, wait a second. Talk to me."

There was no change in his brisk pace ahead of her. He seemed more than eager to ditch her. Desperate to get away from her.

Gabrielle navigated the lightless path as best she could, hands extended out at her sides to help her follow the snaking corridor.

"Where are you going?"

"Out."

"What for?"

"I told you." A latch clicked open from where his voice now sounded. "I've got a job to do. Been lax as hell about doing it lately."

Because of her.

He didn't say it, but there was no mistaking his meaning.

"I need to get out of here," he tossed back at her curtly. "High time I add a few more suckheads to my tally."

"The night's already half over. Maybe you should get some rest instead. You don't seem well to me, Lucan."

"I need to fight."

She heard his footsteps stop, heard a shift of fabric somewhere ahead of her in the dark, as if he'd paused and was stripping out of his clothes. Gabrielle kept moving toward the sound of him, her hands searching, trying to get her bearings in what was an endless pitch blackness. They were in another chamber now; there was a wall to her right. She used it as a guide, sidling along with careful steps.

"In the other room, your face looked flushed. And your voice is . . . strange."

"I need to feed." The words were low and deadly, an unmistakable threat.

Did he sense that she shrank back as he said it? He must have, because he chuckled, brittle with wry humor, as though amused by her unease.

"But you did feed," she reminded him. "Just last night, in fact. Didn't you take enough blood when you killed that Minion? I thought you said you only needed to feed every few days?"

"An expert on the subject already, are you? I'm impressed."

Boots hit the floor with a careless thump, one, then the other.

"Can we turn on some lights in here? I can't see you—"

"No lights," he snapped. "I can see you just fine. I can smell your fear."

She was afraid, not so much for herself right now, but for him. He was worse than on edge. The air around him seemed to pulse with raw fury. It came at her through the dark, an unseen force pushing her back.

"Have I done something wrong, Lucan? Should I not be here at the compound? Because if you've changed your mind about that, I have to tell you that I'm not sure it was a good idea for me to come here, either."

"There is no other place for you right now."

"I want to go back home to my apartment."

She felt a blast of heat skating up her arms as if he had

just turned a deadly look on her. "You just got here. And you can't go back there. You'll stay until I decide otherwise."

"That sounds an awfully lot like a command."

"It is."

Okay, now he wasn't the only one bristling with anger. "I want my cell phone, Lucan. I need to call my friends and make sure they're okay. Then I'm going to call a cab, and I'm going to go home, where I can try to make sense out of the mess my life has become."

"It's out of the question." She heard the metallic clink of weaponry, the rough scrape of a drawer opening. "You're in my world now, Gabrielle. I am law here. And you are under my protection until I deem it is safe to release you from it."

She sucked in the curse that raced to the tip of her tongue. Barely. "Look, the benevolent overlord attitude might have gone a lot further for you back in the day, but don't even think you can use it on me."

The livid snarl that lashed out of him made the hairs on the back of her neck rise. "You won't survive a night out there without me, do you understand? If not for me, you wouldn't have survived your first goddamned year!"

Standing there in the dark, Gabrielle went utterly still. "What did you say?"

Only a long silence answered.

"What do you mean I wouldn't have survived...."

He swore through gritted teeth. "I was there, Gabrielle. Twenty-seven years ago, when a helpless young mother was attacked by a Rogue vampire at a Boston bus station, I was there."

"My mother," she murmured, her heart thudding

hollowly in her chest. She felt for the wall behind her, and leaned against it for support.

"She'd already been bitten. He was draining her when I smelled blood and found them outside the terminal. He would have killed her. Would have killed you, too."

Gabrielle could hardly believe what she was hearing. "You saved us?"

"I gave your mother a chance to get away. She was too far gone from the bite. Nothing was going to save her. But she wanted to save you. She ran away with you in her arms."

"No. She didn't care about me. She left me. She put me in a trash bin," Gabrielle whispered, her throat burning as she spoke the words, felt the old hurt of abandonment all over again.

"The bite would have put her in a state of shock. It's likely she was disoriented, thinking that she was putting you someplace safe. Sheltering you from danger."

God, how long had she wondered about the young woman who'd given birth to her? How many scenarios had she concocted to explain, to herself at least, what might have happened the night she was recovered on the street, as an infant. Never had she imagined this.

"What was her name?"

"I don't know. I didn't care. She was just another victim of the Rogues. I hadn't thought about any of it until you mentioned your mother tonight at your apartment."

"And me?" she asked, trying to put everything together. "When you first came to see me after the killing I'd witnessed, did you know I was the baby you saved?"

He exhaled a dry laugh. "I had no idea. I came to you because I smelled your jasmine scent outside the nightclub and I wanted you. I needed to know if your blood would taste as sweet as the rest of you."

Hearing those words made her think of all the pleasure Lucan had given her with his body. Now she wondered how it would have felt to have him suckling from her neck as he thrust inside of her. To her shock, she realized she was a lot more than curious. "But you didn't. You haven't..."

"And I won't," he replied, his words clipped. Another curse came from his direction in the dark, this one a pained hiss. "I never would have touched you at all, if I'd known..."

"If you'd known what?"

"Nothing, forget it. Just... Christ, my head is pounding too much for me to talk. Just get out of here. Leave me alone now."

Gabrielle stayed right where she was. She heard him moving again, a stiff shuffling of feet. Another rumbling, animal growl.

"Lucan? Are you all right?"

"I'm fine," he snarled, sounding anything but. "I need...ah, fuck." He was breathing harder now, almost panting. "Get out of here, Gabrielle. I need to be...by myself."

Something heavy hit the carpeted floor with a dull thud. He sucked in a sharp breath.

"I don't think you need to be alone right now at all. I think you need help. And I can't keep talking to you in the dark like this." She smoothed her hand over the wall, blindly searching for a light. "I can't see any—"

Her fingers brushed a switchplate, flipped it on.

"Oh, my God."

Lucan was doubled over on the floor near a king-sized

bed. His shirt and boots were off, and he was writhing as though in extreme pain, the markings on his bare back and torso livid with color. The intricate swirls and arcs changed from deep purples to reds to black as he spasmed, clutching his abdomen.

Gabrielle raced to his side and kneeled down beside him. His body contracted savagely, pulling him into a tight ball.

"Lucan! What's going on?"

"Get out." He snarled when she tried to touch him, lashing out like a wounded animal. "Go! Not your...concern."

"The hell it's not!"

"Get...*aagh!*" A convulsion gripped him again, worse than the last. "Just get away from me."

Panic flooded her to see him thrashing with such pain. "What is happening to you? Tell me what to do!"

He flipped onto his back like invisible hands had tossed him over. The tendons in his neck were stretched taut as cables. Veins and arteries bulged on his biceps and forearms. His lips were peeled back in a grimace, baring his sharp white fangs. "Gabrielle, get the fuck out of here!"

She backed off to give him space, but she wasn't about to leave him suffering like this by himself. "Should I get someone for you? I can go tell Gideon—"

"No! Don't...can't tell. Not...anyone." When he lifted his eyes to her, she saw that his pupils were thin slits of black, swamped by pools of glowing amber. That feral gaze went to her throat. Locked onto the place where she could feel her pulse hammering. Lucan shuddered, squeezed his eyes shut. "It will pass. It always does... eventually."

As if to prove his point, after a long moment, he started

to drag himself to his feet. It was hard going and graceless, but the growl he sent Gabrielle's way when she tried to help him convinced her to let him do it on his own. By sheer force of will, he got up and flopped onto his stomach on the edge of the bed. He was still panting, his body still tense and heaving.

"Is there anything I can do?"

"Go." He blew the word out on an anguished gasp. "Just... stay away."

She remained right where she was. Braved a light touch on his shoulder. "Your skin is on fire. You're burning up with fever."

He didn't say anything. She wasn't sure he was capable of words when all his energy was focused on grounding himself and getting free of whatever it was that had him in such a fierce hold. He'd told her he needed to feed tonight, but this seemed to be something deeper than basic hunger. This was suffering on a level she'd never seen.

A chill thought ran through her head, carried there by a term Lucan had used earlier tonight.

Bloodlust.

That was the addiction he had described as being a hallmark of the Rogues. *All that separated the Breed from their savage brethren.* Looking at him now, she had to wonder how difficult it might be to feed a hunger that could also destroy you.

And once Bloodlust had you by the throat, how long before it pulled you under completely?

"You're going to be all right," she told him softly, stroking his dark hair. "Just relax. Let me take care of you, Lucan."

CHAPTER
Twenty-three

He was lying in cool shade, a soft breeze sifting through his hair. He didn't want to wake up from the deep, dreamless sleep. It wasn't often that he found this kind of peace. Never like this. He wanted to nestle down into it, sleep for a hundred years.

But the faint trace of jasmine floating close by made him stir. He sucked the sweet scent into his lungs, tasting it in the back of his parched throat. Savoring it. He peeled open his heavy lids, looked up, and saw beautiful brown eyes gazing back at him.

"Feeling better?"

He was, actually. The searing headache was gone. His skin no longer felt like it was being shredded off of him. The twisting pain in his gut had faded to a hollow gnawing, uncomfortable as hell, but nothing he couldn't handle.

He tried to tell her he was better, but his voice came out in a hoarse croak. He cleared his throat, pushed sound out of his mouth. "I'm okay."

Gabrielle was seated on the bed with him, holding his head in her lap. She pressed a cool, damp cloth softly to his forehead and cheeks. With her other hand, she was stroking his hair, her fingers gentle and soothing.

It felt good. So incredibly good.

"You were in pretty bad shape. I was worried about you."

He groaned at the reminder of what had happened. The attack of blood hunger had knocked him on his ass. He'd been reduced to a sputtering, feeble ball of pain. And she had seen it all. Jesus, he wanted to crawl in a dark hole and die for letting anyone see him laid low like that. Particularly Gabrielle.

Humiliation over his own weakness hit him hard, but it was the sudden jolt of dread that made him rise up, fully awake. "Christ. Gabrielle, I didn't . . . did I hurt you?"

"No." She touched his jaw, not a trace of fear in her eyes or her tender caress. "I'm fine. You didn't do anything to me, Lucan."

Thank God.

"You're wearing my shirt," he said, just now noticing that her sweater and jeans were gone and her slender curves were draped in a shroud of his black tee-shirt. All he wore were his pants.

"Oh, yeah," she said, pulling at a loose thread. "I put this on a while ago, when Dante came by looking for you. I told him you were in bed, asleep." She blushed a little. "I thought he'd be less inclined to ask questions if I answered the door in this."

Lucan sat back, frowning at her. "You lied for me."

"It seemed pretty important to you that nobody see you . . . like you were."

He looked at her, sitting there so trusting with him, and he was leveled with admiration. Anyone else who'd have witnessed him like that would have put a titanium blade through his heart—and rightly so. But she hadn't been afraid. He'd fought through one of his worst bouts so far, and Gabrielle had been there with him the whole time. Taking care of him.

She had protected him.

His chest tightened with respect. With deepest gratitude.

He had never known what that could feel like, being able to trust someone like that. He knew that any one of his brethren would have his back in battle, as he would theirs, but this was different. This was someone looking out for *him*. Protecting him at his most vulnerable.

Even when he'd been spitting and snarling at her, trying to drive her away. Letting her see him for the true beast he was.

She had stayed beside him, despite all of that.

He didn't have the words to thank her for something so profoundly generous. Instead, he leaned in and kissed her, as softly as he could, with all the reverence he could never adequately express.

"I should get dressed," he said, groaning at the thought of leaving her. "I'm better now. I should go."

"Go where?"

"Topside, to take out a few more Rogues. I can't let the others do all of my work."

Gabrielle moved toward him on the bed, putting her hand on his forearm. "Lucan, it's ten o'clock in the morning. It's daylight up there."

He swiveled his head to the bedside clock and saw that she was right. "Shit. I slept through the night? Dante's going to ride my ass for a while about this one."

Gabrielle's lips curved into a sensual smile. "Actually, he's under the impression that you were riding mine all this time. Remember?"

Arousal sparked inside him like flame on dry tinder. *Goddamn.*

Just the thought . . .

She was sitting with her legs folded beneath her, the black tee-shirt bunched high on her thighs, giving him a shadowed glimpse of tiny white panties at the top of all that peachy skin. Her hair fell around her face and shoulders in sumptuous waves, making him want nothing more than to bury his hands in it as he sank down into her body.

"I hate that you had to lie for me," he said, growling the words. He smoothed his hand along the silky curve of her thigh. "I should make an honest woman of you."

She caught his fingers, and held them still. "Do you really think you're up to that?"

He chuckled with dark humor. "Oh, I'm more than up to it."

Although her eyes were warm with interest, she gave him a dubious look. "You've been through a lot. Maybe we should talk about what happened. It might be a better idea for you to get some more rest."

The last thing he wanted to do was talk about his problems, especially when Gabrielle was looking so tempting in his bed. His body was recovered from its earlier trial, and his sex came easily to life. As usual, whenever he was near her. Whenever he so much as thought of her.

"You tell me if I need more rest."

Taking her hand in his, he guided her toward the hard

ridge of his erection, which bulged against the zipper of his pants. She rubbed the aching bulk of his shaft, then rotated her wrist to cup him in her palm. He closed his eyes, losing himself to her touch and the warm perfume of her own arousal as she edged into his arms.

He kissed her, long and deep, a slow joining of their mouths. Lucan slipped his hands under the tee-shirt, letting his fingers travel up the silky skin of her back, then around to her ribs, and the delicious swell of her breasts. Her nipples pinched tight as he stroked them, little buds just begging to be suckled.

She arched into his hands, moaning. Her own fingers were working the button and fly at his waist. Unzipping his pants. Sliding in, then pulling his length into the hot palm of her hand.

"You are so dangerous," he whispered against her mouth. "I like seeing you here, in my domain. I didn't think I would. God knows, I shouldn't."

He gathered up the hem of the tee-shirt, drew it over her head, and tossed it aside so that he could gaze with open appreciation at her nude body. He swept aside her hair, and tenderly stroked the side of her neck with the backs of his knuckles.

"Am I really the first woman you've brought here?"

He smiled wryly, caressing her soft skin. "Who told you that? Savannah?"

"Is it true?"

He bent forward and took one of her rosy nipples into his mouth. Pressed her down beneath him with the weight of his body while he quickly shucked off his pants. His fangs began to stretch out from his gums, desire swiftly burning out of control, pumping through him in hot waves.

"You're the only one," he said thickly, giving her that honesty in return for the trust she had given him hours before.

Gabrielle would be the last female he'd bring here, too.

He couldn't imagine having anyone else in his bed, now. He would never permit anyone into his heart again. Because he had to face some hard facts, here—that's what he'd done. For all his careful control and years of self-imposed solitude, he had let his emotional guard slip, and Gabrielle had filled his void like no other ever could again.

"God, you are so soft," he said, caressing her, trailing his fingers down her side and abdomen, to the delicate flare of her hip. He pressed a kiss to her lips. "So sweet."

His hand traveled lower, between her thighs, coaxing her legs apart for his questing touch.

"So wet," he murmured, plumbing her mouth with his tongue as his finger delved past her panties, into the slick folds of her cleft.

He penetrated her, just a tease at first, then deeper. She clutched at him, arching up as two more fingers entered her body, caressing the plush sheath that gripped him so fiercely. He broke their kiss and removed the lace that covered her sex. Then he inched down the length of her, pushing her legs apart and sinking down between them.

"So beautiful," he rasped, mesmerized by the flushed perfection of her. He pressed his face against her, opening her to him with his fingers, tonguing her clit and the wet crevices that surrounded it. He brought her to a swift climax, relishing the hard tremors that rolled over her as she curled her fingers into his shoulders and cried out in release.

"God, you wreck me, woman. I can never get enough of you."

He was so fevered to be inside of her, he hardly heard her little gasp as he came back up to cover her with his body. He registered the sudden stillness of her, but it was her voice that made him freeze above her.

"Lucan...your eyes..."

Instinctively, he turned his face away from her. Too late. He knew that she had glimpsed the hungered glow of his transformed gaze. It was the same feral look she had seen in him last night—or, rather, close enough that her human eyes would have difficulty telling the difference between blood hunger and the heated intensity of desire.

"Please," she said gently. "Let me see you...."

Reluctantly, bracing himself over her on his fists, he brought his eyes back to hers. He saw the flicker of alarm but she didn't flinch from him. She looked closely, studying him.

"I won't harm you," he said, his voice raspy and thick. He let her see his fangs as he spoke, unable to conceal any of his body's reaction to her now. "This is need, Gabrielle. Desire. You do this to me. Sometimes just thinking about you—" He broke off, cursing low under his breath. "I don't want to frighten you, but I can't stop the change. Not when I want you so damned much."

"And all the other times we've been together?" she whispered, frowning. "You've hidden this from me? You always shielded your face, kept your eyes averted, when we made love before?"

"I didn't want to scare you. I didn't want you to see what I was." He scoffed. "You've seen everything anyway."

She slowly shook her head, her hands coming up to hold his face still. She looked at him deeply, taking in every part of him. Her eyes were moist, glittering, incredibly bright. Tender with affection, and all of it pouring out for him. "You are beautiful to me, Lucan. I will always want to see you. There's nothing you ever need to hide from me."

Her earnest declaration moved him. She held his wild gaze as she stroked his rigid jaw, her fingers tracing down to play across his parted lips. His fangs ached, elongating further as she explored his face with her tender touch.

As if to prove something to him—or maybe, to herself—she slipped her finger past his lips, into his mouth. Lucan groaned deep in his throat, a harsh, wordless snarl. His tongue pressed hungrily against her fingertip, his teeth grazing her skin with tender restraint as he closed his lips and sucked her deeper into his mouth.

He watched Gabrielle swallow hard. He smelled adrenaline jetting through her, mixing with the scent of her desire.

She was so damned beautiful, so soft and giving, so courageous in everything she did, he couldn't help but feel awed by her.

"I trust you," she told him, her dusky eyes darkening with passion as she slowly withdrew her finger from between his sharp teeth. "And I want you. Every part of you."

It was more than he could take.

With an animal grunt of lust, he came down on her, positioning his pelvis between her thighs and spreading them wide with his knees. Her sex was slick and hot against the head of his cock, a welcome he couldn't resist. With a deep thrust, he impaled her, sliding as deep as he could go. She took every last inch of him, her tight channel gripping him like a fist, bathing him in wondrous, wet heat. Lucan hissed sharply as the walls of her sex shuddered with his first slow withdrawal. He filled her again, hooking her knees over his arms so he could get even closer, delve ever deeper.

"Yes," she coaxed him, moving with him in a tempo that was becoming anything but gentle. "God, Lucan. Yes."

He knew his face was harsh with the force of his lust; he had likely never looked more beastly than at that moment, when his blood was running molten, summoning the part of him that was the curse of his father's brutal lineage. He fucked her hard, trying to ignore the thrumming, rising need within him that called for something more than this immense pleasure.

His focus latched on to Gabrielle's throat, where a strong vein pulsed beneath her delicate skin. His mouth watered feverishly, even as the pressure built in the base of his spine, signaling his coming release.

"Don't stop," she said without the slightest tremor in her voice. God help her, but she actually pulled him closer to her, holding his feral gaze as her warm fingers stroked his cheek. "Take as much of me as you need. Just... Oh, God... don't stop."

Lucan's nostrils filled with the erotic scent of her, and the faintly copper tanginess of the blood that was coloring her breasts and flushing the pale skin of her neck and face. He roared in agony, fighting to deny himself—deny them both—the ecstasy that could be had only through a vampire's kiss.

Wrenching his eyes away from her throat, Lucan drove into her body with renewed vigor, bringing her, and then himself, to a shattering climax.

But his release only abated one part of his need.

The other, deeper one remained, worsening with each strong pulse of Gabrielle's heart.

"Damn it." He rolled away from her on the bed, his voice raw and fevered.

"What's wrong?" Gabrielle put her hand on his shoulder.

She moved closer to him, and he felt the plush warmth of her breasts crushing against his spine. Her pulse hammered audibly, vibrating through flesh and bone until it was all that he could hear. All that he knew.

"Lucan? Are you all right?"

"God*damn* it," he growled, shrugging from under her light grasp on his shoulder. He threw his legs over the edge of the bed and sat up, putting his head in his hands. His fingers trembled as he shoved them through his hair. Behind him, Gabrielle was silent; he turned and met her questioning gaze. "You haven't done anything wrong. You feel too right, and I have to ... I can't get enough of you right now."

"It's okay."

"No. I shouldn't be with you like this, when I need ..." *You*, his body answered. "Holy Christ, this is just no good."

He turned away again, about to get up off the bed.

"Lucan, if you're hungry ... if you need blood ..."

From behind him, she moved closer. Put her arm over his shoulder, her wrist hovering just under his chin.

"Jesus, don't offer it to me." Reflexively, he recoiled from her, like he would from poison. He got up, threw on his pants. Started pacing. "I'm not going to drink from you, Gabrielle."

"Why not?" She sounded hurt, rightfully confused. "You obviously need it. And I'm the only human around at the moment, so I guess you're stuck with me."

"That's not it." He shook his head, eyes squeezed

closed to force the feral part of him to heel. "I can't do it. I won't bind you to me."

"What are you talking about? It's okay to screw me, but the thought of taking my blood turns your stomach?" She gave a sharp laugh. "My God. I can't believe I actually feel insulted over that."

"This isn't going to work," he said, furious at himself for digging them into a deeper hole because of his own lack of control around her. "This isn't going to come out right. I should have set things straight between us from the start."

"If you have something to tell me, I wish you would. I know you have a problem, Lucan. Pretty hard to miss it, after seeing you last night."

"That's not it." He cursed. "It's part of it. I don't want to hurt you. And by taking your blood, I will. Sooner or later, if you are bound to me in blood, I will hurt you."

"Bound to you," she said slowly. "How?"

"You bear the mark of a Breedmate, Gabrielle." He gestured toward her left shoulder. "It's there, just below your ear."

She frowned, her hand drifting up to the precise place where the diminutive teardrop and crescent moon rested on her skin. "This? It's a birthmark. I've had it ever since I can remember."

"Every Breedmate has borne the same mark somewhere on her body. Savannah and the other females have it. My own mother as well. You all do."

She had gone very still, now. Her voice was very small. "How long have you known this about me?"

"I saw it the first night I came to your apartment."

"When you took my cell phone pictures?"

"After," he said. "When I came back later, and you were sleeping in your bed."

Understanding dawned in her expression, a mix of surprise and emotional violation. "You *were* there. I thought I had dreamed you."

"You've never felt a part of the world you live in because it's not your world, Gabrielle. Your photographs, the way you're drawn to places that house vampires, your confusion over your feelings about blood and the compulsion to let it—these are all parts of who you truly are."

He could see her struggling to accept what she was hearing, and he hated that he wasn't able to make things easier. Might as well get everything out on the table and be done with it.

"One day, you'll find a worthy male and take him as your mate. He will drink from you alone, and you from him. Blood will bind the two of you as one. It's a sacred vow among our kind. One that I can't give you."

He might as well have slapped her from the look of injury on her pretty face. "You can't... or you won't?"

"Does it matter? I'm telling you that it's not going to happen because I won't permit it. If we share a blood bond, I will be drawn to you for as long as I have breath in my body and you in yours. You would never be free of me because the bond will compel me to seek you out wherever you run."

"Why do you think I would run from you?"

He exhaled dryly. "Because, one day, this thing I'm fighting is going to get me, and I can't bear the idea that you might be in my path when it does."

"You're talking about Bloodlust."

"Yes," he said, the first time he had ever truly acknowledged it, even to himself. All these years, he'd been able to hide it. Not from her. "Bloodlust is the greatest weakness of my kind. It is an addiction—a damnable plague. Once it has you in its grasp, few vampires are strong enough to escape it. They go Rogue, and then they are lost for good."

"How does it happen?"

"It's different for everyone. Sometimes, the disease moves in, little by little. The hunger grows, and so you feed it. You feed it whenever it calls, and one night you realize the need is never filled. For others, one careless indulgence can tip them past breaking."

"And how is it for you?"

His smile grew tight, more a baring of his teeth and fangs. "I have the dubious honor of carrying my father's blood in my veins. If the Rogues are beasts, they are nothing compared to the scourge that started our entire race. For Gen Ones, the temptation is always there, drumming harder in us than in any others. If you want to know the truth of it, I have been staving off Bloodlust since my first taste."

"So, you have a problem, but you got through it last night."

"I was able to hold it back, thanks in no small part to you, but each time it gets worse."

"You can get through it again. We'll get through it together."

"You don't know my history. I've already lost both of my brothers to the disease."

"When?"

"A very long time ago." He scowled, thinking back on a past he didn't like to dredge up. But the words came quickly now, whether he wanted to relive them or not. "Evran, the middle born of us three, went Rogue soon after he reached adulthood. He was killed in combat, fighting for the wrong side in one of the old wars between the Breed and the Rogues. Marek was the eldest, and the most fearless. He and Tegan and I were part of the first cadre of Breed warriors to rise up against the last of the Ancients and their armies of Rogues. We formed the Order around the time of the great human plague in Europe. Less than a hundred years later, Bloodlust claimed Marek; he sought the sun to end his misery. Even Tegan had a close brush with the addiction long ago."

"I'm sorry," she said softly. "You've lost so much to it. And to this conflict with the Rogues. I can see why it terrifies you."

He had a flippant reply perched at the tip of his tongue—some line of bullshit he wouldn't hesitate to trot out for one of the other warriors if they were presumptuous enough to think him afraid of anything. But the dismissive retort stayed stuck in his throat as he looked at Gabrielle, knowing that better than anyone in all his long existence, she understood him best.

She knew him on a level no one else ever had, and part of him was going to miss that once the time came to send her away to the future that awaited her in the Darkhavens.

"I didn't realize Tegan and you went back so far," Gabrielle said.

"He and I go all the way back, to the beginning. We're both Gen One, both sworn in our duty to defend our race."

"You're not friends, though."

"Friends?" Lucan laughed, considering the centuries of animosity that simmered between the two of them. "Tegan doesn't have friends. And if he did, he sure as hell wouldn't count me among them."

"Then why do you let him stay here?"

"He's one of the best warriors I've ever known. His commitment to the Order goes deeper than any hatred he harbors for me. We share the belief that nothing is more important than protecting the future of the Breed."

"Not even love?"

He couldn't speak for a second, caught off guard by her frank question and unwilling to consider where it might lead. He had no experience with that particular emotion. The way his life was going currently, he didn't want to get close to anything resembling it, either. "Love is for the males who choose to lead soft lives in the Darkhavens. Not for warriors."

"Some of the others in this compound might argue that with you."

He met her gaze with a level stare. "I'm not them."

Her chin dropped at once, long lashes shuttering her eyes from his view. "So, what does all of this make me? Am I just a way of passing time for you between killing Rogues and trying to pretend you've got everything under control?" When she looked up, tears were swelling in her eyes. "Am I just some little toy that you turn to whenever you need to get off?"

"I haven't heard you complain."

Her breath caught, a tiny gasp snagging in her throat as she gaped at him, clearly appalled and having every right to be. Her expression fell, then hardened into something as brittle as glass. "Fuck you."

Her contempt for him in that moment was understandable, but that didn't make it any easier to swallow. He would never take such a verbal beating from anyone. Before now, no one had ever had the nerve to try him. Lucan, the aloof one, the stone-cold killer who tolerated weakness in no form whatsoever—least of all in himself.

For all the conditioning and discipline he had mastered in his centuries of living, here he stood, being torn wide open by the only woman he had been foolish enough to let get close to him. And he cared for her, too, far more than he should. Which made hurting her now seem all the more repugnant, regardless of the fact that last night made it clear to him that it was necessary he push her away. It was unavoidable, and he would only make it worse by trying to pretend she would ever fit into his way of life.

"I don't want to hurt you, Gabrielle, and I know that I will."

"What do you think you're doing right now?" she whispered, a slight hitch in her voice. "You know, I believed you. God, I actually believed every lie you've fed me. Even that bullshit about wanting to help me find my true destiny. I really thought you cared."

Lucan felt helpless, the coldest kind of bastard for letting things get so out of hand with her. He strode over to a bureau, took out a fresh shirt and put it on. Heading for the door that led to the hallway outside his private apartments, he paused to look back at Gabrielle.

He wanted so badly to reach out to her, to try to make things better somehow, but he knew that would be a mistake. One touch and he would have her in his arms again.

Then he might not be able to let her go.

He opened the door, about to walk out.

"You have found your destiny, Gabrielle. Just like I said you would. I never told you it would be with me."

CHAPTER
Twenty-four

Lucan's words—all the astonishing things he'd told her—were ringing in Gabrielle's ears as she came out from under the steaming water in his bathroom shower. She cut the tap and toweled off, wishing the hot water could have melted away some of the hurt and confusion she felt. There was so much to deal with, not the least of which was that Lucan had no intention of being with her.

She tried to tell herself he hadn't made any promises to begin with, but that only made her feel like a bigger fool. He had never asked her to put her heart under his boot heels; she'd done that all on her own.

Leaning in toward the mirror that ran the entire width of the bathroom suite, Gabrielle moved her hair back to have a closer look at the crimson-colored birthmark below her left ear. Or rather, the Breedmate mark, she corrected herself, peering at the little teardrop that appeared to be falling into the bowl of a crescent moon.

By some twisted sort of irony, she was connected to Lucan's world by the tiny mark on her neck, and yet, it was also the very thing preventing her from being with him.

Maybe she was a complication he didn't want or need, but it wasn't like meeting him had made life a bowl of cherries for her, either.

Thanks to Lucan, she was involved in a bloody underworld war that made the worst inner city gangbangers look like playground bullies. She had all but abandoned one of the sweetest condos in Beacon Hill and would lose it altogether if she didn't get back and get to work so she could pay her bills. Her friends had no idea where she was, and telling them now would probably only put them in danger of losing their lives.

To top it all off, she was half in love with the darkest, deadliest, most emotionally closed-off man she'd ever known.

Who just so happened to also be a bloodsucking vampire.

And, what the hell, since she was being honest, she wasn't half in love with Lucan. She was full-on, flat-out, head-over-heels, never-going-to-get-over-this-one, in love with him.

"Way to go," she told her miserable reflection. "Just frigging brilliant."

Yet even after everything he'd said to her, she still wanted nothing more than to go to him wherever he was in the compound and wrap herself in his arms, the only place she'd ever found any kind of comfort.

Yeah, like she really needed to add public humiliation to the very personal one she was still trying to deal with. Lucan had made it pretty clear: whatever they had together—if they'd ever truly had anything beyond the physical—was over.

Gabrielle walked back into his bedroom and retrieved her clothes and shoes. She dressed quickly, wanting to be out of his personal quarters before he came back and she did something really stupid. Well, she amended, glancing at the mussed bedsheets still in disarray from their love-making, something even more stupid.

With the idea that she would look for Savannah and maybe try to find a phone line out of the compound, since Lucan hadn't seen fit to return her cell, Gabrielle ducked out of his bedroom. The corridor was confusing, no doubt by design, and she had taken several wrong turns before she finally recognized her surroundings. She was near the training facility, judging by the sharp staccato crack of rounds hitting targets.

She cleared a corner and was stopped abruptly by an unyielding wall of leather and weapons standing in her path.

Gabrielle looked up, and up some more, and met with a chilling blast of menace coming at her from a narrowed green gaze. Those cool and calculating eyes locked onto her through a careless fall of tawny hair, like a jungle cat lurking behind golden reeds as it sized up its prey. She swallowed hard. A palpable danger radiated from the vampire's large body and from within the depths of his un-blinking predator's eyes.

Tegan.

Her mind supplied the name of the unfamiliar male, the only one of the compound's six warriors she hadn't yet met.

The one with whom Lucan apparently shared a barely concealed contempt.

The vampire warrior didn't move out of her way. He hardly reacted at all to her crashing into him, except for the slight quirk of his mouth as he stared down to where her breasts were mashed against the plane of hard muscle just below his chest. He was wearing about a dozen weapons, the threat reinforced by no less than two-hundred pounds of hard-hewn muscle.

She backed up, then sidestepped him just to be safe. "Sorry. I didn't see you there."

He didn't say a word, but she felt as if everything going on inside of her had been laid bare by him in an instant—in that split-second brush of contact when her body had collided with his. He stared down at her with a chilling, emotionless gaze, like he could see her from the inside out. Although he said nothing, expressed nothing, Gabrielle felt dissected.

She felt... invaded.

"Excuse me," she whispered.

When she moved to step by him, Tegan's voice stopped her.

"Hey." His voice was softer than she expected, a deep, dark rasp. It was a peculiar contrast to the starkness of his gaze, which hadn't moved even a fraction. "Do yourself a favor and don't get too attached to Lucan. Odds are real good that vampire's not gonna live much longer."

He said it without a speck of emotion in his voice, just a flat statement of fact. The warrior walked past her, stirring the air of the corridor with an apathy that seeped, cold and disturbing, into Gabrielle's bones.

When she turned to look after him, Tegan and his un-settling prediction were gone.

————

Lucan tested the heft of a sleek black 9mm in his hand, then raised the weapon and squeezed off a series of rounds into the target at the far end of the firing range.

Although it felt good to be back on familiar ground around the tools of his trade, his blood seething and ready for a decent fight, part of him kept straying back to his encounter with Gabrielle. Damn, but the woman had his head in knots. Despite everything he had said to push her away from him, he had to admit that he was in deep with her.

How long did he think he could carry on with her without falling? More to the point, how did he ever think he was going to handle the thought of letting her go? Of sending her away with the idea that she would be paired with someone else?

Things were getting too goddamned complicated.

He hissed a curse. Fired off another bunch of rounds, relishing the blast of hot metal and acrid smoke as his target's chest exploded from the impact.

"What do you think?" Nikolai asked, his crisp wintry eyes glittering. "Sweet little piece, isn't it? Responsive as hell, too."

"Yeah. Feels good. I like it." Lucan flipped on the safety and gave the new handgun another look. "Beretta 92FS converted to full auto with a drop-in unit? Nice work, man. Real nice."

Niko grinned. "I haven't even told you about the custom rounds that bad boy's carrying. I tricked out some hollowpoint polycarbonate-tipped bullets. Took the shot out of the poly tips, added titanium powder in its place."

"That ought to make a nasty mess when it hits a suckhead's blood system," Dante added from where he sat sharpening his blades on the edge of a weapons cabinet.

No doubt, the vampire was right about that. In the Old Times, the cleanest way to kill a Rogue was by separating its head from its body. That worked fine while swords were the weapon of choice, but modern technology brought new challenges for both sides.

It wasn't until the early 1900s that the Breed discovered the uniquely corrosive effect of titanium on the overactive blood systems of Rogue vampires. Thanks to an allergy that was amplified by cellular mutations in their blood, Rogues reacted to titanium the way Alka-Seltzer reacted to water.

Niko took the weapon back from Lucan and pet it like a prize. "What you got here is one kickass Rogue blaster."

"When can we test it out?" Rio asked.

"How about tonight?" Tegan strode in without making a sound, but his voice cut through the room like the growl of a coming storm.

"You talking about that location you scouted down by the harbor?" Dante asked.

Tegan nodded. "Probable lair, housing maybe a dozen individuals, give or take. I'm guessing they're still green, just turned Rogue. Be no big thing to take them out."

"Been a while since we cleaned house on a raid," Rio drawled, his smile broad and eager. "Sounds like a party to me."

Lucan passed the weapon back to Niko and gave the others a scowl. "Why the hell am I just hearing about this?"

Tegan slid a flat stare his direction. "You need to do a little catch-up, man. While you were holed up with your female all night, the rest of us were topside doing our jobs."

"That's a low blow," Rio said. "Even for you, Tegan."

Lucan considered the slam in measured silence. "No,

he's right. I should have been up there taking care of business. I had some things to handle back here. And now they're handled. It's not going to be an issue anymore."

Tegan smirked. "Is that right? Because I gotta tell you, when I saw the Breedmate in the hall a few minutes ago, she was looking pretty upset. Felt like someone had torn the poor girl's heart out. Felt to me like she needed someone to make things better for her."

Lucan roared up on the vampire in a furious, black rage. "What did you say to her? Did you touch her? So help me, if you did anything to her—"

Tegan chuckled, genuinely amused. "Easy, man. No need to come off your chain about it. Your female's none of my concern."

"You remember that," Lucan said. He whirled around to meet the curious gazes of the other warriors. "She's no concern for any of you, are we clear? Gabrielle Maxwell is under my personal protection while she is in this compound. Once she leaves for the Darkhavens, she'll no longer be my concern, either."

It took him a minute to simmer down and not give in to the urge to go head-to-head with Tegan. One day, it was probably going to come to that. And Lucan couldn't totally blame the male for holding a grudge. If Tegan was a mean-ass soulless bastard, Lucan was the one who helped make him that way.

"Can we get back to business now?" he snarled, daring someone to stoke him further. "I need to hear facts about this harbor location."

Tegan launched into a description of what he'd observed about the likely Rogue lair, and offered his suggestions for how the group of them could go about raiding it. Although the source of this information bothered Lucan somewhat, he couldn't think of a better way to cap off his black mood than with an offensive strike on their enemies.

God knew, if he ended up anywhere near Gabrielle again, all his tough talk about duty and doing what was right by her would be scattered like dust. It had been a couple of hours since he'd left her in his bedroom, and she was still foremost in his mind. Need for her still tore through him when he thought about her soft, warm skin.

And thinking about how he'd hurt her made a space like a cold pit open up in his chest. She had proven herself a true ally in covering for him with the other warriors. She had held him through his own bit of personal hell last night, standing by him, as tender and loving as any male could ever want in a cherished mate.

Dangerous thinking, no matter how he chose to look at it.

He let the discussion about the raid continue, agreeing that they needed to start hitting the Rogues where they lived, rather than picking them off individually as they ran across them in the street. "We'll meet back in here at sundown to suit up and head out."

The group of warriors began conversing amongst themselves as they dispersed, Tegan sauntering along at the rear.

Lucan considered the stoic loner, who took such damnable pride in the fact that he didn't need anyone. Tegan willfully kept himself detached, isolated. But he hadn't always been like that. Once, he'd been a golden boy, a born leader. He could have been great—had been, in fact. But all of that changed in the course of one terrible night. From there, a steep downward spiral began. Tegan hit bottom and had never recovered.

And although he had never admitted it to the warrior,

Lucan would never forgive himself for the role he had played in that fall.

"Tegan. Hold up."

The vampire paused with obvious reluctance. He didn't turn around, just stood there in silence, his back held at an arrogant angle as the other warriors filed out of the training facility and into the corridor. When they were alone, Lucan cleared his throat and spoke to his Gen One brethren.

"You and I have a problem, Tegan."

He exhaled sharply. "I'll go alert the media."

"This issue between us isn't going to go away. It's been too long, too much water over the dam. If you need to settle the score with me—"

"Forget it. It's ancient history."

"Not if we can't bury it."

Tegan scoffed, turning to look at him at last. "You got a point here, Lucan?"

"I just want to say that I think I'm starting to understand what it cost you. What I cost you." Lucan slowly shook his head, ran a hand over his scalp. "T, you have to know that if there had been any other way...If things could've gone down differently..."

"Jesus Christ. Are you trying to apologize to me?" Tegan's green eyes were hard enough to cut glass. "Spare me the concern, man. You're about five-hundred years too late. And sorry doesn't change a fucking thing, does it?"

Lucan clamped his jaws together, stunned to feel true anger rolling off the big male, instead of the usual cool apathy.

Tegan hadn't forgiven him. Not even close.

After all this time, he didn't think it likely that he ever would.

"No, T. You're right. Sorry doesn't change anything."

Tegan stared at him for a long moment, then turned away and stalked out of the room.

Live music screamed out of refrigerator-sized amplifiers at the front of the private underground nightclub—although "music" was a generous description of the band's pathetic caterwauling and discordant guitar riffs. The group moved robotically on the stage, slurring their words and dropping far more beats than they hit. In a word, they sucked.

But then, who could expect the humans to perform with any sort of expertise when they were playing before a crowd of bloodthirsty, feeding vampires?

From behind his concealing shades, the leader of the Rogues narrowed his eyes and scowled. He had a thrashing headache when he'd arrived a short while ago; now his temples felt as if they were about to explode. He leaned back against the cushions of his private booth, bored with the gory festivities. A slight lift of his hand brought one of his sentries jogging over. He waved dismissively toward the stage.

"Someone put them out of their misery. Not to mention mine."

The guard nodded, then hissed in reply. He curled back his lips to reveal huge fangs protruding from a mouth that was already watering at the mere mention of more carnage. The Rogue loped off to carry out his orders.

"Good dog," murmured his powerful Master.

He was glad for the sudden trill of his cell phone, and a reason to get up for some air. A new racket had begun onstage, now, as the band came under the sudden assault of a pack of frenzied Rogues.

With the club erupting in full-on anarchy, the leader strode to a private backstage room, and took the ringing cell phone from his inside suitcoat pocket. He had expected to see the untraceable number of one of his many Minions, most of whom had been dispatched to gather information on Gabrielle Maxwell and her apparent involvement with the Breed.

But this was not one of them.

He could tell as much even before he flipped open the device and saw the blocked ID flashing on the display.

Intrigued, he picked up the call. The voice on the other end was not unfamiliar to him. He had done some illicit business with the individual recently and they still had a few things to discuss. At his prompting, the caller relayed details about a raid being hatched that very night on one of the smaller Rogue cells in the city.

In a matter of seconds, he was given everything he needed to make sure the raid turned in his favor—the location, the warriors' intended method and route, their basic plan of attack—all on the condition that one member of the Breed be spared retaliation. This sole warrior was not to be exempt entirely, however, only wounded enough that he would never be able to fight again. The fate of the rest, including the nearly unstoppable Lucan Thorne, was for the Rogues to decide.

Lucan's death had been part of their agreement once before, but execution of the task had not gone quite as planned. This time, the caller wanted assurances that the deed would, in fact, be carried out. Even went so far as to remind him that he had been given considerable compensation for the act, but had yet to make good on his part.

"I am well aware of our bargain," he seethed into the

cell phone. "Do not tempt me to demand further payment from you. I promise you will regret it."

He snapped the device shut on a black curse, cutting short the politic backpedaling that had begun on the heels of his threat.

The *dermaglyphs* at his wrist pulsed with the deep hue of his rage, colors shifting within the pattern of other markings that had been tattooed on his skin as a form of disguise. He scowled at the need to hide his lineage—his birthright—with crude ink and secrecy. He loathed the necessity of his shadowy existence, almost as much as he did all those who stood in the way of his goals.

He was fuming as he stalked back inside the main area of the club. Through the dark, his gaze lit at once on his lieutenant, the only Rogue in recent history to have looked Lucan Thorne in the eyes and lived to tell about it. He gestured for the huge male to come over, then gave him orders for carrying out the night's fun and games.

Regardless of his secret negotiations, when the smoke cleared tonight, he wanted Lucan and all of the other warriors with him to be dead.

CHAPTER
Twenty-five

He avoided her the rest of the day, which Gabrielle figured was probably just as well. Now, just past dusk, Lucan
and the five other warriors strode out of the training facility as a unit, each of them a picture of menace in black
leather and deadly weaponry. Even Gideon was joining in
tonight's raid, going out in place of Conlan.

Waiting in the corridor to see them off, Savannah and
Eva went to their mates and took them in long embraces.
Soft, private words were exchanged in low, loving voices.
Tender kisses spoke of a woman's fear and a man's strong
reassurances that he would return safely to her.

Gabrielle stood some distance away in the hall, feeling
so much an outsider as she watched Lucan say something
to Savannah. The Breedmate nodded and he put a small
object in her hand, his gaze trailing past her shoulder to

light on Gabrielle. He said nothing, made no move to approach her, but his eyes lingered, drinking her in across the wide space that separated them now.

And then he was gone.

Striding ahead of the others, Lucan turned a corner at the far end of the corridor and disappeared. The rest of his cadre followed, leaving nothing but the hard clip of boot heels and the metallic jangle of steel in their wake.

"You okay?" Savannah asked, coming up to Gabrielle and wrapping a gentle arm around her shoulders.

"Yeah. I'll be fine."

"He wanted me to give you this." She held out Gabrielle's cell phone. "A peace offering of some sort?"

Gabrielle took it, nodding her head in agreement. "Things aren't going well between us right now."

"I'm sorry. Lucan said he trusts you'll understand you can't leave the compound, or tell your friends where you are. But if you need to call them..."

"Thank you." She looked up at Gideon's mate and managed a small smile.

"If you want some privacy, just make yourself at home anywhere you like." Savannah hugged her briefly, then glanced to Eva as the other woman came over to join them.

"I don't know about anyone else," Eva said, her beautiful face drawn with worry, "but I could use a drink. Or three."

"Maybe we all could use a little wine and company," Savannah replied. "Gabrielle, you come join us when you're ready. We'll be in my place."

"Okay. Thanks."

The two women moved off together, speaking quietly, their arms linked as they walked up the snaking corridor

toward Savannah's and Gideon's apartments. Gabrielle
wandered in the other direction, not sure where she
wanted to be.

That wasn't actually true. She wanted to be with
Lucan, in his arms, but she'd better get over that desperate
wish, and quick. She wasn't about to beg him to want her,
and assuming he made it back from tonight's raid in one
piece, she had better prepare herself to put him out of her
mind completely.

She strolled toward an open door down one quiet,
dimly lit spoke of the hallway. A candle burned somewhere inside the empty chamber, the only light in the
place. The solitude, and the smells of faded incense and
old wood drew her in. It was the compound's chapel; she
remembered passing it on her tour with Savannah.

Gabrielle walked between two rows of bench seats,
toward a raised pedestal at the front of the chamber. It was
there that the candle burned, a thick red pillar of slow-
melting wax, its flame nestled deep in the core radiating a
soft crimson glow. She sat down on one of the front row
benches and simply breathed for a while, letting the peace
of the sanctuary wash over her.

She flipped open her cell phone. The message symbol
was blinking. Gabrielle hit the voicemail button and listened to the first call. It was from Megan, time stamped
two days ago, around the same time she'd been calling
Gabrielle's apartment following the Minion attack in the
park.

*"Gabby, it's me again. I've left a bunch of messages for you at
home, but you haven't called me back. Where are you? I'm really getting worried! I don't think you should be alone after what happened.
Call me back as soon as you get this—and I mean the very second you
get this, okay?"*

Gabrielle erased it and moved on to the next message, left last night at 11 P.M. Kendra's voice came on, sounding a little tired.

"Hey, there. You home? Pick up if you are. Shit, I guess it's kinda late—sorry about that. You're probably sleeping. So, I've been meaning to call you guys, try to hook up for drinks or something, maybe hit another club? How about tomorrow night? Call me."

Well, at least Kendra was safe as of a few hours ago. That took away some of Gabrielle's concern. But there was still the matter of the guy she'd been seeing. The Rogue, Gabrielle amended, feeling a shiver of fear for her friend's unwitting proximity to the same danger that was currently dogging her own heels.

She skipped to the last message. Megan again, from just a couple of hours ago.

"Hi, sweetie. Just checking in. Are you ever going to call me and tell me how it went at the station the other night? I'm sure your detective was glad to see you, but you know I'm dying to hear in detail just how glad he was."

Megan's voice was calm and teasing, perfectly normal. Completely changed from the panic of her earlier messages at Gabrielle's home and on the cell.

God, that's right.

Because to her, and to her cop boyfriend as well, there was no reason to be alarmed about anything since Lucan had wiped their memories.

"Anyway, I'm meeting Jamie for dinner tonight at Ciao Bella—your favorite. If you can make it, swing by. We'll be there at seven. Save you a seat."

Gabrielle clicked erase and checked the clock on the cell phone: 7:20.

She owed it to her friends to at least call and let them know she was all right. And part of her longed to hear their voices, her only connection to the life she knew before Lucan Thorne turned her entire world upside down. She speed-dialed Megan's cell and waited anxiously as it rang. Muffled talking came over the receiver in the second before her friend said hello.

"Hi, Meg."

"Oh, hey—there you are! Jamie, it's Gabby!"

"Where is that girl? She coming, or what?"

"I don't know yet. Gabby, are you gonna join us?"

Gabrielle listened to the familiar chaos of her friends' chatter and wished she could be there. She wished she could go back to the way things were, before...

"I, ah...I can't. Something's come up, and I..."

"She's busy," Megan told Jamie. "Where are you, anyway? Kendra called me looking for you today. She said she went by your apartment but it didn't look like you were home."

"Kendra stopped by? Have you seen her?"

"No, but she wants to get together with all of us. Sounds like she's done with that guy from the club."

"Brent," Jamie supplied loudly and dramatically over Megan's voice.

"They broke up?"

"I don't know," Megan replied. "I asked her how it was going and she just said she's not seeing him anymore."

"Good," Gabrielle said, so very relieved. "That's really good news."

"So, what about you? What's so important that you can't come out for dinner tonight?"

Gabrielle frowned, staring at her surroundings. The red candle's flame wobbled as the air in the chapel stirred slightly. She heard soft footsteps, then a quietly indrawn breath as whomever walked in realized the chamber was occupied. Gabrielle turned and saw a tall blond in the open doorway. The woman gave Gabrielle an apologetic look, then started to turn away.

"I'm, ah... out of town right now," she told her friends in a hushed voice. "I might be gone for a few days. Maybe longer."

"Doing what?"

"Um, I'm on a commission job," Gabrielle lied, hating to do it, but seeing no other choice. "I'll give you guys a call as soon as I can. Take care of each other. I love you."

"Gabrielle—"

She clicked off the call before she was forced to say anything more.

"I'm sorry," the blond woman said as Gabrielle came toward her. "I didn't realize the chapel was in use."

"It's not. Please stay. I was just..." Gabrielle released a pent-up sigh. "I just lied to my friends."

"Oh." Gentle pale blue eyes settled sympathetically on her.

Gabrielle closed the phone and smoothed her finger over the polished silver case. "I left my apartment in a rush the other night to come here with Lucan. None of my friends know where I am, or why I had to leave."

"I see. Maybe one day you can explain everything to them."

"I hope so. I just don't want to put them in danger by telling them the truth."

The halo of long, golden hair shifted as the woman nodded with understanding. "You must be Gabrielle? Savannah told me that Lucan had brought a female here under his protection. I'm Danika. I am—*I was*—Conlan's mate."

Gabrielle accepted the slender hand Danika offered in greeting. "I'm very sorry about your loss."

Danika smiled, sadness swimming in her eyes. When she withdrew her hand from Gabrielle's grasp, it moved absently to cradle the nearly imperceptible swell of her abdomen. "I've been meaning to come and find you to say welcome, but I fear I'm not the best company right now. I haven't much had the desire to leave my quarters these past few days. It's still very hard for me, trying to make this . . . adjustment. Everything is so different now."

"Of course."

"Lucan and the other warriors have been very generous to me. On their own, they've each sworn their protection if I should ever need it, wherever I am. For me, and my child."

"You're pregnant?"

"Fourteen weeks. I'd hoped this would be the first of many sons for Conlan and me. We were so excited about our future. We'd waited a long time to start our family."

"Why did you wait?" Gabrielle winced as soon as the question left her lips. "I'm sorry. I don't mean to pry. I'm sure it's none of my business."

Danika dismissively clucked her tongue. "There's no need to apologize. I don't mind your questions, truly. It's good for me to talk about my Conlan. Come, let's sit awhile," she said, walking with Gabrielle to one of the chapel's long benches.

"I met Conlan when I was just a girl. My village in Denmark had been sacked by invaders, so we thought. It was actually a band of Rogues. They killed nearly everyone, slaughtered women and children, our village elders. No one was safe. A group of Breed warriors arrived in the middle of the attack. Conlan was one of them. They rescued as many of my people as they could. When my mark was discovered, I was taken into the nearest Darkhaven. It was there I learned all about the vampire nation and my place within it. But I couldn't stop thinking about my savior. As fate would have it, a few years later, Conlan came through the area again. I was so excited to see him. Imagine my shock to discover that he'd never forgotten about me, either."

"How long ago was this?"

Danika hardly paused to calculate the time. "Conlan and I shared four hundred and two years together."

"My God," Gabrielle whispered. "So long…"

"It passed in a blink, if you want to know the truth of it. I won't lie and tell you that it was always easy being the mate of a warrior, but I wouldn't have traded a single moment. Conlan believed totally in what he was doing. He wanted a safer world, for me, and for our children to come."

"And so you waited all this time to conceive?"

"We wouldn't start our family so long as Conlan felt he needed to remain with the Order. The front lines are not the best place for children, which is why you don't see families among the warrior class. The dangers are too great, and our mates need to be able to focus solely on their missions."

"Don't accidents happen?"

"Unplanned pregnancies are all but unheard of among the Breed, because it takes something more sacred than simple sex for us to conceive. The fertile time for blood-bonded Breedmates revolves around the crescent moon. During this crucial period, if we wish to create a child, our bodies must have both our mate's seed and his blood flowing within us. It is a sacred ritual that no mated pair goes into lightly."

The very image of sharing this profoundly intimate act with Lucan made Gabrielle warm deep inside her core. The thought of bonding in that way with anyone else, growing large with anyone's child but Lucan's was a prospect she refused to consider. She would rather be alone, and likely would be.

"What will you do now?" she asked, filling the quiet that made her imagine her own lonely future.

"I'm not sure yet," Danika replied. "I do know that I will never bond to another male."

"Don't you need a mate in order to stay young?"

"Conlan was my mate. With him gone, one lifetime will be long enough. If I refuse to bond in blood with another male, I will simply age normally from now on, like I did before I met Conlan. I will simply be...mortal."

"You'll die," Gabrielle said.

Danika's smile was resolved, but not entirely sad. "Eventually."

"Where will you go?"

"Conlan and I had been planning to retreat to one of the Darkhavens in Denmark, where I was born. He wanted that for me, but now I think I would rather raise his son in Scotland instead, so that our child can know something of his father through the land he loved so much. Lucan has already begun making arrangements for me, so that I can go whenever I decide that I'm ready."

"That was kind of him."

"Very kind. I couldn't believe it when he came to find me and give me the news, along with his pledge that my child and I would always have a direct line to him and the rest of the Order if we ever need anything. It was the day of the funeral, just hours afterward, so his burns were still extremely severe. Yet he was more concerned about my welfare."

"Lucan was burned?" Alarm snaked into her heart. "When, and how?"

"Just three days ago, when he carried out the funeral ritual for Conlan." Danika's fine brows lifted. "You don't know? No, of course, you wouldn't. Lucan would never mention a word of his act of honor, or the damage he suffered in doing it. You see, the Breed's funeral tradition calls for one vampire to carry the body of the fallen to be received by the elements outside," she said, gesturing to a shadowed corner of the chapel, where a dark stairwell was located. "It's a duty of great respect, and of sacrifice, because once topside, the vampire who attends his brethren must remain with him for eight minutes as the sun rises."

Gabrielle frowned. "But I thought their skin couldn't tolerate solar rays."

"No, it can't. They burn severely and quickly, but none so much as the vampires who are first generation. The oldest of the Breed suffer the worst, even under the briefest exposure."

"Like Lucan," Gabrielle said.

Danika gave a solemn nod. "For him, the eight minutes of dawn must have been beyond bearing. But he did it. For Conlan, he willingly let his flesh burn. He might even have died up there, but he would let no one else carry the burden of laying my beloved Conlan to rest."

Gabrielle thought back to the urgent phone call that had taken Lucan out of her bed in the middle of the night. He'd never said what it was about. Never shared any of his loss with her.

Pain twisted in her stomach when she thought of what

he had endured by Danika's description. "I spoke to him—that very day, in fact. From his voice, I knew something was wrong, but he denied it. He sounded so tired, beyond exhausted. You're telling me that he was suffering from extensive ultraviolet burns?"

"Yes, he was. Savannah told me that Gideon found him not long afterward. Lucan was blistered from head to toe. He couldn't open his eyes for the pain and swelling, but he refused any help in getting back to his quarters so that he could heal."

"My God," Gabrielle gasped, astonished. "He never told me, not any of this. When I saw him later that night—just hours later—he seemed perfectly normal. Well, what I mean is, he looked and acted like nothing was wrong with him."

"Lucan's nearly pure bloodlines made him suffer the most, but they also helped him heal more quickly from the burns. Even then, it wasn't easy for him; he would have required a great deal of blood to replenish his system after so much trauma. By the time he was well enough to leave the compound to hunt, he would have been practically ravenous with hunger."

And he had been. Gabrielle understood now. The memory of him feeding from the Minion he'd killed flashed through her mind, but it had a different context now, no longer the monstrous act it had appeared on the surface, but a means of survival. Everything was taking on a different context since she'd met Lucan.

In the beginning, she would have considered the war between the Breed and their enemies to be nothing more than one evil versus another, but now she couldn't help feeling that it was her war, too. She had a stake in its outcome, and not just because her future was apparently linked to this strange otherworld. It was important to her that Lucan won not only the war against the Rogues, but also the equally devastating, very personal war he was struggling with in private.

She worried for him, and couldn't dismiss the niggling fear that had been crawling up her spine since he and the other warriors left the compound for the raid.

"You love him very much, don't you?" Danika asked as Gabrielle's anxious silence stretched between them.

"I do, yes." She met the other woman's gaze, seeing no reason to hide the truth when it was probably written all over her face. "Can I tell you something, Danika? I have this awful feeling about what he's doing tonight. And to make it worse, Tegan said he didn't think Lucan was going to be alive much longer. The longer I sit here, the more afraid I am that Tegan might be right."

Danika frowned. "You spoke with Tegan?"

"I ran into him—literally—a short while ago. He told me not to get too attached to Lucan."

"Because he thought Lucan was going to die?" Danika let out a long breath and shook her head. "That one seems to enjoy putting others on edge. He probably said those things only because he knew it would upset you."

"Lucan has said there is some bad blood between them. Do you think Tegan can be trusted?"

The blond Breedmate seemed to consider it for a moment. "I can tell you that loyalty is a large part of the warriors' code. It means everything to these males, down to a one. Nothing in this world could make them violate that sacred trust." She rose now, and took Gabrielle's hand in hers. "Come on. Let's go find Eva and Savannah. The wait will pass more quickly for all of us if we don't spend it alone."

CHAPTER
Twenty-six

From their observation point on the roof of one of the harbor buildings, Lucan and the other warriors watched as a small pickup truck, spitting gravel under its polished chrome wheels, roared up to the front of their target location. The driver was human. If his sweaty, slightly anxious scent didn't announce him, the country music blaring out of his open window surely would. He got out of the vehicle carrying a stuffed brown-paper bag that reeked of steaming fried rice and pork lo mein.

"Looks like our boys are eating in tonight," Dante drawled, while the unsuspecting delivery man checked the flapping white ticket stapled onto his order and looked around the desolated wharf with dawning wariness.

The driver approached the warehouse's entry door, shot another nervous look around, then swore into the darkness and jabbed the buzzer. There were no lights on inside the building, only a pool of yellow shining down from the bare bulb over the door. The battered steel panel opened, revealing the dark behind it. Lucan could see the feral eyes of a Rogue staring out as the delivery man blurted the take-out order total and thrust the bag into the wedge of blackness in front of him.

"Whaddaya mean, trade for it?" the urban cowboy demanded in a thick Boston accent. "What the hell—"

A large hand seized him by the front of his shirt, jerking him off his feet. He screamed, and in his flailing panic somehow managed to rip away from the Rogue's grasp.

"Oops," Niko hissed from his position near the ledge, "guess he just realized it wasn't Chinese on the menu."

The Rogue flew at the human in a blur of shadows, taking him down from behind, tearing open his throat with savage efficiency. Death was bloody and instantaneous. When the Rogue leaped up and began to heft its kill onto its shoulder to drag it inside, Lucan got to his feet.

"Time to move. Let's go."

In concert, the warriors hit the ground and headed at blinding speed for the Rogues' warehouse lair. Lucan, leading the way, was first to reach the vampire and his lifeless human burden. He slapped a hard hand onto the Rogue's shoulder and spun him around, at the same time drawing one of his slayers' blades from a sheath at his hip. He sliced hard and with unerring aim and severed the beast's head in one clean stroke.

The Rogue immediately began a cellular meltdown, dropping its blood-soaked victim onto the gravel as the kiss of Lucan's blade ran like acid through the vampire's corrupted nervous system. A few seconds later, all that remained of the Rogue was a puddle of putrid blackness seeping into the dirt.

Up ahead at the door, Dante, Tegan, and the three other warriors were locked and loaded, braced to start the real action. On Lucan's "go," the six of them poured into the warehouse with weapons at the ready.

The Rogues inside had no idea what had hit them until Tegan let a dagger fly and nailed one through the throat. As the Rogue shrieked and writhed toward a smoldering disintegration, its enraged companions lunged for cover, grabbing up weapons as they scrambled to evade the barrage of bullets and razor-sharp steel that Lucan and his brethren were now raining down upon them.

Two Rogues bit it in the first few seconds of engagement, but the remaining pair had fled deep into the warehouse's gloomy corners. One of the Rogues blasted gunfire at Lucan and Dante from behind an old pile of crates. The warriors dodged the attack and sent a little love back at the Rogue, driving him out into the open where Lucan finished him off.

At his periphery, Lucan spotted the last of the suckheads trying to make an escape through a maze of tumbled storage barrels and scattered metal pipes in the rear of the building.

Tegan hadn't missed it, either. The vampire went after the fleeing Rogue like a freight train, vanishing into the bowels of the warehouse in deadly pursuit.

"We're clear," Gideon shouted from somewhere in the smoke- and dust-filled darkness.

But no sooner had he said it than Lucan sensed a new threat closing in on them. His ears picked up the quiet scramble of movement overhead. The dingy skylights above the exposed ventilation ducts and steel trusses of the warehouse were nearly opaque with grime, but Lucan was sure that something was advancing across the roof.

"Heads up!" he called to the others just as the ceiling shattered, and seven more Rogues dropped down with weapons blazing.

Where had they come from? The intel on the lair was solid: six individuals, probably turned Rogue only recently, and operating independently, without affiliation. So, who had called in the cavalry to back them up? How did they know about the raid?

"Fucking ambush," Dante growled, voicing Lucan's thoughts aloud.

No way in hell this fresh wave of trouble was coming in purely by chance, and as Lucan's gaze settled on the largest of the Rogues coming at them now, he felt black fury rise to a boil in his gut.

It was the vampire who had eluded him the night of the slaying outside the dance club. The bastard out of the West Coast. The Rogue who might have killed Gabrielle, and might yet one day soon if Lucan didn't take him out right now.

While Dante and the others returned fire on the descending group of Rogues, Lucan gunned for that one target alone.

Tonight, he would finish it.

The suckhead hissed as he approached, the hideous face stretching into a grin. "We meet again, Lucan Thorne."

Lucan gave a grim nod. "For the last time."

Shared hatred made both males discard their guns in favor of more personal combat. In a flash, blades were drawn, one in each hand, as the two vampires prepared to battle to the death. Lucan threw the first strike. And took a vicious slice in his shoulder as the Rogue evaded the blow with stealth speed, having moved in a blink and appearing on the other side of him now, jaws open in triumph at the spilling of first blood.

Lucan leaped around with equal agility, his blades slashing whisper close to the Rogue's big head. The suck-head glanced down to where his right ear now lay, severed at his feet.

"Game on, asshole," Lucan snarled.

With a vengeance.

They flew at each other in a swirl of rage and muscle and cold, deadly steel. Lucan was aware of the battle taking place around him, the other warriors holding their own against the second round of warfare. But his main focus—all of his hatred—was centered on his personal grudge with the Rogue in front of him.

He felt his fangs stretch with the force of his anger, his pupils sharpening, until he knew that there could be little difference between his face and the one snarling back at him. They were equally matched in strength, but Lucan's blood burned hotter than his opponent's.

All Lucan had to do was think of Gabrielle, and of the terror this beast would inflict on her, and he was on fire with rage.

He fed that fury, driving the Rogue back with blow after relentless blow. He didn't feel the strikes he took on his own body, though there had been many. He forced his opponent down. Readied himself to deliver the final, killing blow.

With a roar, he sliced deep into the neck of the Rogue, liberating the huge head from its savaged body. Arms and legs spasmed as the vampire collapsed in a convulsing heap on the floor. Lucan's fury was still hammering hard in his veins; he flipped his blade over in his hand and drove it hard into the suckhead's chest, speeding the disintegration of the corpse.

"Holy hell," Rio said from somewhere nearby, his voice wooden. "Lucan—above you, man! Got another one in the rafters!"

It happened in an instant.

Lucan wheeled around, battle fury tearing through every muscle in his body. He threw a glance up to where Rio had indicated. High above his head, another Rogue vampire was crawling through the trusses of the warehouse ceiling, holding something that looked like a small metal football under his arm. A small red light on the device blinked quickly, then began a steady burn.

"Get down!" Nikolai raised his customized Beretta and took aim. "Dude's about to drop a fucking bomb!"

Lucan heard the sudden blast of the gunshot.

Saw the Rogue take Niko's slug right between its glowing yellow eyes.

But the bomb was already airborne.

Half a second later, it blew.

CHAPTER
Twenty-seven

Gabrielle sat up with a start, jolted out of a fitful doze on the sofa in Savannah's living room. The women had been gathered there for the past few hours—taking comfort in one another's company—with the exception of Eva, who sometime ago had gone to the chapel to pray. The Breedmate had been edgier than the rest of them, spending the good part of the evening pacing and chewing her lip with anxious impatience.

From somewhere above the labyrinth of corridors and rooms, muted sounds of movement and clipped male voices carried down into the living room. The muffled hum of the elevator vibrated the thick air as the vehicle began its descent to the main floor of the compound.

Oh, God.

Something was wrong.

She could *feel* it.

"Lucan."

Gabrielle pushed aside the chenille throw that covered her and swiveled to put her feet on the floor. Her heart was racing, squeezing tight in her breast with every frantic beat.

"I don't like the sound of this, either," Savannah said, sliding a tense look around the room.

Gabrielle, Savannah, and Danika poured out of the apartment to greet the warriors, none of them saying a word, hardly breathing as they hurried toward the arriving elevator.

Even before the steel door slid open, it was apparent from the urgent sounds within that bad news was coming.

Just how bad, Gabrielle had not been prepared for.

The stench of smoke and blood hit her nose like a physical blow. She winced at the foul odor of war and death as she strained to get a clear picture of the situation in the elevator car. None of the warriors were coming out. Two were down on the floor of the car, three others were crouched around them.

"Get some clean towels and blankets!" Gideon shouted to Savannah. "Bring as many as you can, baby!" As she sprang into action, he added, "We're gonna need some wheels, too. There's a gurney in the infirmary."

"On it," Niko answered from within the elevator.

He leaped over one of the two ravaged forms lying supine on the floor. As he passed, Gabrielle saw that his face and hair and hands were black with soot. The warrior's clothing was torn, his skin peppered with easily hundreds of bleeding abrasions. Gideon bore similar contusions. Dante, too.

But their wounds were nothing compared to the

massive injuries sustained by the two Breed warriors who had been carried, unconscious, off the streets by their brethren.

Gabrielle knew from the leaden weight in her heart that one of them was Lucan. She crept forward, and caught her breath to see her fears realized.

Blood pooled beneath him, spilling wine-dark out onto the white marble of the corridor. His boots and leathers were shredded, as was most of the skin on his arms and legs. His face was an ugly mess of soot and crimson cuts. But he was alive. He curled back his lips and hissed through extended fangs when Gideon had to move him in order to apply a makeshift tourniquet to stanch a gash on his arm.

"Shit—I'm sorry, Lucan. It's pretty deep. Jesus, it won't stop bleeding, either."

"Help... Rio." The words came out in a dark growl, a direct command, even though he was lying flat on his back. "I'm good"—he broke off with a pained snarl— "Damn it... want you to... look after... him."

Gabrielle kneeled down beside Gideon. She held out her hand to take the end of the binding from him. "I can do that."

"You sure? It's ugly. You really gotta get your hands right in there to pull it tight."

"I've got it." She nodded toward Rio, who lay nearby. "Do as he says."

The injured warrior on the floor beside Lucan was plainly in agony. He, too, was bleeding profusely from torso wounds and horrific damage to his left arm. The mangled limb was wrapped in a blood-soaked rag that might have been a shirt. His face and chest were burned and lacerated beyond recognition. He started moaning, low in his throat, a piteous sound that brought hot tears to Gabrielle's eyes.

When she blinked them away, she found Lucan's pale gray eyes locked on her. "Nailed...the bastard."

"Shh." She smoothed sweat-dampened strands from his battered brow. "Lucan, just be still. Don't try to talk."

He ignored her, though, swallowing on a dry throat and then pushing the words out. "From the nightclub... son of a bitch was there tonight."

"The one who got away from you?"

"Not this time." He blinked slowly, his look as fierce as it was stark. "Can't ever...hurt you now..."

"Yeah," Gideon drolly piped from where he was working on Rio. "And you're damn lucky to be alive for it, hero."

Gabrielle's throat constricted further as she gazed down at him. For all his protestations that his duty came first and that there never could be a place for her in his life, Lucan had been thinking of her tonight? He was bleeding and injured, partly because of something he did for her?

She picked up his hand and held it to her, cradling the part of him that she could, pressing his bent fingers close against her heart. "Oh, Lucan..."

Savannah ran up with an armful of the requested supplies. Niko followed closely behind, pushing the rolling hospital bed ahead of him.

"Lucan first," Gideon told them. "Get him into a bed, then come back for Rio."

"No." Lucan groaned, a sound of determination more than pain. "Help me up."

"I don't think you sh—" Gabrielle said, but he was already trying to raise himself up from the floor.

"Easy, big guy." Dante stepped in, putting a strong

hand under Lucan's arm. "You got laid pretty low out there. Why don't you take a breather, let us wheel you down to the infirmary."

"Said I'm good." With Gabrielle and Dante each holding a hand, Lucan hoisted himself to a sitting position. He panted a bit, but remained upright. "Took a few hits, but damn it... gonna walk to my own bed. Not letting you... drag me there."

Dante glanced at Gabrielle and rolled his eyes. "You know he's thickheaded enough to mean it."

"Yeah. I know he is."

She smiled, grateful for the stubbornness that kept him strong. Lending the support of her body, she and Dante put their shoulders under his arms and held on to him as Lucan began a slow crawl up to his feet.

"Over here," Gideon told Niko, who moved the gurney into position for Rio, while Savannah and Danika did what they could to stanch his wounds, remove his soiled, tattered clothing and the unneeded bulk of his weapons.

"Rio?" Eva's voice was pitched high as she ran into the chaos, her rosary beads still clutched in her hand. She came up on the open elevator and instantly shrank back, choking on her breath. "Rio! Where is he?"

"He's hanging in there, Eva," Niko said, moving away from the loaded gurney to intercept Eva. He steered her away with firm hands before she could get too close to the carnage. "There was an explosion tonight. He took the worst hit."

"No!" Her hands came up to her face in horror. "No, you're wrong. That's not my Rio! It can't be!"

"He's alive, Eva. But you're going to have to be strong for him."

"No!" She started screaming in wild hysteria, trying to force her way near her mate. "Not my Rio! God, no!"

Savannah came around and took Eva under her arm. "Come away now," she said gently. "They know how to help him."

Eva's broken sobs filled the corridor and pierced Gabrielle with a private anguish that was a mix of relief and stone-cold fear. She worried for Rio, and it shattered her heart to think what Eva must be feeling. Gabrielle knew some of that hurt herself because it could have been Lucan in Rio's place. A few bare millimeters—mere fractions of a second—might have been all that determined which of the two warriors would be lying in a deepening pool of blood, fighting for his life.

"Where's Tegan?" Gideon asked, keeping his attention rooted on his own fast-moving fingers as he continued to inspect and treat the fallen warrior under his care. "Has he come back yet?"

Danika shook her head, but shot an anxious glance at Gabrielle. "Why would he be here? Wasn't he with all of you?"

"We lost track of him soon after we hit the Rogue lair," Dante put in. "Once the explosion went off, our main goal was getting Lucan and Rio back to the compound as quickly as possible."

"Let's roll here," Gideon said, taking the head of Rio's gurney. "Niko, help me get this thing moving."

Questions about Tegan were eclipsed as everyone scrambled to do what they could for Rio. They all made their way down to the infirmary, Gabrielle, Dante, and Lucan moving the slowest along the corridor as Lucan swayed on his feet, holding fast to both of them and working to keep himself steady.

Gabrielle braved a glance at him, wanting so badly to caress his bruised and bleeding face. As she looked at him, heart twisting, his dark lashes flicked up, and he met her eyes. She didn't know what passed between them in that prolonged instant of quiet amid the chaos, but it felt warm and right, despite everything that was terrible about the night's events.

When they reached the room where Rio was being tended to, Eva stood at the side of the gurney, hovering over his broken body. Tears streamed down her cheeks.

"This wasn't supposed to happen," she moaned. "It shouldn't have been my Rio. Not like this."

"We'll do everything we can for him," Lucan said, his breath rasping heavily from his own injuries. "I promise you, Eva. We won't let him die."

She shook her head, staring down at her mate on the bed. As she pet his hair, Rio murmured incoherent words, semiconscious, and in obvious pain. "I want him out of here at once. He should be taken to the Darkhavens. He needs medical care."

"He's not stable enough to be moved from the compound," Gideon told her. "I have the training and the equipment to treat him here for now."

"I want him out of here!" Her head snapped up, her glittering gaze flitting from one warrior to another. "He's no good to any of you now, so let me have him. You don't own him anymore—none of you. He is all mine now! I only want what is best for him!"

Gabrielle felt Lucan's arm tense at the hysterical outburst. "Then you need to stay out of Gideon's way, and let him work," he said, slipping easily into the role of leader despite his own battered condition. "Right now, the only thing that matters is keeping Rio alive."

"You," Eva said, her voice dry as she leveled a teary glare at him. Her eyes took on a wilder sheen, her face transformed into a mask of pure hatred. "It should be you dying right now, not him! You, Lucan. That was the deal I made! It was supposed to be you!"

A chasm opened up in the infirmary, swallowing all sound but the stunning truth of what Rio's mate had just confessed.

Dante and Nikolai's hands went to their weapons, both warriors prepared to strike at the slightest provocation. Lucan lifted his hand to stay them, his eyes holding fast to Eva. He really didn't give a damn that her venom was aimed squarely at him; if he'd been some kind of target for her rage, he had survived it. Rio might not. Any one of his brethren present on the raid tonight might not have survived Eva's betrayal.

"The Rogues knew we were going to be there," Lucan said, his voice held all the more cool by the depth of his fury. "We were ambushed at the warehouse. You arranged it."

Low growls sounded from the other warriors. If the confession had come from a male, there would have been little Lucan could do to keep his brethren from attacking with lethal force. But this was a Breedmate, one of their own. Someone they had known and trusted as kin for more than one lifetime.

Now Lucan looked at Eva and saw a stranger. He saw madness. A deadly desperation.

"Rio was to be spared." She bent over him, cradling his bandaged head in the crook of her arm. He made a noise, something raw and wordless, as Eva tugged him into her embrace. "I didn't want him to be able to fight anymore. Not for you."

"So you would see him maimed instead?" Lucan asked. "This is how you care for him?"

"I love him!" she cried. "What I did—all of it—was out of love for him! Rio will be happier somewhere else, away from all of this violence and death. He will be happier in the Darkhavens, with me. Away from your damned war!"

Rio made the sound in his throat again, more plaintive now. It was unmistakably a sound of agony, although whether it stemmed from physical discomfort or the distress of hearing what was happening around him, was unclear.

Lucan gave a slow shake of his head. "That's a call you can't make for him, Eva. You didn't have the right. This is Rio's war, as much as anyone else's. It is what he believed in—what I know he still believes in, even after what you have done to him. This war belongs to all of the Breed."

She scoffed acidly. "Ironic of you to think so, when you are only a few steps away from turning Rogue yourself."

"Jesus Christ," Dante hissed from where he stood nearby. "You're wrong, Eva. You are fucking disturbed."

"Am I?" Her gaze remained rooted on Lucan, sadistic in her glee. "I've been watching you, Lucan. I've seen you struggle with your hunger when you think no one is around. Your façade of control does not fool me."

"Eva," Gabrielle said, a voice of calm washing over the tension in the room. "You are upset. You don't know what you're saying."

She laughed. "Ask him to deny it. Ask him why he deprives himself of blood until he is nearly starving for it!"

Lucan said nothing in response to the very public accusations, because he knew them to be true.

So did Gabrielle.

It moved him that she would rise to his defense, but this moment wasn't so much about him as it was Rio and the deception that would shatter the warrior. Perhaps already had, judging from the increased sawing of the male's bandaged limbs and his struggling to speak past his injuries.

"How did you strike this bargain, Eva? How did you make contact with the Rogues—one of your day trips topside?"

She exhaled with mocking humor. "It wasn't so hard. There are Minions walking around all over the city. You only have to look. I found one and told him to put me in touch with his Master."

"Who was it?" Lucan demanded. "What did he look like?"

"I don't know. We met just once and he kept his face hidden. He wore dark glasses and kept the lights off in the hotel room. I didn't care who he was or what he looked like. All that mattered was that he is powerful enough to make things happen. I only wanted his promise."

"I can imagine what he made you pay for it."

"It was just a couple of hours with him. I would have paid anything," she said, no longer looking at Lucan, or everyone else who was gaping at her in disgust, but instead staring down at Rio. "I would do anything for you, my darling. I would bear . . . anything."

"You may have made a bargain with your body," Lucan said, "but it was Rio's trust you sold."

A rasp slipped from between Rio's parched lips as Eva cooed and caressed him. His eyelids fluttered open. There was a shallow, gasping breath as he tried to form words.

"I..." He coughed, his wracked body spasming. "Eva..."

"Oh, my love—yes, I'm here!" she cried. "Tell me what you need, baby."

"Eva..." His throat worked in silence for a moment, and then he tried again. "I...denounce...you."

"What?"

"Dead..." He moaned, his mental pain no doubt deeper than the physical, but the fierce look in his bleary, bloodshot eyes said he would not be deterred. "No longer exist...to me...you are...dead."

"Rio, don't you understand? I did this for us!"

"Leave," he gasped. "Never...see you...again..."

"You can't mean that." She lifted her head, her eyes darting frantically. "He doesn't mean that! He can't! Rio, tell me you don't mean that!"

When she tried to reach for him, Rio growled, using what little strength he had to shun her touch. Eva let out a sob. Blood from his wounds covered the front of her clothes. She stared down at the stains she bore, then over to Rio, who had now shut her out completely.

What happened next took only a few seconds at most, but it played out as if time itself had slowed to a merciless crawl.

Eva's stricken gaze lit on Rio's weapon belt lying next to the bed.

A look of resolve crossed her face as she lunged for one of the blades.

She raised the gleaming dagger up near her face.

Whispered to Rio that she would always love him.

Then Eva flipped the weapon around in her hand and pressed it to her throat.

"Eva, no!" Gabrielle screamed, her body jerking in re-flex as if she thought she could save the other female. "Oh, my God, no!"

Lucan held her at his side. He swiftly took her in his arms and turned her face into his chest, shielding her from seeing Eva slice through her own jugular and fall, bleeding and lifeless, to the floor.

CHAPTER
Twenty-eight

Fresh out of the shower in Lucan's bedroom suite, Gabrielle toweled off her wet hair and slipped into a plush white terry-cloth robe. She was exhausted, having spent the better part of the day with Savannah and Danika, the three of them helping Gideon attend to Rio and Lucan. Everyone in the compound moved in a state of numb disbelief over Eva's betrayal and the tragic outcome that left her dead at her own hand and Rio clinging precariously to life.

Lucan was in bad shape as well, but true to his word and his stubborn volition, he had left the infirmary on his own motor to rest in his personal suites. Gabrielle was astonished that he had accepted any care at all, but between the other women and herself, there hadn't been any hope of his refusing.

Gabrielle felt a swelling sense of relief when she opened the bathroom door and found him seated on the massive bed, his back propped up against the headboard with several pillows. Although his cheek and brow were stitched and bandages covered much of his broad chest and limbs, he was recovering. He was whole, and in time, he would be healed.

Like her, he wore nothing but a white terry robe; it was all the women had permitted him to put on after they'd spent hours cleaning and patching up contusions and bloody shrapnel wounds, which peppered so much of his body.

"Feel better?" Lucan asked, staring as she ran her fingers through her damp hair to push it out of her face. "I thought you might be hungry once you came out of there."

"I'm starved."

He gestured to a squat cocktail table in the sitting area of the bedroom, but Gabrielle's nose had already picked up on the impressive buffet. French bread, garlic and spices, tomato sauce, and cheese wafted from across the room. She saw a plate of field greens and a cup of fresh fruit, even something dark and chocolate-looking amid all the other temptations. She wandered over for a closer look, her stomach growling in anticipation.

"Manicotti," she said, breathing in the pasta's aromatic fumes. A bottle of red wine had been uncorked beside a crystal glass. "And chianti?"

"Savannah wanted to know if you had any favorite foods. It was all I could think of."

It was the meal she'd made for herself the night he had come back to her apartment to return her cell phone. The meal that sat cold and forgotten on her counter while she and Lucan went at it like minks. "You remembered what I was cooking that night?"

He gave a mild shrug. "Sit down. Eat."

"There's only one place setting."

"Were you expecting company?"

She looked at him. "You really can't eat any of this? Not even a bite?"

"If I did, I could only stomach a small amount." He motioned for her to take a seat. "Eating human food is merely for appearances."

"All right." Gabrielle sat on the floor cross-legged. She slid the creamy linen napkin out from under the silverware and draped it over her lap. "But it doesn't seem fair for me to stuff my face in front of you."

"Don't worry about me. I've had enough female fussing and concern for one day."

"Suit yourself."

She was too hungry to wait another second and the meal looked far too delicious to resist. Using the edge of her fork, Gabrielle cut off a bite of the manicotti and chewed it in a state of absolute bliss. She ate half of it in record time, pausing only to pour a glass of wine, which she also consumed with ravenous delight.

The whole time, Lucan watched her from the bed.

"Good?" he asked when she flicked a sheepish glance at him over the rim of her wineglass.

"Fantastic," she murmured, shoveling in a mouthful of vinegarette-drenched field greens. Her stomach was much happier now. She swallowed the last bite of salad, then poured another half glass of chianti, and settled back with a sigh. "Thank you for this. I'll have to thank Savannah, too. She didn't have to go to all this trouble."

"She likes you," Lucan said, his studious expression

unreadable. "You were a big help last night. Thank you for looking after Rio and the others. Myself, as well."

"You don't have to thank me."

"Yes, I do." The small, stitched gash in his forehead bunched up with his scowl. "You've been kind and giving all along, and I—" He broke off, muttering something under his breath. "I appreciate what you did, that's all."

Oh, she thought, *that's all*. Even his gratitude came fully equipped with emotional barriers now.

Suddenly feeling too much like an outsider with him at the moment, she was more than willing to change the subject.

"I hear Tegan made it back in one piece."

"Yes. But Dante and Niko nearly tore him apart on sight, after he pulled that disappearing act during the raid."

"What happened to him last night?"

"One of the Rogues tried to slip out a back door at the warehouse as things heated up. Tegan tailed him into the street. He was going to take the suckhead out, but decided to follow him first, see where he might run. He tracked him to the old asylum outside the city. Place was crawling with Rogues. If there was any doubt, now we're certain it's a large colony. Probably an East Coast headquarters."

A chill went through her when she thought that she had been to the asylum by herself—had been *inside* the place—unaware that it was a Rogue location.

"I have some pictures of the interior. They're still in my camera. I didn't have a chance to unload them yet."

Lucan had gone stock-still, staring at her as if she just told him she'd been playing with live grenades. His face seemed to go a bit more ashen beneath its fatigued pallor. "You not only went there, but you broke in to the place?"

She shrugged, guiltily.

"Jesus Christ, Gabrielle." He threw his legs over the side of the bed and sat there for a long moment, just looking at her. It took him a while to form words. "You might have been killed. Do you realize that?"

"I wasn't," she answered, lame observation, but still fact.

"Not the point." He ran both hands deep into the hair at his temples. "Shit. Where's your camera?"

"I left it in the lab."

Lucan picked up the phone beside his bed and speed dialed on intercom. Gideon came on the other end.

"Hey, what's up. Everything good?"

"Yeah," Lucan said, but he was glaring at Gabrielle. "Tell Tegan to put the asylum recon detail on hold for now. I just found out we've got pictures of the interior."

"No shit?" There was a pause. "Ah, fuck me. You mean, she actually went *in* the goddamn place?"

Lucan arched a wry I-told-you-so brow at her. "Load the images from the camera and tell the others we'll meet in an hour to discuss the new strategy. I think we just may have saved some crucial time here."

"Right. See you in sixty."

The call ended with a click of the intercom.

"Tegan was going to go back to the asylum?"

"Yeah," Lucan replied. "A likely suicide mission since he was lunatic enough to insist that he infiltrate solo tonight to gather intel on the place. Not that anyone was going to persuade him differently, least of all me."

He got up off the bed and began inspecting some of his bandages. As he shifted, the top of his robe sagged open, revealing most of his chest and a wedge of his abdomen. The unique markings on his chest were a pale shade of henna, lighter than they had been last night. Now they looked as sallow as the rest of him. Parched and nearly colorless.

"Why are you and Tegan at such odds with each other?" she asked, keeping a close eye on him as she dared the question that had been on her mind ever since Lucan had mentioned the warrior's name. "What happened between you?"

At first, she didn't think he was going to say anything. He kept prodding his injuries, testing the flex of his arms and legs in silence. Then, just about the time she would have given up, he said, "Tegan blames me for taking something from him. Something he cherished." He looked squarely at her now. "His Breedmate died. By my hand."

"Good lord," she whispered. "Lucan . . . how?"

He frowned, glanced away again. "Things were different in the Old Times when Tegan and I first knew each other. Warriors, for the most part, chose not to take Breedmates because the dangers were too great. There were few of us in the Order then, and protecting our families was difficult when combat took us leagues away from them, often for months at a time."

"What about the Darkhavens? Wouldn't they have provided some protection?"

"There were fewer of those then, too. And even less that would welcome the risk of housing a warrior's Breedmate. We, and those we loved, were consistent targets of Rogue violence. Tegan knew all of this, but he bonded himself to a female anyway. Not long afterward, she was captured by the Rogues. They tortured her. Raped her. And before they sent her back to him, they nearly drained her. She was an empty husk—worse than that, she was made a Minion of the Rogue who ruined her."

"Oh, my God," Gabrielle gasped, horrified.

Lucan sighed, as if the weight of the memories pressed hard on him. "Tegan went insane with rage. He became like an animal, slaughtering everything in his path. He would appear so awash in gore that many thought he had bathed in blood. He gorged himself in his fury, and, for nearly a year, he refused to accept the fact that his Breedmate's mind was lost forever. He kept feeding her from his vein, unwilling to see her corruption. He fed to feed her. He didn't care that he was steadily sliding into Bloodlust. For that entire year, he defied Breed law, and would not put her out of her misery. As for Tegan himself, he was slowly, but surely, going Rogue. Something had to be done...."

When he let the statement hang, unfinished, Gabrielle spoke for him. "And as leader, it fell to you to take action."

Lucan gave a grim nod. "I put Tegan in a thick stone cell, and then I put his Breedmate to the sword."

Gabrielle closed her eyes, sensing his regret. "Oh, Lucan..."

"Tegan wasn't freed until his body had withdrawn from its Bloodlust addiction. It took many months of near starvation and absolute agony for him to be able to walk out of that cell on his own legs. When he realized what I'd done, I thought he would try to kill me. But he didn't. The Tegan I knew didn't come out of that cell at all. Something colder did. He's never said the words, but I know he's hated me ever since."

"Not as much as you hate yourself."

His jaw was clenched hard, drawing the lean skin tighter across his cheekbones. "I'm used to making difficult choices. I'm not afraid to take on the hard tasks, or to be the target of anger, even hatred, because of the decisions I make for the betterment of the Breed. I don't give a damn about any of that."

"No, you don't," she said gently. "But you had to hurt a friend, and that has weighed heavily on you for a long, long time."

The look he gave her begged to argue, but maybe he didn't have the strength. After all that he had been through, he was tired, bone tired, although she doubted he would be willing to admit that, even to her.

"You're a good man, Lucan. You've got a very noble heart underneath all that heavy armor."

He grunted, dismissive and sardonic. "Only someone who's known me less than a few weeks would make the mistake of presuming that."

"Really? I can think of a few people here who would tell you the same thing. Including Conlan, if he were alive."

His brows went low, like a thundercloud. "What can you possibly know about that?"

"Danika told me what you did for him. The funeral rite. Bringing him topside as the sun came up. To honor him, you let yourself burn."

"Jesus Christ," he snapped, shooting to his feet. He started to pace in an agitated, halting track near the bed. His voice was coarse, a barely contained roar. "Honor had nothing to do with it. You want to know why I did that? It was guilt. The night of the bombing in the train station, I was supposed to be running that mission with Niko, not Conlan. But I couldn't get you out of my mind. I thought maybe if I had you—if I finally got inside you—it might satisfy my itch and I could move on, forget about you. So, that night I put Conlan on the job in my place. It would have been me in that tunnel, not Conlan. It should have been me."

"My God, Lucan. You're unbelievable, you know that?" She slammed her palms down on the table and let out a sharp, furious laugh. "Why can't you cut yourself some fucking slack?"

The uncontrolled outburst got his attention when nothing else had. He stopped pacing and stared at her. "You know why," he said, his tone level now. "You know, better than anyone else." He shook his head, mouth twisted with self-contempt. "Turns out Eva knew something about it, too."

Gabrielle thought back to the shocking exchange in the infirmary. Everyone had been appalled at Eva's actions, and stunned by her crazed accusations against Lucan. All except him. "Lucan, the things that she said . . ."

"All true, as you have seen for yourself. But you still defended me. That's twice you've kept my weakness from being exposed." He scowled, turning his head away from her. "I won't ever ask you to do that again. My problems are my own."

"And you need to address them."

"What I need is to get some clothes on and go take a look at those pictures Gideon is uploading. If they give us enough info on the asylum's layout, we can hit the place tonight."

"What do you mean, hit it tonight?"

"Take it out. Shut it down. Blow the fucking thing sky-high."

"You can't be serious. You said yourself it's probably full of Rogues. Do you honestly think that you and three other guys will survive going up against unknown numbers?"

"We've done it before. And there will be five of us," he said, as if that should make a difference. "Gideon has said he wants in on whatever we do. He'll be taking Rio's place."

Gabrielle scoffed, disbelieving. "And what about you? You're barely on your feet."

"I'm walking. I'm well enough. They won't be expecting a retaliation so soon, which makes it the best time for us to strike."

"You must be out of your mind. You need rest, Lucan. You can't do anything until you get your strength back. You need to heal." She watched a muscle work in his jaw, a tendon ticking beneath the sallow, drawn slope of his cheek. His features were harder than normal, too lean. "You can't go out there the way you are."

"I said, I'm fine."

The words rushed out of him, a coarse rasp in his throat. When he looked at her again, his silver irises were shot with bright amber flecks of color, like fire licking through ice.

"You're not. Not by a long shot. You need nourishment. Your body's been through too much recently. You need to feed."

She felt a surge of coldness sweep the room and knew it came from him. She was provoking his anger. She'd seen him at his worst before and lived to tell of it, but maybe she was pushing too hard right now. She could sense he'd been itchy and uptight, his temper on a short leash ever since he'd brought her to the compound. Now he was dangerously on edge; did she really want to be the one to shove him past his threshold of control?

Screw it. Maybe that was just what was needed.

"Your body is beaten down, Lucan, not just from your injuries. You're weak. And you're afraid."

"Afraid." He swung an icy look at her, sneered with arctic sarcasm. "Of what?"

"Yourself, for starters. But I think you're even more afraid of me."

She waited for an instant rebuttal, something cold and nasty to match the wintry rage that was rolling off of him like frost. But he didn't say anything. He glared at her for a long moment, then turned away and strode, a bit stiffly, toward a tall bureau on the other side of the room.

Gabrielle sat there on the floor, watching as he yanked open drawers, pulled out clothing and tossed it onto the bed.

"What are you doing?"

"I don't have time to debate this with you. It's pointless."

A cabinet of weapons opened before he reached it, the doors swinging on their hinges with an invisible, violent jerk. He stalked over and pulled out a retractable shelf. At least a dozen daggers and other lethal-looking blades lay in orderly rows on the shelf's velvet liner. With a careless grab, Lucan swiped two large knives in black leather sheaths. He slid open another shelf and selected a big, brushed stainless steel handgun that looked like something out of an action movie nightmare.

"You don't like what I'm saying, so you're going to run away from me instead?" He didn't look at her, or even curse in reply. No, he completely ignored her, and that really pissed her off. "Go ahead, then. Pretend you're invincible, that you're not scared to death of letting someone care for you. Run away from me, Lucan. You're only proving my point."

Gabrielle felt a keen sense of hopelessness as Lucan retrieved an ammunition clip from the cabinet and shoved it into the pistol's hollow grip. Nothing she said would stop him. She felt helpless, like she was trying to wrap her arms around a storm.

She glanced away from him, her eyes straying back to the table where she sat, at the plates and silverware in front of her. She saw the unused knife lying there, the polished blade gleaming.

She couldn't hold him back with words, but there was something else. . . .

She pushed back the long sleeve of her robe. Very calmly, with the same fearless resolve that had served her a hundred times before, Gabrielle picked up the knife and pressed the edge of it to the fleshy part of her forearm. A small pressure, the barest slice of the blade through her skin.

She didn't know which of Lucan's senses responded first, but the roar he let loose when his head came up and he saw what she had done rattled every piece of furniture in the room.

"Goddamn it—Gabrielle!"

The blade flew out of her grasp and across the length of the bedroom, embedding to the hilt in the far wall.

Lucan moved so fast she could hardly track him. One second he was standing several feet away at the foot of the bed, the next he had his large hand clamped down hard around her fingers, hauling her up to her feet. Blood rose from the thin line of her cut, juicy, deep crimson, trickling down her arm. Her hand was still caught in Lucan's crushing grip.

He towered over her, a wall of dark, seething fury.

His chest was heaving, the nostrils flaring as his breath

sawed in and out of his lungs. His handsome face was contorted with anguish and outrage, and his eyes burned with the unmistakable heat of his hunger. Not a trace of gray remained, his pupils narrowed down to the barest slivers of black. His fangs were stretched long, their sharp white tips gleaming behind the vicious curl of his lip.

"Now, try to tell me that you don't need what I'm offering," she whispered fiercely.

Sweat glistened on his brow as he stared at her fresh, bleeding wound. He licked his lips and ground out a word from another language.

It didn't sound friendly.

"Why?" he demanded, accusing. "Why would you do this to me?"

"You really don't know?" She held his feral gaze, weathering his anger as droplets of blood splattered a crimson trail across the snowy white of her robe. "Because I love you, Lucan. And this is all I have to give you."

CHAPTER
Twenty-nine

Lucan thought he knew hunger. He thought he knew fury and desperation—desire, too—but every paltry emotion he'd ever felt in all his ageless life fell away like dust as he stared into Gabrielle's defiant brown eyes.

His senses were swamped, drowning in the sweet jasmine scent of her blood, its source so dangerously close to his mouth. Glossy red, thick as honey, the crimson rivulet pulsed from the small wound she had inflicted on herself.

"I love you, Lucan." Her soft voice broke through the pounding of his own heart and the driving need that now engulfed him. "With or without blood to bind us, I love you."

He couldn't speak, didn't even know what he might have said if his parched throat could form words. With a vicious growl, he thrust her away from him, too weak to be near her when all the darkness in him urged him to make her his in this final irrevocable way.

Gabrielle fell back onto the bed, the loosely tied robe barely covering her nakedness. Bright stains dotted the white sleeve and lapel. There was a red smear on her bare thigh, vivid scarlet on peaches-and-cream skin.

God, how he wanted to put his mouth on that silky wedge of flesh, all over her. Only her.

"No."

The command came out of him, dry as ash. His gut was clenched in a vise of pain, knotted and twisting. It pulled him down. His knees collapsed beneath him when he tried to turn away from the tempting sight of her, sprawled and bleeding like a sacrifice laid out before him.

He dropped to the carpeted floor in a slump of bone and muscle, fighting back a need like he had never known before. She was killing him. This yearning for her—the shattering in his chest when he thought of her ever being with another male.

And then there was his hunger.

Never more intense than when Gabrielle was near, now that his lungs were filled with the perfume of her blood, he was ravenous.

"Lucan..."

He sensed her moving off the bed. Her feet crushed softly on the carpet and then came slowly into his view, pink-lacquered toenails like smooth little shells. She knelt down next to him. Gentle hands sank into his hair, then cupped his tense jaw as she slowly brought his head up to face her.

"Drink from me."

He squeezed his eyes shut, but it was a weak attempt to deny what she was saying. He didn't have the strength to fight the tender, yet unrelenting pull of her arms as she lifted him toward her.

He could smell the blood on her wrist; this close it sent a furious rush of adrenaline coursing through him. His mouth watered, fangs stretched longer, tearing his gums. She coaxed him higher, bringing his torso up off the floor. With one hand, she moved aside her long hair, baring her neck to him.

He flinched, but she held him firmly. Guided him closer.

"Drink, Lucan. Take what you need."

She leaned forward until there was only a breath of space between his slack mouth and the delicate pulse that fluttered beneath the pale skin below her ear.

"Do it," she whispered, and brought him to her.

Pressed his lips forcibly against her neck.

She held him there for an anguished eternity. Then again, maybe it took only a slim fraction of a second for the hook to set. Lucan couldn't be sure. All he knew was the warm crush of her skin against his tongue, the beat of her heart, the rapid panting of her breath. All he knew was the longing he felt for her.

No more denial.

He wanted her—*all of her*—and the beast was too far gone to be merciful now.

He opened his mouth...and sank his fangs into the yielding flesh of her throat.

She gasped at the sudden penetration of his bite, but she didn't release her hold on him, not even when he gulped in the first greedy pull from her open vein.

Blood rushed into his mouth, hot and earthy-sweet, ex-quisite. Beyond anything he could ever have imagined.

After nine hundred years of living, he was finally tasting heaven.

He drank urgently, deeply, need overwhelming him as Gabrielle's quenching blood surged down his throat, into flesh and bone and cell. His pulse hammered with renewal, pumping blood into fatigued limbs and healing his recent wounds.

His sex had come alive with the first taste; now it throbbed heavy and hard between his legs. Demanding even more possession.

Gabrielle was stroking his hair, holding him close as he drank from her. She moaned with each hard tug of his mouth, her body melting, her scent going dark and humid with desire.

"Lucan," she gasped, shuddering around him. "Oh, God..."

With a wordless snarl, he pressed her down beneath him on the floor. He drank deeper, losing himself to the erotic heat of the moment and to a frantic desperation that terrified him.

Mine, he thought, selfish and utterly savage with the idea.

It was too late to stop now.

This kiss had damned them both.

While the initial bite had been a shock, the sharp nick of pain had quickly dissipated into something lush and intoxicating. Pleasure bloomed all over her body from the inside out, as if each long pull of Lucan's mouth at her neck sent a shaft of warm light back into her, reaching down through her core to stroke her soul.

He covered her with his naked weight, their robes

askew as he took her to the floor with him. His hands were rough as they sank into her hair, holding her head to the side as he drank from her. Heedless of any pain his injuries might be causing him, he pressed his bare chest against her breasts. His lips never broke contact with her neck even for a second. She could feel the intensity of his need in every hard draw.

But she felt his strength, too. It was coming back, bit by bit, renewing because of her.

"Don't stop," she murmured, speech slowed for the mounting ecstasy that was building in her with each pulsating movement of his mouth. "You won't hurt me, Lucan. I trust you."

The wet, succulent sounds of his hunger was the most erotic thing she'd ever heard. She loved the heat of his lips on her skin. The ungentle graze of his fangs as he drew her blood into his mouth was a sensation that was both dangerous and exciting.

She was already soaring toward a splintering orgasm when she felt the thick head of Lucan's erection nudging against her sex. She was wet, aching for him. He drove in deep with one thrust, filling her completely with rigid, volcanic heat. Detonating her in an instant. Gabrielle cried out as he plunged hard and fast, his arms like a cage around her, clutching her tightly. He was mindless in his rhythm, a force of raw, magnificent desire.

And still he remained fastened at her neck, pulling her into a blissful, creamy darkness.

She closed her eyes and let herself float away, toward a beautiful obsidian fog.

From someplace distant, she felt Lucan buck and pound above her, his strokes urgent, his large body vibrating with the power of his own release. He shouted something harsh and went completely still.

The delicious pressure at her neck abruptly eased, then vanished, leaving coldness in its wake.

Still drifting, still awash in the heady feel of Lucan sheathed inside her, Gabrielle lifted her heavy lids. Lucan was poised over her on his knees, staring down at her as though frozen. His lips were bright red, his hair wild around his head. His feral eyes were throwing off amber sparks, they were so bright. His skin color was healthier, the network of markings on his shoulders and torso glowing a deep crimson-black.

"What is it?" she asked him, worried. "Are you okay?"

He didn't speak for a long moment.

"Jesus Christ." The rough growl of his voice was tremulous, a pitch she'd never heard in him before. His chest was heaving. "I thought you were...I thought I had—"

"No," she said, giving a lazy, sated shake of her head. "No, Lucan. I'm fine."

She couldn't read his intense expression, but then he didn't give her a chance. He recoiled, sliding out of her. There was a stricken look in his transformed eyes.

Her body felt cold and empty without his warmth. She sat up, rubbing off her sudden chill. "It's okay," she assured him. "Everything's okay."

"No." He shook his head and vaulted to his feet. "No. This was a mistake."

"Lucan..."

"I never should have let this happen!" he bellowed.

With a furious roar, he stalked to the foot of the bed to retrieve his clothes. He yanked the black camo pants and nylon shirt on, then grabbed his weapons and boots, and left the room in a tempest of seething rage.

Lucan could hardly catch his breath for the way his heart was banging in his chest.

When he'd felt Gabrielle go slack beneath him as he drank from her, a stark fear had torn through him, shredding him from the inside out.

She trusted him, she had said while he had been drinking feverishly at her neck. He'd felt the spurs of Bloodlust jabbing into him as Gabrielle's blood flowed into him. Her voice had eased some of the pain. She was tender and caring, her touch, her naked emotion—her presence itself—grounding him when the animal part of him might have slipped its reins.

She trusted him not to harm her, and that trust gave him strength.

But then he'd felt her drifting away from him and he feared... God, in that instant, how he'd feared.

It still gripped him, the black, cold terror that he might have harmed her—could have killed her—if he'd let things go any further than they had.

Because, for all his pushing her away, all his denial, he belonged to her. Gabrielle owned him, down to his soul, and not simply for the fact that her blood was nourishing him now, healing his wounds and strengthening his body. He had bonded to her, long before now. But the irrefutable proof of it had come in that bleak instant a moment ago when he feared he might have lost her.

He loved her.

Down to the darkest, loneliest part of him, he loved Gabrielle.

And he wanted her in his life. Selfishly, dangerously, he wanted nothing more than to keep her with him for all the rest of his days.

The realization made him weave in the corridor outside the tech lab. In truth, it nearly sent him to his knees.

"Whoa, easy there." Dante came up to Lucan almost without warning and grabbed him under the arm. "Damn. You look like holy hell."

Lucan couldn't speak. Words were beyond him.

But Dante didn't need an explanation. He took one look at Lucan's face and fangs and Dante's nostrils flared as they picked up the obvious scents of blood and sex. He blew out a low whistle, a gleam of wry amusement flashing in the warrior's eyes.

"You gotta be kidding me—a Breedmate, Lucan?" He chuckled, shaking his head as he clapped Lucan on the shoulder. "Shit. Better you than me, brother. Better you than me."

CHAPTER
Thirty

Three hours later, with night full upon them, Lucan and the other warriors were geared up and sitting in a black SUV parked about a half mile down the road from the old asylum.

Gabrielle's photographs had proven extremely useful in planning the hit on the Rogue lair. In addition to several exterior and ground-level, entry-point photos, she'd taken interior shots of the boiler room, various corridors, stair-wells, and even a few containing inadvertent images of mounted security cameras that would need to be disabled once the warriors gained access to the place.

"Getting in's going to be the easy part," Gideon said, as the group of them began the final review of the operation. "I'll interrupt the security signal on the ground-level cam-eras, but once we're inside, planting those two dozen bars of C4 in critical areas without alerting the entire colony of suckheads will prove a little trickier."

"Not to mention the added problem of unwanted publicity with the humans," Dante said. "What the hell's taking Niko so long to locate that gas main?"

"Here he comes," Lucan said, spotting the vampire's dark shape nearing the SUV from the ridge of trees outside.

Nikolai opened the back door and climbed in next to Tegan. He pulled off his black head covering, wintry blue eyes alive with excitement. "Piece of cake. The main line is in a lockbox on the west end of the complex. The suckheads may not need heat, but public service has plenty of gas running to the buildings."

Lucan met the warrior's eager look. "So, we get in, set up our party favors, clear the location—"

Niko nodded. "Signal me when the shit's in place. I'll flip the main line, then detonate the C4 once we all rendezvous back here. On the surface, it'll look like a gas leak caused the explosion. And if Homeland Security wants to get involved, I'm sure some of Gabrielle's photos of gangbanger graffiti will send the humans sniffing around in circles for a while."

Meanwhile, the warriors would be sending a big message to their enemies, particularly the Gen One vampire who Lucan suspected was at the helm of this new Rogue insurgency. Blowing their headquarters into the next century ought to be a sufficient invitation for the bastard to come out into the open and dance.

Lucan was anxious to get started. Even more anxious to finish the night's mission because he had his own unfinished business back at the compound. He hated leaving

Gabrielle like he had, knowing she had to be confused and probably more than a little upset.

There were things to be said, certainly, things he hadn't even been prepared to think about much less discuss with her in that moment when the stunning reality of his feelings for her had hit him.

Now, his head was full of plans.

Reckless, stupid, hopeful plans, all of them centered on her.

Around him in the vehicle, the other warriors were checking their gear, loading up the bars of C4 into zippered duffel bags and making final adjustments to the earpieces and mics that would keep them in contact with one another once they breached the asylum perimeter and split up to place the explosives.

"Tonight, we do this for Con and Rio," Dante said, flipping one of his curved blades with nimble, black-gloved fingers and stabbing it into the sheath on his hip. "Vengeance time."

"Hell, yeah," Niko replied, a sentiment echoed swiftly by the others.

When they started to go for the doors, Lucan lifted his hand.

"Hold up." His grim voice stilled them all. "There's something you need to know. Since we're about to go in there and possibly get our asses handed to us, I suppose now's as good a time as any to be straight with you about a couple of things...and I need a promise from each of you."

He met the faces of his brethren, warriors who'd been fighting beside him, as tight as kin, for what seemed like forever. They had always looked to him to lead, trusting him to make the hard calls, certain he would never be at a loss for strategy or decision.

Now he wavered, hesitant, unsure of where to begin. He raked a hand over his jaw, blew out a sharp sigh.

Gideon frowned at him, concerned. "Everything good, Lucan? You took a pretty massive hit in the ambush last night. If you want to sit this out—"

"No. No, that's not it. I'm fine. My injuries are healed…thanks to Gabrielle," he said. "Earlier today, she and I…"

"No shit," Gideon replied when Lucan's explanation trailed off. Damn the vampire, but he was actually grinning about it.

"You drank from her?" Niko asked.

Tegan grunted in the backseat. "That female's a Breedmate."

"Yes," Lucan said, answering with serious calm. "And if she'll have me, I mean to ask Gabrielle to take me as her mate."

Dante smirked at him, rolling his eyes. "Congrats, man. Seriously."

Gideon and Niko offered similar responses, clapping Lucan on the shoulder.

"That's not all."

Four pairs of eyes fixed on him, everyone but Tegan looking at him with grim expectation.

"Last night, Eva had some choice things to say about me—" There was an immediate defensive vocal barrage from Gideon, Niko, and Dante. Lucan spoke over the angry rumbles. "Her betrayal of Rio and the rest of us is inexcusable, yes. But what she said about me…it was the truth."

Dante gave him a narrow look. "What are you talking about?"

"Bloodlust," Lucan replied. The word fell hard into the silence of the SUV. "It's ah ... it's a problem for me. Has been for a long while. I'm dealing with it, but there are times ..." He dropped his chin, stared at the unlit floor of the vehicle. "I don't know if I can beat it. Maybe, with Gabrielle at my side, I might stand a chance. I'm going to fight it like hell, but if it gets worse——"

Gideon spat a vivid obscenity. "Ain't gonna happen, Lucan. Of all of us sitting here, you're the strongest. Always have been. Nothing's gonna pull you down."

Lucan shook his head. "I can't pretend to be the one always in control anymore. I'm tired. I'm not invincible. After nine hundred years of living the lie, it took Gabrielle less than two weeks to tear my mask off. She's forced me to see myself as I truly am. I don't like a lot of what I see, but I want to be better ... for her."

Niko scowled. "Damn, Lucan. You talking about love here?"

"Yeah," he said solemnly. "I am. I love her. Which is why I need to ask something of you. All of you."

Gideon nodded. "Name it."

"If things get bad with me—sometime soon, or down the road—I need to know that I can count on you guys to have my back. You see me lose it to Bloodlust, if you think I'm going to turn ... I've got to have your word that you'll take me out."

"What?" Dante recoiled. "You can't ask that of us, man."

"Listen to me." He wasn't accustomed to begging. The plea was like gravel in his throat, but he needed to spit it out. He was tired of carrying the burden alone. And the

very last thing he ever wanted was to fear that in his weakness he might do anything to harm Gabrielle. "I need to hear you swear it. Each of you. Promise me."

"Shit," Dante said, gaping at him. Finally, he nodded gravely. "Yeah. Okay. You're fucking crazy, but okay."

Gideon shook his head, then held out his fist and knocked his knuckles against Lucan's. "If that's what you want, you got it. I swear to you, Lucan."

Niko voiced his agreement, too. "That day will never come, but if it does, I know you'd do the same for any one of us. So, hell yeah, you have my word."

Which left Tegan, sitting stoically in the backseat.

"What about you, T?" Lucan said, pivoting to meet the warrior's flat green stare. "Can I count on you in this?"

Tegan held him in a long, contemplative silence. "Sure, man. What the fuck, whatever you say. You turn, and I'll be first in line to take you out."

Lucan nodded, satisfied as he looked around at the sober stares of his brethren.

"Jesus," Dante interjected when the heavy quiet in the vehicle seemed endless. "All this touchy feely is making me itchy to kill something. How about we quit jerking each other off and go blow the roof off this mutha?"

Lucan returned the vampire's cocky grin. "Let's do it."

The five Breed warriors in head-to-toe black poured out of the SUV as a unit, then began the stealthy approach toward the asylum on the other side of the moonlit trees.

CHAPTER
Thirty-one

"Come on, come on. Open, damn it!"

Gabrielle sat behind the wheel of a black BMW coupe, waiting impatiently for the massive gate at the compound's estate entrance to slide open and let her out. She hated that she'd been forced to take the car from the fleet without permission, but after what had happened with Lucan, she was desperate to get away. Since the entire grounds were circled with high-voltage fencing, that left just one alternative.

She'd figure out some way to return the Beemer once she was home.

Once she was back where she truly belonged.

She had given all she could to Lucan tonight, but it wasn't enough. She had been prepared for him to push and resist her attempts to love him, but there was nothing she could do if he shut her out. As he had tonight.

She had given him her blood, her body, and her heart, and he had rejected her.

She was all out of energy now.

All out of fight.

If he was so determined to be alone, then who was she to force him into changing? If he wanted to crash and burn, she sure as hell didn't intend to stand around waiting to see it happen.

She was going home.

The heavy iron gates finally parted wide enough to let her out. Gabrielle punched the gas and sped out onto the quiet, unlit street. She had no clear idea of where she was until she drove a couple of miles and found a familiar intersection. There she took a left onto Charles Street, and headed for Beacon Hill in an autopilot daze.

Her block seemed so much smaller to her as she parked the car at the curb outside her apartment. Her neighbors' lights were on, but despite the ambient yellow glow, the brick building seemed dreary somehow.

Gabrielle climbed the front steps and fished her key out of her purse. Her hand knocked against a small dagger she'd taken out of Lucan's weapon cabinet—a bit of insurance in case she ran into any trouble on the way home.

The apartment phone was ringing as she came inside and turned on the foyer light. She let the machine get it, turning to set all the locks and deadbolts on the door.

From the kitchen, she heard Kendra's clipped voice come over the message intercom.

"It's very rude of you to ignore me like this, Gabby." Her friend sounded strangely shrill. Pissed off. *"I need to see you. It's important. You and I really need to talk."*

Gabrielle walked through the living room, noting the blank spaces on her walls where Lucan had removed some of her framed photographs. It seemed like a year had passed since the night he'd come to her apartment and told her the stunning truth about himself and the battle that was raging among those of his kind.

Vampires, she thought, surprised to find that the word no longer shocked her.

Probably very little could shock her now.

And she no longer feared that she was losing her mind like her mother had. Even that tragic history had taken on new meaning now. Her mother hadn't been crazy at all. She'd been a terrified young woman, caught up in a violence that few human minds could grasp.

Gabrielle was not about to let that same violence destroy her. She was home, such as it was, and she would figure out some way to make her old life fit again.

She dropped her purse on the counter and walked over to the answering machine. The message indicator was blinking the number 18.

"You've got to be kidding me," she murmured, hitting the *Play* button.

As the machine did its thing, Gabrielle went into the bathroom to inspect her neck. Lucan's bite glowed dark red below her ear, right near the teardrop and crescent moon that marked her as a Breedmate. She probed the twin punctures and vivid bruise that Lucan had left on her, but found it didn't hurt at all. The dull, empty ache between her legs was the worse pain, but even that paled next to the cold rawness that settled in her chest when she thought of Lucan recoiling from her tonight as if she were poison. Stumbling out of the room like he couldn't get away from her fast enough.

Gabrielle ran the water and washed up, vaguely aware of the messages playing in the kitchen. As the machine advanced to the fourth or fifth one, she realized something odd.

All of the messages were from Kendra, all within that past twenty-four hours. One after the other, some with less than five minutes between them.

And Kendra's tone had soured significantly from her first message when she had been playfully casual, offering to take Gabrielle out to lunch or drinks or anything else that sounded good. Then the tone of the invitation had gotten a bit more insistent: Kendra saying that she had a problem and needed Gabrielle's advice.

The last couple of messages were strident demands that Kendra expected to hear from her soon.

When Gabrielle ran to her purse and checked her cell phone's voicemail, she found more of the same.

Kendra's repeated calls.

Her weirdly acid tone of voice.

A chill crept along her limbs when she thought of Lucan's warning about Kendra. That if she'd fallen victim to the Rogues, she was no friend of hers anymore. That she was as good as dead.

The phone started ringing again in the kitchen.

"Oh, my God," she gasped, gripped in a mounting terror.

She had to get out of there.

Hotel, she thought. Somewhere remote. Somewhere she could hide for a while, decide what to do.

Gabrielle grabbed her purse and the keys to the BMW, practically running for her front door. She threw the locks free and twisted the knob. As the door swung open, she found herself staring at a familiar face that had once been friendly.

Now she was certain it belonged to a Minion.

"Going somewhere, Gabby?" Kendra brought her cell phone away from her ear and closed it. The ringing in the apartment ceased. Kendra smiled thinly, her head cocked at an odd angle. "You're awfully hard to catch lately."

Gabrielle winced at the lost, vacant look in those un-blinking eyes. "Let me past you, Kendra. Please."

The brunette laughed, a loud, open-mouthed chortle that faded into an airless hiss. "Sorry, sweetie. No can do."

"You're with them, aren't you?" Gabrielle said, sick with the understanding. "You're with the Rogues. My God, Kendra, what have they done to you?"

"Hush," she said, her finger to her lip as she shook her head. "No more talking. We have to go now."

When the Minion reached for her, Gabrielle pulled away. She thought of the dagger in her purse, and won-dered if she could retrieve the blade without Kendra's no-tice. If she could, would she be able to use it on her friend?

"Don't touch me," she said, inching her fingers under the leather flap of her bag. "I'm not going anywhere with you."

Kendra bared her teeth, a terrible parody of a smile. "Oh, I think you should, Gabby. After all, Jamie's life de-pends on it."

Cold dread pierced her heart. "What?"

Kendra nodded her head toward the waiting sedan. A tinted window eased down, and there was Jamie, sitting in the backseat beside an enormous thug.

"Gabrielle?" Jamie called out, a panicked look in his eyes.

"Oh, no. Not Jamie. Kendra, please don't let anyone hurt him."

"That'll be entirely up to you," Kendra said politely. She grabbed Gabrielle's purse out of her hands. "You won't be needing anything in here."

She motioned for Gabrielle to walk ahead of her toward the idling car. "Shall we?"

Lucan set two bars of C4 under the huge water heaters in the asylum's boiler room. Crouched down behind the utility equipment, he flipped up the transmitter antennas, then spoke into his mic to report his progress.

"Boiler room is a check," he told Niko on the other end. "I've got three more units to set and then I'm out—"

He froze, hearing the scuff of footsteps outside the closed door.

"Lucan?"

"Shit. Company coming," he murmured quietly as he rose from his position and crept near the door to prepare to strike.

He wrapped his gloved hand around the hilt of a nasty serrated blade sheathed across his chest. He had a gun on him, too, but they'd all agreed no firearms on this mission. No need to alert the Rogues of their presence, and with Niko throwing the gas main outside, pumping fumes into the building, the spark of a bullet firing was liable to set the whole works off prematurely.

The latch on the boiler room door began to twist.

Lucan smelled the stench of a Rogue, and the unmistakable coppery scent of human blood. Muffled animal grunts mingled with wet smacking and the faint whine of a victim being bled dry. The door opened, letting in a huge gust of putrid air as the Rogue started to drag its dying plaything into the dark alcove.

Lucan waited to the side of the door until the Rogue's big head came into full view. The suckhead was too involved in its prey to notice the threat. Lucan brought his hand up, burying the blade in the Rogue's rib cage. It roared, huge jaws gaping, yellow eyes bulging as the titanium sped through its blood system.

The human fell to the floor in a slump, boneless, spasming in the throes of death while the Rogue who'd been feeding off of him began to sizzle and shake, blisters rising like it had been doused with acid.

No sooner did the Rogue collapse into swift decomposition than another came pounding up the corridor. Lucan leaped to meet the new attack, but before he could deliver the first blow, the suckhead came up short, yanked off its feet from behind by a black-clad arm.

A blade flashed, as crisp and quietly as lightning, across the Rogue's throat, severing the big head in one clean strike.

The huge body was dropped to the floor like rubbish. Tegan stood there, blade dripping gore, green eyes steady. He was a killing machine, and the grim set of his mouth seemed to reiterate his earlier promise to Lucan that if Bloodlust ever got the better of him, Tegan was going to make sure Lucan got his own taste of titanium fury.

Looking at the warrior now, Lucan had no doubt that if Tegan ever came for him, it would be over before he even knew the vampire was in the room.

He met that cool, lethal look and gave a nod of acknowledgment.

"Talk to me," Niko said over Lucan's earpiece. "You good in there?"

"Yeah. All clear." He cleaned his dagger on the human's shirt, then sheathed it. When he glanced up, Tegan was already gone, vanished like the specter of death that he was.

"Heading to the north entry points now to place the rest of these party cakes," he told Nikolai as he ducked out of the boiler room and crept down an empty stretch of corridor.

CHAPTER
Thirty-two

Gabrielle, what's happening? What's wrong with Kendra? She came to the gallery and told me you were in an accident and that I had to come with her right away. Why would she lie about that?"

She didn't know how to answer Jamie's anxious, whispered questions from beside her in the backseat of the sedan. They were speeding away from Beacon Hill, toward downtown. Financial District skyscrapers loomed ahead in the dark, office lights twinkling like Christmas bulbs. Kendra sat in the front seat next to the driver, a thick-necked bouncer type in a thug's dark suit and sunglasses.

Gabrielle and Jamie had a similar companion in back with them crowding them onto one side of the slick leather bench seat. She didn't think they were Rogues; they didn't appear to be hiding huge fangs behind their tense lips, and from what little she knew of the Breed's deadly enemies, she didn't expect that she or Jamie would have gone so much as a minute without getting their throats ripped out if the two men were, in fact, blood-addicted Rogues.

Minions, then, she reasoned. Human mind slaves of a powerful vampire Master.

Like Kendra was.

"What are they going to do with us, Gabby?"

"I'm not sure." She reached over and squeezed Jamie's hand. She kept her voice low, too, but she knew their captors were listening to every word. "It'll be okay, though. I promise."

They had to get out of the car before they reached their destination, that much she did know. It was the most basic rule of self-defense: *never let yourself be taken to a secondary location*. Then you were on your attacker's turf.

Odds of survival would go from poor to nil.

She glanced at the sliding lock on the door next to Jamie. He watched her eyes, brow pinching in question as she stared at him then back to the lock. Then he got it. He gave her a nearly imperceptible nod.

But when he started to shift his hands into place to unlock the door, Kendra chose that moment to turn around and taunt them from the front seat. "Almost there now, kiddies. Are you excited? I know I am. I can't wait for my Master to finally meet you in the flesh, Gabby. Mm, mmm! He's just gonna eat you right up."

Jamie leaned forward, practically snarling with venom. "Back off, you lying bitch!"

"Jamie, don't!" Gabrielle tried to hold him back, fear seizing her at his naive display of protectiveness. He had no idea what he was doing, agitating Kendra or the other two Minions in the car with them.

But he wouldn't be swayed. He made a lunge from his seat. "You touch either one of us and so help me, I'll claw your eyes out!"

"Jamie, stop, it's okay," Gabrielle said, pushing him back down. "Calm down, please! It'll be okay."

Kendra had hardly flinched. Staring at them both, she let out a sudden, shrill giggle. "Ah, Jamie. You always have been Gabby's faithful little terrier. Arf! Arf! You're pathetic."

Very slowly, obviously very full of herself, Kendra resituated herself in the front seat, giving them her back. "Turn up at the light," she told the driver.

Gabrielle blew out a tremulous sigh of relief as she settled back against the cold leather. Jamie was bunched up against the car door, fuming. When their eyes met, he slid a fraction to the side, letting her see that the door was now unlocked.

Her heart jumped at his ingenuity and courage. She could hardly contain her hopeful smile as the vehicle slowed for the traffic light a few yards ahead. It was red, but based on the line of cars stopped in front of them, it was due to change at any second.

This was their only chance.

She glanced at Jamie, and saw that he understood the plan perfectly.

Gabrielle waited, watching the light, the seconds seeming like hours. The red light blinked off, then went to green. The cars started moving ahead of them. As the sedan began to accelerate, Jamie grabbed the door handle. Pushed it open.

Fresh night air rushed in, and the both of them made a

headlong move for freedom. Jamie hit the pavement and immediately moved to grab Gabrielle's arm to help her escape.

"Stop her!" Kendra shrieked. "Don't let her get away!"

A heavy hand clamped down on Gabrielle's shoulder and hauled her back inside the car. She crashed against the Minion's massive chest. His arms wrapped around her, trapping her in an iron hold.

"Gabby!" Jamie screamed.

A desperate sob choked out of her throat. "Get out of here! Jamie, go!"

"Punch it, you idiot!" Kendra yelled to the driver as Jamie reached for the door handle, trying to come back for Gabrielle. The engine roared, tires screeching as the car joined the other traffic.

"What about him?"

"Leave him," Kendra ordered sharply. She smiled at Gabrielle, who was struggling in vain in the backseat. "He's already served his purpose."

The Minion held her in a bruising grip until Kendra ordered the car to a stop outside a sleek corporate building. They got out of the car and forced Gabrielle toward the glass entrance. Kendra was talking to someone on her cell phone, purring with self-satisfaction.

"Yes, we've got her. We're coming up now."

She pocketed the phone and led the way across a vacant, marble lobby to a bank of elevators. Once inside, she pressed the button for the penthouse suite.

Gabrielle immediately thought back to the private showing Jamie had done for her photographs. As the elevator stopped on the top floor and the mirrored doors slid open, she had a dreadful feeling that her anonymous buyer was about to make himself known.

The Minion thug who had her by the arms shoved her into the suite. She stumbled forward and, in mere seconds, Gabrielle's dread became fact.

A tall, dark-haired figure in a long black coat and sunglasses stood in front of the wall of glass, Boston's nighttime skyline glowing behind him. He was as big as any one of the warriors, and he projected the same air of confidence. The same cool menace.

"Come in," he said, the boom of his deep voice rolling like a storm. "Gabrielle Maxwell, it is a pleasure to finally meet you. I've heard so much about you."

Kendra went to his side and pet him adoringly.

"You brought me here for a reason, I assume," Gabrielle said, trying not to mourn the loss of Kendra's humanity or fear the dangerous being who made Kendra what she was.

"I've become quite a fan of your work." He smiled without baring his teeth. Kendra was brushed aside with a rough hand. "You take some interesting photographs, Miss Maxwell. Unfortunately, I need you to stop. It's not good for my business."

She tried to hold the calm, predatory gaze that she knew was peering at her from behind the dark glasses. "What's your business? You know, aside, from being a diseased, bloodsucking leech."

He chuckled. "World domination, of course. Really, is there anything else worth fighting for?"

"I can think of a few things."

A dark brow arched over the rim of his shades. "Oh, Miss Maxwell, if you say love or friendship, I may have to end this pleasant little introduction right now." He steepled his fingers, the rings on them sparkling in the dim light. She didn't like the way he was staring at her, sizing her up.

His nostrils flared slightly, and then he leaned forward. "Come closer."

When she didn't move, the big Minion at her back shoved her into motion. She drew up just an arm's length away from the vampire Master.

"You smell delicious," he hissed slowly. "Like a flower, but there is something...else. Someone has fed from you recently. A warrior? Don't bother to deny it, I can smell him on you."

Before she realized it, he grabbed her wrist, yanking her to him. With rough hands, he pushed her head to the side, moving the hair that concealed Lucan's bite and the other, more damning mark, beneath her left ear.

"A Breedmate," he growled, smoothing his fingertips over her skin. "And newly claimed at that. You grow more fascinating by the second, Gabrielle."

She didn't like the intimate way he whispered her name.

"Who bit you, Breedmate? Which one of the warriors did you permit between those long, lovely legs?"

"Go to hell," she said, through gritted teeth.

"Not going to tell me?" He clucked his tongue, slowly shook his head. "That's all right. We can find out soon enough. We can make him come to us."

He drew back from her at last, and motioned for one of the Minion guards. "Bring her to the roof."

Gabrielle fought the grip of her captor, but she was no match for his brute strength. She was forced toward a red exit sign and a door with an information placard affixed to it, marked "Helipad Access."

"Wait! What about me?" Kendra complained from within the suite.

"Oh, yes. Nurse K. Delaney," her dark Master said, as

if just now remembering her. "After we leave, I want you to come out to the roof. I know you'll find the view from the ledge to be spectacular. Enjoy it for a moment . . . then step off."

She blinked at him dully, then bobbed her head, completely under his spell.

"Kendra!" Gabrielle shouted, still desperate to reach her friend. "Kendra, don't do it!"

The one in the black coat and dark shades strode past without a care in the world. "Let's go. I'm finished here."

With the last block of C4 in place at the northern end of the asylum, Lucan navigated his way through a ventilation duct that led to the outside. He removed the loosened grid and hoisted himself out onto the ground. The grass crushed beneath him as he rolled onto it, fresh air crisp in his mouth as he came up on his feet and started to jog toward the perimeter fence.

"Niko, how're we doing?"

"We're good. Tegan's on his way back and Gideon should be right behind you."

"Excellent."

"Got my finger on the detonators," Nikolai said, his voice nearly drowned out by the low chop of a helicopter encroaching on the area. "Say the word, Lucan. I'm dying to light this sucker up."

"Me, too," Lucan said. He scowled up into the night sky, searching for the bird. "We've got incoming, Niko. Sounds like a chopper heading right for the asylum."

As soon as he said it, he saw the dark shape appear over the tree line. Small lights flashed as the helicopter angled for the roof of the asylum and began its descent.

A breeze kicked up as the propeller beat its steady rhythm. Lucan smelled pine and summer pollen...and another perfume that made his blood run cold in his veins.

"Oh, Jesus," he gasped as the trace scent of jasmine registered. "Do not touch the detonators, Niko! For chrissake, whatever you do, you can't let that fucking building blow!"

CHAPTER
Thirty-three

A volatile mix of adrenaline, rage, and absolute, marrow-chilling fear vaulted Lucan to the roof of the old asylum. The helicopter had barely touched down on its landing rails as he thundered toward it from the edge of the building. Lucan was vibrating with fury, more explosive and unstable than a tractor trailer packed with C4. He fully intended to rip the limbs off of whomever was holding Gabrielle.

He approached from behind the helicopter, careful not to be seen as he rolled under its tail, then came around to the passenger side of the cockpit, gun drawn.

He glimpsed her inside. She was in the backseat next to a big male dressed in black and wearing dark glasses. She looked so small, so terrified. Her scent swamped him. Her fear tore at his heart.

Lucan yanked open the cockpit door, shoved his weapon into the face of Gabrielle's captor, and made a grab for her with his free hand. She was jerked back before he could latch onto her.

"Lucan?" Gabrielle gasped, her eyes wide with surprise. "Oh, my God, Lucan!"

He did a quick visual assessment of the situation, noting the Minion pilot and another mind-slave human next to him in the front. The Minion in the front passenger seat spun around to knock away Lucan's arm, and got a bullet in his head instead.

When Lucan looked back to Gabrielle not even an instant later, the calm one with her had put a savage-looking blade to her throat. Peeking out from the sleeve of his long black trenchcoat were the *dermaglyphs* Lucan had seen in the surveillance photos from the West Coast.

"Let her go," he told the Gen One leader of the Rogues.

"My, my, this is a faster response than I could have imagined, even for a blood-bonded warrior. What are you up to? Why are you here?"

The low, arrogant voice took him aback.

Did he know this bastard?

"Let her go," Lucan said, "and I'll show you why I'm here."

"I think not." The Gen One smiled broadly, baring his teeth.

No fangs. A vampire, but not a Rogue at all.

What the hell?

"She's lovely, Lucan. I rather expected she was yours."

Christ, he knew that voice. It came from somewhere buried deep in his memory.

Deep in his past.

A name cut through his mind, as sharp as a blade.
No. It couldn't be him.
Impossible...
He shook off the momentary confusion, but the slip in focus cost him dearly. Creeping up on him from the side, a Rogue had come up on the roof from within the asylum. With a snarl, it seized the helicopter door and slammed the edge of it into Lucan's skull.

"Lucan!" Gabrielle screamed. "No!"

He staggered, one knee sinking beneath him. His gun was kicked out of his grasp. It skittered across the rough surface of the roof, several yards out of reach.

The Rogue punched him, a massive fist connecting with his jaw. A second later, a brutal kick smashed into his ribs. Lucan went down, but he swung out with his booted foot and collapsed his attacker's leg. He leaped on the Rogue, one hand going for the blade sheathed at his torso.

A few feet away, the helicopter's rotors began a high-pitched whine. They were speeding up. The pilot was preparing to take off again.

He couldn't let that happen.

If he let Gabrielle off this roof, he had no hope that he would see her alive again.

"Get us out of here," Gabrielle's captor ordered his pilot, as the chopper's blades whirred faster and faster.

Outside, scrabbling on the roof, Lucan fought the Rogue who'd attacked him. Through the dark, Gabrielle spotted another one coming up from a hatch in the roof.

"Oh, no," she breathed, hardly able to speak for the cutting edge of steel that was biting into the skin at her throat.

The big male leaned past her to see what was happening on the roof. Lucan had returned to his feet. He sliced the first Rogue who had jumped him, lacing open the big vampire's gut. The Rogue's scream was audible even over the loud drone of the helicopter's rotors. Its body started convulsing, spasming ... *melting*.

Lucan's head pivoted around to the helicopter. Fury blazed out of his eyes, glowing like twin embers lit by hellfire. He lunged forward, roaring, shoulders bunched. Coming at the vehicle like a freight train.

"Get us out of here now!" shouted the male beside Gabrielle, the first true trace of worry she'd heard in him. "Now, goddamn it!"

The helicopter started lifting.

Gabrielle tried to shrink away from the bite of the blade by pressing her spine into the back of the small rear seat. If she could just find a way to knock his arm away, she might be able to reach the cockpit door—

There was a sudden lurch of the helicopter, as if they had snagged on some part of the building. The engine whined, straining.

Her captor was fuming now. "Take off, you idiot!"

"I'm trying, sire!" said the Minion at the controls. He pulled a lever and the engine protested with a terrible groan.

There was another lurch, a sharp downward tug that rattled everything inside the helicopter. The cockpit rolled forward. Gabrielle's captor lost his grounding on the seat, a momentary inattention.

The blade left her throat.

With a burst of sheer determination, she threw herself backward and kicked out with both legs, shoving him into the back of the pilot's seat. The vehicle pitched sharply forward. She scrambled for the latch on the cockpit door.

It swung open wildly, flapping on its hinges as the whole compartment shook and wobbled. Her captor was righting himself, about to grab for her again. His sunglasses had fallen off in the chaos. He glared at her with icy gray eyes, full of malice.

"Tell Lucan this is far from over," the leader of the Rogues ordered her, hissing the words through an evil smile.

"Go to hell," Gabrielle shot back at him. In that same instant, she lunged for the open space of the door and dropped the several feet down onto the roof.

As soon as he saw her, Lucan let go of the helicopter's landing rail. The vehicle jolted upward, spinning crazily as the pilot struggled to gain control of his ascent.

He raced to Gabrielle's side and pulled her to her feet, hands roaming all over her to make sure she was in one piece. "Are you okay?"

She nodded jerkily. "Lucan behind you!"

On the roof, another Rogue was heading for them. Lucan met the challenge with pleasure, now that Gabrielle was with him, every muscle in his body primed for dealing death. He drew another blade and pounded toward the approaching threat.

The fight was savage and swift. With fists flying, blades slashing, Lucan and the Rogue engaged in a deadly hand-to-hand combat. Lucan took more than one hit, but he was unstoppable. Gabrielle's blood was still strong within him, giving him a fury that would have been a match for ten opponents at once. He struck hard and with lethal efficiency, dispatching the Rogue with a vertical slice to its body.

Lucan didn't wait to see the titanium do its thing. He spun around and ran back to Gabrielle. Once he was in reach of her, all he could do was pull her into his arms and hold her fast against him. He could have stayed there all night, just breathing her in, feeling her heart beat, stroking her soft skin.

He lifted her chin and placed a fiercely tender kiss on her lips. "We have to get out of here, baby. Right now."

Above their heads, the helicopter was rising higher.

From out of the clear cockpit, the Gen One vampire who'd taken Gabrielle stared down through the glass enclosure. He gave Lucan a vague salute, grinning as his ride ascended into the night sky.

"Oh, God, Lucan! I was so scared. If anything had happened to you..."

Gabrielle's whisper made him forget all about his escaping enemy. The only thing that mattered to him was that she was able to talk to him. She was breathing. Gabrielle was with him, and he hoped to God he could keep her that way.

"How the hell did they get to you?" he asked, his voice shaking with urgency and the sharp aftershocks of his fear.

"After you left the compound tonight, I needed to get away and think. I went home. Kendra showed up. She had Jamie held hostage in a car outside. I couldn't let them hurt him. Kendra is—was—a Minion, Lucan. They killed her. My friend is dead." Gabrielle gave a sudden sob. "But Jamie got away, at least. He's somewhere downtown, probably scared out of his mind. I need to find him and make sure he's all right."

Lucan heard the low clip of the helicopter as it rose

higher above them. He had to give Niko the signal to blow the place before the Rogues inside had a chance to escape, too.

"Let's get out of here, then we'll deal with the rest." Lucan scooped Gabrielle off her feet and up into his arms. "Hold on to me, sweetheart. Tight as you can."

"Okay." She wrapped her arms around his neck.

He kissed her again, relief flooding him to have her in his arms.

"Don't ever let go," he said, looking into the shining, beautiful eyes of his Breedmate.

Then he stepped over the edge of the roof and dropped with her, as soft as he could manage, down to the ground below.

"Lucan, talk to me, man!" Nikolai called over the earpiece. "Where are you? What the fuck is going on out there?"

"Everything's all right," he answered, carrying Gabrielle swiftly across the darkened grass of the property, toward where the warriors' SUV waited. "Everything's going to be all right now. Hit the detonator and let's finish this thing."

Gabrielle was huddled under the strong curve of Lucan's arm as the SUV pulled onto the road leading to the compound's estate. He'd been holding her close to him since they'd escaped the asylum grounds, shielding her eyes as the entire complex of buildings had gone up in a hellish ball of fire.

Lucan and his brethren had actually done it—they'd taken out the Rogues' headquarters in one awesome strike.

The helicopter had managed to elude the explosion, vanishing skyward into the black smoke and cover of night.

Lucan was pensive, staring out the tinted window, up into the canopy of stars. Gabrielle had seen his look of surprise—of stunned disbelief—when he'd been up on the roof and thrown open the helicopter's cockpit door.

It was as if he'd seen a ghost.

The mood carried with him even now as they entered the estate and Nikolai drove toward the garage. The warrior pulled the vehicle to a stop inside the huge hangar. When he cut the engine, Lucan finally spoke.

"Tonight we scored an important victory against our enemies."

"Hell yeah," Nikolai agreed. "And we avenged Conlan and Rio. They would've loved to have been there to see that place blow."

Lucan nodded in the dark vehicle. "But make no mistake, we are entering a new phase of conflict with the Rogues. This is war now, more than ever. Tonight we've stirred the hornet's nest. But the one we needed to get—their leader—is still alive."

"Let him run. We'll get him," Dante said, grinning confidently.

But Lucan gave a grim shake of his head. "This one is different. He won't make it easy. He'll anticipate our moves. He'll understand our tactics. The Order is going to need to strengthen its strategies and increase its numbers. We need to organize the few remaining cadres around the world, bring in more warriors, the sooner the better."

Gideon pivoted around in the front seat. "You think it's the Gen One out of the West Coast who's leading the Rogues?"

"I'm sure of it," Lucan answered. "He was in the

helicopter on the roof tonight, where he was holding Gabrielle." He stroked her arm with tender affection, pausing to look at her as if the mere sight of her reassured him in some way. "And the bastard's not a Rogue—not now, if he ever was. Once, he was a warrior, like us. His name is Marek."

Gabrielle felt a cold blast coming from the SUV's third row of seats and knew that Tegan was looking at Lucan.

Lucan knew it, too. He swiveled his head to meet the other warrior's stare. "Marek is my brother."

CHAPTER
Thirty-four

The weight of Lucan's revelation followed them as they exited the vehicle and took the hangar's elevator down into the compound. Standing beside Lucan, Gabrielle laced her fingers through his as they descended. Shock and sympathy clawed at her heart, and when he glanced over at her, she knew he could read the worry in her eyes.

Gabrielle saw similar looks of concern reflected in the eyes of Lucan's warrior brethren as well, an unspoken acknowledgment of what the night's discovery meant.

The time was going to come that Lucan would have to face killing his own brother.

Or be killed by him.

Gabrielle hardly had a chance to absorb that cold fact before the elevator doors opened on Savannah and Danika, who were waiting anxiously for the warriors' return. There were relieved welcomes, dozens of questions about the outcome of the night's mission, as well as worried inquiries into what on earth had made Gabrielle leave the compound without a word to anyone. Gabrielle was too tired to answer, too exhausted from the entire ordeal to even try to express what she was feeling.

But she knew she would have to provide some answers soon, to Lucan at least.

She watched as he was ushered away by the other warriors amid talk of war tactics and new battle strategies to be used against the Rogues. Gabrielle was swiftly pulled in an opposite direction by Savannah and Danika. They fretted over her sundry scrapes and bruises, insisting that she take a warm meal and a long, hot bath.

Gabrielle reluctantly agreed, but not even Savannah's amazing cooking or the fragrant heat of the soak that followed could relax her.

Her mind was spinning with thoughts about Lucan, Jamie, and everything that had happened that night. She owed Lucan her life. She loved him more than anything, would always be grateful to him for his rescuing her, but it didn't change how she felt about the way things had been going between them. She couldn't stay at the compound like this. And no matter what he said, she wasn't about to enter one of the Darkhavens.

So, what did that leave? She couldn't go back to her apartment, either. Her old life no longer fit. To return to it meant she would have to deny everything she'd experienced with Lucan these past weeks and work to forget him. She would have to deny all that she now understood about herself, and her connection to the Breed.

The truth was, she didn't know where she belonged now. She didn't know where to begin looking, but as she walked the compound's maze of corridors, Gabrielle found herself standing outside Lucan's private quarters.

The door to the main apartment was ajar; a soft light glowed from within. Gabrielle pushed it open, then stepped inside.

Candlelight flickered in the adjacent bedroom. She followed the ambient warmth to the threshold and paused there, marveling at what she saw. Lucan's austere bedroom had been transformed into something out of a dream. Four tall black pillar candles set into intricate silver sconces burned in each corner. Red silk draped the bed. On the floor before the fireplace was a cushioned nest of fluffy pillows and even more crimson silk. It looked so romantic, so inviting.

A room intended for lovemaking.

She took a step farther inside. Behind her, the door closed softly on its own.

No, not quite on its own. Lucan was there, standing on the other side of the room, watching her. His hair was damp from a shower. He wore a loosely tied, satiny red robe that skated around his bare calves, and there was a heated look in his eyes that melted her where she stood.

"For you," he said, indicating the romantic setting. "For us tonight. I want things to be special for you."

Gabrielle was moved, instantly aroused by the sight of him, but she couldn't bear to make love the way things had been left between them.

"When I left tonight, I wasn't going to come back," she told him from the safety of distance. If she went any closer, she didn't think she'd have the strength to say what had to be said. "I can't do this anymore, Lucan. I need things from you that you can't give me."

"Name them." It was a soft command, but still a command. He moved toward her with careful steps, as though he sensed she might bolt on him at any second. "Tell me what you need."

She shook her head. "What would be the use?"

A few more slow steps. He paused just beyond an arm's length. "I'd like to know. I'm curious what it would take to convince you to stay with me."

"For the night?" she asked quietly, hating herself for how badly she needed to feel his arms around her after what she'd been through these past several hours.

"I want you, and I'm prepared to offer you anything, Gabrielle. So, tell me what you need."

"Your trust," she said, tossing out something she felt was well out of reach. "I can't...do this anymore, when you don't trust me."

"I do trust you," he said, so solemnly she actually believed him. "You are the only one who's ever really known me, Gabrielle. There is nothing I can hide from you. You've seen it all—the worst, certainly. I'd like the chance to show you some of the good in me." He moved closer. She could feel heat coming off his body. She could sense his desire. "I want you to feel as safe with me as you've allowed me to feel with you. So, the question is, can you trust me, knowing everything about me that you do?"

"I've always trusted you, Lucan. I always will. But that's not—"

"What else, then?" he asked, cutting her denial short. "Tell me what else I can give you to make you stay."

"This isn't going to work," she said, inching backward. "I can't stay. Not like this. Not when my friend Jamie..."

"He is safe." When Gabrielle looked at Lucan, confused, he said, "I sent Dante topside to find him soon after we arrived. He reported back a few minutes ago that he retrieved your friend from a police station downtown and took him home."

Relief flared in her, but it was quickly followed by concern. "What did Dante tell him? Did he wipe Jamie's memory?"

Lucan shook his head. "I didn't think it would be fair to make that decision for you. Dante merely told him that you were safe as well and that you would be in contact with him soon to explain. Whatever you wish to tell your friend is up to you. You see? Trust, Gabrielle."

"Thank you," she murmured, warmed by the consideration. "Thank you for helping me tonight. You saved my life."

"Then why are you afraid of me now?"

"I'm not afraid," she said, but she was moving away from him, hardly aware of that fact until the bed came up behind her, blocking her escape. In an instant, he was right there in front of her.

"What more do you want from me, Gabrielle?"

"Nothing," she said, hardly more than a whisper.

"Nothing at all?" he replied, his voice dark, demanding.

"Please. Don't make me want to stay with you tonight when you will only wish me gone tomorrow. Let me go now, Lucan."

"I can't do that." He took her hand and lifted it to his lips. His mouth was warm and soft on her fingertips, weaving a spell around her as only he could do. He brought her hand closer, pressing her palm to his chest, to the heavy throb that beat against his ribs like a drum. "I can't ever let you go, Gabrielle. Because whether you want it from me or not, you have my heart. You have my love, too. If you'll accept it."

She swallowed hard. "What?"

"I love you." The words were low and earnest, a caress she felt deep inside of her. "Gabrielle Maxwell, I love you more than life itself. I've been alone for so long, I didn't know enough to recognize that until it was nearly too late." He stopped talking then, searching her eyes intensely. "It's not . . . too late, is it?"

He loved her.

Joy, pure and bright, poured through her to hear those words coming from Lucan.

"Say it again," she whispered, needing to know that this moment was real, that it would last.

"I love you, Gabrielle. With every ounce of life in me, I love you."

"Lucan." She sighed his name, tears rising, swelling, spilling over to run down her cheeks.

He pulled her into his arms and kissed her deeply, a passionate joining of their mouths that sent her head spinning, her heart soaring, her blood pulsing like fire in her veins.

"You deserve so much better than me," he told her, reverence in his voice and in his bright, amber-flecked gray gaze. "You know the demons in me. Can you love me—would you have me—even though you know my weakness?"

She cupped his strong jaw in her palm, letting him see the love she held for him reflecting in her eyes. "You're never weak, Lucan. And I will love you no matter what. Together we can get past anything."

"You make me believe that. You've given me hope." Lovingly, he caressed her arm, her shoulder, her cheek. His gaze roamed over her face, following the reverent path of his hands. "My God, you are so exquisite. You could have any male, Breed or human—"

"You're the only one I want."

He smiled. "God help you, but I will have no other. I've never wanted anything so selfishly as I want this moment. Be mine, Gabrielle."

"I am."

He swallowed, glancing down as if suddenly uncertain. "I'm talking about forever. I can't settle for anything less. Gabrielle, will you have me as your mate?"

"Forever and always," she whispered, leaning back onto the bed and bringing him down with her. "I am yours, Lucan, forever and always."

They kissed again, and when they drew apart this time, Lucan reached for a slim gold dagger lying on the table next to the bed. He brought it toward his face. Gabrielle started a bit, seeing him bring the edge of the blade up to his mouth. "Lucan—"

His eyes were soft, serious, yet tender as he held her anxious gaze. "You've given me your blood to heal me. You strengthen me and protect me. You are all that I ever want, all that I could ever need."

She'd never heard him speak so solemnly. His irises just about glowed, the pale gray mingling with amber and the depth of his emotion.

"Gabrielle, will you honor me now and take my blood to complete our bond?"

Her voice was the barest gasp. "Yes."

Lucan bowed his head and moved the dagger to his lower lip. When he set the blade aside and looked at her once more, his mouth was glossy with dark red blood.

"Come here. Let me love you now," he said, and pressed his scarlet kiss to her lips.

Nothing could have prepared her for that first sweet taste of Lucan's blood.

Richer than wine, instantly intoxicating, his blood flowed over her tongue like an elixir crafted for the gods. She felt all of Lucan's love pouring into her, all of his power and strength. Light filled her from deep within, giving her a taste of the future that awaited her as Lucan's Breedmate. Happiness flooded her, leaving her flushed with its heat, and a feeling of contentment like she had never known before.

She felt desire, too.

More intense than it had ever been.

With a low growl of need, Gabrielle braced her hand against Lucan's bare chest and rolled him onto his back. She stripped out of her clothes in little more than an instant and climbed on top of him, straddling his hips between her thighs.

His sex thrust up in front of her, thick and solid as stone. The beautiful web of markings on his skin were deep purple shot with vivid red, pulsing in stronger hues as she gazed upon him in hunger. Gabrielle leaned down and let her tongue trace along the swirling, intricate lines that decorated him from thigh to navel, and higher, up his muscled chest and shoulders.

He was hers.

The thought was fiercely possessive, primal. She had never wanted him more than she did in that moment. She was panting and wet, burning up with the need to mount him and ride him hard.

God, was this what Savannah meant when she said the blood-bond would enhance lovemaking?

Gabrielle looked at Lucan with pure carnal need, hardly knowing where to begin with him. She wanted to devour him, worship him, use him up. Slake the coiling need that was churning inside of her.

"You should have warned me you were feeding me an aphrodisiac."

Lucan grinned up at her. "And spoil the surprise?"

"Laugh it up, vampire." Gabrielle arched a brow, then gripped his stiff erection and sheathed him to the hilt in one long move. "You just promised me eternity, you know. I can make you live to regret it."

"Yeah?" The word was more of a strangled groan as she rocked on him, making his hips buck sharply beneath her. Eyes blazing now, he gave her a glimpse of fang as he smiled, clearly enjoying his torture. "Breedmate, I'm going to love seeing you try."

ABOUT THE AUTHOR

With family roots stretching back to the *Mayflower*, author Lara Adrian lives with her husband in coastal New England, surrounded by centuries' old graveyards, hip urban comforts, and the endless inspiration of the broody Atlantic Ocean. To learn more about Lara and her novels, please visit *www.LaraAdrian.com*.

Read on for a preview of
Lara Adrian's next novel in her
heart-stopping *Midnight Breed* series. . . .

Kiss *of* Crimson

b y

LARA ADRIAN

On sale June 2007

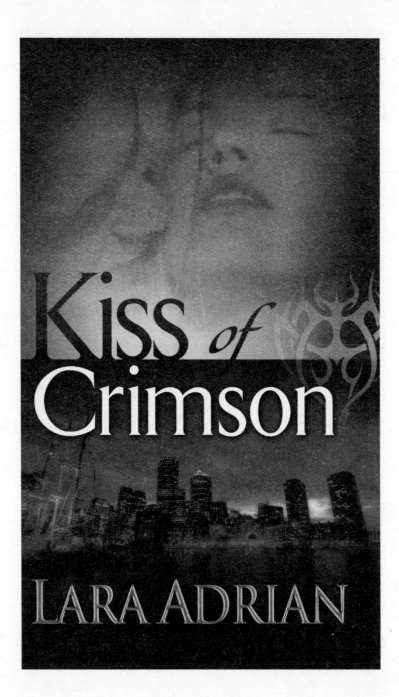

Kiss of Crimson

Lara Adrian

Kiss of Crimson

On sale June 2007

CHAPTER
Three

Tess came awake with a start.

Shit. How long had she been dozing? She was in her office, Shiva's case file open beneath her cheek on the desk. Last she recalled, she'd fed the malnourished tiger and put it back in its containment so she could begin writing up her findings. That was—she glanced at her watch—two and a half hours ago? It was now a few minutes before 3 A.M. She was due back in the clinic at 7 o'clock.

Tess groaned around a big yawn and a stretch of her cramped arms.

Good thing she woke up before Nora reported back to work, or she'd never hear the end of—

A loud bump sounded from somewhere in the back of the clinic.

What the hell?

Had she been jolted out of her sleep by a similar noise a minute ago?

Oh, jeez. Of course. Ben must have driven past and saw the lights on in the clinic. It wouldn't be the first time he'd come around on a late-night drive-by to check in on her. She really didn't feel like getting a lecture on her crazy hours, or her stubborn streak of independence.

The noise came again, another clumsy bump, followed by an abrupt clatter of metal as something got knocked off a shelf.

Which meant someone was in the back storage room.

Tess rose from her desk and took a few tentative steps toward her office door, ears tuned to any disturbance at all. In the kennels off the reception area, the handful of post-op cats and dogs were restless. Some of them were whining; others were issuing low warning growls.

"Hello?" Tess called into the empty space. "Is someone here? Ben, is that you? Nora?"

Nobody answered. And now the noises she'd heard before had gone still as well.

Great. She'd just announced her presence to an intruder. *Brilliant, Culver. Absolutely frigging brilliant.*

She tried to console herself with some fast logic. Maybe it was just a homeless person looking for shelter, who found his or her way into the clinic from the back alley. Not an intruder. Nothing dangerous at all.

Yeah? So why were the hairs on the back of her neck tingling with dread?

Tess shoved her hands into the pockets of her lab coat, feeling suddenly very vulnerable. She felt her ballpoint pen knock against her fingers. Something else was in there as well.

Oh, that's right. The tranq syringe, full of enough Telazol to knock a four-hundred-pound animal out cold.

"Is someone back there?" she asked, trying to keep her voice firm and steady. She paused at the reception station and reached for the phone. The damn thing wasn't cordless—she'd gotten it cheap on closeout—and the receiver barely reached to her ear from over the counter. Tess went around the big U-shaped desk, glancing nervously over her shoulder as she started punching 9-1-1 on the keypad. "You'd better get out of here right now, because I'm calling the cops."

"No . . . please . . . don't be afraid. . . ."

The deep voice was so quiet, it shouldn't have reached her ears, but it did. She heard it as surely as if the words had been whispered right up next to her head. *Inside her head*, strange as that seemed.

There was a dry croak and a violent, wracking cough, definitely coming from the storage room. And whomever the voice belonged to sounded like he was in a world of hurt. Life and death kind of hurt.

"Damn it."

Tess held her breath and hung up the phone before her call connected. She walked slowly toward the back of the clinic, uncertain what she was going to find, and really wishing she didn't have to look at all.

"Hello? What are you doing in here? Are you hurt?"

She spoke to the intruder as she pushed open the door and stepped inside. She heard labored breathing, smelled smoke and the briny stench of the river. She smelled blood, too. Lots of it.

Tess flicked the light on.

Harsh fluorescent tubes buzzed to life overhead, illuminating the incredible bulk of a drenched, heavily injured man slumped on the floor near one of the supply shelves. He was dressed all in black, like some kind of goth nightmare—black leather jacket, tee-shirt, fatigues, and lace-up combat boots. Even his hair was black, the wet strands plastered to his head, shielding his down-turned face from view. An ugly smudge of blood and river water traveled from the back door, partially opened onto the alley, to where the man lay in Tess's storeroom. He had evidently dragged himself inside, maybe unable to walk.

If she hadn't been so accustomed to seeing the grisly aftermath of car accidents, beatings, and other bodily trauma in her animal patients, the sight of this man's injuries might have turned Tess's stomach inside out.

Instead, her mind switched from alarm and the instinctual fight-or-flight mode she'd been feeling out in the reception area, to that of the physician she was trained to be. Clinical, calm, and concerned.

"What happened to you?"

The man grunted, gave a vague shake of his dark head like he wasn't going to tell her anything about it. Perhaps he couldn't.

"You're covered in burns and wounds. My God,

there must be hundreds of them. Were you in some kind of accident?" She glanced down to where one of his hands was resting on his abdomen. Blood was seeping through his fingers from a fresh, deep puncture. "Your gut is bleeding—and your leg, too. Jesus, have you been shot?"

"Need . . . blood."

He was probably right about that. The floor beneath him was slick and dark from what he'd lost just since his arrival at the clinic. He'd likely lost a good deal more before he got there. Nearly every patch of his exposed skin bore multiple lacerations— his face and neck, his hands, everywhere Tess looked, she saw bleeding cuts and contusions. His cheeks and mouth were pale white, ghostly.

"You need an ambulance," she told him, not wanting to upset him, but damn, the guy was in bad shape. "Just relax now. I'm going to go call 911 for you."

"No!" He lurched from his slump on the floor, thrusting his hand out to her in alarm. "No hospitals! Can't . . . can't go there . . . they won't . . . can't help me."

Despite his protest, Tess started to run for the phone in the other room. But then she remembered the stolen tiger hanging out in one of her exam rooms. Hard to explain that to the EMTs, or, God forbid, the police. The gun shop had probably already called in the theft of the animal, or would by the time the store opened that morning, just a few short hours away.

"Please," gasped the huge man bleeding all over her clinic. "No doctors."

Tess paused, regarding him in silence. He needed

help in a big way, and he needed it now. Unfortunately, she looked like his best chance at the moment. She wasn't sure what she could do for him here, but maybe she could patch him up temporarily, get him on his feet and get him the hell out of there.

"Okay," she said. "No ambulances for now. Listen, I'm, ah—I'm actually a doctor. Well, more or less. This is my veterinary clinic. Would it be all right if I come a little closer and have a look at you?"

She took the quirk of his mouth and ragged exhaled sigh as a yes.

Tess inched down beside him on the floor. He seemed big from across the room, but crouched next to him, she realized that he was immense, easily six-and-a-half feet, and 250-plus pounds of heavy bone and solid muscle. Was he some kind of bodybuilder? One of those macho meatheads who spent his life in the gym? Something about him didn't quite fit that mold. With the grim cut of his face, he looked like the kind of guy who could tear a gym rat to pieces with his teeth.

She moved her hands lightly over his face, feeling for trauma. His skull was intact, but her touch told her that he'd suffered a mild concussion in some fashion. Probably was still in a state of shock.

"I'm just going to check your eyes," she informed him gently, then lifted one of his lids.

Holy shit.

The slit pupil cutting through the center of a large, bright amber iris took her aback. She recoiled, freaked out by the unexpected presentation.

"What the—"

Then the explanation hit her, and she instantly felt like an idiot for losing her cool.

Costume contacts.

Chill out, she told herself. She was getting jumpy for no good reason. The guy must have been at a Halloween party that got out of hand or something. Not much she could tell from his eyes so long as he was wearing those ridiculous lenses.

Maybe he'd been partying with a rough crowd; he certainly looked big and dangerous enough to be part of some kind of gang. If he was rolling with gang-bangers tonight, she didn't detect any evidence of drugs on him. She didn't smell alcohol on him, either. Just some heavy-duty smoke, and not from cigarettes.

He smelled like he'd walked through fire. Just before he took a dive into the Mystic River.

"Can you move your arms or legs?" she asked him, moving on to inspect his limbs. "Do you think you have any broken bones?"

She skimmed her hands over his thick arms, feeling no obvious fractures. His legs were solid, too, no real damage beyond the bullet wound in his left calf. From the look of it, the round appeared to have passed clean through. Same with the one that hit him in the torso. Luckily for him.

"I'd like to move you to one of my exam rooms. Do you think you can walk if I help hold you up?"

"Blood," he gasped, his voice thready. "Need it . . . now."

"Well, I'm sorry, but I can't help you there. You'll need a hospital for that. Right now we need to get you off this floor and out of those ruined clothes. God knows what kind of bacteria you picked up in that water out there."

She put her hands under his armpits and started to lift, encouraging him to stand. He growled, something deep and animalistic. As the sound left his mouth, Tess caught a glimpse of his teeth behind his curled upper lip.

Whoa. That's weird.

Were those monstrous canines actually . . . *fangs*?

His eyes came open as if he had sensed her awareness. Her unease. Tess was instantly blasted by piercing bright amber light, the glowing irises sending a bolt of panic straight into her chest. Those sure as hell weren't contacts.

Good Lord. Something wasn't right with this guy at all.

He grabbed her upper arms. Tess cried out in alarm. She tried to pull out of his grasp, but he was too strong. Hands as unyielding as iron bands clamped tighter around her and brought her closer. Tess shrieked, wide-eyed, frozen in fear as he drew her right up against him.

"Oh God. No!"

He turned his bloodied, battered face toward her throat. Sucked in a sharp breath as he neared her, his lips brushing her skin.

"Shhh." Warm air skated across her neck as he spoke in a low, pained rasp. "I won't . . . not going to . . . hurt you. I promise. . . ."

Tess heard the words.

She almost believed them.

Until that split second of terror, when he parted his lips and sank his teeth deep into her flesh.

CHAPTER
Four

Blood surged into Dante's mouth from the twin punctures in the female's neck. He drew from her with deep, urgent pulls, unable to curb the feral part of him that knew only need and desperation. It was life pulsing over his tongue and down his parched throat, silky, cinnamon-sweet, and so very warm.

Maybe it was the severity of his need that made her taste so incredible, so indescribably perfect to him. Whatever it was, he didn't care. He drank more of her, needing her heat when he was chilled to his marrow.

"Oh God. No!" The woman's voice was heady with shock. "Please! Let me go!"

She clutched at his shoulders reflexively, fingers digging into his muscles. But the rest of her body was slowly going still in his arms, lulled to a boneless sort of trance by the hypnotic power of Dante's bite. She sighed a long gasp of breath, sagging limply as he eased her down onto the floor beneath him and took the nourishment he so badly needed.

There was no pain for her now, not since the initial penetration of his fangs, which would have been sharp but swiftly fleeting. The only pain here was Dante's own. His body shuddered from the depth of its trauma, his head splitting from concussion, his torso and limbs laced open in too many places to count.

It's okay. Don't be afraid.

You are safe. I promise.

He sent the reassurances into her mind, even as he held her tighter, brought her more firmly into the cage of his arms, his mouth still drawing hard from the wound at her throat.

Despite the ferocity of his thirst, a need amplified by the severity of his injuries, Dante's word was good. Beyond the bite that startled her, he would not harm the female.

I'll take only what I need. Then I'll be gone, and you will forget all about me.

Already his strength was returning. Torn flesh was mending from the inside out. Bullet and shrapnel wounds were healing over.

Burns cooling.

Pain fading.

He eased up on the female, willing himself to slow, even though the taste of her was beyond enticing. He'd registered the exotic note of her blood scent on his first draw, but now that his body was rejuvenating, his senses coming back online fully, Dante couldn't help but savor the sweetness of his unwilling Host.

And her body.

Beneath the shapeless white lab coat, she was strong, lean muscle and long, graceful limbs. Curvy in all the right places. Dante felt the mash of her breasts pressing against his chest, where he pinned her on the storeroom floor, her legs tangled with his. Her hands were still gripped hard on his shoulders, no longer pushing against him, but simply holding on to him as he took a final sip of her life-giving blood.

God, she was so exquisite he could drink from her all night.

He could do a hell of a lot more than that, he thought, suddenly aware of the erection that was wedged hard and demanding at her pelvis. She felt too good beneath him. His blessed angel of mercy, even if she'd come into the role by force.

Dante breathed in her spicy-sweet scent, gently dropping a kiss on the wound that had fed him a second chance at life.

"Thank you," he whispered against her warm, velvet-soft skin. "I think you saved my life tonight."

He smoothed his tongue over the small punctures, sealing them closed, and erasing all traces of his bite. The female moaned, stirring from her temporary thrall. She moved under him, the subtle shifting of her body only heightening Dante's desire to be inside her.

But he'd already taken enough from her tonight.

In spite of the fact that she would remember none of what occurred, it seemed less than sporting to seduce her in a puddle of stale river water and spilled blood. Particularly after going at her neck like an animal.

He moved slightly off of her, and brought his right hand up near her face. She flinched, understandably wary. Her eyes were open now—mesmerizing eyes, the color of flawless aquamarine.

"My God, you are beautiful," he murmured, words he'd casually tossed out to numerous females in the past, but surprisingly never meant more than he did now.

"Please," she whispered. "Please, don't hurt me."

"No," Dante said gently. "I'm not going to hurt you. Just close your eyes now, angel. It's almost over."

A brief press of his palm against her brow, and she would forget all about him.

"Everything's all right," he told her as she shrank back from him on the floor, her eyes locked onto his as if she waited for him to strike her. Dared him to. Dante smoothed her hair off her cheek with the tenderness of a lover. Her felt her tension ratchet a little tighter. "Relax now. You can trust—"

Something sharp stuck him in the thigh.

With a vicious snarl, Dante rolled away, flipping onto his back. "What the hell?"

Heat spread from that stabbing point of contact, burning through him like acid. A bitter taste gathered at the back of his throat, just before his vision began to swim crazily. Dante tried to heave himself upright on the floor, but fell back again, his body as uncooperative as a lead slab.

Panting rapidly, those bright blue-green eyes wide with panic, Dante's angel of mercy peered over him. Her pretty face warped in and out of his vision. One slender hand was pressed to her neck, where he'd bitten her. The other was raised up at shoulder level, holding an empty syringe in a white-knuckled grip.

Holy Christ.

She drugged him.

But as bad as that news was, Dante registered something even worse as his blurring gaze struggled to hold on to the small hand that had managed to fell him with one blow. Between her thumb and forefinger, in that fleshy juncture of soft skin, the female bore a small birthmark.

Deep scarlet, smaller than a dime, the image of a teardrop falling into the bowl of a crescent moon seared into Dante's brain.

It was a rare mark, a genetic stamp that proclaimed the female sacred to those of Dante's kind.

She was a Breedmate.

And with her blood now pulsing within him, Dante had just completed one half of a solemn bond.

By vampire law, she was his.

Irrevocably.

Eternally.

The very last thing he wanted or needed.

In his mind, Dante roared, but all he heard was a low, wordless growl. He blinked dully, reaching out for the woman, missing her by an easy foot. His arm dropped like it was weighted down with irons. His eyelids were too heavy to lift more than a fraction. He moaned, watching his erstwhile savior's features blur before his eyes.

She glared down at him, her voice edged with defiant fury.

"Sleep tight, you psychotic son of a bitch!"